David Braham

FORGOTTEN STARS OF THE MUSICAL THEATRE

Kurt Gänzl, Series Editor

Lydia Thompson BY KURT GÄNZL

Leslie Stuart BY ANDREW LAMB

William B. Gill BY KURT GÄNZL

David Braham BY JOHN FRANCESCHINA

Alice May BY ADRIENNE SIMPSON

Harry B. Smith BY JOHN FRANCESCHINA

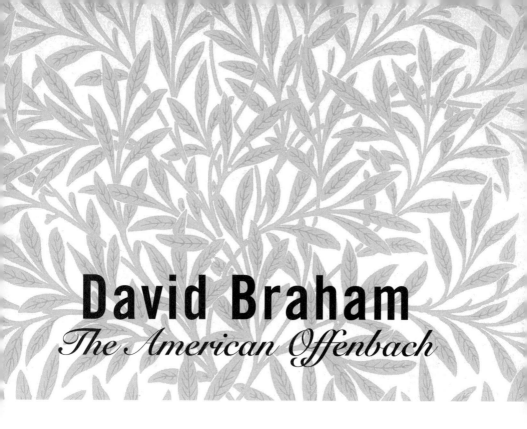

David Braham
The American Offenbach

John Franceschina

FORGOTTEN STARS OF THE MUSICAL THEATRE

SERIES EDITOR: KURT GÄNZL

ROUTLEDGE
NEW YORK AND LONDON

Published in 2003 by
Routledge
29 West 35th Street
New York, NY 10001
www.routledge-ny.com

Published in Great Britain by
Routledge
11 New Fetter Lane
London EC4P 4EE
www.routledge.co.uk

Routledge is an imprint of the Taylor & Francis Group.
Printed in the United States of America on acid-free paper.

10 9 8 7 6 5 4 3 2 1

Library of Congress Cataloging-in-Publication Data

Franceschina, John Charles, 1947–
    David Braham : the American Offenbach / [by John Franceschina].
      p. cm. — (Forgotten stars of the musical theatre ; 4)
    Includes index.
      ISBN 0–415–93769–8 (hardcover : alk paper)
      1. Braham, David, 1838–1905. 2. Composers—United States—Biography.
    I. Forgotten stars of musical theatre ; 4.
    ML410 .B792 F73 2003
    782.1'4'092—dc21   2002152095

For Ann Connolly

David Braham, a photograph from the collection of Ann Connolly.

Contents

Acknowledgments

An almost obsessively private man, David Braham left only a few clues to the story of his life, preferring to be remembered by his extensive legacy of published music. Uncovering and interpreting the clues was facilitated by the continued and energetic support of Ann Connolly, Braham's great-granddaughter, who provided access to family documents, photographs, and memories that would have otherwise been unattainable. A travel-research grant from the Institute for the Arts and Humanistic Studies at The Pennsylvania State University enabled visits to the New York City Municipal Archives, the New York Public Library, the Museum of the City of New York, the Library of Congress, and the National Archives in Washington, D.C., where friendly curators were helpful in solving problems caused by a mass of conflicting information. Librarians at Bird Library at Syracuse University; the Boston Public Library; the Rare Book, Manuscript, and Special Collections Library at Duke University; the Harry Ransom Humanities Research Center at the University of Texas at Austin; and the Pattee-Paterno Library at The Pennsylvania State University also provided quick and expert help in this study. Dave Moran of Olde Music and Cokery Books in Australia provided a wealth of information and a fair amount of sheet music, and Jack Kopstein was an important source of information on the military bands of the period. Marguerite Lavin of the Museum of the City of New York and Janie C. Morris of Duke University were instrumental in securing permissions for materials from their collections, and Robert Davis, Inc., graciously provided scans of images for use in this volume. Finally, Kurt Gänzl, the editor of this series, and Robert Byrne, Richard Carlin, and Lisa Vecchione of Routledge have consistently been helpful and efficient nurturers of this project. To everyone, my deepest gratitude.

"Sic transit gloria spectaculi"
Some Famous but Forgotten Figures
of the Musical Theatre

Kurt Gänzl

Over the past few years, I have spent most of my time researching, writing, and otherwise putting together the vast quantity of text involved in the second edition of my now three-volumed *Encyclopedia of the Musical Theatre*. And, as the Lord Chancellor in *Iolanthe* exhaustedly sings, "thank goodness they're both of them over!" Part of this extremely extended extending exercise involved my compiling bibliographies of biographical works for the hundreds (or was it thousands?) of people whose careers in the musical theatre warranted an entry in the *Encyclopedia*. As I duly compiled, however, I became surprisedly aware of just how many outstanding figures of the historical stage have never, ever been made the subject of even a monograph-sized "life and works." Time and time again, I found that the articles that I have researched (from scratch, not only by choice but quite simply because no-one has ever, it seems, done it before) and written for the *Encyclopedia* are the largest pieces of biographical copy up till now put together on this or that person or personality. And I do not mean nobodies: I mean some of the most important and most fascinating theatrical figures of the nineteenth and early twentieth century theatres.

This series of short biographies is intended to take the first small step towards rectifying that situation. To bring back to notice and, perhaps, even to their rightful place in the history of the international theatre, a few of the people whose names have—for all but the scholar and the specialist—drifted into the darkness of the past, leaving too little trace.

This is a very personal project and one very dear to my heart. And because it is so personal, even though the majority of the volumes in the series are written by my closest colleagues in the theatre-books world, rather than by myself, you will find that they have me stamped on them in some ways. And I take full responsibility for that.

These books are not intended to be university theses. You will not find them dotted with a dozen footnotes per page, and hung with vast appendices of sources. I am sure that that is a perfectly legitimate way of writing biography, but it's a way that has never appealed to me and, because I am being allowed to "do it my way" in this series, the paraphernalia of the thesis, of the learned pamphlet, has here been kept to a minimum. My care, in these biographies, is not to be "learned"; it is to tell the story of Lydia, or Willie or Alice, of Tom or Harry or of Dave, of her or his career in the theatre and (as much as is possible at a century's distance) on the other side of the footlights as well: to relate what they did and what they achieved, what they wrote or what they sang, where they went and with whom, what happened to them and what became of them. Because these people had fascinating lives—well, they fascinate me, and I hope they will fascinate you too—and just to tell their stories, free of any decoration, any theorizing, any generalities, any "significance" (oh! that word)—seems to me to be thoroughly justified.

The decoration, the theorizing, the generalities, and an exaggerated search for (shudder) significance will all be missing. Perhaps because I've spent so much of my life as a writer of reference works and encyclopedias, I am a thorough devotee of fact, and these books are intended to be made up wholly of fact. Not for me even the "educated guess." Not unless one admits it's just a guess, anyhow.

So, what you will get from us are quite a lot of dates and places, facts and figures, quite a lot of theatre-bills reproduced word for word from the originals, quite a lot of songwords from the songwriters and singers, of text from the playwrights and actors and, where we have been able to dig it up, as much autograph material from the hands of our subjects as is humanly possible.

What you won't get any more than can be helped is the "he must have felt that . . ." (must he, who says?), or the "perhaps she . . . ." There will be no invented conversations. No "Marie Antoinette turned to Toulouse-Lautrec and said 'you haven't telephoned Richard the Lionheart this week . . . '" Direct speech in a biography of a pre-recording-age subject seems to me to be an absolute denial of the first principle of biography: the writing down of the content and actions of someone's life. Indeed, there will be nothing invented at all. My theory of biography, as I say, is that it is facts. And if the facts of someone's life are not colorful and interesting enough in themselves to make up a worthwhile book, then – well, I've chosen the wrong people to biographize.

Choosing those people to whom to devote these first six volumes was actually not as difficult as I'd thought it might be. When Richard, my editor, asked me for a first list of "possibles" I wrote it down—a dozen names—in about five minutes. It started, of course, with all my own particular "pets": the special little group of a half-dozen oldtime theatre folk who, through my twenty years and more working in this field, have particularly grabbed my interest, and provoked me to want to learn more and more and indeed everything about them. The only trouble was . . . I was supposed to be editing this series, not writing the whole jolly thing. And there was no way that I was handing over any of my special pets to someone else—not even Andrew, Adrienne, or John—so I had to choose. Just two.

Lydia Thompson, to me, was the most obvious candidate of all. How on earth theatre literature has got to its present state without someone (even for all the wrong reasons) turning out a book on Lydia, when there are three or four books on Miss Blurblcurble and two or three on Miss Nyngnyng, I cannot imagine. Lydia chose herself. Having picked myself this "plum," I then decided that I really ought to be a bit tougher on myself with my second pick. Certainly, I could take it easy and perhaps pot the incomplete but already over-one-million-word biography of the other great international star of Lydia's era, Emily Soldene, which is hidden bulgingly under my desk, into a convenient package. But then . . . why not have a crack at a really tough nut?

When I said I was going to "do" Willie Gill, almost everyone—even the most knowledgeable of my friends and colleagues—said "who?" Which seems to me to be a very good reason for putting down on paper the tale of the life and works of the man who wrote Broadway's biggest hit musical of his era. Tough it has been and tough it is, tracking him and his down, but what satisfaction to drag from the marshes of the past something which seemed so wholly forgotten. A full-scale biography of a man about whom *nothing* was known!

Having realized that these two choices were pinned to the fact that it was I who was going to be writing about them, I then also realized that I ought to be considering my other choices not from own "pet" list, but to suit the other authors who were going to take part in the series. First catch your author.

Well, I caught three. The fourth, pretexting age, overuse, and retirement, got away. But I got the other three—my three (since the fourth is retired) favorite and most respected writer colleagues in the theatre-books business. Enter Andrew, Adrienne, and John: one from England, one from New Zealand, and one from America. A very judicious geographical spread. And the subjects for the four final volumes were, of course, chosen in function of what enthused them.

For Andrew, the not-so-very-forgotten English songwriter Leslie Stuart, whose *Florodora* songs stunned Broadway, and the rest of the world, in the earliest years of this century. For Adrienne, the mysterious Alice May, whose career ranged from Australia and New Zealand to the West End and Broadway and who has gone down in history—when anyone reads that bit of history—as Gilbert and Sullivan's first (full-length) prima donna. For John, two very different American writers: the musician Dave Braham who, while his wordsmith Ned Harrigan has attracted repeated attention down through the years, has been himself left puzzlingly in the shade, and the prolific, ebullient Harry B Smith, the writer who flooded Broadway with over two hundred musicals in an amazing and amazingly successful career.

I feel bad about the ones who have got left on the cutting-room floor . . . but, maybe later? If we all survive what I've discovered with some apprehension is the intensive work needed to extract from the past the life and works of someone long gone, and largely forgotten.

But it has been worth it. Worth all the work. I've enjoyed it enormously. I know my colleagues have enjoyed it, and are still enjoying it. And I hope those of you who read the stories of Lydia, Willie, and Alice, of Dave, Harry, and Tom, will enjoy them too. And that you will remember these people. Because I really do reckon that they deserve better than to be forgotten.

Chapter 1

Overture: "My Brother's Violin"

The summer following the opening of *Reilly and the Four Hundred*, the greatest success to emerge from the collaboration between composer David Braham and his son-in-law Edward Harrigan, the authors were scheduled to be interviewed by the *New York Herald* at Braham's town house at 75 West 131st Street in Harlem. Inside the house, to the accompaniment of a banjo and a piano, three of Braham's eight children were singing "Maggie Murphy's Home," the runaway hit from the score, while Braham sat on the front stoop, waiting for his son-in-law and the interviewer to arrive, nodding his head in time to the music and merrily smoking a cigar. The black and red tennis cap he always wore made him look more like a character out of a 1920s musical comedy than a major figure in the American musical theater. The *Spirit of the Times* (August 19, 1882) had dubbed him "the American Offenbach," claiming he could make all of New York City "keep time" to his music.

The comparison of Braham to the famous composer of French musical comedies was more than simple hyperbolic publicity. Both composers began their careers writing music for satirical burlesques; both arranged and orchestrated all of the songs and incidental music in their productions; both employed popular dance styles in their musical comedy scores; both traded on existing musical forms from both the popular and classical traditions; both wrote for specific performers, designing their musical ideas to hide the limitations of the one and exploit the potential of another; and, because of their phenomenal popularity, both became the archetype (consciously or otherwise) for the musical theater they created. Associations with Mozart (with whom Braham shared an unusual fecundity of musical ideas and a facility for orchestration) and with Sir Arthur Sullivan (because Harrigan and Braham were considered America's answer to Gilbert and Sullivan during the *HMS Pinafore* craze in 1879) came and went, but David Braham would ever be linked with Offenbach. Though he never publicly mentioned the connection, the subtle and witty inclusion of phrases from one or another of Offenbach's melodies in his overtures and incidental music suggests that, at the very least, Braham was not adverse to the tag.

Harrigan and the interviewer finally arrived and were ushered into the house, swept away immediately by the waves of music emanating from the old upright piano in the parlor. David's wife, Annie, rushed in from the kitchen to greet her husband's guests, and the four adults began a lively conversation, unconsciously shouting over the voices of the children singing—another musical comedy scene.

Braham lead the way to his "office," where his desk was crowded with sheet music and Harrigan's play manuscripts, and the walls were covered with music manuscript paper half-littered with notes and scratches. That's the way he arranged music, he explained. He would compose a line of the violin part, then do the same line for flute, clarinet, cornet, and all the other instruments. Sometimes he would not even write down the notes. He would simply play the part on his violin, and his son, George, would copy it down: quick and efficient. The interviewer appeared surprised and impressed. Harrigan, used to his father-in-law's working habits, was not, thinking that if Braham could read his son-in-law's handwriting—something few other people could decipher—Braham could certainly orchestrate music on the wall!

The men found themselves seated in comfortable chairs, worn with wear, but cozy nonetheless. Suddenly the children stopped singing, and the house was still. The office was filled with a quiet expectation like the kind experienced in the theater after the opening number when the audience is waiting for the plot to get under way. And so the story begins.

David Braham was born in February 1834 in the parish of St. George's, Middlesex, then a prosperous middle-class neighborhood in the East End of London. His father, Joseph John Braham, was born in Rochester, Kent, in 1801 and had gone to London in his teens to apprentice in the watch making profession under Thomas Cook, in whose business the elder Braham would remain for the rest of his professional career. His future and trade secure, Joseph turned to domestic matters and swiftly charmed and married Elizabeth Ann Mary Atkinson, a dressmaker. Typical of the artisans of the period, the couple took residence adjacent to Cook's shop at 565 Grosvenor Place, at the intersection of Commercial Road.

In the early 1820s, at about the time of the Brahams' marriage, St. George's had become a haven for merchants and traders at the height of their prosperity. The area around Wellclose Square, with its manicured gardens and well-appointed houses and carriages, was the most fashionable place to live, and not only because that was where the Danish ambassador held court. Centrally located, across from the parish church, Wellclose Square was the place where the rich could flaunt the merchandise carefully crafted for them by the tradesmen of Commercial Road, the thoroughfare that separated St. George's from nearby Whitechapel and its predominantly Jewish neighborhoods. Based on what is believed to have been the genesis of the Braham name, Joseph Braham's choice of locales was anything but accidental. According to Braham family tradition, members of an Orthodox German Jewish family named Abraham migrated to England in the mid-eighteenth century, dropping the initial "A" of the name in the spirit of assimilation. A letter to the *New York Herald* dated June 13, 1923, and bearing the headline "Dave Braham a Jew" attempted to reinforce the story. Without providing any corroborative evidence, the author, John J. MacIntyre of Port Richmond, argued: "[It] may interest readers of your attractive letter columns to learn that David Braham, composer of the music of the famous Harrigan and Hart songs, was a Jew. His real name was Abraham. By dropping the 'A' he made 'Braham.'" Although it is doubtful that Joseph held on to many of the Orthodox beliefs of his ancestors, he was profoundly ecumenical in his ethical and commercial philosophies and raised his children to be tolerant and appreciative of ethnic differences—traits that would eventually come to fruition in his son David's work in New York City.

David's exposure to ecumenism was not limited to his father's lectures at home but extended well into his grammar-school education. Many of the schools operating in Middlesex during the second quarter of the nineteenth century were experimental, non-denominational schools, aiming to solve the "religious question" by avoiding sectarianism and promoting liberalism. The British Union School established by Joseph Fletcher in 1816 on Farmer Street, Shadwell, was one such school. Designed to serve the areas of Wapping, St. George's, Middlesex, Limehouse, Shadwell, and Radcliff, the school registered 550 boys and girls of various religious beliefs on its rolls by 1819. By 1845, nearly half the population under sixteen years of age attended schools preaching varying degrees of liberalism.

But it was not the ethics of a grammar-school education that spurred the interest of the young Braham boy, nor the obligatory lessons in reading, writing, and doing sums. What David enjoyed most was what many other children viewed as a waste of time: clapping and singing, an elementary musical education. So proficient had David become at reading notes and marking rhythms that he began creating his own melodies, and by the time he was a teenager, he announced that his ambition was to become a professional harpist. It is unknown whether young David engaged in formal training beyond the simple performance skills he acquired at school, but certainly he was adept enough on the harp to entertain the monied merchants of Wellclose Square, and to be invited to perform at the country estates of their friends.

It was on the way to the first of these "engagements" in the English countryside that David Braham experienced a career (if not life)-changing event. About to board a crowded coach hastening to his destination, Braham was informed by the driver that he was permitted to ride in the vehicle but his cumbersome instrument was not. Momentarily daunted by the loss of the engagement, David remembered that, as a lad, he often used to pick out tunes on his older brother Joseph's fiddle. Greater was Braham's ambition to be a musician than specifically to be a harpist, and he switched to the much more practical (and portable) violin for the remainder of his life.

By the time he was eighteen, David Braham had acquired an almost virtuosic mastery of the violin; still, he had no ambition to tour as a professional artist, preferring the more popular venues of the music hall, theater, and salon to the concert hall. Perhaps he felt he lacked the "formal" training necessary for the concert stage. Perhaps his own musical tastes drew him more to parlor songs and theater music than to symphonies and concertos; theater memorabilia dating back to the days of the Royalty and Brunswick Theatres located at Wellclose Square in the 1820s still could be found in the households of St. George's as late as 1845. Ever since the celebrated English vocalist and composer John Braham (who bore no relation to David except in family name) debuted as Cupid at the Royalty in 1787, the community was bitten by the theater bug, and David Braham may have been among its happy victims. Perhaps he preferred the role of accompanist rather than soloist. Perhaps he was warned by his father about the difficulties of earning a living as a serious musician. Whatever the reason, Braham chose to live the life of a part-time performer, like many of the tradesmen and merchants in St. George's, and devote his daylight hours to practicing a trade.

According to the 1851 British Census, David Braham's "trade" was that of a "Brass turner," fashioning, among other things, the brass tubing for trombones, cornets, and horns in conjunction with the firm of Rudall, Rose, Carte and Co., the oldest manufacturers of brass instrument in Britain and winners of a prize medal at the 1851 Great Exhibition in London. The years between 1851 and 1854 passed quickly and enjoyably for David Braham, making instruments during the day, making music at night. But the happy surroundings of St. George's had begun to change, and David began to itch for a new environment. The prospect of work on the docks of London brought throngs of unskilled laborers into the community. By the 1840s, the low rate of pay and the impermanence of employment brought great poverty to the district, a misery intensified by the outbreak of cholera in 1849. Brother Joseph's infant son John narrowly escaped becoming a victim to the first epidemic, but many other children were not as fortunate.

In 1854, Braham's mother became another victim of the cholera epidemic that ravaged St. George's through 1855. Faced with the loss of his favorite parent and the diminishing possibilities of a working-class lifestyle, David began to consider immigrating to America. Joseph had departed for New York City a few years earlier, hoping to find a better life, and David determined the time was right for him to do the same. In April 1856, violin in hand, David Braham boarded the *Empire State* at Liverpool and set sail for the New World, where he arrived on April 28.

New York in 1856 was everything that David Braham had hoped for. Not only was it the musical and theatrical center of America where a musician of talent could earn an honest living, it also was a place of endless variety, a cultural melting pot able to stir young Braham's musical imagination. On May 5, the French Ravel troupe was performing the acrobatic spectacle *Mazulm* at Niblo's Garden; on May 7, Henrietta Behrend made her debut in Italian opera in *Norma* at the Academy of Music; on May 12, the Franklin Museum opened at 127 Grand Street, with living statuary (twenty-seven of Mme. Warton's models, billed as the "finest artistic living females"); May 16 ushered in *Er muss auf's Land; oder, der Ball im Methodisten-Hause* at the Stadt Theater; on May 20, a Family of Mountaineer Singers (Béarnais) appeared at the Tabernacle for three performances; on May 24, Dion Boucicault and Agnes Robertson appeared in Boucicault's new play, *Violet; or, The Life of an Actress* at Burton's Chambers St. Theatre; and on May 26, English soprano Louisa Pyne could be heard concertizing at Niblo's Saloon.

Braham's work as a musician in the theater orchestras and bands of London was merely a prelude to the nights of subbing in various orchestra pits throughout the city until he could acquire some permanent position. His self-effacing, pleasantly cooperative nature, combined with his meticulous sight-reading skills and near-virtuosic ability on the violin, made him a great favorite with musicians, conductors, and patrons—a reputation that would follow him for nearly fifty years. Playing in pit orchestras also had a profound effect on Braham's future as a composer and arranger. He knew about brass instruments from having constructed them back home in England. Now he became more aware of performers' needs: how to minimize mistakes (or "clams," as bad notes are often termed by pit musicians) and maximize orchestral color in ensembles of varying sizes. Moreover, the different styles of music that were now available to him stirred his creative imagination. Braham's early compositions in England had been merely imitative childhood exercises; he needed the musical melting pot of the big city to stimulate him to create a sound that was his alone.

In the summer of 1857, sporting his characteristic mustache, the redheaded, bespectacled David Braham accepted a position as violinist in the orchestra accompanying Matt Peel's Campbell's Minstrels, a company of blackface "Ethiopian delineators" preparing for an East Coast tour to begin in late August. Included in the company were the "Irish Minstrel" Matt Peel; end man George Washington ("Pony") Moore; comic dancer Mert Sexton; English jig dancer Tommy Peel; guitarist, vocalist, and pantomimist A. M. Hernandez; violinist and orchestra leader John B. Donniker; banjoist Frank B. Converse; and harpist and tenor Raffaele Abecco. It was a serendipitous opportunity for Braham because the tour promised him a decent wage at the very time New York City was experiencing a major financial crisis—the "Panic of 1857"— caused by the failure of the New York branch of the Ohio Life Insurance and Trust Company. Throughout the fall, banks failed, businesses closed, attendance at theaters and concerts dropped significantly, and thousands of New Yorkers ended up unemployed and homeless.

When the panic struck, Campbell's Minstrels were in New Haven, Connecticut, playing to large crowds. From New Haven they traveled to Albany, New York, and on to Cleveland, Ohio, where the *New York Clipper* (October 3, 1857) reported consistently crowded houses at the Melodeon Hall, where they performed on September 23 and 24. Mert Sexton's peculiar style of dancing was singled out as being particularly effective in Cleveland, from which the minstrels headed south for New Orleans by way of Cincinnati. The company found New Orleans audiences especially amenable to its brand of jokes, songs, dances, and satirical sketches, and remained in Louisiana until the New Year. During this leg of the tour, Braham's musicianship won him the respect of John Donniker, the company's celebrated minstrel fiddler, and the friendship of tambourinist "Pony" Moore ("Mr. Tambo"), who would later, at the helm of the English "Moore and Burgess Minstrels," popularize several of Braham and Harrigan's songs in London.

In January 1858 Campbell's Minstrels began working their way up North with stops in Memphis, Tennessee, and Savannah, Georgia, where the *New York Clipper* (February 13, 1858) reported excellent business. From Savannah, the minstrels moved to Augusta, Georgia, where their popularity apparently caused a lack of attendance at a performance by a more serious company led by a "Mr. Marchant." The situation prompted this news item in the *Evening Dispatch* (February 5, 1858):

> In consequence of the Campbell Minstrels, *there was no audience at [Mr. Marchant's] theatre last night.* The splendid bill—"School for Scandal," "Marseilles Hymn," and the farce of "Slasher and Crasher,"—will be offered again Monday night. It is a standing reproach to the liberality and taste of lovers of amusement in a city like this, that such a company as Mr. Marchant's should play to empty benches night after night, as they have done so often for two weeks, while other amusements of far less merit will fill a hall in inclement weather. Tell it not in Gath or elsewhere—but it is so. We mean to cast no reflection on the Campbells—they are deservedly

popular—but simply to express surprise and regret that while there are so many admirers of that class of amusement, there are so few among us who appreciate the drama.

Before leaving Augusta for Goldsboro, North Carolina, and Norfolk, Virginia, Matt Peel was reported to have made some kind of "arrangement" with Mr. Marchand to enable both companies to complete their engagements in that city.

By March 23, 1858, Campbell's Minstrels had reached the Maryland Institute where good houses were reported. In addition to praising the comic antics of Peel and Moore and the singular jig dancing of Master Tom Peel, reviewers singled out the instrumental performances as the high point of the evening. Although David Braham had yet to see his name in print, he was connected to a popular success that was soon to open in New York City. Following two performances at the Music Hall in Brooklyn on April 9 and 10, Matt Peel's Campbell's Minstrels opened at 444 Broadway on April 12 for an extended run.

In New York City, as well as on the road, the minstrel show was divided into three parts. In the first part, the curtain rose on a rousing company number, after which the performers seated themselves in a semicircle, the "interlocutor" presiding in the center, and the comedians Mr. Tambo and Mr. Bones (named for the instruments they played) seated at opposite ends (hence the name "end men"). The comic antics of the end men were interrupted by serious romantic songs performed by a lyric tenor balladeer, and the segment concluded with another ensemble number that, in the case of Peel's Campbell company, was invariably the celebrated "Anvil Chorus" from Verdi's *Il Trovatore*. The second part of the performance was an "Olio," a kind of variety show in which the members of the company took solo turns performing their individual specialties. The program for May 2, 1859, lists "Fantasia–Clarionette," "Heel and Toe Exercise," "Cornet Solo," "Banjo Peculiarities," "Negro Eccentricities," and the "Highland Fling" among the variety performances. The evening's performance ended with a farce, typically satirizing the fashions of the day or other popular entertainments, followed by the walk-around, a spectacular production-number finale. Though Braham's creative contribution to the Campbells' shows was limited to his participation in the ten-piece orchestra that accompanied the performance, the experience would have a considerable impact on his later career. From it he learned about comic timing; musical variety; the way to build production numbers both vocally and instrumentally; and, most importantly, ways to make serious music palatable to a popular audience. It would be his integration of European musical idioms with a folklike popular style that created the characteristic musical style of Harrigan and Hart and developed the template for the musical comedy "sound" of the twenieth century.

Peel's Campbell's Minstrels closed for a short time in the middle of July but reopened on August 30 under the management of Mr. Sniffen, who retained most of the original company but began adding performers from other minstrel companies. On October 24, 1858, the *New York Clipper* announced that internal problems within the organization had led Peel to sever his relationship with Sniffen and to organize a new touring company. Although many of the members of Peel's original company left with him, "Pony" Moore and David Braham remained in New York with Sniffen's company, to which Cool White (after a five-year absence in New York City) was added on November 15. On December 27, 1858, the company began to be advertised as "Sniffen's Campbell's Minstrels" with an ensemble that included the popular Cool White, Ben Cotton, and "Pony" Moore, but with the New Year, Sniffen's troupe was almost entirely reorganized. On January 3, 1859, the "new arrangement" went into effect with the following company: Billy Birch, bones; E. Bowers, Shakespearean jester and "middle man"; "Pony" Moore, "'tother end" and tambourinist; John B. Donniker, "fiddle man"; B. Golden, clog dancer; J. B. Herman, the "golden-mouthed ballad singer"; Raffaele Abecco, harpist and tenor; A. M. Hernandez, pantomimist; Ben Cotton, eccentric dancer; R. M. Carroll, jig and fancy dancer; and Master Charles, fancy dancer. "Pony" Moore found the new company at odds with his efforts and left New York on February 12, 1859, to rejoin Matt Peel's touring troupe where he would remain until Matt Peel's death on May 4, 1859. Braham remained with the New York Company until March, when the minstrels left 444 Broadway.

Braham next became the leader of the string section of Robinson's Military Band, one of many popular instrumental ensembles concertizing in and around New York City. Bands had always been a staple of civic holiday festivities, and as military and paramilitary groups began to proliferate around the United States, so did the bands that accompanied them. During the summer months, military bands performed in tandem with concerts of operatic and sacred music at Jones's Wood and Clifton Park. During this phase of his New World apprenticeship, Braham refined his understanding of orchestral writing and learned new ways of blending serious and popular musical elements for the continued pleasure of an audience comprised of many different ethnic and cultural backgrounds. His participation in Robinson's Military Band also developed an association with the New York City Volunteer Fire Department that in later years would be ironically fortuitous. On October 17, 1859, the Third Grand Triennial Parade of the New York City Volunteer Fire Department took place, starting at Fifth Avenue and Thirty-fifth Street and ending at Union Park. Braham and Robinson's Band led the Guardian Engine Company #29 and the Index Hose Company #32 in the seventh of eleven divisions of the parade.

During his tenure as a bandmaster, Braham continued to be a familiar face in all of the pit orchestras in New York City. During this period David Braham fell in love with Annie Hanley, the teenage daughter of an Irish army officer. Braham met the girl through her brother, Martin, who had joined the Ravel family of acrobats and pantomimists at age fifteen, serving them first as an apprentice pantomime and later as manager of the company. The explosively talented Ravels had been a staple at Niblo's Garden well before Braham had arrived in the United States. When Braham started performing regularly in Niblo's orchestra, he was befriended by the teenage Hanley, whose mother had immigrated with her four children to the United States in 1846 when Martin was barely over two years old and Annie was said to be only an infant of three months. Given the lack of surviving records, Annie Hanley's early years are a matter of conjecture. Family tradition suggests that she was born in the barracks at Nenagh, where her father, William, was stationed, but there are great discrepancies in the year of her birth. The New York Census for 1900 gives Annie Hanley's birth date as April 1846 and the place of birth as New York City, while the 1890 "Police Census" for Manhattan suggests that she was born as early as 1840. Annie Braham's obituary in the *New York Times* gives her age as seventy-nine as of October 1920, placing her birth date in 1841.

According to Adelaide Harrigan, Annie recalled living near Canal Street in the late 1840s with her mother, sister Mary, and brother Martin—the oldest son, Dennis Flanigan, from an earlier marriage, having moved to Chicago, where he lost his life in the fire of 1871. As young girls, Annie worked as a bookbinder and Mary worked at "chromos," hand-coloring printed copies of famous paintings. Mary eventually married a genial and solvent Irishman named Patrick Maguire in the livery stable business whose able horsemanship won him the honor of driving the hearse carrying Lincoln's body in procession through New York City. Teenage Annie was much more impressed with David Braham's mild manner and striking good looks than his bank account, and after a brief courtship the couple were married in a private ceremony. Although no legible record of the marriage seems to exist in the records of Manhattan County, family tradition argues that the wedding took place late in 1859, after which David Braham began the search for professional employment commensurate with his duties as a husband and father.

Chapter 2

Act One: "Leader of the Orchestra"

After his experiences with Campbell's Minstrels and Robinson's Military Band, David Braham felt ready to step into the role of orchestra leader. The fluid nature of minstrelsy taught him to be flexible, able to cover performers' missed cues or sloppy entrances, while leading the string section of the band sharpened his skills as a conductor. He would not turn down pit performance work if it came his way, certainly; he had a family to support. But he knew he was qualified to conduct in New York City, and he felt certain that there was a place for his talents.

At the beginning of the 1859–60 season, New York City had nine theaters, nine places of variety entertainment, five concert saloons, three minstrel houses, two halls devoted to opera, and a menagerie and circus, all of which employed orchestras, if only to provide overtures and entr'acte entertainment. Many of the best positions were already taken: Thomas Baker was the musical director of Laura Keene's Theatre; Edward Mollenhauer had the same position at the Winter Garden; Robert Stoepel wielded the baton at Wallack's; and William Peterschen and Henry Beissenhertz conducted the bands at the Old and New Bowery Theatres, respectively. Braham bided his time throughout the season, continuing to play in pit orchestras and writing specialty arrangements for celebrities on tour, not the least (though the shortest) of which was General Tom Thumb (Charles Stratton), Barnum's famous midget, in residence at the Hope Chapel in April 1860.

Just as Braham began to think he would have to wait until the next season to realize his goal, Robert Fox and John C. Curran took over Mozart Hall on 663 Broadway, rechristened it "Canterbury Music Hall," and hired "Dave" (as he will become known to others from this point on) Braham as leader of the orchestra. Ads announcing the June 21, 1860, opening of the new theater boasted that the Canterbury was the "largest, coolest and most magnificent hall in the city" capable of seating two thousand people, with the "largest and best company in the United States" and an "Orchestra of Fifteen talented Musicians, Under the Management and Direction of Mr. D. Braham, Whose ability is too well known to require any comment" (*New York Clipper,* June 16, 1860). Even though his debut as a New York City conductor was heralded by an overly hyperbolic fanfare, Braham quickly demonstrated that he was suited to the task of directing the music in a theater specializing in variety entertainment. A later advertisement in the *Clipper* (July 21, 1860) trumpeted that the theater's interior featured "large and elegantly designed chandeliers, of the most elaborate and costly workmanship, enriched with globes, brilliantly illuminated by gas, resemble massive pyramids of light, with 'inter-tissued robes of gold and pearl.'" Certainly Braham's first appointment as a musical director in New York City was at no mean establishment.

At this point it is important to stop and address just what musical directors did in the 1860s. Obviously they rehearsed and conducted the orchestra, often playing as part of the orchestra as well. It was not unusual for conductors to direct from the piano or the violin (as was Braham's preference). Musical directors also functioned as contractors, hiring and firing musicians, librarians, copyists, instrumental and vocal arrangers, orchestrators, and composers. They provided necessary continuity between variety acts, as well as supplying performers with new material and updating the old. Although typically, in today's musical theater, each of the above duties is assigned to a separate specialist, in David Braham's day musical directors were jacks-of-all-trades whose single program credit belied the true extent of their creativity. The *Clipper*

(December 15, 1860), discussing the pantomimes popular during the Christmas holiday season, provides a provocative caricature of the conductor and orchestra and the effect they have on both audience and play:

> From the first note of the overture to the last in the grand crash that precedes the fall of the curtain, we are held, as it were, in a spell, which is a happy alternation from the sombre reality of our common destiny. A sort of fine insanity seems to have seized upon the musicians, the conductor, with baton in hand, being the most insane of the lot. How he and his associates can undergo the mere bodily movement inseparable from their duties in connection with a pantomime, seems extraordinary—the same with the facility with which they change from tune to tune. Every instrument has been brought into requisition, to give grandeur to the commencement of the said overture, and to impart expression to the earlier passages; but, presently there is a pause, and then a simple violin discourses for a minute about the Last Rose of Summer, Black-Eyed Susan, or some darkie romance; and so exquisitely, too, that the crowded audience, so noisy a few seconds since, is hushed into perfect silence. All eyes are fixed upon the player, not a word is spoken, even the breath seems to be held in suspense, until it might be thought that the dropping of a pin would be heard. On goes the magician or musician (for then he is both), finishing with a sweet, lingering note, that seems to lament its own ending. And then, how emphatic is the outburst of applause which stops the overture for a time, and is only relinquished to allow the loud, merry measure next on the orchestral score to be heard. The finish of that overture comes—fiddles, bassos, flutes, drums, trumpets, cymbals, triangles, and everything else joining in the final crash. . . .

The typical orchestra of the period was comprised of three violins, one each of viola, cello, and bass, flute, clarinet, trumpet (cornet), two horns, and percussion. Some orchestras added a trombone as well as a second clarinet and an additional cornet, and musical directors had to be creative in writing arrangements that could be adapted to varying orchestra sizes, particularly if the company went on tour.

Braham had his hands full during the summer season at the Canterbury. Not only did he occasionally have to conduct a full military band in addition to his regular orchestra, he also had to accompany the performances of a number of "stars" on the variety stage. Among the performers his orchestra accompanied were the celebrated Orrin family of acrobats and gymnasts (Professor G. E., George, Robert, and Master Ned Orrin); T. D. Rice, whose engagement for six nights beginning on July 28 was his last performance in New York City before his death; Charley White, the long-revered Ethiopean comedian; and the ever-popular Sam Cowell, advertised in July as "The Most Celebrated Comic Singer Of the present century."

The flexibility demanded of a variety conductor was well in evidence on August 6, when Sam Cowell's performance was encored again and again, ultimately holding up the rest of the show. As the *New York Clipper* (August 18, 1860) observed:

> Sam Cowell's reception at Canterbury Hall, on Monday night, 6th inst., was very enthusiastic. He was down for two songs on the bills, and after the first he had to come out twice more, amidst thundering applause. But the second appearance, at about 11 o'clock, took the shine out of everything—once, twice, thrice he was tally hoed out, and even then the folks were not satisfied, keeping up an incessant clapping, stamping, and halloaing. Three times the curtain rose for the next piece—a pretty harvest dance by all the girls—but it would-n't go, and after going through half the dance, they were compelled to beat a retreat, such was the hi-hi-ing. Cowell apologized, and the proprietors dittoed, but it took half an hour to stop the commingled cheering and whistling. Sam is on again this week.

Braham kept his composure and kept the music flowing throughout the melee, securing his credibility as a musical director and maintaining the reputation of the Canterbury as the site of respectable and well-executed entertainments.

Without a break, the summer season merged into the 1860–61 season on September 3 with a lineup that featured some of the best variety entertainers in the business: J. H. Ogden, the "Irish Ambassador, the comic singer of the age"; Eva Brent, singing operatic arias in English; Cool Burgess; and dancers Kate Pennoyer, Mary Partington, Kate Harrison, Annie Chester, and Marietta Ravel, who, according to the *Clipper* (September 15, 1860), "takes the house by storm night after night, being possessed of very attractive understandings, and is not at all backward in making known that fact." Plump, feisty, and curly-headed, Ravel was a frequent guest at the Braham home at 129 Laurens Street in Greenwich Village even before she joined the roster at the Canterbury.

Sam Cowell, a photograph from a Carte de Visite.

Her ongoing relationship with Braham's brother-in-law, Martin Hanley, whom she met during his apprenticeship with the Ravel Family, made her one of the family.

Throughout the fall, celebrities came and went, never failing to please the diversified tastes of the audience, never failing to challenge Dave Braham's creativity in the monumental preparation of new arrangements with every change of bill. Knife throwers, trapeze artists (some of them having only a single leg), "fancy-jig-and-shake-down" dancers, acrobats, strongmen, ballet dancers, and singers of every style imaginable crossed the boards at the Canterbury Music Hall, and each was accompanied on his or her journey by "Dave" Braham and his orchestra. Performers were especially pleased with Braham's composure in the pit. Such diversified entertainment involving acrobatics and weaponry is always fraught with accidents and requires a conductor who can handle a great deal of stress. The *Clipper* (September 15, 1860) noted one incident in which Professor Orrin's son Ned fell on his head after failing to catch the trapeze with his toes. Though momentarily everyone

Ballet at Rehearsal.

thought he was badly injured, he jumped to his feet and proceeded as if nothing had happened. Braham led the orchestra in a fanfare, and the audience cheered in the belief that the incident was a well-rehearsed part of the act.

On November 5, the bill included the Italian dancer and choreographer Antonio Grossi. Grossi particularly enjoyed Braham's ability to conduct for dancers and would work with him many times as their careers developed. Advertised as the "celebrated *danseuse* and singer," Adah Isaacs Menken arrived at the Canterbury on December 17 to perform with the tremendously propular Sam Cowell, Emma Frothingham, the Carlo family of knife throwers, and J. H. Ogden. The orchestra was advertised to number fourteen and the *corps de ballet* boasted twenty, and a portion of the hall had been refurbished with marbletop tables where, for thirty-seven cents, a patron could order drinks and watch the performance.

By the end of the year, Braham's life was thriving at work and at home. On November 30, 1860, his young wife gave birth to their first child, Annie Theresa, and Braham quickly learned to balance the responsibilities of being a professional musical director with the joys of being a father. For the remainder of his career Braham would be a "family" man, simultaneously nuturing a private household, overseen by his devoted though highly assertive wife, and the more public family of the theater. Already the public and private households were intermingled through his association with the Hanleys and the Ravels, but little did Braham know of the personal and professional musical theater dynasty that would follow from the birth of his daughter.

While David was building his reputation at the Canterbury, his brother, Joseph (recently having sired a son, Harry, destined for fame as a composer and conductor in his own right), was billed as musical director for Smith and Harrison's Art Union Concert Hall, 497 Broadway. Advertised as "The most popular place of amusement in the city," with "the largest and most efficient Orchestra in the city," the Art Union traded on the same kind of variety entertainment that made the Canterbury so successful. In addition to an ensemble of "fifteen first class performers," headliners included soprano Annie Bordwell, who sang ballads, Scotch songs, and operatic arias; champion jig dancer Kate Partington; little Nelly Grey, the Infant Wonder; Cool Burgess, the "original Bob Ridley"; Billy Jacobs, comic vocalist and eccentric comedian; and young Dan Williams, advertised as the "greatest banjoist in the world."

Back at the Canterbury, the irrepressible Sam Cowell gave his 102nd performance on March 16, 1861, accompanied by Marietta Ravel and the other house mainstays. The more headliners Braham's orchestra accompanied, the easier his job became and, by the end of March, the work became less about preparing new material for unfamiliar faces than about polishing numbers that had become audience favorites. As Braham began to relax into the comfortable pattern of Monday morning rehearsal (for the orchestra to run through the new material for the week) and evening performances, his delight was shattered on Sunday, March 24, when the Canterbury Music Hall was destroyed by fire. Fox and Curran immediately sought other quarters to house their popular variety bills. By April 1, they managed to take over the floundering French Theatre at 585 Broadway and the new Canterbury opened on April 15 with Marietta Ravel, J. H. Ogden, Agnes Sutherland (the "Scottish nightingale"), and David Braham leading an orchestra of eighteen "first-class musicians." On July 31 another tragedy struck the Canterbury when Mlle. D'Aubrey (Ida Crippin), playing Desdemona in a burlesque satire of Shakespeare's *Othello*, stepped too close to the sidelights, causing her dress to catch fire. Although every effort was made to protect the actress from the blaze, the injuries she sustained were so great that she died the following day. In the theater, the audience was unaware of the severity of the incident. The actress was hurried offstage and the evening's entertainment continued, the buoyant music arising from the pit keeping the audience from suspecting the worst. Ever calm and efficient, David Braham again managed to avert the disaster of a panicked audience.

During the summer season, Braham was joined by old friends from his Campbells days, Raffaele Abecco and A. M. Hernandez, whose pantomimic spectacle *The Southern Refugee; or, False and True* allowed Braham the opportunity to fashion a score that was both dramatic and patriotic by evoking the music of the Civil War. *The Southern Refugee* ran to the end of August to complete the summer season, and the new fall lineup began on September 2 with minstrel Charley Fox and the Nelson brothers, gymnasts. By the end of September, Hernandez and Abecco were back in the bills as was Ravel, who returned in October. Into the new year, Braham found himself accompanying spectacular pantomimes—*The Magic Laurel, The Southern Refugee*, and *Mazulm*—all filled with "wonderful transformations" and "startling tricks," and the ever-popular burlesque, *Battle of Farnborough*, as well as singers, dancers, acrobats, tightrope artists, and blackface comedians. Finally, late in January 1862, Braham provided the entertainment for a wedding celebration when Marietta Ravel officially became part of the Braham family, marrying Martin W. Hanley, now her manager, in a Roman Catholic ceremony celebrated by Bishop Hughes.

Old friends from the minstrel circuit came and went, and the new Canterbury chugged along until the end of April 1862, when the New York State legislature passed the Concert Saloon Law, forbidding the sale of liquor in places of entertainment. Prompted by the proliferation of waitresses of questionable morals, the "belles of the concert saloon," the law substantially curtailed the popularity of many of the variety houses in the city, and by the end of May most of the minor houses, including the Canterbury, had closed up shop. Considered by proprietors as a kind of puritanical witch-hunt, the controversy was the first of many David Braham would encounter in his long career. In an attempt to resist passage of the bill, the *Clipper* (January 25, 1862) argued:

> The orchestra at the Canterbury, ably led by Mr. Braham, is judiciously composed of gentlemen who might have become more famous with more opportunities. Now, what does the Canterbury do for them? It not only gives them employment, but it affords the

opportunity for artistic distinction which all true artists are continually seeking. Let the genius of art stand upon such an American platform, and art will then be properly worshiped. Therefore, let Brother Braham continue to sound his A with his usual grace, and "more power to his elbow."

Fortunately, musicians in such establishments were the last to be indicted, though the performers onstage were not as lucky.

On a Tuesday evening, between ten and eleven o'clock, a wide-awake officer thought he discovered the bartender at the Stadt Theater, at 39 Bowery, selling lager beer, as was his usual practice. Informing his superior, Captain Davis, of this alleged infraction of the Concert Saloon Law, the captain paid a visit to Police Superintendent Kennedy, who promptly ordered the arrest of proprietor, bartender, and players. With half a dozen patrolmen, Captain Davis entered the theater, which was quite crowded, and arrested Edward Harman, the proprietor; his wife, who was behind the bar at the time; and Christian Hanz, the bartender. Then, climbing onto the stage, to the intense disgust of all the audience, the police took into custody four actors and three actresses and conveyed them to the station house at Essex Market. Needless to say, the actors protested vociferously against their arrest, as illegal and unnecessary. One young actress claimed that she had a sick husband at home, who had no means to support his family. In an attempt to provide for her husband and offspring, she had gone upon the stage. "Was it just," she cried, "for a respectable woman to be locked up in a prison all night for Mr. Harman's offense?" However, because of the superintendent's orders, the captain had no right to act in the matter, and the actors were detained until morning. When they were brought before Justice Steers, he pronounced their arrest unlawful, and immediately ordered the discharge of all the players, who, in consequence, threatened a suit for false imprisonment, holding the officers responsible.

During his finals days at the Canterbury Music Hall, Braham participated in a benefit performance at the Academy of Music, the proceeds of which went to Billy Birch, the "King of the Negro Minstrels," and Ben Cotton, who were about to depart for Australia. Among those appearing at the May 13 benefit were blackface comic M. Ainsley Scott, Gustave Bideaux (who would ultimately give up minstrelsy for the life of a homeopathic doctor), and some of Braham's acquaintances from the minstrel circuit: Raffaele Abecco, a recent colleague at the Canterbury, and jig dancer Tommy Peel. In his first years as a professional conductor and arranger in New York City, Braham learned that even in the seemingly endless variety of music hall entertainment, there is a continuous repetition of faces, and he began to make mental notes about the strengths and weaknesses of individual performers so that the next time they appeared he could anticipate their musical needs. Sensitivity to performers' abilities was a hallmark of Braham's compositional style. In a rare interview for the *New York Dramatic Mirror* late in his career, after he had written his last collaboration with Edward (Ned) Harrigan, Braham described his songwriting process:

> My main difficulty while with Ned was to get the music to fit the voices and characters of the actors. It's a very different thing from writing a song for the general public. It's not uncommon, as you know, for a good actor to have a poor voice, and that naturally makes it difficult to devise an effective song for him. When poor Tony Hart was with the company we had to nurse his voice very carefully. And the songs for Johnny Wild had also to be very, very simple to suit the compass of his voice.

It was, indeed, his sensitivity to performers that led to Braham's next employment. On June 7, 1862, the *Clipper* announced that Henry Wood had acquired the old Jewish synagogue at 514 Broadway, opposite the St. Nicholas Hotel, and was hiring a company of minstrels—including Cool White, Raffaele Abecco, M. Ainsley Scott, and Gustave Bideaux (all performers familiar with Dave Braham and his violin)—with which to open on or about July 1. It is not surprising, therefore, in a business that turns on connections as much as talent, that when Wood's Minstrel Hall opened on July 7, 1862, David Braham and his brother Joseph (of the recently closed Art Union Hall) were advertised as members of the company. At Wood's, Braham acquired further experience with the minstrel-show format, especially in the satirical sketches that ended the evening's entertainment. On December 1, 1862 there was a spoof of *Othello* (complete with the popular "Ethiopian" comedian Eph Horn cross-dressed as Desdemona), followed on December 22 by *Dinah, or The Pardon Pell Mell*, a burlesque of Meyerbeer's recent grand opera *Dinorah; or, The Pardon of Ploërmel*.

Braham continued as a member of Wood's company until March 1863, when Braham's old friends Fox and Curran from the Canterbury Music Hall took over management of Wallack's old theater at 485

Eph Horn.

Broadway and converted what had become a German opera house into a variety hall christened "The New Idea." David Braham was hired as musical director for the enterprise, which opened on March 16, 1863, with a long list of headliners from minstrelsy and ballet. On March 23, the Melville Family of gymnasts from Australia were added to the list, followed by a tightrope walker, Albertini Chiriski; a strongman, Otto Wentworth; and pantomimists Marietta Zanfretta and A. M. Hernandez in April. In May, Braham was reunited with Agnes Sutherland, whom he had met through his brother, Joseph, at the Art Union Hall, and later with Antonio Grossi, who appeared with Hernandez and Zanfretta in a new production of *The Southern Refugee*.

The summer season began on June 1 with Grossi, Hernandez, and Zanfretta appearing in the pantomime *The Unfortunate*, and on July 6, the famous trick and fairy pantomime featuring the Martinetti Family, *The Green Monster and White Knight*, was given a lavish production with new scenery, refurbished musical arrangements, and a grand *corps de ballet*. The *Clipper* (July 18 1863) noted that Julien Martinetti played the role of the knight, Philippe played the chevalier, and Verlarde danced the role of Harlequin. The reviewer concluded that "the Martinettis for versatility, quickness of perception, grace and elegance of performance, are really excellent. We should have been pleased to have seen a larger attendance, for the artists engaged here deserve patronage, and ought to be rewarded nightly with crowded audiences."

Like the Ravels, the Martinettis were passionate, temperamental, and obsessively meticulous in their work. During a performance at the Howard Athenaeum in Boston in 1854, a six-foot-tall supernumerary from Vermont was standing in the wrong place. In broken English, Julien Martinetti reprimanded the lad for standing there. Defensively, the boy stood his ground, claiming that the captain of the supes had given him explicit directions and that he was not going to move. The blood rushing to his cheeks, Julien threatened to kick the Vermonter out of the way. A shouting match ensued, both sides hurling epithets that would have escalated to blows but for the appearance of the captain of the supes who convinced the lad to stand in another place so Martinetti could get his way. Once in his accustomed place onstage, Julien immediately became affable and continued the performance as if nothing had gone wrong. The young supernumerary's career in the theater, however, was short-lived.

The Martinettis reappeared in a ballet titled *La Sylphide,* and their celebrated animal-impersonation pantomime called *Jocko, the Brazilian Ape,* before leaving the bills on August 3. Although reviews of the summer productions were generally favorable, audience attendance was low and, on August 17, with a benefit performance for John Curran, the company manager, the season at "The New Idea" ended abruptly. David Braham had reaffirmed old friendships in the business and continued to perfect his craft, but once again consistent employment had eluded him. For nearly a year, Braham's name disappears from theater advertisements and reviews in New York City. The 1863–64 *New York City Directory* lists Braham as residing at 499 Broome Street during this period, and it is likely that David relied on the strength of his violin virtuosity to provide for the needs of his wife, Annie, and his three-year-old daughter, Annie Theresa.

The light at the end of the tunnel came with Robert W. Butler, the proprietor of the American Theatre at 444 Broadway. Butler's American Concert Hall, which had opened on August 8, 1860, with twenty-six-year-old actor Josh Hart as stage manager, had been the single variety establishment to survive the Concert Saloon Law of 1862. While Fox and Curran were struggling with "The New Idea," Butler was building his American Theatre into the finest variety house in New York, advertising talent such as Tony Pastor, Charley White, Bob Hart, Johnny Wild, Florence Wells, and Julia Melville. Advertisements at the end of April 1864 boasted a mammoth Ethiopian troupe, a great pantomimic

The Boston Museum in 1856.

ensemble, and a splendid ballet company, with a complete change in the bills every week. Butler was listed as manager; Monsieur La Thorne (who succeeded Hart during the 1860–61 season) was the stage manager; Paul Brilliant, late of the Ravel Troupe, acted as the balletmaster; and Albert Braham was the musical director. A month later, Albert was replaced by David Braham in the bills, and Antonio Grossi, Braham's favorite choreographic collaborator, was listed as balletmaster.

After a six-week summer engagement at the Boston Museum beginning on July 6, 1864, Butler's company returned to 444 Broadway, advertising a stellar assortment of talent along with Dave Braham and a magnificent *corps de ballet*. Beginning with creating the underscore for the first pantomime of the new season, *Old Granny Grumpy*, Braham was immediately in his element, accompanying farces and pantomimic spectacles such as *Turn Him Out, Slasher and Crasher, Buried Alive, The Goose with the Golden Eggs, The Laughing Hyena*, and *The House That Jack Built*, well into the New Year. In June 1865 Braham scored another patriotic pantomime, *The Scout of the Potomac*, a Civil War–inspired work that anticipated Braham's work ten years later with Harrigan on *The Blue and the Grey*.

Tony Pastor, who had been a staple of the American theater, left before the end of the season to create his own theater company, hiring many of the performers who had shared the bills with him at 444 Broadway, including Sheridan and Mack, who performed Irish songs and dances; James Gaynor, a singer and banjoist; Ida Duval, a seriocomic singer; and Johnny Wild, a blackface comedian and his singing wife, Blanche Stanley. Because David Braham was contracted for the full season at Butler's theater, David's brother, Joseph, was hired by Pastor as the musical director of a small orchestra of five to eight pieces. On March 22, the Pastor company began its tour with a two-night engagement in Paterson, New Jersey, in preparation for a July 31 opening at the Bowery Minstrel Hall, rechristened Tony Pastor's Opera House. Suddenly faced with the prosperity of consistent employment, Joseph and his family moved into larger quarters, at 12 Spring Street, and brother David moved nearby, to 283 Elizabeth Street.

Both Brahams had spent a month in Boston during the summer of 1865, Joseph in June at the Morris Brothers Opera House with the Pastor Company, David in July at the Boston Museum with Butler's Company. During the company's absence, 444 Broadway was cleaned and repainted for the new season. On opening night, August 17, 1865, such a large crowd assembled waiting for the theater to open that every seat in the house was taken within fifteen minutes of the doors opening. When it became evident that even standing room was overcrowded, barrels were stacked in the alley by the stage door to allow spectators outside the theater a view of the proceedings through the open windows of the building. Many old favorites reprised their acts, to the continued delight of their fans. Antonio Grossi created a ballet that was judged "one of the best seen in this city for a long time" and "one of the great attractions" of the theater.

Braham was certainly part of an immensely successful team, so it is difficult to understand what led him to give up the reins at 444 Broadway and pick them up at 720 Broadway, the old Hope Chapel, rechristened the "Theatre Comique," under the management of Harry Leslie, a pantomimist and tightrope walker. It was a variety hall like the American Theatre, but without the reputation or the stars. Perhaps the birth of his son George in November drove David to seek more lucrative employment and, leaving an established theater for a new venture, he most certainly could name his own price. In any event, the "Theatre Comique" opened on December 23 with the typical fare: acrobatics, songs, ballets, pantomimes, and Ethiopian delineations—material with which Braham was more than familiar—and disappeared from advertisements in April

Mechanics' Hall, from the Museum of the City of New York, The E.B. Marks
Collection. Used with permission.

1866. The new season at the American Theatre met with an even more
unfortunate end: on February 15, 1866, 444 Broadway was completely
destroyed by fire.

At some point during the 1865–66 season, David Braham and his
family moved to 137 Orchard Street, less than half a mile away from
Joseph's new residence, at 111 Forsyth. Joseph had found secure employment with the Pastor Combination and would remain with it until 1875,
when he left to travel with the Harrigan and Hart company. David was
less fortunate in long-term employment, and in May 1866 he was in the
market for a new job.

Braham's next employment came from his old friend Charley
White, whom he had known since the "old days" at the Canterbury
Music Hall. Beginning June 25, 1866, White had assumed the manage-
ment of Mechanics' Hall (formerly Bryant's Minstrel Hall) at 472
Broadway and hired Antonio Grossi to stage the dances and Braham to

conduct the musical continuity for a variety bill. The summer season that included such luminaries as Mlle. Belle Rosa (a *danseuse* from Paris), the Clinetop Sisters, Millie Flora, Bob Hart, Fanny Forest, Signor Henrico (the "Hercules of the age"), and Charley White himself, closed on September 1 and was immediately followed on Monday, September 3, by the fall lineup that advertised Josh Hart (Butler's former stage manager at the American Concert Hall) and a bevy of faces familiar to the variety circuit in New York City. The fact that Braham had worked with many of the performers at one or another theater since he began conducting in 1860 simplified somewhat his responsibilities in maintaining a polished orchestra in the midst of continually changing bills.

The program for the closing night of the season, April 30, 1867, suggests the kind of variety available at Mechanics' Hall, and the range of music for which Braham was responsible. The evening commenced with an overture arranged by David Braham from popular songs of the day. George Winship and George Warren followed in a blackface sketch, after which came Lizzie Shaw in a dance, the Broadway Boys in a song and dance, and Viro Farrand in a "Fancy Dance." This terpsichorean spectacle was followed by a comic sketch called "The Skillegans," performed by Frank Kerns, George Winship, and George Warren, and a ballet choreographed by Antonio Grossi titled "The Coquette," danced by Millie Flora, Helene Smith, Florence Wells, Laura Leclaire, Viro Farrand, Jennie Lorraine, Lizzie Shaw, Millie Young, and Georgie Natalie. Charley White then took the stage in a farce titled "The Stupid Servant," in which he played the character of John Breakall. Millie Flora followed with a dance, Dick Ralph with a song and dance, Florence Wells with another dance, and the Broadway Boys with a "Clog Dance." Another orchestral overture introduced the concluding burlesque, *Streets of New York*, featuring White, Winship, Kerns, Ralph, Warren, and H. Jones. All in all, Braham had to prepare seven dance numbers, a complete ballet, two full overtures, and whatever musical continuity was required for the sketches—and this was but a single evening's musical requirements!

During his tenure with Charley White, David Braham moved his family to a larger, more comfortable apartment, at 86 Carmine Street, a home he would maintain until the fall of 1876. Another daughter, Adelaide, had been born on March 15, 1867, and the Brahams welcomed the additional space afforded by the new residence. After White left the management of Mechanics' Hall, Braham found himself once again looking for work, and once again he found employment at the hands of old friends, this time Josh Hart and singer-dancer Frank Kerns, who had just acquired the management of the Eighth Avenue Opera House at Thirty-fourth Street. Beginning on July 20, Hart and Kerns attempted to re-create the Mechanics' Hall company, advertising the "best variety in the city," with the familiar faces of Dick Ralph, George Warren, the Broadway Boys, Laura Leclaire, Helene Smith, and Florence Wells, all accompanied by Braham's orchestra in the pit. By the end of the year, Johnny Thompson, Maggie Vernon, Crissie Canenen, Harry Bloodgood, and Little Mac (in the "Essence," an act he had popularized at Bryant's Minstrel Hall) had all appeared in the bills that featured, among the usual variety entertainments, a burlesque of Daly's melodrama *Under the Gas Light* titled *Under the Lamp Post*; an Irish drama, *Paudeen Rhue; or, The Hero of '96*; and a farce called *The Rescue of Colonel Kelly; or, The Manchester Riot.*

One of David Braham's earliest published compositions dates from this period, "Adolphus Morning-Glory," which was written expressly for Harry Bloodgood, the blackface singer and dancer who appeared regularly at the Eighth Avenue Opera House in the fall of 1867. It is unknown whether Braham set J. B. Murphy's text during Bloodgood's performance at the opera house, or whether Braham composed the song earlier, having witnessed and enjoyed Bloodgood's performances as early as 1865, at Hooley's Opera House in Brooklyn. In any event, the song's cover, published in 1868 by Ditson and Company, announces that it was "sung with great success by Harry Bloodgood, the popular song and dance man," so it is likely that it was part of Bloodgood's repertoire during the 1867–68 season.

Braham's composition evokes the characteristic style of postwar American music. An eight-bar introduction in a schottische style states the tune, a simple triadic structure comprised of two four-bar phrases, accompanied by traditional tonic-subdominant-dominant harmonies. The sung portion of the piece, little more than an eight-bar ditty, reiterates the infectious and easily memorable melody previously heard in the instrumental introduction. Each verse of the lyric is followed by a repeated dance section that not only utilizes the original melodic material but also intersperses it with rhythmically accented chords, to add variety to the musical texture and to emphasize the different dance steps employed in the choreography. Although the work is simple and typical of the period, it remains theatrically effective and demonstrates the technique of a composer familiar with working with dancers. "Adolphus

Morning-Glory" remained popular into the next decade, even reappearing at the Theatre Comique on July 11, 1870, when it was performed as a duet by Johnny Queen and Billy West.

Ever since Hart and Butler parted company at 444 Broadway during the 1860–61 season, there existed a rivalry between them to secure the best variety entertainers. At the Eighth Avenue Opera House, Hart, on many occasions, outbid Butler in acquiring star performers, but these proved to be Pyrrhic victories because Hart's theater, lacking a balcony, could not produce the revenue required to pay the exorbitant salaries he promised. Giving Johnny Thompson $150 a week, for example, for a single song and dance was an extravagance that could not be maintained indefinitely. In December 1867, a month after Kerns relinquished the partnership, leaving Josh Hart the sole proprietor of the establishment, the Eight Avenue Opera House closed. Once again out of a permanent position, Braham would have to wait for the arrival of a fellow countryman from England for his luck to change dramatically.

Chapter 3

Olio: "W. H. Lingard"

W hile David Braham, Josh Hart, and Frank Kerns were busy at the Eighth Avenue Opera House, Charley White, in association with Sam Sharpley (the leader of Sharpley's Minstrels), took over management of the Theatre Comique, the old Wood's Minstrel Hall, at 514 Broadway, and commenced yet another season of variety entertainment. A piece of doggerel verse published by the *New York Clipper* on January 24, 1868, suggests the kind of entertainment to be had:

> At the Theatre Comique, up in famed Broadway street,
>> Where three men are a flying in air,
> If you are not noodles, you will see some fine poodles
>> Doing tricks that are funny and rare;
> There's one little fellow, neither white nor yet yellow—
>> We believe he's the star of the troupe—
> Who jumps over girdles, and garters and hurdles,
>> Likewise through a flaming big hoop.

Charley White in character.

Although White had employed many of the established entertainers who were also appearing at other variety venues in the city, the Theatre Comique's revenues from August through December ($36,406) compared quite favorably with those of the more established houses. So, after the demise of the Eighth Avenue Opera House, David Braham applied to White for employment. Braham now had a wife and three children to provide for, and he looked forward to the return to a familiar hall with familiar performers doing familiar routines. It was not his old American acquaintances, however, who would have the most profound effect on Braham's future, but an English comic singer named William Horace Lingard.

Lingard made his New York City debut on April 6, 1868, at the Theatre Comique and was immediately heralded as one of the funniest men of his time. His act was in two parts: a series of comic sketches or characterizations accompanied by songs, and a "Statue Song" that embodied impersonations and "vocal illustrations" of a variety of different historical personalities, with an extraordinary diversity of dialects and physical mannerisms displayed in instantaneous changes of voice, look, demeanor, and costume. Among the characters represented in the first part were a henpecked husband forced to become a teetotaler against his will; an overstuffed diner attempting to make a speech; a British executioner lamenting his trade; and a young lady at the seaside chirping the song "On the Beach at Long Branch," an Americanized version of "On the Beach at Brighton," a British music hall favorite. The *Clipper*'s (April 18, 1868) review of Lingard's opening performance was characteristic of the critical praise lavished upon him:

> Nothing is strained or overacted. The delineations are marked by intelligence throughout, and in some cases there are refined touches which belong to the highest class of comedy acting, while his talent for mimicry and power of adaptation, nay, of identification of character, are wonderful. His representation, both in make-up and acting, of a young lady at the sea side, is one of the best things of the kind we have ever witnessed, and is alone worth seeing, and sufficient to make him an attractive card. This concludes the first part of his entertainment, and has been hailed with great enthusiasm each evening. His second part, called the "Statue Song," consists of singing one verse of a song relative to some particular person, and then he appears in a most capital make-up for that personage, as follows: Fabian in the duel scene in the "Corsican Brothers," King Theodore, Sir Robert Napier, Louis Napoleon, Bonaparte, Andrew Johnson, General Grant and George Washington—eight in all. The quick changes from one to the other, and the truthful likenesses to each, were really wonderful, the most successful of which was Andy Johnson, which created roars of laughter and three hearty cheers. In fact, after he had made the change and re-appeared, the applause was so great that he was obliged to disrobe himself of the brass button coat of Grant and reappear as Andy Johnson. Taken altogether, Mr. Lingard has met with one of the heartiest receptions that has greeted any performer from across the water for some time.

Lingard concluded his tremendously successful run at the Comique on May 30. On the twenty-ninth, he gave a farewell benefit performance to the second-largest crowd ever assembled in the building, and received from his grateful fans several bouquets of flowers, a diamond ring, a valuable lace handkerchief, and a "magnificent silk dress" for his performance of "On the Beach at Long Branch." By the time Lingard departed the Comique for a brief American tour, he had clearly won the adulation of the New York City public and fired the imagination of David Braham, who signed on as musical director for the Lingard combination. The two Englishmen were immediately compatible. In Braham, Lingard found a musician who could change musical styles as quickly as he could change costumes. In Lingard, Braham discovered a comedian who challenged him intellectually, and whose sense of humor recalled his youthful experiences at the theaters in London.

Lingard's Mimic Company opened at the Griswold Opera House in Troy, New York, on June 1, 1868, followed by engagements in Newark, Philadelphia, and Boston. Until the Boston leg of the tour, business was only fair, reports suggesting that Lingard was making a good impression, but not a lot of money. At the Boston Museum, however, the Lingard troupe—consisting of European magician Signor Logrenia, "Professor" William Hilton, Monsieur Airec, Lucy Egerton, Lizzie Wilmore, and Minnie Geary, along with Lingard and Braham—boasted of good business for a month-long run (July 6 to August 8). An advertisement for the Theatre Comique on August 15, 1868, in the *Clipper* boasts that Lingard "Has just concluded his First Season in Boston, where, for five weeks, the Museum has been crowded to overflowing, and on the occasion of his Benefit, on August 7th, hundreds were unable to gain admission." On August 11, Lingard's company opened a three-night engagement at the Academy of Music in Brooklyn during which Lingard's wife, Alice Dunning, made her first appearance in America as the Widow White in a farce, *Mr. and Mrs. Peter White.*

When the Theatre Comique reopened on August 17, 1868, Charley White, now associated with Sandy Spencer, who had bought out Sharpley's interest, turned over the managerial duties to Lingard, who immediately installed Braham as musical director. The theater itself had been refurbished during the summer, with the seats in the parquet, dress circle, and gallery stuffed and upholstered with a tasteful, red-striped fabric. The entire auditorium was repainted in blue and gold, and 186 patent-iron folding chairs were installed in the orchestra. The lobby was given a fresh coat of paint, and new rugs were installed throughout in an attempt to render the theater one of the most comfortable and well appointed in the city. As reported by the *Clipper* (August 15, 1868), it was the intention of the management to wipe out all trace of the "music hall business" and to conduct the Comique as a "vaudeville and variety theatre."

After the obligatory "Overture" by Braham and the orchestra, evoking the popular music of the day, the opening bill began with a ballad by British vocalist Lucy Egerton, followed by Joseph Kline Emmet (soon to make his mark as Fritz in Charles Gayler's play *Fritz, Our Cousin German*) performing a song and dance in whiteface titled "The Happy Dutchman." Lingard then appeared in several of the sketches that had made him a celebrity the previous season, followed by the ventriloquist Professor Hilton, with his three singing and talking heads. Alice Dunning sang a song, and for an encore, reappeared in a short-cut, Chinese-style dress that allowed the audience a good look at her legs. Lingard continued the evening's entertainment with his "Statue" routine, followed by Emmet with more Dutch comedy, another overture by Braham's orchestra, and the farce *Mr. and Mrs. Peter White* that concluded the performance.

Throughout his career, Braham would compose and arrange hundreds of overtures, some based on his own original melodies, others employing popular tunes, but all were expertly crafted medleys designed to transport the audience into the spirit of the entertainment. Unlike the conductor of legend who unwisely chose to construct an overture around the theme of "Home, Sweet Home," driving the audience into a kind of nostalgic melancholy, Braham always displayed expert judgment in his choice of marches, jigs, polkas, and waltzes, arranging them to fulfill and challenge the expectations of the house. So successful would Braham become in his choice of music that reviewers, typically unaccustomed to mentioning the incidental music in the bill, more often than not made special note of the overtures, praising their appropriateness, originality, and performance.

The bill for September 28 began with Braham's orchestra playing the overture to Donizetti's opera *La Figlia del Reggimento* (1840), followed by a farce, *The Day after the Wedding*. Next, Lingard appeared in his sketches, including Captain Jinks, "Walking Down Broadway" (a new "lady" song), the Guinea Pig Boy, a Young Lady at the Sea-Side (singing "On the Beach at Long Branch"), "Fifth Avenue," and "The Grecian Bend," satirizing a popular style of feminine posture, consisting of a

AND OTHER NEW SONGS BY

Wᵐ HORACE LINGARD.

PLAIN.

1. *THE GRECIAN BEND.*
2. *FIFTH AVENUE.*
3. *GUINEA PIG BOY.*

4. *FUNNY FELLOW.*
5. *SERGEANT COP!*
6. *YOU COULDN'T DO WITHOUT US.*

COLORED.

NEW YORK:

PUBLISHED BY WM. A. POND & CO., 547 & 865 BROADWAY.

W. H. Lingard demonstrating the "Grecian Bend."

mincing walk, with the head held high, bosom thrust forward, and the rear stuck out as far as possible.

In 1868, Wm. A. Pond published a medley drawn from Lingard's repertoire titled "The Lingard Quadrille," with David Braham credited as composer and arranger. "The Grecian Bend" was published by Pond in the same year, with Lingard credited as the author and composer. Twenty-eight years later, in 1896, Braham took out his own copyright on "The Lingard Quadrille" and, the following year, applied for a copyright for "The Grecian Bend." How much Braham had a hand in the original song is unknown, because the copyright copy is no longer extant. Attributions are often difficult to make with certainty during this period because performers often appropriated songs they performed and published them under their own names. In *Sing Us One of the Old Songs*, for example, Michael Kilgarriff attributes "The Grecian Bend" to "Pony" Moore, who seemed particularly fond of appropriating other composers' works.

In October and November, the Galton Sisters (Susan and Blanche) came across the boards of the Comique performing operetta, but the bill remained pretty much focused on Lingard's impersonations, Hilton's ventriloquisms, Emmet's Dutchisms, and Alice Dunning's legs. Singing actress (and soon-to-be manageress of her own theater at 720 Broadway) Lina Edwin appeared on November 9, and so impressed David Braham that he set her lyrics for, "Waiting at the Ferry" to music. Another fine example of Braham's early work utilizing easily accessible diatonic harmonies and repetitive melodic phrases, the song is in a simple verse/chorus form, where the chorus melody is a repetition of the first two phrases of the verse. The contour of the melody is designed to demonstrate Lina Edwin's vocal agility within a fairly conservative range (an octave and a third). Unlike the chorus of "Adolphus Morning-Glory," which was published as a solo vocal line, the chorus of "Waiting at the Ferry" was arranged for a vocal quartet. Like "The Grecian Bend," "Waiting at the Ferry" was recopyrighted by David Braham in 1897, twenty-eight years after the original publication in 1869 by White, Smith, and Perry.

During the early morning hours of Friday December 4, the Theatre Comique was partially destroyed by fire caused by the night watchman's failure to turn off the heat after the Thursday night performance. Undaunted, the Lingard Company moved to the Brooklyn Academy of Music (where it had performed occasionally during the fall), while the management (having incurred a loss of fifteen thousand dollars with no insurance) took the opportunity to refurbish and improve the theater building, adding an extra row of chairs in the orchestra, a ladies toilet room off the dress circle, new machinery for the stage, and an arch in the lobby between the box office and the auditorium, making the entrance one of the handsomest of any theater in the city. On February 6, 1869, the *Clipper* detailed the various improvements at the theater. There were now 225 iron chairs in the orchestra painted blue and upholstered in brown leather. The benches in the parquet, seating 220 patrons, and those in the dress circle, seating 270, were newly upholstered in green leather. At the front of the circle were 45 balcony chairs, painted blue and upholstered in red. The gallery benches, accommodating 220 people, also were painted, but no color was specified. The facings of the two balconies were painted with a blue ground pinked with gold, with sixteen brackets for gas, each with three burners. The private boxes were papered in imitation gold and tastefully decorated.

The new building was advertised to open on Monday, February 1, 1869, with the Lingard company in a "mythological, musical, local burlesque extravaganza" titled *Pluto; or, The Young Man who Charmed the Rocks* by H. B. Farnie, based on H. J. Byron's burlesque *Orpheus and Eurydice; or, The Young Lady who Charmed the Rocks*. The cast included Alice Dunning as Orpheus, Ethel Norman as Aristaeus, W. H. Lingard as Pluto, Dickie Lingard as Apollo, Lina Edwin as Eurydice, Lillie Hall as Proserpine, and George Atkins as Clotilda. Costumes were designed by Samuel May of London, scenery by Richard Marston, props and furnishings by Waldron and Donnelly, and music by David Braham.

In this version of the Orpheus tale, Eurydice complains of being married to a very poor young author (Orpheus), preferring the charms of one Aristaeus, a "sporting party, fast and loose," who ingratiates himself with her husband by promising to introduce him to a publisher. While Orpheus is out buying wine, Aristaeus makes love to Eurydice, but as he is about to speed her away in a "handsome cab," she complains that something has bitten her. The maid, Clotilda (called Tilda or Tilly), enters with Eurydice's wailing baby just in time to find her mistress dying and on her way to "Charon's Ferry." When Orpheus returns with the wine, Tilly tells him what has transpired, and Orpheus sets off to Hades in quest of his wife—much to the bemusement of Apollo, who, believing any husband insane for wanting his wife back, gives Orpheus a magical lyre to take on his journey.

In Hades, Pluto is discovered complaining about the extravagances of his wife, Proserpine, threatening to divorce her unless she become more frugal in her spending. His mood changes immediately upon the entrance of Eurydice, who leads him on a merry chase right into the arms of Proserpine, who claims that her husband's infidelity gives her just cause for divorce (and a huge settlement). Orpheus enters looking for his wife and immediately succumbs to Proserpine's advances. Pluto and Eurydice's attempts to disengage their respective spouses lead to a general melee that is quieted only when Orpheus begins to play the magic lyre, causing everyone to dance. Gradually the dancing becomes more and more spirited until the entire *dramatis personae* collapse from exhaustion. In the end, Pluto agrees to let Eurydice leave Hades with her

"Up in a Balloon," printed in Wm. A. Pond and Co.'s *Spirit of Burlesque*, edited by Henry B. Farnie.

husband only if Orpheus can make his exit without looking back, but the sound of Pluto's kissing Eurydice good-bye is too much for Orpheus to bear. He turns around, condemning himself and his wife to an eternity of the attentions of Pluto and Proserpine.

While the original burlesque by Byron traded on familiar English ditties and operatic airs, Farnie's version—revising lyrics to include up-to-date topical references—employed "Up in a Balloon," credited to G. W. Hunt and introduced by Alice Dunning, "Tommy Dodd," credited to Ernée Clarke; a cancanlike galop called "The Broadway Toff," advertised "As sung by Miss Lydia Thompson"; and a polka titled "Farewell to Proserpine." Farnie's lyrics to "Up in a Balloon" suggest the kind of anachronistic fun that was in play in mythological Hades:

I am, as you know a Madison belle,
Who did captivate once a magnificent swell,
He was envoy, ambassador, or something rare,
To king-what's-his-name, of I-do-not-know-where!
'Twas at Saratoga, a year come next June,
We walk'd and we talk'd by the light of the moon;
There was squeezing of hands, follow'd up by a kiss,
And as far's I remember, I felt just like this . . . Ah!
Chorus:
Up in a balloon, boys,
Up in a balloon . . .
All among the little stars
Sailing round the moon . . .
Up in a balloon, boys,
Up in a balloon . . .
It's something very jolly
To be up in a balloon!

The wedding was fixed, the presents were bought,
And from Tiffany's, jewelry was to be brought,
But alas, when the bill to my dear lover went,
By some misadventure he had not a cent!
My guardian, a broker a-way down in Wall,
Provided him plenty of funds at my call;
But when the old gentleman questioned him where
His securities were, why, he answered "up there!" Ah!
Chorus

Although Ditson's 1869 publication of the "Pluto Quadrille, Containing all the Popular Airs in the Burlesque of that Name" credits Lingard as composer, his actual contribution to the score is unknown. Braham's contribution appears to have rested with the arrangement and orchestration of songs and the composition of dance and incidental music for the burlesque.

Pluto did not open to good notices. One bright spot, according to the critics, was the scenery and costumes, which were praised highly. In fact, the closing scene was considered the best of any burlesque finale being performed in the city because the stage was not overcrowded with ballet girls hiding the scenery. However, the text was criticized for its weak and far-fetched puns, bad rhymes, poor taste in political satire, and unfunny jokes. The *Clipper* (February 13, 1869) noted that even Lingard had to explain several punch lines to the audience. In spite of the criticism, however, *Pluto* continued to run throughout the spring, reappearing in a "reconstructed" form on April 26, when the Theatre Comique hyperbolically advertised the "Grand Reconstruction and Eighty-eighth time" of *Pluto*, now subtitled "The Magic Lyre." Calling the work "The liveliest and best burlesque extant," the ad employed a standard marketing technique and stressed the word "new." There was to be new music, new dialogue, new costumes (this time from Parisian designs), and the production promised to be on a "scale of magnificence" that would surpass the previous production in every respect. Although J. C. Williamson (the Dutch-dialect comedian who would establish musical theater in Australia) had succeeded Lingard in the role of Pluto through the run, Lingard reprised the role for six performances, beginning on April 26. This time the critics were less demanding, emphasizing the pleasant new songs—particularly "The Velocipede" sung by Alice Dunnings and her sister Dickey Lingard—and the blondes in the cast.

While David Braham was conducting *Pluto* at the Theatre Comique in May, "lightning song and dance" artists Hank Mudge and Joe Lang were performing another of his early compositions, "The Footprint in the Sand," during the week of May 24, 1869 at Hooley's Opera House in Williamsburgh, Brooklyn. With lyrics by W. E. McNulty, "The Footprint in the Sand" is another schottische tune with a much richer harmonic palette than "Adolphus Morning-Glory" or other Braham songs of the period. Although typical of the verse/chorus pattern of the period, where the chorus simply reiterates the first phrase of the verse, the melody makes great use of harmonic alterations and leaps to create a "tripping" and "rolling" effect in the music. Since the lyrics speaks of breakers rolling on to the beach, and a young maiden tripping lightly on the shore, this work constitutes an early example of Braham's character-istic word-painting through music, which would flourish during his cel-ebrated collaboration with Edward Harrigan.

The Theatre Comique closed its regular season on June 5 when the company, including David Braham and his orchestra, traveled to Boston for a nine-week summer engagement (June 7 to August 5) at Selwyn's Theatre. Lingard and his wife had left on June 1, necessitating a change in the cast of *Pluto*, and business was not good for the final week of the run. The first week of the engagement in Boston began with a continu-ation of *Pluto* to middling business. The second week added a farce called *Who Speaks First?* as well as Lingard in his popular impersonations. The third week introduced the transvestite farce *The Captain's Not Amiss*, and continued the run of *Pluto* to only fair business. The fourth week adver-tised *Captain of the Watch* to open the bill, and it was announced that *Pluto* would be withdrawn from production on July 3. Finally, claiming that Lingard was completing one of the most successful seasons in Selwyn's history with receipts for three weeks totaling $16,124, an adver-tisement in the *Clipper* on July 17, 1869, announced the 178th and last performance of *Pluto* on that day, a Saturday.

As the Lingard company was completing its season in Boston, it was announced in New York City that B. A. Baker had accepted the position of stage manager at the Theatre Comique for the coming season, replac-ing Lingard who had become the sole lessee of the Theatre Comique in Boston. Charley White, who had attempted a summer season at the Comique presenting burlesques and pantomimes but little of the old variety fare, hoped to make the establishment a legitimate place of amusement. Variety entertainment, it seemed, was destined to be replaced by "straight" plays. Braham's old friend in variety entertainment Josh Hart was now the business and stage manager for the Howard Athenaeum in Boston.

Anticipating a dearth of employment opportunities back home in New York City, David Braham signed on for a short engagement with the Lingard Combination at the Holliday Street Theatre in Baltimore, commencing on August 9. The company consisted of Alice Dunning, Dickie Lingard, Edward Righton, Edith Challis, Conway Cox, Belle Howitt, Lillie Hall, and Agnes Wood. The seemingly inextinguishable burlesque *Pluto* was the mainstay of the first week of the engagement.

The Baltimore review cited in the *Clipper* of August 21, 1869, was especially praiseworthy of Braham's contribution, noting that the "only real interest that centres in the piece is the many beautiful airs and grotesque dances with which it abounds. . . .The orchestral music, directed by Prof. Braham, was very fine, some of the best musical talent of Baltimore comprising a portion of the orchestra."

At the end of the first week of the Baltimore engagement, Braham was called back to New York City to resume his post as musical director of the Theatre Comique. Even though Charley White had hoped to make the establishment a "legitimate" place of amusement, he was not above including dancers and farces as curtain-raisers and orchestral entr'acte entertainment. The new venture opened on August 16 with a production of Tom Robertson's play *David Garrick*, introduced by a "grand fantasie solo" by the celebrated danseuse Mlle. Diana, and the American premier performance of a new farce titled *The Pretty Horse Breaker*. Braham's contributions to the evening's entertainment were duly noted by the *New York Herald* (August 17, 1869) in a review that rejoiced at seeing the "popular orchestra leader, back in his old place."

Before returning to New York City, Braham had arranged the music for the second week of Lingard's run in Baltimore, scheduled to include a burlesque, *The Maid and the Magpie; or, The Fatal Spoon*; the farce *The Captain's Not Amiss*; and Alice Dunning's "Bouquet of Melodies." The new burlesque afforded Braham much opportunity for ersatz melodrama in the musical underscore and ample possibilities for comic ballads and ensembles. In *The Maid and the Magpie*, Alice Dunning performed the trouser role of Pipo, a stagestruck young man, while Edward Righton took on the drag role of Ninetta with the song "I Am a Village Beauty." Conway Cox assumed the role of an old clothes man named Isaac, and Edith Challis cross-dressed as his rakish son, Gianetto. J. S. Edwards played the funniest character in the burlesque, Ninetta's father, who entered dressed in the dilapidated uniform of a French corporal, accompanied by the most lugubriously melodramatic music. His tearful reunion with his daughter after years of absence, and his singing of the ballad "I'm Hard Up since my Well Run Dry," were considered the comic high points of the evening. The plot abounded with ludicrous situations interspersed with political and topical satire, exotic dances, and highly entertaining vocal ensembles, one of which, performed by Pipo, Ninetta, Gianetto, and Isaac, merited four encores.

When the engagement closed in Baltimore on August 21, Lingard;

his wife, Alice Dunning; and her sister Dickie Lingard went up to Boston to open Lingard's Adelphi Theatre (formerly the Theatre Comique). Because David Braham had chosen to return to his position at the Theatre Comique, he encouraged Lingard to hire as musical director his nephew John, who had recently completed his studies at the Boston Conservatory and was working as a musician in Boston. Lingard took Braham's advice and, after postponing the scheduled September 1 opening to allow for more rehearsals, the Adelphi Theatre raised its curtain on September 6 with the burlesque extravaganza *Kenilworth*.

Back at the Theatre Comique in New York City, David continued to intersperse the "legitimate" drama with his highly touted musical interludes, but the novelty of the experiment was quick to wear off, and even the critics who found much delight in August were substantially less enthusiastic in September. A sharp decline in business marked the beginning of the end and, on September 18, 1869, barely a month after *David Garrick* opened to good reviews, the Theatre Comique closed, casting David Braham again among the ranks of the unemployed.

Chapter 4

Act Two: "Variety Virtuosos"

David Braham did not have to wait long for new employment. Following the failure of the Theatre Comique, it was closed "for alterations" during the week of September 20, and Robert W. Butler, Braham's employer at 444 Broadway, replaced Charley White as manager. Seemingly unaffected by "Black Friday," the stock market crash on September 24 that struck a crippling blow to the city's economy, the Theatre Comique reopened on Monday, September 27, as a variety house to a densely crowded audience, with a number of familiar faces on the roster: Antonio Grossi was on board as balletmaster, and the orchestra was under the direction of "Professor" Dave Braham, recently elevated to academic status in all the advertisements.

After a spirited overture in the characteristic Braham style, the opening-night curtain rose to reveal the company dressed like ordinary people, led by Maurice B. Pike in a rendition of "The Star-Spangled Banner." Lizzie Whelpley followed in a dance, G. F. McDonald and Lew Brimmer in a blackface sketch, Sallie Clinetop in a dance, D. L. Morris in a Dutch stump speech, Dick Ralph with a song and dance, Rita Percy impersonating classical statuary, and Maude De Lasco offering "vocal stylings." British entertainer, Rita Percy, "one of the best formed women ever seen on the stage," made her American debut in statuesque performances representing "Joan of Arc"; "Rebecca at the Well"; "Faith"; "Hope"; "Memory"; a "Greek Slave," in two different poses; the "Queen of Night"; and "Columbia." Reviewers complained that the lighting effects did a disservice to the young lady's charms which were draped so beautifully and modestly that no one could be offended. De Lasco's efforts were not appreciated by the audience, and she did not appear after Wednesday, September 29. A ballet devised by Antonio Grossi, featuring Mlles. Venturoli and Augusta, interrupted the proceedings, which concluded with Sheridan and Mack in their character delineations followed by a "Dutch" farce titled *Forty Winks*.

For Sheridan and Mack, David Braham produced the seriocomic ditty "Little Green Veil," with lyrics by W. E. McNulty (who had already provided the text for "The Footprint in the Sand"). The tale of love at first sight between the singer and a flirtatious young lady who hides her charms behind a "little green veil," the song develops the theatrical device of interrupting the vocal line with an instrumental interlude that Braham had previously introduced in "Footprint." Interpolating two-bar musical interludes into the sung chorus not only provided musical variety to the tune, it also gave the performers the opportunity to add stage business to their songs. It demonstrates a remarkable sensitivity to the proclivities of comic performers, who typically pack their routines with physical gags, satirical postures, and audience interplay that often break the flow of the melody. Braham solved the problem by working the business into the structure of the song. In addition, Braham provided a lilting eight-bar dance break using music that was distinct from, though evocative of, the sung portion of the piece. Braham would repeat this trick many times in his compositions for Edward Harrigan.

By the November bills, David Braham had been reunited with his old friends the La Pointe (or Lapointe, as they were then billed) Sisters and the gifted stage manager Monsieur La Thorne, who replaced George F. McDonald late in October. Surrounded by familiar and trusted collaborators, Braham was back in his element, providing the underscore to spectacles such as *A Night in Dreamland*, and the ballet *Demonio*, featuring Kate Pennoyer. On December 13, the Lingard Combination, back on tour since October 14, began performing the indefatigable *Pluto; or, The Magic Lyre* during their month-long engagement at the Grand Opera House in New York, which would also include *The Maid and the Magpie*. Suddenly Braham's work was being performed simultaneously at several theaters in the city.

The New Year's Eve performance of *Pluto* was particularly newsworthy because it marked the onstage reconciliation between W. H. Lingard and his wife, Alice Dunning, who, according to the press, had been having their share of marital problems. The January 8, 1870, issue of the *Clipper* described the event:

> In the scene where Orpheus (Miss Dunning) demands of Pluto (Mr.
> Lingard) her release from Hades, Mr. Lingard appeared very nervous
> and excited . . . and just as Miss Dunning began to sing, "Fare Thee
> Well, Dove," he flung aside all restraint, and catching her in his arms,
> kissed her again and again. Miss Dunning, rushing from his embrace,
> disappeared behind the scenes, leaving Mr. Lingard apparently in a
> fainting condition, while resting on the shoulders of Miss Harris
> [Proserpine]. In a few moments he made his exit, when the audience
> burst forth in thunders of applause at witnessing this little scene
> between man and wife. . . . On reaching the *finale* and using the
> words "Remember Pluto," the audience again became very enthusias-
> tic over the reconciliation. The curtain descended, but so loud were
> the calls for the hero and heroine that Mr. Lingard appeared before
> the curtain and said: "Ladies and Gentleman—I thank you for your
> good wishes. Mrs. Lingard and I will get along nicely now. And I
> desired to commence the New Year well, and to do better for the
> future. But (in great agitation) I fear my conduct on the stage this
> evening has only offended her whose regard I value more than the
> good opinion of all the world."

January 1870 brought more than peace to the Lingards: It ushered in the Clodoche troupe to the Theatre Comique, providing Braham with the opportunity of accompanying yet another ballet, *The Silver Knights*, and George H. Coes, who would figure prominently in Braham's career at the Eagle Theatre.

With the month of February came the pantomime *The Village Blacksmiths* and the ballets *Les Echos du Tyrol* and *The Isle of Nymphs*, in addition to the Original Comique Minstrels including George Coes, John Hart, Master Barney, and Add Ryman. On February 19, Lizzie Whelpley and Lottie La Pointe performed a "Lingard Medley" arranged by David Braham; Jennie Kimball performed in songs and sketches, and the entire company sang and danced "Shoo Fly, Don't Bodder Me," the walk-around that had infected the Comique since November 8.

With Jennie Kimball (or Kimble, as it is on the published music), David Braham composed "Flirting in the Twilight," a buoyantly seductive and rangy melody designed to demonstrate the entire compass of Kimball's lyric soprano voice. Virtually a companion piece to "Little Green Veil," "Flirting in the Twilight" exhibits the same general structure, interspersing sung chorus lines with musical interludes and following each chorus with an eight-bar dance break in a distinctively *schotissche* style. In both compositions, while maintaining the standard verse/chorus structure, Braham has exhibited an adventuresome use of chromatic alterations of diatonic scale tones and a rather sophisticated harmonic texture accompanying his characteristically memorable melodies.

As the season continued into the summer months, Braham accompanied more pantomimes (*Jocrisse; or, Harlequin and the Genius of Plenty, The Fairy's Gift, Jack and Gill* [*sic*], *Knick-Knack; or, Harlequin Will-o'-the-Wisp of the Mystic Dell*); ballets (*The Water Nymphs, The Holiday Sports of Spain*), spectacles (*Warriors of the Sun*); and the "four dancing blondes," Rose Lucille, Ida Greenfield, Emily Herbert, and Fannie Lucille, performing the "Shoofly Cancan," a number designed by its brazen abandon to ignite the blood of the most lethargic of audiences. Certainly J. H. Wallack, scene painter; T. Bowers, theater machinist; W. Kohler, gas specialist (lighting designer); M. La Thorne, stage manager (director); Antonio Grossi, choreographer; and David Braham, musical director, had put in a full season at the Comique. Audiences received a lot for their money in 1870. Admission to the gallery was twenty-five cents; and to the dress circle, fifty cents. Orchestra seats and balcony chairs cost a dollar, and private boxes were advertised at six dollars and five dollars.

At some point during the rigorous weekly schedule of eight performances (matinees on Wednesday and Saturday), staging rehearsals, and orchestra read-throughs, Braham found time to compose and arrange a "medley quadrille" for concert band titled "Par Excellence." The work, published as part of the *Band Master's Repertoire* by E. H. Harding in 1870, consists of five movements of various dance meters, including a spirited polka, a flowing barcarole, a military quick step, and a galop. Each movement is marked by a distinctively memorable tune, suggesting that Braham's prodigious melodic gifts were not only directed to the creation of popular vocal music.

The summer season closed on Saturday, September 3, 1870, followed immediately by the fall lineup on the following Monday. Although late in the summer Butler had formed a partnership with E. G. Gilmore in the management of the Theatre Comique, little had changed in the artistic management of the theater. La Thorne continued to function as stage manager, Grossi as balletmaster, and Braham as musical director, with Edward Simmons replacing Wallack as scenic artist. Among the featured performers for this season were comics Master Barney, J. F. Wambold, and George Coes; *danseuses* Giovanna Mazzeri and Mlle. Venturoli; seriocomic vocalist Emma Grattan, formerly a member of the Elise Holt and Lydia Thompson burlesque troupes; Braham's previous employer, the minstrel Charley White; the Australian Ethiopian "professor" J. E. Taylor; the Siegrist Family, with their trained dogs; and the Lauri Family, internationally acclaimed pantomimists. Braham and Grossi produced more ballets, including *The Black Dwarf*; *Crystalline; or, The Fairies of the Mist*; *The Brigand's Daughter*; and the holiday spectacular, *Jolly Santa Claus; or, The Fairy of the Mistletoe*, which featured J. C. ("Fatty") Stewart as Santa Claus. Reviews were consistently good for La Thorne, Grossi, and Braham with critics making special note of the excellence of the orchestral sound and the superior quality of the musical arrangements.

While Braham was laboring at the Theatre Comique in the spring of 1871, William Horace Lingard and company had settled into 720 Broadway (now called Lina Edwin's Theatre) for an extended engagement beginning on March 6. A month later, on April 3, the Lingard-Braham burlesque *Pluto* commenced a two-week run with Lingard, Alice Dunning, and Dickie Lingard reprising the roles of Pluto, Orpheus, and Aristaeus, respectively, and Louise Terry making her American debut as Proserpine. Not untypically, *Pluto* carried the Lingard company to the end of its engagement on April 15.

Down the street at 514 Broadway, during the afternoon and evening of Monday, April 24, 1871, two benefit performances took place on behalf of stage manager La Thorne. Although the theater was only about two-thirds full for the matinee, the evening show was crowded to the rafters, with spectators anxious to pay their respects to the stage director who had kept things moving at an unflagging pace for the past two seasons. At the termination of the evening's ballet, "Fatty" Stewart called La Thorne out onstage, where he was received with a great ovation. Once he could be heard over the cheering crowd, Stewart presented the stage manager with a gold medallion worth more than two hundred dollars as a token of the esteem in which he was held by the actors and staff of the Theatre Comique. On the medal measuring two and a half inches in diameter, was a gold playbill inscribed with the words "Programme. Presented to Mons. La Thorne by his friends, N.Y., April 24, 1871." After the stage manager expressed a few words of heartfelt thanks, the scenery parted to reveal the entire company assembled onstage to congratulate him, and Braham led the orchestra in the performance of one of the popular melodies of the day.

Three days later, on Thursday evening, April 27, it was David Braham's turn to appeal to the generosity of the public who, according to the *Clipper* (May 6, 1871), responded in a most liberal manner. For his benefit, Braham requested a "business as usual" performance. Not wishing to make a speech, he wanted no special accolades or presentations beyond the hearty appreciation of the audience for his work in the pit and the extra money the benefit would generate. He enjoyed the work he did, and it enabled him to provide for his family. For David Braham, that was enough; he had no need to be in the spotlight.

The season closed at the Theatre Comique on Wednesday, May 31, 1871, with a sketch titled "The Last of the Mohicans"; J. F. Wambold in songs and a banjo solo; Ashcroft and Morton performing a new and original song and dance called "Darling Little Emeline"; a burlesque of Shakespeare's *Richard III* called "Bad Dickey"; Lisle Riddell singing seriocomic songs; a ballet titled *Saffronilla*; George C. Davenport's Irish comic songs; Geraldine and Leopold performing gymnastic feats; and J. W. Morton's Dutch song and dance. The only new attractions were the reappearance of Lisle Riddell and a dramatic sketch written by J. C. Stewart titled "Our Country Cousins," which concluded the performance. Beginning on June 1, the Theatre Comique Company began a summer tour, stopping in New Jersey at Elizabeth and Paterson, then on to Hartford, Connecticut; Springfield and Worcester, Massachusetts; and Providence, Rhode Island, ending in a month-long engagement at the Boston Theatre in Boston starting on June 19.

As the Theatre Comique troupe was loading into the Boston Theatre, the 1870–71 season at Boston's Howard Athenaeum was drawing to a close. John Stetson was the manager, replacing Josh Hart, who had become the acting and stage manager at the Globe Theatre in New York City. John Braham, late of Lingard's Adelphi Theatre, was billed as the musical director, leading a twelve-piece orchestra. The headliners at the Athenaeum included D. L. Morris; Jennie Engle; J. S. Murphy;

The exterior of the Boston Theatre in 1854.

Charles Howard; Harry Bloodgood; Ada Richmond; the Bedouin Arabs; Maffitt and Bartholomew; and the team of Harrigan and Hart, who made their first appearance at the theater on May 1 in a sketch titled "The Little Fraud." John Braham would leave a lasting impact on the career of Harrigan and Hart. Not only would he arrange Harrigan's simple melodies for use in the performances, he actually composed the music to several of Harrigan's early lyrics. In addition, when Harrigan and Hart were ready to leave Boston en route to the "big time" in New York City, John provided Harrigan with a letter of introduction to his Uncle, David, suggesting that he might be of some help to them in the future. Little did he know the extent of his prophecy!

Because the Athenaeum was closing as the Comique company began its Boston season, David Braham did not have the opportunity to see Harrigan and Hart perform that season. Nephew John, on the other hand, often visited the Boston Theatre to see what his uncle was up to. During the week of July 3, John saw a military spoof called "Obeying Orders"; James Wambold playing the banjo and imitating the sounds of birds and frogs; Ashcroft and Morton in songs and dances; Lisle Riddell in a selection of character songs; a comic sketch titled "Not to Be Shaken"; the ventriloquist Professor Hilton, with his three talking heads; a "Plantation" sketch; Jennie Engle's medley of popular songs; a grand ballet; Hughey Dougherty's "Essence of Old Virginny"; Geraldine and

Edward Harrigan and Tony Hart.

Leopold in their gymnastic feats; and Ashcroft and Morton in a routine called "Gens d'armes," singing the famous duet from Offenbach's *Geneviève de Brabant*. The evening's performance concluded with "The Other Fellow," a comic sketch by "Fatty" Stewart. Three performances were advertised on July 4: at two-thirty, six, and after the fireworks.

After the Theatre Comique Company concluded its engagement in Boston on July 15, the company dispersed for the summer, and David Braham returned to his family at 86 Carmine Street. Another daughter, Alice (more familiarly known to the family as Ida), had been born late in 1870, and David was anxious to help his wife look after the baby. The children were growing up quickly: Annie Theresa was almost eleven, George was six, and Adelaide had just turned four. Braham looked forward to spending the next season in New York surrounded by his wife and children.

David Braham did not return to the Theatre Comique for the 1871–72 season. Instead he followed Robert W. Butler, who had recently become manager of the Union Square Theatre, a new place of entertain-

The Union Square Theatre, from the Museum of the City of New York, The J. Clarence Davies Collection, 29.100.844. Used with permission.

ment built by Sheridan Shook on the southern side of Union Square, between Broadway and Fourth Avenue. Typical of the long-standing rivalry between Butler and Josh Hart, who now held the management of the Theatre Comique, both managers bid for Braham's services, and Butler won. He also succeeded in stealing away George H. Coes as stage manager and Antonio Grossi as balletmaster, and hired William W. De Milt as machinist and H. Southerton as propmaster. Braham had spent the month of August composing and arranging the music for *Ulysses; or, The Return of S. G.*, a tasteless *mélange* of Greek myth, ethnic caricature, and social satire, set in the context of the Civil War, which was advertised to open the season. The weeks prior to the September 11 opening were spent rehearsing the new burlesque, auditioning new orchestra members, orchestrating the score, copying parts, and rehearsing the orchestra.

When the doors finally opened to the new theater, the audience beheld an elegant auditorium painted in French gray, with moldings and bas-reliefs in pink, white, and gold. An elaborate fresco depicting Cupids and wreaths of flowers adorned the ceiling of the central dome, and large figures, representing Comedy and Music, were painted on opposite sides of the dome, just over the proscenium arch. Two private boxes, one above the other, were on each side of the stage between two columns painted light green, with bases and capitals ornamented in white and gold, with a pink relief. A large sunburst chandelier in the dome, augmented by numerous sconces hanging from the side walls, provided a tasteful soft light throughout the auditorium. The orchestra was fitted with iron folding chairs, upholstered in crimson leather, each row being a step higher than the one before it to allow for perfect sight lines throughout the main seating level. The front rail of the balcony circle, as well as those enclosing the private boxes and orchestra pit, were upholstered in a crimson plush fabric.

Outside the theater, over the portico leading to the street, was a large and elegant sign that read "Union Square Theatre," created with glass prisms that reflected sunlight during the day and were illuminated by gas at night, casting a rainbow of variegated colors along the street. Inside, the acoustics were advertised as excellent, and the ushers and ticket sellers were praised for their affability and politeness, offering yet another proof that every effort was being made by the manager to secure the comfort and enjoyment of the patrons.

The opening bill began with *Ulysses*, featuring Felix Rogers in the title role; Belle Howitt as Penelope, Emma Grattan as Eurymachus, Penelope's suitor; Lizzie Wilmore as Medon, the slavemaster; and a chorus consisting of Schwicardi, Kelly, Morgan, Waddleton, Hurley, and Coes. Rogers played Ulysses like a Jew for the first part of the burlesque, then reappeared impersonating General Grant. Reviews of his performance provide an acute indication of the sensibilities of the day: his usage of racial stereotypes was lauded as a great success, while his representation of the demeanor and personality of General Grant was considered in questionable taste. The closing scene of the burlesque presented a *divertissement* titled "The Home of the Butterflies," featuring the celebrated prima ballerina Marie Bonfanti, the most famous ballet dancer in America, as well as Mlle. Bertha and the entire *corps de ballet*, elegantly costumed in white and crimson silk and decorated with silver lace.

The *New York Herald* of September 13, 1871, had little good to say about the production: "The language is wretched, the music execrable and the acting decidedly poor. There is neither fun nor point, and the announcement that the piece has come to an end is a kind of pleasurable surprise." Only two musical numbers were mentioned specifically: "Villikins and His Dinah," sung and danced by Ulysses, and "He Wants a Kiss," performed by a drunken chorus watching Eurymachus attempt to make love to Penelope. While the first song was judged the "only creditable performance" of the evening, the second was found to be in very poor taste, "across the verge of decency." Since the only "hit" of the production was a riot in the audience that arose spontaneously when a reference to a police matter on July 12, 1871, created opposing factions among the crowd, it is no wonder that the author of the play chose to remain anonymous, leaving Braham and the rest of the creative staff to fend off the critical diatribes.

The burlesque lasted nearly an hour and a half (newspapers report that it was cut to about an hour by the end of the week), and was followed by first-class variety entertainment: the ear-splitting Annie Adams with seriocomic songs; Hughey Dougherty with his familiar dissertation on "Love"; and handsome tenor Fred Foster singing "Piccadilly," and "Don't Stop My Beer" as an encore, then reappearing as a girl singing a medley that included "A Young Girl of the Period," "Tommy Dodd," and "I Dote on the Military." The transvestite routine was followed by the American debut of the Matthews Family (one man, two ladies, four boys, and a little girl) performing songs, dances, and acrobatics, James Wambold with his banjo, Ashcroft and Morton singing and dancing (plus two encores), Geraldine and George Leopold with their aerial acrobatics, and the pantomime *Pat-a-cake-Baker's Man; or, The Adventures of Paul and Virginia*, presented by the flamboyant Martinetti-Ravel Troupe. Although reviewers complained about the length of the program, they found it to be a "propitious commencement" to the Union Square Theatre that presaged a happy and successful season. The *Clipper* of September 23, 1871, was particularly pleased to note that a large portion of the audience were ladies.

The following week saw little change in the bill with the exception that *Ulysses* was replaced by the ubiquitous farce, *Mr. and Mrs. Peter White*, and an Ethiopian sketch titled "He Would Be an Actor" was performed by Lew Rattler, Johnny De Angelis, and J. Myers. In the next several weeks, an extravaganza called *Babes in the Wood*; a ballet, *Pearl of Italy*; a pantomime, *Jocko, the Brazilian Ape*; and burlesques of *Cinderella* and *Pocahontas* were added to the bills. The theater appeared to be an artistic and commercial success in spite of a notice in the *Clipper* on November 11, 1871, that announced:

> The Union Square Theatre, having proved a failure as a variety hall,
> is now in the market for rent, and will no doubt be speedily opened
> as a dramatic theatre. Considerable excitement is manifested among

well known managers as to who will be able to secure the lease of it. Rumor on Saturday night asserted that Mr. John Brougham was the fortunate individual, but it lacked confidence. The applicants are numerous.

However, no change in the management was reported as of November 20, when Harrigan and Hart were advertised in a performance of their popular sketch "The Little Fraud." The pair had come to New York with John Stetson, the manager of Boston's Howard Athenaeum, for a two-week engagement at the Globe Theatre, 728 Broadway, beginning October 16. Armed with the letter of introduction from John Braham, Harrigan presented himself to David Braham, who took an interest in the pair. He secured for them an immediate engagement at the Union Square Theatre and an interview with Tony Pastor (for whom brother Joseph was the musical director), who would employ them at his theater early in the 1872–73 season.

The story has often been told about Harrigan's early visits to 86 Carmine Street. Although they began as an attempt to establish a firm connection with one of New York's most popular and "efficient" musical directors, they quickly evolved into friendly visits focused more on the Braham household than on Harrigan's immediate career. Certainly the discussions centered around the theater and songwriting because that is what both men loved, but gradually Harrigan found himself charmed by twelve-year-old Annie Theresa Braham, and he soon found himself creating excuses to visit the Braham family, not to further his career, but to see Braham's pretty, black-haired daughter. After the week's run at the Union Square Theatre, Harrigan and Hart went back on the touring circuit. The performances in New York City had not caused their careers to skyrocket, but Harrigan had found a new and willing collaborator in David Braham and the love of his life in Annie Theresa.

The holidays brought Gus Williams, W. H. Ashcroft, and John Mulligan to the Union Square Theatre as well as a "comic trick pantomime" titled *The Red Witch; or, The Goose and the Golden Egg*. In January 1872, David Braham received the lyric to "The Mulligan Guard," a song idea that Edward Harrigan had developed in Boston. Harrigan conceived of the song to accompany his satire of paramilitary "target" companies that had been proliferating around New York City since the 1830s, because the city's existing military organizations had refused to enlist immigrants. Typically, these groups adopted exotic names and costumes indicative of the nationality of the members. They would set off for target practice, parading interminably through the streets of New York City, led by a brass band hired for the occasion and followed by an African-American boy carrying an oversized target bearing the name of the company's patron in large letters. The first stop on the way invariably was the home of the patron who was serenaded and subsequently expected to supply the prizes for the shooting match at a nearby picnic area. By the time the company reached the target range, however, most of the members were too drunk to shoot straight and ended up maiming one another rather than hitting the bull's-eye.

Harrigan's Irish Mulligan Guards depicted an organization of three, with Harrigan leading the parade in an oversized military outfit, with a sword strapped to his belt, so enormous that it dragged along the ground. Next in line came Tony Hart, carrying a musket and wearing a uniform several sizes too small, a huge, furry shako on his head. Bringing up the rear was a young African-American boy named Morgan Benson, wearing a Confederate Army cap and carrying a lollypop-looking target.

Harrigan's lyrics satirized these groups' peripatetic tendencies, in addition to paying tribute to one Jack Hussey, an Irish longshoreman from County Cork who had acquired a reputation as a lifesaver and a favorite of the Seventh Ward:

> We crave your condescension,
> We'll tell you what we know
> Of marching in the Mulligan Guard from Sligo ward below.
> Our Captain's name was Hussey,
> A Tipperrary man,
> He carried his sword like a Russian duke, whenever he took
>   command.
> We shoulder'd guns, and march'd, and march'd away,
> From Baxter street, we march'd to Avenue A,
> With drums and fife, how sweetly they did play,
> As we march'd, march'd, march'd in the Mulligan Guard.
> When the band play'd Garry Owen,
> Or the Connamara Pet;
> With a rub a dub, dub, we'd march
> In the mud, to the military step.
> With the green above the red, boys,
> To show where we come from,

Our guns we'd lift with the right shoulder shift,
As we'd march to the bate of the drum.
Chorus
Whin we got home at night, boys,
The divil a bite we'd ate,
We'd all set up and drink a sup
Of whiskey strong and nate.
Thin we'd all march home together,
As slippery as lard,
The solid min would all fall in,
And march with the Mulligan Guard.
Chorus

Braham's music begins with a side-drum roll and a single beat of the bass drum. This figure is played three times and followed by eight bars of a drum-and-fife duet. The fife tune is then repeated with full orchestra leading into a four-bar military fanfare. The voice follows in an idiomatic Braham melody outlining the harmony with almost no dissonant nonchordal tones. Following the indication "Forward march" comes the chorus anticipating many of the trios in the marches of John Philip Sousa, with its easily memorable, constantly soaring melody. After the last verse and chorus are sung, the introductory fife tune reappears, followed by the opening side drum and bass drum duet (with the indication "Present arms"). The musical interlude is completed with an eight-bar Irish jig borrowed from the Irish ballad "St. Patrick's Day in the Morning" (with the indication "Target excursion band"), leading into a final reprise of the chorus (with the indication "Forward march").

Harrigan was so delighted with the music Braham had supplied for the lyrics that he attempted to convince William A. Pond to publish the song even before it had been performed on any stage. Harrigan felt (and Braham certainly agreed) that it would be excellent publicity for the act to have the song in the public's ear in advance, but the publisher did not agree. It was only after seeing "The Mulligan Guard" in performance that Pond finally decided to publish it, paying Harrigan and Braham a mere fifty dollars for the rights.

While Braham was sketching out melodies for Edward Harrigan during the day, Braham's evenings were crowded with ever-changing bills at the Union Square Theatre, which included two extravaganzas, *The Pirates of Barnegat* and *The Court of Common Split Peas; or, Will the Band*

Begin to Play; a pantomime, *Tit for Tat*; and two burlesques, *Bad Dickey*, satirizing *Richard III*, and *Ernani*, spoofing the Hugo play and the Verdi opera, and featuring the "Hokey-Pokey." On his way to and from the theater, Braham read with interest the reports that it had been leased to impresario Maurice Grau for twelve months beginning September 1, 1872, for a season of opera, and that the property on which the Theatre Comique stood had been put up for auction on February 20. With his future appearing less and less secure, Braham especially looked forward to a reunion with his old friend "Pony" Moore, who had left for England after Matt Peel's death in 1859 and who was due to return to New York City on April 3. And even though the celebrated Vokes Family began a long and successful engagement at the Union Square Theatre on April 15—opening with their "signature piece," *The Belles of the Kitchen*, a farce depicting the antics of servants bit by the theater bug when the master is away—Braham knew that his days there were numbered.

On June 1, Robert Butler left the management of the Union Square Theatre and signed on as manager of the Vokes Family, accompanying them on their summer engagement in Boston. The *Clipper* (June 1, 1872) reported that Butler's tenure at the Union Square Theatre was not personally remunerative and that he undoubtedly left the position without regret. He was replaced with Albert M. Palmer, who, in turn, brought in Frank A. Howson as musical director. On June 1, the day when both Butler and Braham were "retired" from the Union Square Theatre, William Horace Lingard reappeared in New York City after forty weeks on the road. Closing in Wilmington, Delaware, on May 31, Lingard boasted that the tour was the most profitable of any since he came to the United States and, almost as if to prove his claim, he purchased a brownstone, 130 East 37th Street, at the corner of Lexington Avenue. If Braham's future seemed uncertain as the summer began, at least he had old friends nearby to offer their condolences.

Chapter 5

Act Three: "Josh Hart and the Theatre Comique"

The summer was hardly warm when Josh Hart, the manager of the Theatre Comique, paid David Braham a visit at 86 Carmine Street. David's wife, Annie, had been anxious to bring the men together, hopeful that their reminiscences of past glories might lead to future employment. Braham was hesitant at first. He had often been involved in the bidding wars for talent between Hart and Butler, and the previous season had turned down Hart's generous offer at the Comique for Butler's more lucrative contract at the Union Square. Besides, his friend Henry Wannemacher had been hired as musical director for the Comique, and Braham was strongly disinclined to push anyone out of a job.

If there was any tension lingering between Hart and Braham, it disappeared the moment Hart stepped through the door. Swept away by the music and laughter of the Braham household, Hart jovially asked what it would take to bring Braham back to work at the Theatre Comique. Annie chimed in with a dollar amount (she knew better than her husband what it cost to raise a family), and by the end of supper, David had signed on as musical director for the 1872–73 season. Although Braham had been happy at the Union Square Theatre, with its comfortable appointments and nearly perfect acoustics, he was delighted to be back at the Comique, hoping that, under Hart's deft management, it would be his home away from home for many seasons to come. Another daughter, Henrietta, was born during the summer of 1872 and now, as the father of five healthy children, David sought permanent employment more than ever before.

Hart's Theatre Comique opened on August 19, 1872, with a first-class variety company. In September, leather-lunged Annie Adams (advertised as receiving $250 per week in gold), blackface comedian Johnny Wild, Macklin and Wilson (changing roles from male to female and vice versa as they sang and danced), and Frank Kerns (of the ill-fated Eighth Avenue Opera House) were added to the roster of performers for whom Braham provided vocal arrangements, accompaniment, and musical continuity (introductions, exits, and incidental music). October saw the burlesque *Arrah na Brogue*, satirizing the flamboyant Irish playwright Dion Boucicault, and featuring a spectacular "Barn Door Reel," arranged and orchestrated by Braham and danced by Johnny Queen and Larry Tooley. Braham's expertise as a conductor was further tested by Professor Shonel's trick mules when the orchestra was required to accompany the mules' antics with appropriate musical punctuations. November added the "celebrated" Worrell Sisters and the burlesques *Ixion, Ag-i-nes,* and *King of Carrots*, and with December came Neil Warner and John F. Poole's burlesque *Africa; or, Livingstone and Stanley*, featuring a "cocoa nut dance" for eight blackface dancers arranged by Braham.

The first week of December also brought Harrigan and Hart to the Theatre Comique after playing three months at Tony Pastor's, with their sketches "The Day We Went West," and "The Big and Little of It," both winning generous applause from the audience. On December 9, the team continued their increasingly successful engagement at the Comique with their signature routine, "The Little Fraud" (henceforth billed as "The Little Frauds" in all the advertisements), and a new Civil War sketch, "After the War." The week of December 23 introduced the Christmas pantomime *Ding Dong Bell, Pussy in the Well*.

On New Year's Eve, Josh Hart was presented with a gold watch by the company and staff of the theater as a token of their appreciation of his efficiency and good taste. Such sentiments were anticipated in the *Clipper* (December 14, 1872) when the reviewer noted:

Josh Hart, the manager, has, by untiring energy, made this theatre one of the most successful of its class in this city, if not in the entire country. The performances are ever filled with novelty and the star attractions are rapidly changed. During a season one is almost certain to see all the most celebrated performers of the variety profession. Obscenity, vulgarity and profanity are carefully expurgated from the performances, which insures the continued attendance of the fair sex, who already represent a large portion of the audiences.

With the new year came Master Barney singing and dancing a jig, Henry S. Page and his virtuoso cornet, the Tracy Brothers clog dancing, the Matthews Family acrobats, and Harrigan and Hart as "The Fiji Island Cannibals." The week of January 27 advertised three burlesque extravaganzas, each with Harrigan and Hart in the cast: *Ali Baba; or, The Forty Thieves; Lalla Rookh;* and *Keno and Loto.* During the following week of February 3, Harrigan and Hart portrayed two Irishwomen quarreling over the right to use a particular clothesline in their original sketch "Who Owns the Clothes Line?" On February 10, when members of the Theatre Comique company, including Harrigan and Hart, left the theater for a week's engagement in Brooklyn, Braham prepared new musical routines for the Majiltons—Charles, Frank, and Marie—performing their grotesquerie "Les Trois Diables," John and Maggie Fielding with their specialty musical sketch "Blarney," and William Forner performing difficult music on an instrument fashioned of wood and straw, in addition to the arrangements for the remaining Comique regulars. On February 17, when Harrigan and Hart rejoined the company, John F. Poole's dramatic sketch *Spaniards; or, The Lone Star of Cuba* was advertised, featuring the appearance of a full brass band on stage. Mirroring a similar experience at the Canterbury Music Hall, not only did Braham have to concern himself with his thirteen-member orchestra in the pit, he also had to coordinate a marching brass band on stage as well.

Among the constantly changing programs in the spring requiring Braham's musical expertise, March brought *Robinson Crusoe and His Man Friday* and J. H. Budworth performing Edward Harrigan's version of *Rip Van Winkle,* while April introduced the Flalzettie Pantomime Troupe; Ling Look, the "Chinese Wonder"; and Yamadiva, the serpent-man, all requiring specialty and exotic musical accompaniment. The final week of the regular variety season at the Theatre Comique began on May 5 with a bill that included Frank Kerns, the Ethiopian comedian just returned from a winter's stay in Florida, in a sketch called "The Baby Elephant"; James Bradley in a song and dance; Harrigan and Hart in a original sketch called "Ireland versus Italy"; Cool Burgess in assorted songs; a character dance by Kitty O'Neil; Dutch songs and dances by Larry Tooley; Professor T. W. Tobin's sketch "Frankenstein Mystery"; and John Wild, among others, in comic routines. The long evening of entertainment concluded with John F. Poole's dramatic sketch *Joe Russett; or, The Life of a Newsboy,* which was introduced by another of Braham's specialty overtures.

Because the regular company was scheduled to open a two-month summer season at the Academy of Music in Chicago on Monday, May 12, the Friday night, May 9 performance was the last for about half the company at the theater. On Saturday they boarded a train to Illinois while a series of guest artists were added to the performers left behind to complete the variety season on Saturday afternoon and evening. The final performance in New York City again displayed the highly eclectic musical demands placed on Braham and his orchestra: the Martens performing their "Cat Duet" and a burlesque violin solo; Ling Look, specializing in fire-eating and sword swallowing; G. W. Jester in feats of ventriloquism; Little Jennie Yeamans performing character songs; Monsieur Le Tort with his sleight of hand; Cool Burgess in blackface comedy; Professor Tobin in his "Frankenstein Mystery"; and a sketch titled "P. P. P. Podge." After the Saturday evening performance, the rest of the troupe, including David Braham and a few key members of the orchestra, collected their bags and headed west, for Chicago.

During the summer, Braham composed three songs for Jennie Yeamans to lyrics by Gordian K. Hyde, which were published by William A. Pond in 1874 under the generic title *The Songs of Little Jennie Yeamans.* "Sailing on the Lake," chronicling the courtship between the singer and her "cousin Joe" while sailing in Central Park, marks a departure from the traditional verse/chorus structure Braham used in his earlier character songs. Here the melody of the chorus is quite distinct from that of the verse, anticipating the independence between verse and chorus that would characterize later nineteenth-century popular vocal music. Once again, Braham employs a readily memorable melody that outlines the basic harmonic structure with a musical accompaniment that evokes the chirping of birds and rippling water. Even in early compositions, Braham displayed a remarkable adeptness at word painting in both his melodies and his accompaniments. "The Boot Black; or, I'm As Happy As Any One Can Be" is a more traditional verse/chorus jig in triple time employing a long musical introduction borrowing melodic motifs from the chorus. The song proper begins with a highly rhythmic sung verse followed by a chorus using longer notes, but drawing on much of the melody of the verse. A dance break of completely different musical material is then introduced.

The most interesting song in the set is "The Idol of My Heart," a double song and dance advertised as having been sung by Jennie Yeamans and her sister, Lydia. Set to a "Tempo di Galop," this duet depicts the courtship and subsequent engagement between Johnny and Kitty, who is the idol of his heart. Although this song has often been compared to "Sweet Adeline" (because of the lyric "You're the Idol of my heart, Sweet Adeline"), neither the tone of the music nor the lyrics display any similarity to the more familiar tune. Hyde's lyrics to the chorus depict a youthful romance, free of any hint of sorrow:

> We will ever be so happy free and gay,
> We will sing and dance the happy hours away,
> I will call you then the Idol of my heart,
> We shall then so happy be and never, never part.

Braham set these sentiments to a cheerfully busy melody with many leaps and nonchordal tones to suggest a playfulness rather than pathos. Following the A-B-C structure of the song (three separate melodies of equal length) is an extended dance section utilizing new melodic material filled with busy chromatic runs and rapid notes suggesting the "chase" music characteristic of the Keystone Kops films. Especially noteworthy is the song's highly "independent" instrumental introduction, which makes no thematic reference to any of the melodic material that is sung.

When not composing, Braham put the musicians at the Academy of Music through their paces, nightly accommodating the vicissitudes of a variety bill that included Harrigan and Hart in "The Fiji Island Cannibals"; "The Comique Quartet," laughably performed by Harrigan, Hart, Johnny Wild, and Frank Kerns; John Williams in a virtuosic clog dance; and *Arra na Brogue*, the concluding burlesque. News reports in the *Clipper* (June 7 and July 5, 1873) complained of light business, blaming the lack of variety in the bills, claiming that "unless new attractions are soon offered the engagement here will be unsuccessful, as lady audiences demand new faces occasionally."

When the Chicago engagement closed on July 5, the company headed for a week's stay at Wood's Theatre in Cincinnati, where a new bill was offered to generally crowded houses. A Dutch farce featuring Larry Tooley and Kitty Tilston followed Braham's energetic overture and led to Harrigan and Hart in "The Little Frauds," and Ada Wray in a selection of songs (which evidently failed to match her costume, since the reviews complained about the length of the train on her dress). Next, an Ethiopian farce was acted by Frank Kerns, Johnny Wild, Larry Tooley, and G. L. Stout, followed by Little Jennie Yeamans in seriocomic songs; her mother, Annie Yeamans, in a Chinese song and dance; and the farce "Brown's House Dog," concluding the evening.

On July 14, the company opened at the Opera House in Pittsburgh for one week with basically the same bill as the one performed in Cincinnati. Ed Gooding was incapacitated for the entire Pittsburgh run, and at the end of the week, John Hart was unable to appear because of the illness of his wife, Mary Jane. The absences in the company caused hurried revisions of the running order, but the ever-imperturbable Braham took the changes in stride, rewriting musical introductions and playoffs minutes before the performance. After a week of good business in spite of very hot weather, the company made their way northeast to Boston for an engagement at the Boston Theatre from July 21 to August 16.

Opening night in Boston drew an immense crowd. The bill, varying only slightly from the Cincinnati and Pittsburgh programs, again displayed the depth and breadth of Braham's musical responsibilities. After one of Braham's characteristic overtures came "The Dutch Shoemaker" sketch, Annie Yeamans with Chinese songs and dances, and a "sour" performance on the Chinese fiddle, and J. H. Budworth with songs and animal sounds (encored several times). Another sketch, "The Baby Elephant," featuring Frank Kerns and John Wild, continued the comedy, followed by Kitty O'Neil dancing, Ada Wray singing, Cool Burgess in blackface, and John Williams in "Lancashire Songs and Dances." The farce "Brown's House Dog" again ended the long evening of variety entertainment.

In August the burlesque *Keno and Loto* and the sketch "One Night in a Bar-room," were added to the bill, along with Harrigan and Hart's "German Emigrants," a routine that proved very popular with audiences. Equally pleasing was Harrigan's impersonation of an aged African American named Uncle Pete in the sketch "Massa's Old Friend," and John F. Poole's drama *Joe Russet*, which concluded the entertainment.

John Hart had been absent throughout the Boston run, caring for his wife. On Thursday, August 7, Mary Jane Hart died in New York City. The weekend bill in Boston was rearranged to allow Hart's closest friends in the company to travel to New York City to console him in his bereavement. Although fond of Hart and his wife, Braham was forced to remain at his post, to ensure smooth and seamless performances in the wake of all the changes.

On August 11, as Braham and members of the Comique Company were beginning the final week of their engagement in Boston, the 1873–74 season of the Theatre Comique began in New York City, with Herr Bernhard leading the Theatre Comique Orchestra. The advertisement for the opening in the *Clipper* (August 16, 1873) indicated the grand scale to which Josh Hart aspired in his productions:

THEATRE COMIQUE,
No. 514 Broadway.
Mr. Josh Hart . . . . Sole Proprietor
John F. Poole . . . . Business-manager
John R. Topham . . . . . . Treasurer
G. L. Stout . . . . Stage-manager
David Braham . . . . Orchestra Director
Nelse Waldron . . . . .Machinist and Properties
Richard Doyle . . . . Engineer and Gas Man
R. L. Weed . . . . Scenic Artist
GRAND REOPENING.
This favorite establishment and popular family resort will reopen for the season of 1873 and '74 upon
MONDAY EVENING, AUGUST 11.
Having undergone an entire and complete renovation and reconstruction throughout, the Theatre Comique will take rank as one of the most beautiful, complete and comfortable Theatres in America.
BRIGHT, FRESH AND SPARKLING!
Painting, Frescoing and Ornamentation by Messrs. Monroe and McCormack, No. 41 Centre street. Upholstery, Tapestry and Lace Curtains, by James Sharnburg. Gas Fixtures and Appointments, by R. Doyle. Cocoa Mats and Matting, by E. Greenland, Koscinsko Factory, Brooklyn. New Stage and Stage Machinery, by Nelse Waldron. New Drop Curtain and Proscenium Decorations, by Mr. R. L. Weed.

The New Drop Curtain is an artistic representation of
WASHINGTON CROSSING THE DELAWARE.
Mr. Josh Hart takes pride and pleasure in announcing to his patrons,
the public, the opening of his regular Fall and Winter Season, assur-
ing them that he is determined to make it eclipse all his former
efforts in the production of meritorious and Attractive Novelties. All
that long experience, untiring energy, and liberal outlay can accom-
plish, shall be done to present to the patrons of the Theatre Comique
the very best entertainment that can possibly be collected together on
any one stage in the world. The Inaugural Company will consist of
the following Star Artists:
CHAPMAN SISTERS,
BLANCHE, ELLA, and BELLE,
in their sparkling Burlesque,
DON GIOVANNI; Or LEPORELLO AND THE STONE
STATUE.
Incidental to the Burlesque,
MISS ELLA CHAPMAN
will appear in New Songs and Dances; Banjo Solos, and in her
Unrivaled Clog Dance.
MISS BLANCHE CHAPMAN
in operatic selections.
MISS BELLE CHAPMAN,
in her Champion Parlor Skating Act.
The celebrated and talented Burlesque Actor and Vocalist,
MR. HARRY ALLEN,
Engaged expressly to perform the character of Zerlina.
The Queen Dancers of the World, the
RIGL SISTERS,
BETTY and EMILY.
These ladies will execute one of their
GRAND PAS DE DEUX.
The Wonders of the World,
THE GREAT HUMAN FEMALE SERPENTS,
AND YOUNG LADY BOA CONSTRICTORS,
So-called throughout the large cities by their marvelous perform-
ances. Writhing, serpent-like, into all kinds of imaginable
Contortions and Posturing. Each a Paragon of Beauty, Youth and
Loveliness of form. The Anomalies of the Medical World, Twisting,

Untwisting, Bending, Springing, Coiling and Uncoiling with all the
elasticity of Rattlesnakes, famously known as the great
CLAIRE SISTERS
MISS MINNIE and MISS MAGGIE.
First appearance at this Theatre of the Monarchs of the Profesion,
EAGAN and EDWARDS, LITTLE JENNIE YEAMANS, the
Child Wonder of the World, Mrs. ANNIE YEAMANS, in her
Wonderful Chinese Performance, DICK RALPH, the favorite
Ethiopian Comedian, Mr. JOHN WILLIAMS, the Favorite Irish
Vocalist and Dancer. Everybody's Favorite, Mr. LARRY TOOLEY,
in a collection of New Songs. Miss Kitty Tilston, Mr. J.A. Graver,
Mr. D. L. Kelley, Mr. J. F. Crossen, Mr. G. L. Stout, &c. Concluding,
every Evening and Matinees, with the Chapman Sisters' Burlesque,
LITTLE DON GIOVANNI,
Or LEPORELLO AND THE STONE STATUE.
Little Don Giovanni, a pocket edition of Lover—always in debt, in
love, in spirits, and invincible, Miss BLANCHE CHAPMAN
Leporello, his page boy, who from his chronic nervousness, may be
considered even more funkey than flunkey, Miss ELLA CHAPMAN
Donna Anna, Don Pedro's daughter—a lady with a high voice, high
breeding, and high temper; in fact, the daughter of hi-dalgo, Miss
BELLE CHAPMAN
OUR STANDING NOTICE,
ENTIRE CHANGE EVERY MONDAY.
Look out for first appearance of the
THEATRE COMIQUE FAVORITES:
John Hart, Cool Burgess, John Wild, Frank Kerns, Harrigan and
Hart, Miss Jennie Satterly, Miss Jennie Hughes, Miss Ada Wray,
Miss Kitty O'Neil, J. H. Budworth, and several artists who will make
their first appearance in this country.
MATINEES WEDNESDAY AND SATURDAY.
ADMISSION . . . . FIFTY CENTS
RESERVED SEATS . . ONE DOLLAR
FAMILY CIRCLE . . . . TWENTY-FIVE CENTS

Hart was true to his word and changed bills with weekly regularity,
so David Braham—who rejoined the New York company on 25 August,
after the tour closed in Providence—was anticipating his most challeng-
ing season yet. Not only did he have to keep the orchestra rehearsed to

perform an inordinate amount of music, but also the ongoing presence of Harrigan and Hart meant continued opportunities to compose music. Braham once again found himself trying to balance two families: one at 86 Carmine Street and the other at 514 Broadway. Not surprisingly, Edward Harrigan carved a place for himself in both, finding every excuse to visit the Brahams and spend time with Annie Theresa. Of course, he had business with her father: he wanted to learn about writing songs, along with David's advice about the new routines he had been writing for Hart and himself, but such things could have been dispensed with at the theater. Harrigan was a constant guest in the Braham household because he enjoyed the comfortable family atmosphere, the unpretentious home life that was so rare among professionals in the theater. He appreciated Braham's consummate professionalism at work and his affectionate, paternal demeanor at home, for, although David was well known for his red hair, he seemed to have little of the well-known redheaded personality. Harrigan and Braham quickly developed a professional bond that would operate, virtually uninterrupted, for the next twenty-five years and a familial tie that would continue for the rest of their lives.

Harrigan and Hart returned to the stage of the Theatre Comique on September 8, 1873 with a sketch they had debuted during the summer tour, "The Mulligan Guards." Little more than a staged performance of the song Braham and Harrigan had written a year before, the sketch was praised as one of the best of their career, eliciting screaming fits of laughter from the audience. Not long after, however, New Yorkers had little to laugh about when the most significant economic disaster of the nineteenth century hit the city, caused by the bankruptcy of the Northern Pacific Railroad line. On September 18, Jay Cooke and Company, the brokerage firm that had underwritten the Northern Pacific Railroad, went out of business, and stock prices took a nosedive on the New York Stock Exchange. Two days later, the stock exchange closed for the first time in eighty-one years, in an attempt to get the market under control. When the attempt failed, panic began to sweep across the country as commercial businesses, railroads, and brokerage firms went under. Although thousands of people became unemployed and homeless because of the "Panic of 1873," inside the Theatre Comique it was business as usual, with Josh Hart promising exorbitant salaries to performers. E. Jump, billed as the "greatest living caricaturist," was hired at a weekly salary of $250 in gold, while Maud Gray was expected to receive $500 a week for her period statue routine.

During the first week of the financial panic, Harrigan and Hart reprised their successful Mulligan Guard sketch and appeared in *The Italian Padrone; or, Slaves of the Harp*, a local drama by John F. Poole that anticipated the urban ethnic musical plays that later became associated with Harrigan, Hart, and Braham. In the following weeks, the team added the original sketch "The Absent-Minded Couple," roles in *Arrah na Brogue*, and the burlesque of *Uncle Tom's Cabin* (in which Harrigan played Uncle Tom and Hart played Topsy) to their list of credits. Among the featured performers in November were Little Jennie Yeamans singing Braham's "The Boot Black"; Alexander Davis, a celebrated ventriloquist with whom David Braham developed a lifelong friendship; and Thomas Harper, a one-legged jig dancer of incomparable ability for whom Braham designed a number of specialty turns. Tony Hart's illness the week of November 17, forcing the postponement of "The Blackball Sailors" sketch, afforded Harrigan the opportunity to introduce his "Shamus O'Brien At Home," a short play with music he had written in Syracuse in February 1872. Among a myriad of holiday delights, December ushered in the Worrell Sisters in the ever-popular burlesque *Ixion*; Eph Horn and his Ethiopian delineations; R. M. Carroll and his three sons in the uproarious sketch "The McFadden Family"; and Edward Harrigan with his satire of Tony Pastor's song "The Flags of All Nations," in which Harrigan introduced (in a flour barrel) the flag of quarantine, the flag of the auctioneer, and the Irish flag, all to the great delight of the audience. Through what appeared to be an endless maze of songs, routines, dances, and sketches, Braham continued composing and arranging during the day and leading his well-rehearsed orchestra at night.

By now the responsibilities of being the musical director of a major variety theater had crystallized into a kind of pattern. Late Monday morning, the orchestra assembled to rehearse the major orchestrations for the week. Typically these included two "overtures" (one at the beginning of the program, the other preceding the drama or burlesque that ended the show), pantomime or ballet music, the melodramatic (or comical) underscore that often accompanied the evening's sketches, and the musical continuity (fanfares or "buttons") that would sweep the entertainers on and off the stage. Solo performers of songs and dances normally traveled with their arrangements that ranged in complexity from fully orchestrated parts to the piano-vocal copy of the song from which the musicians would improvise during the performance. After the

The Majilton Family: Frank, Charles, and Marie.

orchestra rehearsal, the performers arrived for a "dress rehearsal," during which the routines were performed in the advertised order—a decision made by proprietor Hart, business manager Poole, stage manager Stout, and musical director Braham sufficiently in advance to allow for the printing of the bill—followed by a break for dinner and the Monday evening performance. When a brand new work was introduced, rehearsals were held during the week, in the early afternoon, with a run-through scheduled for Sunday, the usual day off.

Because Braham had grown accustomed to the rigors of this schedule, he found himself with the time to work on several projects simultaneously. In December, for example, he composed and arranged the music for *Gabriel Grub; or, The Story of the Goblins who Stole the Sexton*, adapted from the story by Charles Dickens by the Majilton and Raynor Families, with dialogue added by Fred Lyster, and produced at the Olympic Theatre beginning Tuesday, December 23, 1873, and closing Saturday, January 17, 1874. Although *Gabriel Grub* was advertised to open on Monday, December 22, 1873, the *Clipper* (January 3, 1874) notes that the theater was dark on the Monday night because of a rehearsal. It is unlikely that David Braham was in attendance at the rehearsal, because the Theatre Comique holiday pantomime, *Tell-Tale Tit*, gave its first performance on that Monday evening. Monsieur F. Rochow conducted the performance at the Olympic Theatre. Advertised as a "Fantastical, Farcical, Demoniacal, Comical, Musical, Legendary and Terpsichorean Imagination," in two acts and a prologue, Dickens's Christmas tale was transformed into a holiday spectacle heavy on songs, gymnastics, and puns, and light on dramatic structure. This was the program handed to the audience for the evening's entertainment:

PROLOGUE.
Christmas Eve at the Old Sexton's. A cold night for Gravedigging.
Polly Dark and her Lovers; "How happy could I be with either."
Tobacconist versus Tailor. A social evening with Mirth, Music, and Dance, and "Laughter holding both his sides."
Concertina and Banjo Duet,—Messrs. Harry and Charles Raynor.
Chit-chat and Conversation. "Mr. Golightly will oblige."
Song and Chorus, "We are so Volatile." Messrs. Harry Raynor, Charles Majilton, Charles Raynor, Frank Majilton, Mlles. Marie and Carrie Majilton.
Singing is dry work. What ho! some Drink! Making the punch and punching the maker. In at the Head and out at the Bung-hole. The light fantastic toe.
Quadrille Domestique,—By all the Company.
"The Mysterious Stranger." A grave subject. The man without a heart. The "Wassail Bowl." Come, fill your Glasses. A Christmas Toast. "Mr. Golightly will oblige again."
Christmas Chimes,—Messrs. Harry and Charles Raynor.
Song, "A Jolly Christmas Party,"—Mr. Harry Raynor and Company.
and now a Story round the Christmas Fire—a tale to make the hair stand upright and the skin to creep. "The Mysterious Stranger will oblige." The Legend of Gabriel Grub, and the Goblins who Stole the Sexton. Shocking effect of the Legend on the Company. Polly Dark frightened. The Search for Nat Dark. Polly alone. "Her eyelids close in balmy slumber."
HUSH!
ACT FIRST.—POLLY'S DREAM.
The Dark Lane. Old Gabriel on his way to his Farm. Christmas Carols and Gabriel's disgust. "The man that hath not music in himself, who is not moved with concord of sweet sounds, is fit for

Treason, Strategy and Spoils." Shall we have Corporal Punishment! Gabriel gives a practical answer. Low Spirits and High Spirits. "He keeps his spirits up by pouring Spirits down." To work! To work! Scene 2d.—The Old Church Yard.

(Gabriel's Farm.) A Fat Soil. Rich Crops and Splendid Statues. "Rank Grass Overhead, and Damp Clay around." Brave Lodgings for one, this in holy ground. Gabriel at his "Farming Work." "Hark, the Vesper Hymn is Stealing." Gabriel finds the Truth of the Old Adage: "'Tis conscience that makes cowards of us all." "Hollands to the rescue." Entrance of Polly Grub from the Church. "Father, Come Home." The Cross drop. "Begone, I disown you." Discomfiture and Retreat of Polly. Gabriel recognizes Old Friends, makes a "Grave Joke," and Refreshes himself. "The Echoes." "JIX." A Pleasant Chat and Lively Company. "Who digs graves when others are Merry!" "Gabriel Grub; Gabriel Grub." Spiritual appearance of Polly. A Solemn Warning. "Ah! you will have it then!"

THE PARRICIDAL BLOW!

And terrific appearance of Mestigris, the Gnome of Earth. Fearful Dialogue and Terror of Gabriel. Gabriel, you're wanted.

ACT SECOND.—PANDEMONIUM.

Marcofax, King of the Goblins. "Uneasy lies the head that bears a crown." "His Majesty is lonely and pines for his Consort's return." "Ha! she comes, my life, my love, my Melusine." Appearance of Melusine as "The Thunderbolt."

Dance—Diabolique,—Miss Marie Majilton.

Entrance of the Will o' the Wisps dragging in Gabriel Grub. "So please you, sire, dismay has struck him dumb." What, ho! Some Wine! "We'll drink to our Dumb Guest." A warm welcome and a comfortable seat. "The Goblin King will oblige."

Song, "Our Welcome Guest,"—Mr. Harry Raynor and Company. "A drop of something hot." The Beauteous Melusine. An obedient Wife, no need for a Divorce.

Song, "Eccentrique,"—Miss Marie Majilton.

The Tycoon's fiddle. Its effects. "If Music be the Food of Love, play on."

Solo—Japanese Fiddle (On one String.),—Mr. Harry Raynor.

And now to amuse our Welcome Guest, "Let the Sports begin." Diabolical Gymnastics,—Messrs. Frank Majilton and Charles Raynor.

Sports Eccentric,—Messrs. Charles Majilton and Harry Raynor.
Goblin's Revels,—Prof. Nelson and Sons.
"Again soft slumber coming." The Emperor ceases to speak. The
Saucy Fly comes humming, and lit upon his cheek. The Saucy Fly
and the Terrible Tarantulas.
Duet—Entomologique, "The Spider and the Fly,"—Miss MARIE
MAJILTON and Mr. CHARLES RAYNOR.
Terrific Combat and Death of the Saucy Fly. Grief of the Goblin
King and Lament.
Dirge,—Mr. HARRY RAYNOR.
What the Goblin King shows to Gabriel Grub. Tableaux. A Happy
Home. A Child's Deathbed. Pleasant old age. The Demon's Post
Bag. "What means this insult?" Slave, uncover! Gabriel's Hat; what
became of it? Final Satanic yell of the Sexton and his Dreadful
Doom. "AND I AWOKE, AND LO! IT WAS A DREAM!"

Emma Lewis performed the role of the Mysterious Stranger. Marie
Majilton played Polly Dark, Polly Grub, Melusine, Thunderbolt, and the
Saucy Fly. Harry Raynor acted Nat Dark, Mr. Golightly, Gabriel Grub,
and Marcofax; Charles Majilton appeared as Luke Twist, Jix, Mistigris,
and Forcepanto, a Tarantula. Charles Raynor played Anky Slender, Xit,
Antennae, a Tarantula, and Ghurrh, secretary to Marcofax; Frank
Majilton acted Frank Dark, Polly's brother, Nip, and Pipifax, an Imp of
Darkness. Carrie Majilton appeared as Mlle. Nadelgewehr, a French
Milliner from Berlin; Prof. Nelson and Sons performed the Goblin
Gymnastics, and vocal ensembles were provided by the celebrated
Russian Quartet.

The *Clipper* (January 3, 1874) found fault with the dialogue, claiming that the show was simply a vehicle for the performers to display their
specialties. Although there was "plenty of singing, grotesque dancing,
hat-spinning and performances upon a number of musical instruments,"
it was noted that most of the routines had been used previously by the
Majiltons and Raynors in their variety acts. The reviews did not harm
Braham in the least: he had steady employment at the Comique, income
slowly accumulating from a growing catalog of published songs, and now
money coming in from his work at the Olympic Theatre. Slowly he was
achieving financial security for his family and becoming a household
name in the bargain.

Early in January, Josh Hart advertised that a real tribe of Comanche

Indians would appear at the Theatre Comique to perform in dances indigenous to their race and in Fred G. Maeder's melodrama *The Scalpers; or, Life on the Plains.* This afforded a new challenge to the musical director, who was no stranger to musical ethnicity, having made use of Irish, Italian, Dutch, German, Jewish, and African-American idioms in his variety-show arrangements and compositions. Now he would add a Native-American sound to his palette of musical colors.

The winter season merged into the spring with few surprises. "The Mulligan Guards" continued throughout the season along with other Harrigan and Hart sketches, "Who Owns the Line," and "A Terrible Example," a satire of Temperance societies, during which Harrigan introduced a new Braham-Harrigan collaboration, "I'll Never Get Drunk Any More." February brought Nully Pieris with her "Beautiful Collection of Songs," Jennie Engel with her seriocomic repertoire, the world-renowned Madrigal Boys, and *The Brigand Chief!,* a remake of the musical burlesque satirizing Hugo's play *Hernani,* and Verdi's opera *Ernani,* that Braham had conducted at the Union Square Theatre in the spring of 1872. In early May, Harrigan performed "Muldoon, the Solid Man" and introduced another sketch, "Who's Got de Flo? or, Scenes from the South Carolina Legislature." The week of May 11 brought back "The Mulligan Guards," followed by a new sextet written and composed by Harrigan, "The Regular Army, Oh!," and "A Terrible Example," during which Harrigan sang his new song "Tom Collins," the music of which—following the traditional verse/chorus pattern—was adapted and arranged by Braham. Kate O'Connor and Alice Bennett were also on hand with seriocomic songs and ballads, as well as Kitty O'Neil with a character dance, R. M. Carroll in his original Irish song and dance titled "Mortar and Bricks," and Jennie Engel in another collection of original songs.

The last week of the season in New York City, May 18, 1874, overlapped with the first week of the Comique Company tour. Harrigan and Hart, along with other members of the company were in Newark that week, leaving David Braham and the remaining regulars (augmented by artists specially engaged for the week) to complete the run at home. Because Braham was otherwise engaged, a French-Canadian conductor, Emil Wesmer, was hired to conduct the first leg of the tour. Everything went wrong from the outset. On May 19, just as the tour began, the company was attached by a New Jersey sheriff, who impounded all the box-office receipts, costumes, and props. Apparently an attachment had been brought against Josh Hart by George W. Childs of the *Philadelphia Ledger*, for the recovery of seventeen hundred dollars he claimed was due for printing expenses. No sooner had the manager recovered his property when the tour moved to the Academy of Music in Brooklyn where, returning to his dressing room during the Saturday, May 23, evening performance, Edward Harrigan noticed that his watch and chain, valued at five hundred dollars, and seven dollars in cash were missing. Believing the theft to be a company prank, Harrigan made no mention of it until after the show, when he began a search for the culprit. He was informed that the newly engaged musical director, Emil Wesmer, had a questionable reputation and notified Detective Dunn of the New York Police of the situation. The following day, Dunn tracked Wesmer down at a hotel in East Houston Street, where the musical director was discovered wearing Harrigan's property. After being arrested and taken to the police station, Wesmer attempted to throw the evidence out of the window in the detective's office but was prevented from doing so and immediately incarcerated to await prosecution.

Fortunately, David Braham rejoined the company as musical director in Harrisburg, Pennsylvania, on May 28, and fortune began to shine on the Comique tour. After the engagement in Harrisburg, the company moved to Columbus, Ohio, on June 2 and then for three days beginning Thursday, June 4, to Cincinnati, where Harrigan and Hart's performance of "The Mulligan Guards" at Wood's Theatre followed a Tuesday night performance of the same sketch by Edward J. Fennessy, C. E. Ulmer, Frank Deneal, and H. J. Klemm. Following brief stays in Louisville, Kentucky, and Indianapolis and Lafayette, Indiana, the tour landed on June 27 in Chicago, where it was quickly eclipsed by John Stetson's company, then playing at the Academy of Music. Unable to meet expenses because of small houses and lukewarm reviews, the company pulled up stakes early in July and returned to New York City for a short hiatus before returning to the Boston Theatre on July 27 for a five-week engagement. Braham particularly enjoyed having a break in the tour, because his sixth child, a son, David Jr., had been born late in June.

Notable at the Boston Theatre was James W. McKee's performance of "Over the Hill to the Poor-House," composed "expressly" for him by Braham, with lyrics by George L. Catlin. An excellent example of a "pathetic" ballad, the song relates the sad story of an old man driven from his home by his ungrateful children and forced to wander "over the hill to the poorhouse," where he will die alone and destitute. The third verse

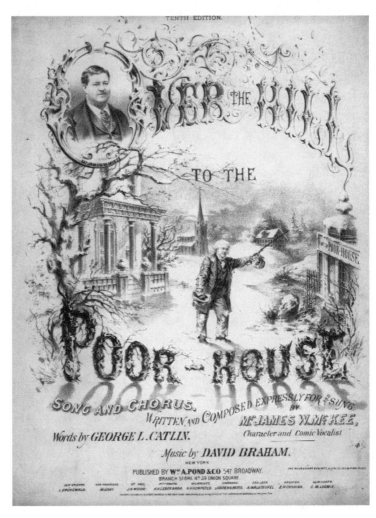

Sheet music cover to Braham and Catlin's "Over the Hill to the Poor-House," Music B-934, Rare Book, Manuscript, and Special Collections Library, Duke University. Used with permission.

(of five) especially tugs at the heartstrings in its descriptions of the narrator's woes:

> It's long years since my Mary was taken,
> My faithful, affectionate wife;
> Since then I'm forlorn and forsaken,
> And the light has died out of my life.
> The boys grew to manhood; I gave them

A deed for the farm! aye, and more,
I gave them this house they were born in!
And now I'm turned out from its door.
Chorus
For I'm old, and I'm helpless and feeble,
The days of my youth have gone by!
Then over the hill to the poor house,
I wander alone there to die.

The music Braham created for this tearjerker employed a flowing arpeggiated accompaniment, anticipating that used in musical theater "hymns" such as Rodgers and Hammerstein's "You'll Never Walk Alone" from *Carousel*. The melody of the verse begins in typical Braham fashion, outlining the harmony through broken triads and diatonic scale passages, alternating downward motion with upward leaps. The harmony itself is quite sophisticated, especially in the "B" section of the verse, where it modulates to the relative minor and makes an effective use of an augmented sixth chord in its classical cadential function, a device Braham would use again and again. The chorus begins with four bars of new melodic material, alternating between chromatically altered lower neighbor tones and broken triads, and ends with a repetition of the last four bars of the verse. The simplicity of the melody and harmony in the chorus lend a subtle emphasis to the pathos of this composition, which more resembles a classical art song than the typical fare of the variety stage.

The 1874–75 season at the Theatre Comique in New York City began on August 10. Newspaper advertisements announced a thoroughly cleansed and redecorated house that would continue to be the "resort of ladies and children," free from objectionable material that could "taint the public morals or foster coarse instincts." Part of the company was still performing in Boston—the Boston Theatre season closed for the summer almost two weeks later, on 22 August—but Braham was back with his orchestra, even if many of the old standbys were not. The opening-night performance featured former gymnast Mlle. Zitella in a variety of seriocomic songs and costume changes, the four Breban Swiss Bellringers, Kate Brevoort eliciting "harmonious sounds from musical glasses," the acrobatic Wilson Brothers, Nully Pieris in her celebrated vocal stylings, Diamond and Ryan in their highly touted Irish specialties, and comedian Luke Schoolcraft, in addition to the bevy of Theatre

Comique regulars. James W. McKee performed "Over the Hill to the Poor-House," for the first time in New York City, and the song was rapturously received by both audiences and critics, who praised its heartfelt sentimentality and well-crafted music.

On August 17, the "Wonder," Master Martin, in his "India Rubber Song and Dance," and the exotic new sensation drama *Mungo, the Ape*, featuring Martin in the title role and new overtures and incidental music by Braham, were introduced. On August 31, Ada Laurent appeared in a terpsichorean presentation, "The Mystery; or, Dancing as It Was and Is," which offered Braham every opportunity to display his abilities as a dance arranger and conductor. The *Clipper* (September 12, 1874) provided an account of this highly original and innovative performance:

> A dressing-room had been constructed at the rear and in the centre of the stage, which had an open door on either side. Miss Laurent entered upon the stage clad in the customary apparel of a lady of society, her dress being of light-colored silk. She then gave to the audience a brief description of her forthcoming performances, and recited some three or four stanzas of poetry appealing to their judgment for fair criticism, entered the dressing-room from the stage-right, and, after a very few seconds had elapsed, emerged from the left door, clad in full male attire, and made up as a French ballet-master. We were then informed that he had advertised for a number of ladies for the ballet, and, after performing a graceful dance, he retired within the dressing-room. Miss Laurent then impersonated a number of ladies who came to reply to the advertisement, giving a characteristic dance with each character assumed. These included Mlle. Larent, a premiere danseuse, with "La Gavotte"; Mrs. Brown, an elderly lady of the old school, with a "*minuet de la cour*"; Mlle. Brownesso, with an illustration of ballet dancing sixty or seventy years ago; Fraulein Freitag, with a wooden-shoe dance; Sophronia Smuggett, from Vermont, with a contra-dance; and the Goddess of Liberty, with an American dance.

Even if Braham merely adapted existing material to the needs of the program or simply conducted from arrangements that Ada Laurent provided, his effortless realization of the quick changes of musical styles demanded by the act showed him to be a conductor who was not only sensitive to dancers but also capable of meeting highly sophisticated musical challenges.

While waiting for Harrigan and Hart to reappear on the stage of the Theatre Comique on September 14, Braham dusted off the incidental music to Maffitt and Bartholomew's comic pantomime *Flick and Flock* and began working on new songs Harrigan had penned while on the summer tour. When Harrigan and Hart returned, they introduced New York City to "Patrick's Day Parade," a sketch they had tried out in Chicago during the summer. Tony Hart performed the transvestite role of Johanna McCann, a servant in the employ of a well-to-do family, who has invited a coachman named Hogarth Higgins (played by James Bradley) to spend time with her, thinking her boyfriend, Fitzgerald Conroy (Ned Harrigan), would not be likely to visit her on St. Patrick's Day because of his habit of marching in the parade. Just as Higgins and Johanna begin to get acquainted, Conroy is heard outside, drunkenly singing an Irish ditty. Higgins is hidden in a closet and Conroy enters, quickly discovering the hat Higgins forgot to take with him. Conroy becomes uncontrollably jealous, but Johanna manages to calm him by asking for a description of the parade. Conroy dresses her in a man's coat and hat and puts an Irish flag in her hand, and, while he carries the Stars and Stripes, they sing a duet, "Patrick's Day Parade," between each verse of which the couple march across the stage. During these intervals Higgins attempts to escape, only to be noticed by Conroy and Johanna, who beat him as the curtain falls.

The song "Patrick's Day Parade," with music by Braham, was, in fact, a rewrite of Bob Hall's music for the same lyrics, arranged by M. De Donato, for "The Day We Celebrate," an earlier version of the sketch, and published in 1874. Both musical settings of Harrigan's lyric employ a duple-meter verse and melodically independent triple-meter chorus, followed by an extended duple-meter march. But the differences in melodic contour and harmonic complexity are significant, particularly in the chorus, where Braham managed to convince Harrigan to rewrite the text to allow for a more varied and interesting melody. The original lyric to the chorus was:

We shout hurrah for Erin Go Bragh
The harp and shamrock and the stripes and stars
Up Broadway wid banners gay
We tramped, tramped, tramped, tramped,
In the Patrick's Day Parade.

The revised version introduces entirely different rhythmical and rhyming patterns:

We shout hurrah for Erin-go-bragh,
And all the Yankee nation,
Stars and Stripes, and Shamrock bright arrayed.
The Irish shout, the girls turn out
To see the celebration,
We march stiff as starch,
In the Patrick's Day Parade.

Throughout his career, Braham would be continually concerned with creating rhythmically interesting, hummable melodies. As a result, it was not unusual for the composer to take an active part in fashioning the text, often requesting changes in versification for the sake of musical interest, a practice to which Harrigan usually acceded, if, at times, only begrudgingly.

On September 28, a "new" overture was introduced by David Braham, and "Who Owns the Line?" returned with Harrigan singing his original songs, "Muldoon, the Solid Man," and "Swim Out, You're over Your Head," neither of which appears to have been composed by Braham. On October 5, yet another "new" overture arranged by David Braham was advertised, and Charles Sullivan and Maggie Seymour made their American debut with their "Original Protean Irish Sketches." Harrigan and Hart appeared in "A Terrible Example," during which Harrigan sang "When the Soup House Moves Away" (introduced the previous season), and a "new song," "When the Soup House Comes Again," neither of which seems to have been composed by Braham. (By this point in their careers, David Braham was as recognizable a name as Edward Harrigan and would certainly have helped in the advertising of a song or a sketch. Braham is even credited on the bills with the composition of incidental music, so the absence of his name in connection with a Harrigan song suggests that Braham did not compose it.) Harrigan and Hart were followed by Monsieur and Mademoiselle d'Omer, French athletes; Mr. and Mrs. A. R. Brenna, burlesque operatic vocalists and dualogists; and the children Venus and Adonis, in their velocipede act. Another Braham overture preceded the local sensation drama *Who Stole the Monkey?*, which completed the performance.

In the following weeks, Harrigan and Hart performed an original musical sketch, "The Invalid Corps," and revived "Patrick's Day Parade," "The Regular Army Oh!," and "The Mulligan Guards," in a revised form that included new lyrics to Braham's popular melody. Another new musical sketch, "The Scandal Club," was introduced during the last week of October, featuring a thrice-encored burlesque sextet sung by Harrigan, Hart, Wild, Kerns, White, and Carter in grotesquely comic costumes. In November, Harrigan and Hart arrived with the "The Clancys," and "The Raffle for Mrs. Hennessy's Clock," in which Harrigan introduced a new song written and composed by him, "The Lockout; or, The Longshoreman's Strike." Although Braham did not compose the music for all of Harrigan's songs during the early days of their career together, it is perhaps noteworthy that Braham did write or arrange the music for all of the more popular, and repeatedly revived, sketches.

Also present in the fall 1874 season was John Williams, the "Lancashire Lad," with his Irish songs and dances. Taken with Braham's musicianship and musical inventiveness, Williams asked Braham to set some of his original lyrics to music. A letter written by John Williams to "Friend Dave," dated September 8, 1876, inquiring whether Braham had "put any music to my song," suggests a collaboration by that date, though it is unknown when the music was actually completed. Although it is likely that the song in question was performed in the fall of 1876, the set of four *Lancashire Songs and Dances* composed by Braham for John Williams was not published until 1885. Two of the songs, "Don't I Love My Dolly?" and "Jolly Factory Boy," had lyrics by Edward Harrigan, while "The Lancashire Dance" and "The Boys of Lancashire" were written by John Williams. Each of the numbers was in the schottische style, with melodic material shared by both verse and chorus, followed by an extended, musically independent, dance break.

Productions of *The Black Crook*, with its scantily clad chorines, and *The King of Carrots*, with the cast dressed as animals against a realistic picture of the menagerie in Central Park, kept Braham busy well into December, when Harrigan appeared with yet another original sketch. "The Skidmores" depicted Harrigan in blackface, commanding an African-American military company, with Tony Hart as a dark-skinned drum major. The song associated with the sketch, "Skidmore Guard," was composed by William (Billy) Carter, and arranged by Braham in obvious imitation of his popular "Mulligan Guard" with its drum breaks and parade music interludes. Critics found the marching and presentation of arms during the number to be first-rate and prophesied that the song would become as popular as its model.

On December 21, in addition to "Patrick's Day Parade" and "The Skidmores," a new burlesque, *Fee-G!*, written by Edward Harrigan, with new music composed by "Professor" Braham, appeared. Marking the state visit of King Kalakaua, the ruler of the Sandwich Islands, (today's state of Hawaii) to the United States, Harrigan produced a tropical absurdist burlesque, satirizing cannibals, P. T. Barnum, Christian evangelists, and current events. The almost undecipherable plot involved an Irishman who is a cannibal king, with a daughter named Princess Mutton Chops (Tony Hart). In addition to the obligatory "Overture" that preceded the performance of the burlesque, the playbill advertised a number of provocative musical numbers within the action: "Midnight Song and Chorus of real vicious Cannibals," a "Serenade" (after which the scene changes), a duet celebrating the beauties of "Muffin Nine," and a "Grand March of Dresses" ("sure to be mentioned in the morning papers"). It is unfortunate that none of Braham's music has survived for this protoabsurd sketch, which anticipates the antics of Alfred Jarry's *Ubu Roi* by two decades. The bill also advertised that two new Harrigan sketches were in preparation, "Down Broadway; or, From Central Park to the Battery!" and "The London Comic Singers," both of which would have the advantage of Braham's music.

The new year brought large audiences to the Theatre Comique to see Gilmore and Smith roller-skating; J. W. McAndrews, assisted by William Carter, in his famous act, "The Charleston Girls"; James Collins and Martha Wren in their comic sketch "Late Hours"; and Therese St. John singing Italian arias. Alice and Clara Coleman performed banjo and cornet duets, imitated the ringing of chimes, and finished with a complicated clog dance. Mlle. Realta performed feats of strength; the handsome Ben Dodge sang popular songs and was given two encores; and Harry Sefton, "The Dancing Spider," sang, danced, and engaged in a number of physical contortions. Ella Wesner, dressed as a man, sang three of her most popular character songs, displayed an appropriate number of silk handkerchiefs, and danced a hornpipe, followed by Ernest Byne, with the assistance of Gerard Byne, who did female impersonations in the sketch "The Four Cousins." Harris and Carrol appeared in the blackface routine "The Slave's Return," and Harrigan and Hart presented "The Day We Went West" and "Lo! The Poor Engine." By now Braham had grown accustomed to the variety fare at the Comique.

On January 11, 1875, Martha Wren and James Collins opened the performance with their Irish operetta "Barney's Courtship!," with Braham and his orchestra accompanying the songs "Mother, He's Going Away," "Barney O'Neil," "Come with Me," and "Molly Darling."

Harrigan and Hart were back with the indomitable "Who Owns the Line?," with Harrigan introducing a new non-Braham song, "Pat Maloney's Family," in addition to a new musical sketch, "King Calico's Body Guard!," with music supplied by Braham. The week of January 18 added more character dances, Ethiopian songs, Irish songs, athletic feats, and the sketch "Poverty's Trials," during which Harrigan introduced another non-Braham song, "No Irish Wanted Here."

The last week of the month brought Harrigan's new musical sketch, "The London Comic Singers," for which Braham composed the lilting title song in waltz time, and his nephew, John, provided the music for "Little Old Dudeen," an Irish drinking song. In the sketch, Tony Hart appeared in evening clothes singing the title song, explaining the premise of the routine. Harrigan followed, made up to look like an old Irishman, similarly dressed in evening attire, singing "Little Old Dudeen." Hart then reappeared as an Italian flower girl and sang a song using an Italian dialect, followed by Harrigan, made up as an English music-hall singer, who sang a music-hall number. At the end of the song he was joined by Hart, costumed as an English gentleman, and the pair engaged in comical banter interspersed with snatches of songs. As in so many routines before, Braham demonstrated his adept mastery of varied musical styles. Later in the performance, Harrigan and Hart performed the prison lament "The Black Maria, Oh!," dressed in the striped suits typically worn by convicts. The routine was a success, but the standard verse/chorus song, set to music by Braham, was not. Considered unmemorable, the tune was not published until its reuse in Harrigan's *McNooney's Visit* in 1887.

For the first two weeks in March 1875, Harrigan and Hart appeared at the Olympic Theatre in Brooklyn, where they performed "The Skidmore Guards" and "The Mulligan Guards" as well as the non-Braham routines "The Clancys" and "The Roadside Murder." When they returned to the Comique on March 15, they reprised "The Mulligan Guards," and introduced, the following week, a sketch called "Slavery Days," for which Braham produced a Stephen-Foster–like title song. Typical of many popular songs of the period, the chorus of "Slavery Days" is an exact repetition of the last eight bars of the verse, with the same rolling eighth-note accompaniment and complex chromatic harmonies complementing a melody that alternated between scale patterns and arpeggios. Even though Braham's melodies remained simple, memorable, and easy to sing, his harmony was becoming subtly more sophis-

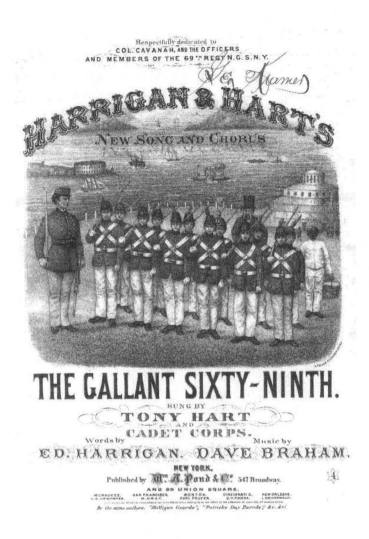

Respectfully dedicated to
COL. CAVANAH, AND THE OFFICERS
AND MEMBERS OF THE 69TH REG. N.G.S.N.Y.

HARRIGAN & HART'S
NEW SONG AND CHORUS

THE GALLANT SIXTY-NINTH.

SUNG BY
TONY HART
AND
CADET CORPS.

Words by   Music by
ED. HARRIGAN.   DAVE BRAHAM.

NEW YORK.
Published by **Wm. A. Pond & Co.** 547 Broadway.

AND 39 UNION SQUARE.

By the same authors, "Mulligan Guards", "Patricks Day Parade," &c. &c.

Sheet music cover to Braham and Harrigan's "The Gallant '69th.'"

ticated as he developed a viable balance between the popular American folk style and the European classical idioms.

On April 19, the night that King Sarbro, the "Wonderful Japanese Artist," debuted, Harrigan's sketch "Down Broadway; or, From Central Park to the Battery," was introduced with new scenery, properties, costumes, and "New and Beautiful Music by Dave Braham." Featuring an exact replication of the 69th Regiment uniforms, the routine starred Kitty O'Neil as the colonel of the regiment and Edward Harrigan as a rube who is dumbfounded by the sight of the statue of George

Dan Bryant.

Washington in Union Square. The marching song designed for the boys impersonating the 69th Regiment was titled "The Gallant '69th'" and composed in imitation of "The Mulligan Guard," complete with the introductory military cadence, and the extended parade music after the chorus. Here, however, Braham is more harmonically ambitious than in the earlier march, using surprising chord changes and chromatic alterations to lend emphasis to Harrigan's lyrics. A fine example of this is found in the first verse, when the peaceful narrative is interrupted by the line "It was there with bayonets bristling." To add to the tension of the lyric, Braham accompanies the phrase with an unexpected harmony that has not yet been heard in the song and that will not be repeated. Not only does this offer musical interest and variety, it also helps fix the lyric in the audience's minds.

On the afternoon of Thursday April 29, the performers and musicians of the Theatre Comique paid tribute to a recently deceased star of the minstrel stage, Dan Bryant, by adding a special matinee performance to benefit Bryant's wife and family. Braham's orchestra was increased to nineteen members for the event, which featured two Braham overtures,

Harrigan and Hart performing "Patrick's Day Parade," and a myriad of sketches, vocalists, acrobats, and performing birds.

A month later, on May 29, 1875, the variety season at the Theatre Comique closed, and the company opened a summer season at Wallack's Theatre on May 31 with an unattributed play called *The Donovans*, with incidental music composed and arranged by Braham. The *New York Times* of June 1, 1875, found *The Donovans* to be one of the worst plays ever performed in New York City, with a threadbare story, inept dialogue, and characters so familiar they are "worse than contemptible." The plot, involving the recovery of a kidnapped child, ended with a railroad sensation scene in which the hero (Harrigan), having rescued the heroine (Tony Hart) from a blazing building, saves her child from a train speeding down the tracks. The melodrama was set in a variety of familiar city settings, the likes of which had become the trademark of the Harrigan and Hart sketches, and accompanied by other variety acts, including the Peak Family of Bell Ringers, and Charles and Carrie Austin in their "celebrated musket drill and bayonet combat," which ultimately received much friendlier reviews.

A title song written by Harrigan and Braham survives from *The Donovans*, published by E. H. Harding in 1876. A duet designed to be sung by Harrigan and Hart as Michael and Norah Donovan, the song has the self-revelatory kind of lyric typical of Harrigan's early sketches:

> We came from dear old Ireland,
> We're strangers in this land,
> We know that all Americans,
> Put forth a welcome hand
> To the poor of suff'ring Ireland,
> Time and time again.
> We thank you for our countrymen,
> And Donovan is our name!
> *Chorus:*
> We're the Donovans!
> We're the Donovans!
> From the Emerald Isle across the sea.
> We're the Donovans!
> We're the Donovans!
> From a noble family!

Braham set the lyric to a bright folklike tune more closely resembling a galop than a jig. Characteristically, the melody of the verse outlines a rather unambitious harmony, and the real "hook" of the song emerges in the melodically independent chorus (published for vocal quartet), with the word "Donovans!" allowing for greater metrical variety than the squarely repetitive patterns of the verse.

In the third week of the run, the sketch "The London Comic Singers" and the Royal Yeddo Jap Troupe were added to the bill, presumably to boost sagging ticket sales. Unfortunately, the attempt failed, and *The Donovans* closed on June 19, prompting the *Clipper* of June 19, 1875, to quip: "'*The Donnovans*' [*sic*] made such a mess of it, at Wallack's, that Harrigan and Hart *dunno* when they'll try another campaign 'Down Broadway.'" Harrigan and Hart responded to the failure by setting off on a national tour, under the management of Martin W. Hanley, Braham's brother-in-law. That Braham supported them in this enterprise is clear: an advertisement posted in the June 19 *Clipper* provided an address where interested parties could engage the tour: it was Braham's address at 86 Carmine Street.

Chapter 6

Intermezzo: "Olios at the Eagle"

N either David Braham nor Edward Harrigan was defeated by the failure of *The Donovans* at Wallack's. Braham's compositions had become so popular that they were sung and played with great regularity throughout New York City. Even the great Gilmore's Band kept Braham's "March Militaire, S.G." (based on the "Skidmore Guard") in a featured position of its repertoire during the month of June in concerts at Gilmore's Garden and on board *Plymouth Rock*, Jarrett and Palmer's floating palace that cruised around upper New York Bay. By the summer of 1875, indoors and outdoors, rare was the establishment that did not include at least "The Mulligan Guard" in its concert program.

Harrigan and Hart had decided that it was time to strike out on their own again, this time at the head of a large combination company that bore their names: "The Original and Only Harrigan and Hart's Combination, consisting of Thirty First Class Artists." Because Braham chose to remain in New York to maintain his position as musical director of the Theatre Comique, William Lloyd Bowron was engaged as musical director for the tour. Joseph Braham, who had been Tony Pastor's musical director at 201

Bowery since 1865, left at the end of the 1874–75 season to join the Harrigan and Hart company as a violinist along with his teenage son, Harry. Amid the bustle and chatter of six children, some practicing the piano, others struggling on the violin, Martin Hanley handled the bookings for the tour at the Braham home, which functioned as a kind of nerve center for all of the Braham-Harrigan enterprises.

The months that followed were filled with correspondence from Harrigan to 86 Carmine Street, chatting about the tour, asking about the Brahams, and revealing a deepening affection for Annie Theresa. He also appeared to have developed a particular fondness for Annie's cousin, Harry, the Braham who would never escape the notoriety of being the first of Lillian Russell's husbands. In a jovial letter dated October 20, 1875, Harrigan replied to one of Annie's criticisms of her cousin:

> Harry Braham is a garlic eater? I never heard of that before. I have heard of opium eaters, landonum [*sic*] takers . . . and bad negro performers, but I have never heard of a garlic eater before. Oh, Annie, how could you speak of your cousin in that manner? Harry too, the darling! You wrong him. He's a nice boy, and should always try to be on hand for any lady. So forgive him. . . . I like Harry. He is so nice to the young ladies—always willing to let them get under his umbrella.

In New York City, it was business as usual for David Braham. The Theatre Comique opened on August 23 under the proprietorship of Josh Hart, with Colonel T. Allston Brown assuming the management and George L. Stout continuing as stage manager. The house was packed for opening night, but attendance fell off almost immediately. Even though the theater still engaged some of the top stars of the variety circuit performing in musical sketches, character songs and dances, and blackface routines—the kinds of entertainment that had made it famous—something was missing, and that something was Harrigan and Hart. To bolster flagging business, on September 6 Stout created a new sketch, "The Great Shooting Match between the Picked Teams of the Mulligan and Skidmore Guards," capitalizing on the popularity of the Harrigan and Hart routines, but attendance continued to wane.

Where was Josh Hart, the master of variety entertainment, while his theater was floundering? Building another theater on Sixth Avenue, between thirty-second and thirty-third Streets, which would feature the same first-class variety performers currently appearing at the Theatre Comique (and often on the same night). In the years immediately following the Panic of 1873, New York City did not appear ready for a new theater, particularly one that promised the kind of entertainment available at a preexisting house, but evidently Josh Hart had a plan, and David Braham would be the last to question it. On October 18, when the new Eagle Theatre opened its doors, Braham found himself in the enviable position of being musical director for two variety theaters simultaneously.

Believed to be the "handsomest theatre" in the country, the Eagle Theatre was built by Josh Hart and ex-Judge Dowling at a cost of $175,000. Five hundred iron folding chairs upholstered in red plush fabric and arranged in twenty-two rows constituted the orchestra seating area, facing a stage that was forty feet deep, seventy-five feet high, and a hundred feet wide. On either side of the proscenium were four private boxes, two above and two below, each with an excellent view of both the auditorium and the stage. The dress circle consisted of three rows of iron folding chairs in front of nine rows of benches, all upholstered in red fabric, and the gallery had eleven rows of unupholstered benches. The proscenium opening, thirty-two feet square, was surrounded by a picture-frame molding decorated in pale pink, blue, and gold, with a carved golden eagle at the top. The drop curtain, said to be the best work of artist Matt Morgan, was painted in imitation of maroon velvet curtains, parted at the center to reveal a medallion on which a young eagle was painted, with the letters "J. H." dropping from its beak. Below this, and against a background painted in imitation of white satin, was a large central medallion painted as a landscape depicting George Washington's birthplace on the Potomac River. The orchestra pit was sunk well below the level of the auditorium floor so that the heads of the musicians would not obstruct the view of the stage.

The premiere performance at the Eagle Theatre began with a spirited overture composed and arranged by Braham, followed by John Wild in his original sketch "My Wife and My Mother-in-law," and Jennie Hughes singing "fresh" seriocomic songs. Wild's performance in the comedy was ironically poignant. His only son, just over fourteen months old, had died on September 13, and the audience, which had mourned his loss a month earlier, now supported Wild's efforts with peals of laughter. A new and original song, "The Eagle," composed by Braham to lyrics by stage manager George L. Stout, was sung by George Coes, Jennie Hughes, H. L. Franklin, and Edna Markley, leading the rest of the company, supported by a number of professional chorus singers. For Stout's patriotic lyrics, anticipating the Centennial celebration of 1876,

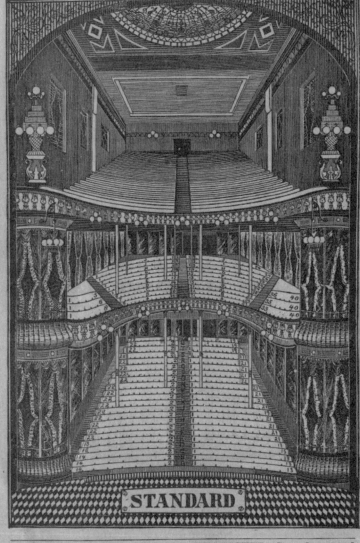

The interior of the Eagle (later called the Standard) Theatre, from the collection of Robert Davis Inc., Theatre Consulting Services.

John Franceschina

Braham composed a harmonically conservative anthem, commencing with a hymnlike verse and ending in a full chorale. Although Braham drew upon the musical characteristics of traditional patriotic songs in "The Eagle," he created a work that is more than simple parody. Contrasting accented nonchordal notes with his customary triadic melodies, Braham composed an effective anthem that, even a century and a quarter later, remains stirring in its simplicity.

The evening's entertainment continued with songs and dances performed in whiteface by Commodore Nutt. Walters and Morton performed Ethiopian songs and dances, A. W. Sawyer played operatic arias on his glass harmonica, the Garnella Brothers "amazed the audience" with their acrobatic feats, Edna Markley sang ballads, "The Tennesseans" sang quintets, and Jolly Nash sang "laughing songs" and played the cornet. The evening concluded with an extravaganza titled *Robinson Crusoe, His Man Friday, Monkey and the King of the Caribee Islands,* which featured Louise Franklin as Crusoe and the midget, Little Mac, as Monkey.

On November 15, London-born George H. Macdermott (also billed as MacDermot), formerly of the Julia Mathews Opera Company and later a staple of the British musical hall, was advertised to perform the judge in Gilbert and Sullivan's *Trial by Jury*, the first performance of a Gilbert and Sullivan operetta in the United States. Although the operetta was not particularly well received, and little attention would be directed to Gilbert and Sullivan until *HMS Pinafore* opened in Boston in 1878, it is important to note that Braham conducted the first performance of *Trial by Jury* in the United States, and his nephew, John, led the orchestra for the first performance of *HMS Pinafore*.

By the end of November, Josh Hart discovered that the proprietorship of two theaters was more than he could handle. As a result, he left management of the Theatre Comique in the hands of Matt Morgan, and focused all his time on the Eagle. Once in charge of the Theatre Comique, Morgan inaugurated a series of "Classical Tableaux and Living Pictures of Art and Nature," which were popular additions to the changing bills of dramatic sketches, pantomimes, and burlesques. Braham found himself creating miniballets to accompany "The Battle of the Amazons," "The Destruction of Pompeii," "The Deluge," "The Slave Market," "The Shower of Gold," and "The Judgment of Paris," wordless tableaux that were displayed at intervals within the variety bill. Whereas he used to be called on to supply different musical styles for dancers, now Braham was required to provide "mood music" for living pictures, all the while still arranging, accompanying, and composing tunes for the olio performances of the stars at the Eagle Theatre.

For Louise Franklin (or Franklyn, as she was often advertised), Braham composed a pretty lullaby to George L. Stout's poem "Rest, My Darling, Slumber Now." Depicting a mother watching over her restless child during a storm, the song is another example of Braham's amalgamation of European musical technique with the simplicity of an American folk song. An *Alberti bass* figure (broken triads in eighth notes) accompanies the entire composition, providing a subtle rocking movement, while unexpected melodic leaps accent key words in the text. Braham's use of an arpeggiated melody based entirely on chordal tones is still in evidence but is much less obvious than in his earlier work.

For performer George Coes, Braham and Stout produced an Irish ballad titled "Eily Machree," depicting the familiar situation of an Irish immigrant saying good-bye to his beloved before sailing off to the "Land of the stranger, the home of the free." Written in triple meter and simple AABA structure, the melody alternates between scale patterns and arpeggios (a favorite Braham device), with a few surprising leaps for lyrical emphasis. A short vocal cadenza before the final phrase of the melody evokes the legitimacy of an art song or operatic aria, and gives the performer an opportunity to demonstrate his vocal virtuosity, in a characteristic Irish tenor style.

With George H. Macdermott, Braham produced "Money the God of the Purse," an ironic, comic patter song about greed:

Now some are fond of studying,
And some are fond of sport;
And some are fond of ignorance,
While some love being taught.
We all have hobbies, more or less,—
But tho' you'll own it funny,
This one affects both rich and poor,
The grasping after money.

Because Braham is credited only with the "arrangement" of the music, his exact contribution to the song is unknown, although the harmonic structure is very typical of Braham's compositions, as are the virtuoso passages in the instrumental introduction. Even if Braham produced only a piano-vocal copy of Macdermott's original tune, his presence in the work is still distinctive.

George H. Macdermott on the cover of *Macdermott's Awfully Loose Songster*.

Another composition associated with Macdermott is the provocatively titled "I Do Feel so Awfully Loose," copyrighted as part of Macdermott's repertoire in 1875 and attributed to Braham in William A. Pond's 1879 catalog of comic and character songs. Depicting the marital squabbles between a man-about-town and his suspicious wife, the lyric by Edwin T. Page begins:

I've been dining and wining to-day, you can see,
    In a style that's deucedly loose;
And to go on the spree now I know would suit me,
    For I musn't go home, 'tis no use.
So I do feel so gay—so reckless and gay,
    My spirits so lively and spruce,
That I fancy that I shall go on the fly,
    For I do feel so awfully loose.

Because *Macdermott's "Awfully Loose" Songster* (1875) cites Vincent Davies as the original composer of the work, it is likely that Braham once again functioned as the adapter and/or arranger of the song—one of his several duties as musical director at the Eagle Theatre, where Macdermott performed the material.

In addition to songs written especially for stars, David Braham produced a number of ballads during the 1875–76 season, capitalizing on the success of "Over the Hill to the Poor-House." Advertised as a companion piece to "Poor House," "To Rest Let Him Gently Be Laid" was composed to a lyric by George Cooper, the author of "Sweet Genevieve" and one of the most prolific lyricists of his day. In unabashed sentimentality, the text describes the death of a man forsaken by his loved ones on earth, but welcomed among the angels in heaven:

For him there was no sweet caressing,
For him there was no gentle tear;
Yet fondly he pray'd for a blessing
On those who had wrong'd him so here.
 Though none o'er his pillow are weeping,
Though rude is the grave they have made;
God loves him so peacefully sleeping,
To rest let him gently be laid.
Chorus:
Oh, softly he murmur'd forgiveness,
And bow'd his grey head on his breast;
They're bringing him back from the poorhouse,
To yonder fair mansions of rest.

Braham set the lyrics to the verse in a stepwise ascending melodic phrase that resolved to a chordal tone in the first statement and to an unexpected appoggiatura when the phrase was repeated. As in the other songs written during this period, Braham was exploring the dramatic use of leaps and nonchordal tones to provide variety, tension, and pathos in his compositions. The chorus melody, borrowed from the final phrase of the verse, follows Braham's typical compositional formula: a triadic melody accompanied by predictable harmony to emphasize the simplicity of the lyric. The unexpected upward leap to a nonchordal tone on the word "poor-house" reinforces the tension in that image in opposition to the peace and tranquillity of the "fair mansions of rest" represented by stepwise chordal tones and underscored by traditional harmony.

Whereas "To Rest Let Him Gently Be Laid" dealt with the death of an old man, "Sway the Cot Gently for Baby's Asleep," written by Hartley Neville, depicts the death of a child in his sleep. What is particularly interesting about the lyrics is the fact that the first verse appears entirely positive, describing a happy child, smiling and dreaming. Only in the second verse do we understand the morbid implication of the sleeping child. Not to detract from this effective change in tone, Braham produced an almost generic lullaby, written again according to the standard verse/chorus formula, where the chorus tune (arranged for vocal quartet) is borrowed from the verse. Throughout the composition, Braham maintained a tonal and melodic simplicity, the only hint of pathos arising in the use of a deftly placed minor harmony in the chorus.

"Gliding Down the Stream," written by Braham to Edward Harrigan's lyric, appears to have been intended as a companion piece to "Sailing on the Lake," originally written for Jennie Yeamans. Once again a female narrator describes a riparian courtship and proposal of marriage:

> Last evening I met Harry,
> My steady company,
> He took me out a sailing
> And whispered, I love thee.
> Of course I blushed and answered,
> Oh! Harry don't be mean;
> He kissed my cheek, the rascal did.
> When gliding down the stream.
> *Chorus:*
> Gliding down the stream,
> Beneath the bright moonbeams,
> When love's a float in Cupid's boat,
> Its beauty's summer's dream.

Gliding down the stream,
When silver spray doth gleam,
My joy you know is with my beau,
When gliding down the stream.

Braham set Harrigan's poem to a jaunty tune, filled with unanticipated harmonies and nonchordal tones to emphasize the playfulness of the dramatic situation. Particularly interesting is the shift of tonal centers in the melodically independent chorus, moving back and forth from the original key to its relative minor, providing a subtle forward "gliding" motion.

In December, in the midst of his own creative activity, Braham found himself conducting more living pictures and "The Gallant '69th'" at the Theatre Comique, and a one-act version of Lecocq's operetta *Giroflé-Girofla*; the pantomime *Harlequin Demon Statue*; and the sensation drama *From St. Louis to New Orleans,* at the Eagle. The drama, anticipating Kern and Hammerstein's *Show Boat* fifty-two years later, was set on a steamboat traveling down the Mississippi River, with a cast in blackface singing minstrel songs and spirituals, the likes of which Braham recalled from his days as a minstrel-show fiddler.

In the middle of the month, the Eagle produced another patriotic song composed by the team of Braham and George L. Stout. "Emancipation Day," dedicated to Josh Hart and celebrating the abolition of slavery in 1863, is a rollicking triple-meter verse/chorus march filled with unexpected melodic leaps and accented nonchordal tones. While the accompanying harmonies remain conservative, Braham's melodic structure relies much less on scales and triads than on upward leaps to suggest the exuberance (if not stereotypical racism) of Stout's colloquial lyric:

In April when de proclimation [*sic*]
Set us people free,
And proclaim Emancipation,
From mountains to de sea.
Equality should be de law, dat Massa Lincoln say,
All us darkies in de nation bless Emancipation day.

The melody of the verse recalls the fourth movement of "Par Excellence," Braham's earlier work for concert band, and provides a telling example of his reworking and developing thematic material as he matured as a composer.

The New Year was filled with chatty, almost illegible correspondence from Harrigan, continuing his running account of the tour, inquiring about the Braham family, and maintaining his romantic correspondence with Annie Theresa. Beyond the time spent deciphering Harrigan's handwriting, Braham continued to divide his creative energies between the Theatre Comique and the Eagle, rehearsing and/or conducting the orchestras in the olio entertainment at both houses. As the winter wore on, Braham accompanied Egyptian jugglers, "callisthenic comets," female minstrels, and a production of *Uncle Tom's Cabin*, embellished by the Wilmington Jubilee Singers, in addition to the usual fare of singers, dancers, and ethnic comedians. Braham looked forward to the end of March, when Harrigan planned to spend a week with his family at Carmine Street: perhaps he and Ned would knock out a few tunes while enjoying a carton of fried oysters and a mug of hot ale. Coincidentally, during the week of March 27, when Harrigan wrote that he would be coming to visit, Braham was conducting "The Skidmore Guards" sketch at the Eagle.

During his week with Harrigan, Braham probed Ned's plans for the future, on both the professional and personal levels. Braham noted sadly—and pointedly—that the Theatre Comique was enduring a rocky season in the absence of Harrigan and Hart. Not only was the team sorely missed, but also the theater itself had begun to acquire a reputation for indecency because of some of the double entendres employed by the variety entertainers. Certainly, Harrigan's brand of decent, socially relevant entertainment would be a welcome relief to the sagging fortunes at the Comique, but Braham's interest in keeping Harrigan close to home was not entirely professional. For some time now, he knew of his daughter's attraction to his collaborator and friend and of Harrigan's fondness for Annie Theresa. A year or two previously, Braham and a group of the performer's friends decided that it was time for him to get married, so they arranged a party at 86 Carmine Street to introduce Ned to a girl they thought would be his perfect mate. When the girl (a rather attractive chorine) arrived, the guest of honor had disappeared, only to be discovered later in the kitchen, eating bacon and eggs with Braham's daughter! If, in fact, Harrigan was seriously interested in Annie Theresa, Braham was seriously interested in keeping him working in New York City.

April brought Minnie Palmer and Nat C. Goodwin (both from the Lyceum Theatre) to the Eagle, and Mlle. Urban and "her sensational

Parisian dancers" and the spectacular *Americans at Home and Abroad*, complete with scenic reproductions of Parisian landmarks, to the Comique, now under the management of one M. Campbell, who immediately began advertising for ballet ladies and specialty performers. In May the irrepressible *Ixion* was back on the boards at the Comique, and a cross-dressed production of *Cinderella* appeared among other burlesques at the Eagle as the season drew to a halt. The long-standing professional relationship between David Braham and Josh Hart was finally challenged in the last weeks of April when the rumor of a quarrel between them reached the Harrigan and Hart tour. On April 24, 1876, Harrigan wrote Annie: "So J. H. and D. B. has [*sic*] had a miff. Well, I hope not serious. Let me know further." Because Annie's reply is lost, and because the newspapers published no word about the dispute, the cause of the trouble remains a matter of speculation. Whatever the cause—artistic, financial, or personal—Braham and Hart parted amicably at the end of the season, never to work together again.

As if in reference to the conversations between Braham and Harrigan the previous spring, on July 15, 1876, the *Spirit of the Times* reported that Harrigan and Hart had taken over the proprietorship of the Theatre Comique, with Martin W. Hanley as manager. New York would now be Edward Harrigan's permanent home, and the Theatre Comique—where David Braham was still employed as musical director—would be Harrigan and Braham's theater. The Braham family responded by moving from 86 Carmine Street around the corner to larger quarters at 222 Varick Street, likely in anticipation of Harrigan's habit of living under their roof.

Chapter 7

Act Four: "Harrigan, Hart, and Braham"

The opening of the 1876–77 season at the Theatre Comique on August 7 inaugurated a new phase in the careers of Harrigan and Hart and solidified the collaboration between Harrigan and David Braham who, for the next twenty years, would be Harrigan's resident composer, arranger, conductor, and friend. Maintaining the variety policy that had brought the Theatre Comique to prominence, the opening night featured the usual array of star performers, many of whom Braham had accompanied in the past. From this point on, however, the attention of both audiences and critics would focus less on the supporting acts than on the routines performed by Harrigan and Hart, flowing in a seemingly inexhaustible stream from the pens of Edward Harrigan and David Braham.

On August 7, assisted by the "69th Boys," Harrigan and Hart performed a Civil War sketch, *The Blue and the Grey*, depicting the reconciliation between brothers who fought on opposites sides during the war. The act had been performed during Harrigan and Hart's tour, finding a less than cordial reception in the southern states, especially when

Harrigan, playing the Union brother, sang a song about his loneliness for the North, "When I Go Marching Home." The title song, however, preaching peace, harmony, prosperity, and brotherhood, won over all audiences not only because of Harrigan's conciliatory lyrics but also because of the infectious melody of Braham's triple-time march. Introduced by a military fanfare of trumpets and drums, followed by a drum cadence, the composition attempts to recapture the spirit of the popular "Mulligan Guard" march, with surprising harmonic changes (now somewhat characteristic of Braham) and a catchy tonal tune.

Also on the program was a revised version of *The London Comic Singers,* introducing three new Braham-Harrigan songs: "Are You There, Moriarty?," a jaunty Irish folklike tune, sung by Harrigan in a policeman's uniform; "*Parlez-vous français?*," sung with "naïveté and vivacity" by Harrigan, cross-dressed as a French girl; and "The Broadway Statuettes," a bright character number sung by Harrigan and Hart dressed as fashionable young men. Later, a group of boys, dressed as an African-American military unit, the Ginger Blues, sang a self-revelatory dialect number reminiscent of the Mulligan and Skidmore Guards:

> Bowing, smiling, just aspilin',
> When de Captain gives command;
> 'Taint no use, as slick as juice,
> We march behind de band. (Umph!)
> Talk about your "Skidmore Guard,"
> We h'ist dem on de hip!
> Raise a dust or else we bust,
> As down de street we skip.
> Turn de heel just like an eel,
> In patent leather shoes;
> Yaller girls in Balmorals,
> Dey love de "Ginger Blues!"

Because the number required a fair amount of marching and close-order drill, Braham produced a playful triple-time march filled with unexpected leaps and unusual dissonances juxtaposed with his favorite device, the tonal triadic melody. The tune was an immediate success and encored several times. The popular songstress Alice Bennett followed with a number of character songs, the most popular of which among audiences and critics was Braham's "To Rest Let Him Gently Be Laid," written the previous summer but heard for the first time in New York.

On August 14, "The Bradys" was added to Harrigan and Hart's list of routines, accompanied by another infectious title song. In "The Bradys," Braham sets Harrigan's lyric in an almost free-form style, repeating melodic phrases at surprisingly irregular intervals, rather than in the more traditional two- and four-bar mirrored phrases. Because of the structural uniqueness of the composition, the harmonic and melodic material is quite conservative, using a mostly predictable accompaniment and a tonally unchallenging melody. The next week introduced Harrigan's *Darby and Lanty*, a comedy without musical accompaniment, and Miss Adah Richmond singing Braham and Harrigan's "I'm Going Abroad with Pa." It tells the story of Miranda, the daughter of a wealthy banker, who dreams of traveling to Europe to complete her education, but whose dreams are dashed when her father goes bankrupt. Braham set the lyric as an engaging "Bowery" waltz, the chorus of which is filled with unusual and surprising harmonies, dramatically emphasizing the emotional changes in the lyrics.

On August 28, the sketch "S.O.T. (Sons of Temperance)" introduced a title song boasting another memorable Braham march. Then, on September 11, "Down Broadway; or, The Miniature 69th" returned with a new specialty two-step titled "The Veteran Guard," featuring a company of boys, marching, close-order drill, and an eminently hummable Braham melody. Capitalizing on the sudden popularity of Braham marches, the next week brought the burlesque *Centennial Marksmen; or, The International Rifle Match by the Four Picked Teams*, with the Mulligan Guards, the Queen's Invincibles (from Canada), the Skidmores, and the Ginger Blues as the contestants represented, each performing its signature routine.

On September 25, Harrigan followed with *The Italian Ballet Master*, drawing upon Braham's expertise as a dance arranger and conductor. On October 2, "Walking for Dat Cake" was introduced, capitalizing on the popularity of the old minstrel show walk-around or "cakewalk," and demonstrating Braham's apparent mastery over every popular musical idiom. *Malone's Night Off; or, The German Turnverein Festival* was Harrigan's new work on October 9, mining the comic potential of feuding Germans and Irishmen in the Bowery and introducing "Duffy to the Front," a satirical political ditty destined for immediate popularity. The final scene of the sketch depicted the German Turnverein Festival in Jones Wood, with Harrigan appearing as Awfulbach Gilmore, satirizing operetta composer Jacques Offenbach's highly publicized visit to New

York City the previous May, when he conducted concerts of his music at Gilmore's Garden. Gilmore's Band was impersonated onstage, and the boys of the Miniature 69th, led by Tony Hart, appeared as German gymnasts and performed a series of complicated military maneuvers while singing a new Braham march, "The German Turnverein." October 23 brought the "Bold Hibernian Boys!," yet another self-revelatory march introduced by drum cadences and a virtuosic orchestral introduction, and a week later, *The Maloney Family* crossed the boards, performing a Harrigan song not attributed to Braham called "Pat Maloney's Family."

During the fall season at the Theatre Comique, Braham and Harrigan were virtually inseparable. The need to turn out new material week after week and the similarity of their work schedules—both leaving for, and returning from, the theater at the same time—resulted in Harrigan's taking a room in the Braham household. No one seemed to mind. Harrigan's presence stimulated Braham's creativity, and the house was filled with music—and romance, as Annie Theresa's youthful infatuation for Harrigan blossomed into love.

On September 13, 1876, while he was living with the Brahams on Varick Street, Edward Harrigan completed his first full-length play, *Iascaire*, an Irish romantic comedy in seven scenes portraying the incarceration, sensational escape from prison, and ultimate vindication of a young Irishman unjustly convicted of political crimes. On November 20, the play was finally produced at the Theatre Comique, featuring an Irish drinking song, composed by Braham to Harrigan's lyrics and titled "Sweet Potteen." *Iascaire* opened two days after Harrigan was married to Annie Theresa by Father Fritz Harris at St. Joseph's Church at Sixth Avenue and Washington Place in Greenwich Village. It was a simple Roman Catholic ceremony, attended by David and Annie Braham; their children George, Adelaide, Ida, Etta, and Dave Jr.; Martin Hanley and his wife, Marietta Ravel; William Harrigan, the groom's father; Tony Hart; and a small gathering of friends from the Theatre Comique. After the ceremony, a carriage was hired to carry the sixteen-year-old bride and her thirtyish husband back to 222 Varick Street and the wedding reception that awaited them. David Braham left the festivities early, since he had a matinee to conduct and, with a Saturday night performance and the dress rehearsal of *Iascaire* on Sunday night, the newlyweds had little time for a honeymoon.

In December, "Patrick's Day Parade," "Ireland vs. Italy; or, Who Owns the Line?," "The Bradys," and "April Fool" demonstrated Braham and Harrigan's penchant for reworking and revising old material and presenting it side by side with new sketches and songs. The "Patrick's Day Parade Quadrille," for example, published by Pond in 1876, adds Braham's "Regular Army O!" and "Sailing on the Lake" to the sketch as well as Charles D. Blake's "Sweet Dora Dare," Henry Tucker's "Sweet Genevieve," and the unattributed "Love Birds Kiss." In subsequent revivals of the sketch, a new Braham march following the usual formula, "Knights of St. Patrick," augmented the score.

In addition to the old favorites, the New Year brought in the first version of *Christmas Joys and Sorrows*, character sketches titled "The Two Young Fellows," in which Harrigan and Hart impersonated the young men who hang about the street corners on the East Side; "Her Majesty's Marines," a naval spoof; "The Maguires" and "The Goats" (both anticipating *Squatter Sovereignty*); and "Monahan's Dream," depicting the Miniature 69th Boys as policemen—all with music by Braham. On April 16, *Old Lavender Water; or, Around the Docks* introduced the first version of one of Harrigan's favorite roles and most often revived plays, although this incarnation did not have the benefit of Braham's music, used in subsequent versions.

After the season closed at the Theatre Comique on May 19, Harrigan and Hart's Combination Company, with Braham as musical director, began its summer tour, opening at W. J. Gilmore's Holliday Street Theatre in Baltimore on May 21. The touring program featured the Gallant 69th Boys, the usual blackface routines, female impersonations, character songs and dances, operatic arias, ventriloquism, and sketches, along with Braham's popular Irish songs "Patrick's Day Parade," "Under the Green," and the showstopping minstrel number "Walking for Dat Cake." In addition, the "superb orchestra, under the direction of Dave Braham" was advertised as "one of the principal features of the entertainment."

After a week in Baltimore, the tour moved to the Arch Street Theatre in Philadelphia, the Park Theatre in Brooklyn, and various one-night stands in New Jersey, Connecticut, and Rhode Island before settling into a two-week run at the Globe Theatre in Boston, beginning on June 25. Everything ran smoothly for Braham through the first week of the Boston engagement. His songs continued to earn the praise of critics throughout the East Coast, and even his orchestra had been singled out in the reviews. On Monday, July 2, however, his luck changed. During the morning rehearsal for the weekly change of bill, John

Braham appeared with a telegram from New York City reporting the death of his father, David's brother, Joseph. Edward Harrigan asked him not to show it to David until the rehearsal was over. He knew how the news would affect his father-in-law and the rest of the company who had toured with Joe the year before.

Everyone in the cast who knew Joe anticipated his death. Even John told Harrigan that when his father left New York, he did not expect to live. Still, the news came as a shock to his brother, who spent the afternoon with his nephew reminiscing about the old days in London, and trying to comfort John. At the evening performances, however, Braham led the orchestra with his usual efficiency, permitting few members of the audience any awareness of his private sorrow. The funeral was scheduled for Thursday, July 5, and, on that day only, David left his orchestra so that he might travel back to New York City to eulogize his brother. He returned to Boston early Friday morning and was back in the orchestra pit that night.

Following the Boston run, the Harrigan and Hart Combination Company traveled west into upstate New York, where poor attendance—audiences had been diminishing throughout the Northeast—forced Harrigan to consider disbanding the tour. Because of the encouragement of David Braham and other members of the company who volunteered to cut their salaries, the tour continued through the end of July, where it was derailed by a violent "railroad war" that had erupted while the company was performing in Buffalo. Unable to meet its future engagements and concerned about the safety of its performers, the Harrigan and Hart Combination Company decided to cut its losses and traveled to Rochester in a tugboat in order to catch a train back to New York City. Although the tour was not a financial success, the experience was not a total loss for Braham and Harrigan. During the tour, the team continued to perfect the symbiotic collaboration that was their trademark: the pair worked, ate, and drank together, and wrote letters home at opposite ends of the same table. So intrinsically connected were their professional and private lives that it was difficult to discern where the interests of one left off and those of the other took over.

Back home in the early days of August, the Harrigan and Hart Combination Company commenced rehearsals for the 1877–78 season, scheduled to open on August 11 at the Theatre Comique. Following Braham's overture, the entertainment began with Sanford and Wilson's familiar musical act "The Jolly Tramps," followed by vocalist Adrienne

Grey, and Harrigan and Hart in character duets, introducing the songs "Roscoe Claude Montveldo," "The Seedy Actors," and the "Plain Gold Ring," all composed by David Braham and immediately popular with the audience. Alice Somers next appeared, singing and dancing in male attire, followed by Cardelia and Victorelli performing on the horizontal bar, Will H. Morton in a number of songs, the "Big Four" in an act called "Wonders," and the Dutch comedian George S. Knight. The comedy *Our Irish Cousins* and a military drill by the Miniature 69th Regiment closed the evening's bill.

The fall season continued to be the traditional variety fare, with Harrigan reviving old sketches in tandem with the new. *Christmas Joys and Sorrows* returned on August 20 and *Malone's Night Off* appeared the following week, with *The Blue and the Gray* reappearing on October 15. Harrigan's new *Old Lavender*, with a song, "College Days," composed by company member G. W. H. Griffin, opened the week of September 3, while *The Rising Star*, Harrigan's new satire about show business in general and the Theatre Comique in particular, opened on October 22. This last piece provides an interesting look into the subtle integration of music and variety entertainment into Harrigan's nonmusical plays. In the first scene, the characters Patsy and Tommy—both entertainers—dance to the music of an unspecified tune. In the fourth scene, there is a comic dialogue between Philip, a violinist and theater conductor, and De Aubrey, an actor who owes him five dollars. In scene five, the character of Mart Hanley is discovered (a self-consciously theatrical device connecting the audience's experience with Hanley the manager to Hanley the character), and the "Overture" is heard playing from offstage. The faint sound of the overture continues through scene six until, in scene seven, Philip is discovered leading the orchestra in the pit. Comic business ensues involving an alligator attempting to get through the stage door (claiming he had been booked for a pantomime) and actors missing their cues, and the conductor throwing music at the stage to remind the actors of their timing, and gesticulating wildly to keep the orchestra together. In typical burlesque fashion, the melee ends with Philip breaking his violin over De Aubrey's head.

On October 12, a matinee to benefit the widow of Edwin Adams was performed at the Academy of Music and featured a great number of star performers from all of the theaters in the city. Harrigan and Hart, accompanied by Braham leading the orchestra, performed a sketch titled "The Crushed Actors" (likely a version of "The Seedy Actors," which opened the season at the Comique). On November 1, the Academy of Music hosted another benefit, this time for the Roman Catholic Orphan Asylum. Harrigan and Hart performed "The Bradys," again accompanied by Braham as leader of the orchestra. Back at the Theatre Comique, the month of November saw the debut of Braham's song "The Water Mill," a "quaint and striking" melody to the lyrics of J. J. Kelly, and revivals of "S.O.T. (Sons of Temperance)" and "The Bradys." Meanwhile, Harrigan and Braham continued to collaborate on individual olio numbers, sketches (notably "The Pillsbury Muddle" about the misadventures aboard a sleeper car traveling to Albany), and a longer play with music that would appear in January. The lowering of prices at the Comique in December appeared to be as popular as the entertainment onstage: orchestra seats were reduced to seventy-five cents; the parquet, fifty cents; the dress circle, thirty-five cents; and the balcony, fifteen cents. The lower prices and the appearance on December 31 of Harrigan's new sketch "Sullivan's Christmas" made the holidays especially merry.

In "Sullivan's Christmas," Catherine and John Sullivan invite Captain Krautsmyer, the leader of a German band, to join them for turkey dinner during the holidays. Preferring the more substantial German cuisine he had planned to share with his band, the captain refuses. In typical farce fashion, the band gets confused in the directions to Captain Krautsmyer's and ends up in Sullivan's parlor, spoiling his meal. "Sullivan's Christmas" was enriched by a new song, "Our Front Stoop," composed by Braham that bore more than a slight resemblance to his own home life:

> I'm the father of a fam'ly, six girls and one big boy,
> With the neighbors they are friendly, they are their mother's joy;
> It's ev'ry summer's evening when the heat would make you droop,
> Old friends would meet from every street to talk on our front stoop.

Employing the verse/chorus formula, Braham set the conversational lyric in characteristic fashion, beginning with an ascending triadic phrase, efficiently outlining the simple, predictable harmony, followed by a descending, mostly stepwise melody. What is most interesting about the work is the chorus, sung entirely to "Tra la la," reflecting the use of nonsense syllables in opéra-bouffe and operetta ensembles and anticipating their employment in crowd scenes in twentieth-century musicals.

On January 14, 1878, the Theatre Comique produced a full-length version of an earlier sketch by Edward Harrigan called *Christmas Joys and*

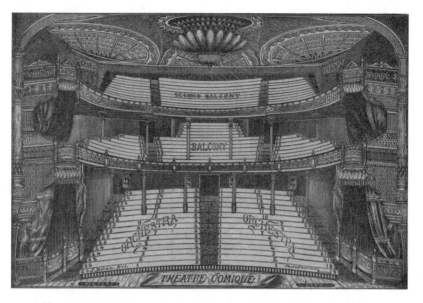

The interior of the Theatre Comique, from the collection of Robert Davis Inc., Theatre Consulting Services.

Sorrows, with new music by David Braham, "freshly painted" scenery by R. L. Weed, mechanical effects by James Gifford, and props supplied by G. W. Burnton. Harrigan and Braham had been rehearsing the spectacular melodrama for some weeks, and the production was something of an innovation for their theater, because it comprised the entire bill, dispensing entirely with any variety entertainment. The drama opens at Ravenswood Estate, where Ira Mellerton (J. W. Somers), the son of the Reverend Theodore Mellerton (Welsh Edwards), is betrothed to Emily Goodall (N. Jones), the reverend's adopted daughter. Their happiness is dimmed by the presence of Chauncy Darrell (H. Fisher), a friend and legal adviser to the minister who convinces him to fashion two wills: the first making his son, Ira, his sole heir (and Darrell executor), and the other leaving his entire estate to Emily, in the event that Ira does not marry her. Covetous of Emily's affections and impending fortune, Darrell hides the second will in the Mellerton family vault and causes Ira to be accused of murdering Nancy Meggs (Annie Mack), an invalid dancer with a husband, Jack (Edward Burt), who beats her. As executor of the first will, Darrell controls all of the money and property belonging to the estate as long as Ira is plagued by a murder charge.

The second act opens three years later. Ira has escaped prison and his supposed victim has been discovered to be alive by Jeremiah McCarthy (Edward Harrigan), a quick-witted, warmhearted Irish undertaker who has accepted the now-impoverished Emily into his household, much to the dismay of his shrewish wife, Margaret O'Dooley (Annie Yeamans). At the New York Undertakers' Masquerade Ball, Emily is abducted by Darrell's henchmen, Jack Meggs, Nancy's brutal husband, and Bill Merritt (C. Sturges), conveying her to a run-down apartment house, using McCarthy's own carriage. In the third act, Emily is rescued from the villains by the undertaker and an African-American woman, Caroline Long (Tony Hart), who are attending a wake in the same squalid tenement, and Ira is recaptured, charged this time with attempted murder.

The fourth act resolves the complications at the Mellerton vault, where Darrell and Meggs are discovered stealing the second will. Nancy, now insane, appears to make a final plea with her husband to give up his life of crime but is choked to death by him in the process. Wild with remorse, Meggs suddenly loses his mind and attempts to stab Darrell, who shoots him in self-defense. McCarthy rushes in with the police and snatches the will from Darrell's hands. Ira is finally exonerated by the testimony of Berrian Soil (Joseph Wilkes), the sexton, who was an eyewitness to Meggs's attack on his wife, and the curtain falls as the undertaker returns to his profession, taking the dead man's measurements.

Christmas Joys and Sorrows was an ambitious experiment to be sure, but the approbation it earned from audiences and critics alike suggested to Harrigan and Braham that the time was right to move away from the time-worn olio formula. The *Clipper* review of January 26, 1878, put the matter succinctly:

> The piece was finely mounted, and so admirably played as even on
> the first night to lighten the hearts of all who were apprehensive as to
> the results of what may be termed a dangerous experiment in a house
> whose patrons have learned to expect the kaleidoscope of a variety
> show, rather than the connected story and the comparative drone of a
> four-act drama. The feelings of the auditors in this respect were
> abundantly shown on the first night by the applause with which, in
> the last act, they hailed the announcement that McCarthy would sing
> a song. In one sense the piece was out of place in a variety house; but
> in another it carried out the very idea which is the keystone of estab-
> lishments of this class. It was of itself variety in the sense that it was a

departure from programmes that are apt, with all their varied acts, to become monotonous when adhered to year in and year out. In that aspect it was graciously accepted by the regular patrons of the Comique, who were thankful for it. In or out of place, as opposing theorists may be pleased to regard it, "Christmas Joys and Sorrows," scored an unmistakable success. The attendance was excellent throughout the week, and on some nights it amounted to a jam.

Although Harrigan and Braham were pleased with their success, Braham recalled the problems at both the Eagle Theatre and the Comique when straight plays threatened to take over theaters that were advertised as variety houses. He advised his son-in-law to move cautiously when attempting to alter an audience's expectations. Still convinced of the value of his experiment but unwilling to jeopardize his success, Harrigan heeded Braham's advice and returned to the variety bill format on January 21, 1878. The following week, Harrigan offered "The Italian Junkman," a new original sketch that may have inspired another charming Braham-Harrigan ballad, "Up at Dudley's Grove," and revived the song "Our Front Stoop," this time sung by the popular entertainer Little Rosebud. On February 4, 1878, among a long list of variety luminaries, Pat Rooney reappeared, spoofing a Lancashire clog dance, and singing a new song and dance written for him by Harrigan and arranged by Braham and called "I'm All Broke Up To-Day." The alternation of sketches and olios continued through the winter, with an early version of Harrigan's melodrama *The Lorgaire* appearing as part of the variety bill on February 18. "Sullivan's Christmas" was revived on 25 February along with the ever popular "Our Front Stoop." Both managed to remain in the bills until March 18, when *A Celebrated Hard Case*, Harrigan's parody of Cormon and Dennery's *A Celebrated Case*, with music by Braham, accompanied the olios.

Written in rhymed couplets (typical of the burlesque genre), *A Celebrated Hard Case* turns on a jewel robbery, murder, and false imprisonment (somewhat reminiscent of *Christmas Joys and Sorrows*), happily resolved in song. However, it is the music cues for this work that provide the greatest interest. The placement of several songs is designated throughout the work, always without lyrics and often without even a title. The only title specified comes at the end of the first scene, when the music of "Don't You Tell My Father" is indicated. In every other instance, the song cues read "Song and March," or "Play lively music. Forward

March. Mardi Gras," or "Song by John [John Rainard, played by Harrigan] and Convicts," or "Adrienne [Adri-Anna, played by Tony Hart] introduces song," or Lather (James F. Crossen) "Does a fancy turn and strikes a song and dance." Helpfully, the incidental underscore or musical punctuation is always associated with some stage business or piece of dialogue. As a result, we find indications such as: "Music—chord. John falls in bass drum," or "Orphans—Music," or "Mysterious business of looking around. Music," or "Gets over to chair on which is a padlock: chord," or "Tremulous music, all intently listening." Once again, Braham had been called on to provide more than popular songs, but it was one of these songs, an infectious waltz, "The Isle of Blackwell," sung by John and the convicts, that helped keep the burlesque running for four weeks.

On Thursday afternoon, April 11, 1878, Martin W. Hanley was honored with a benefit at the Theatre Comique. In spite of bad weather, the theater was filled, and receipts for that single performance were said to have exceeded a thousand dollars. Not only did the audience want to pay tribute to the popular manager of the theater, but also to hear Braham's orchestra, increased to sixteen members as an extra-added attraction. On the following Monday, April 15, Harrigan's sketch "The Doyle Brothers" was presented in a revised three-act form, incorporating some of the material from "The Bradys," as well as a number of Harrigan and Hart (and Braham) specialties. In the first act, the musical routines "Plain Gold Ring," "Dancing in the Ballet," and "London Comic Singers" were added. In the second act, the pair performed a modified version of the sketch "Ireland vs. Italy," and the Miniature 69th Regiment displayed its skill in marching and military drills. In the last act, "Patrick's Day Parade" was added as an energetic finale. Braham's orchestra took the opportunity of the act breaks to display their musical abilities in medleys of popular songs, which included a virtuosic xylophone solo and a series of cornet variations, both of which were lavishly applauded. Harrigan and Braham had mastered ways of integrating variety entertainment into a cohesive dramatic story, and as a result, no olio was added to the bill. A more developed version of *Old Lavender* followed on April 22, and the season closed on April 27 with the account books showing a profit of forty-five thousand dollars.

The season had been a crowded one for Harrigan and Braham. Not only had they churned out a score of songs, sketches, and experimental pieces, organized the weekly bills, and kept them dramatically and musically in top form, but in the midst of rehearsals and performances, they packed up their families and moved from 222 Varick Street to more spacious quarters, at 26 King Street. With six children under the Brahams' care, another daughter (Rose) on the way, and the Harrigans beginning their own family, space was always at a premium in the Braham-Harrigan household.

The day after the season closed at the Theatre Comique, Harrigan, Hart, and Braham, the "Gallant 69th Boys," and forty actors and musicians boarded a train for Pittsburgh where their 1878 summer tour would begin the following day, April 29. Stops at Hooley's Theatre in Chicago; Lot's Opera House in Council Bluffs, Arkansas; the Academy of Music in Omaha; and four nights in Utah led the company to the Bush Street Theatre in San Francisco, where they began a month-long engagement on June 3. Critical reviews of the tour were unanimously complimentary and emphasized the important role played by Braham and his orchestra. The *Omaha Republican* of May 22, 1878, noted that "what most surprised the audience was the orchestra, led by the famous Dave Braham. Nothing like it has ever traveled this way before, and, instead of the dreary and monotonous bit of discord which people inwardly curse, this time they heard something that set their hands and feet going wild." The *Salt Lake Evening News* of May 28, 1878, added that:

> [T]he orchestra introduced several novelties to this part of the country, and the musical part of the entertainment was thoroughly enjoyable. As soon as the curtain was down, "the band began to play," and as soon as the orchestra rested the curtain was rung up again, so that the interest of the audience was maintained throughout the evening. Dave Braham is the prince of musical conductors, and the cornet-player is equal to Levy.

The *Salt Lake Daily Herald* of May 28, 1878, added, "[T]he orchestra accompanying the combination is a treat in itself, some of their selections introducing such novelties, and the music being so good, that they divided the applause with the performance." Among the novelties cited as memorable were the soloists on the violin, cornet, bells, and bagpipes, and an especially effective "mocking-bird solo" on the xylophone. Newspapers across the country praised Braham's melodic gifts as a composer as well, reminding readers that he had not only written the music for the touring entertainment but also was the composer "of many airs that are familiar to every person who ever walks upon the streets."

Due in no small part to the quality of Braham's songs and orchestra, the tour was extended to forty-six performances in San Francisco and advertised as the greatest triumph ever achieved by a touring company in California. The Harrigan and Hart Combination Company actually outdrew Joseph Jefferson's performance in *Rip Van Winkle* and managed to maintain a weekly gross of more than thirty thousand dollars. So hilarious was the entertainment that an occasional mishap befell a happy audience member, whose plight was memorialized by the *Clipper* (June 29, 1878) advertisement for the tour:

> HE LAUGHED HIS TEETH OUT.—Some appreciative individual sitting in a front scat of the balcony of the Bush-street Theatre, last night, just over the orchestra, laughed so heartily at the comicalities of Harrigan and Hart that he laughed his teeth out and dropped them in the orchestra below. Joe, in cleaning up this morning, found them, whole and uninjured. They are a rather expensive full set of upper teeth, which the owner can have by applying for and proving property at the box-office.

Following the extraordinarily successful run in San Francisco, the Harrigan and Hart Combination Company slowly worked its way back East, playing Oakland, San Jose, Stockton, Marysville, Sacramento, Virginia City, Omaha, Council Bluffs, St. Joseph, Kansas City, and St. Louis, and ending with a three-night engagement at the Grand Opera House in Cincinnati. Before leaving California, Braham arranged with the San Francisco-based California Music Publishing Company to publish "I'm Going Abroad with Pa," a seriocomic song performed on tour by a cross-dressed Tony Hart, and "Stem the Tide," dedicated to the California Theatre Boat Club, both with lyrics by Edward Harrigan, and "Garfield Our Best Man," a political song and chorus with lyrics by O. E. Henning.

Both "Stem the Tide" and "Garfield Our Best Man," dedicated to the Garfield Invincibles and published with a engraved portrait of James A. Garfield on the cover, were occasional pieces, composed on order for the organizations they supported. Although each song was written by a different lyricist, both employed the identical verse/chorus march tune vaguely evocative of the earlier hit "The Ginger Blues." Braham had become so popular that it evidently did not matter to either publisher or public that he was blatantly recycling melodies.

Back in New York City, the 1878–79 Theatre Comique season

opened on August 19 with a performance of *The Doyle Brothers*, without an olio. *Old Lavender* followed on August 26, with an advertisement that "Mr. Dave Braham and his famous orchestra" would perform a "Grand Musical Selection" before the drama. *A Celebrated Hard Case* appeared on September 2 with the traditional variety entertainment. On September 16, *Malone's Night Off; or, The German Turnverein* was revived with the addition of a new song, "Sweet Mary Ann (Such an Education Has My Mary Ann)," a simple diatonic patter song extemporizing on the heroine's scholarly, intellectual, and practical acumen. Evidently Mary Ann knows Greek, Latin, and a bevy of other foreign languages, she plays the piano and all sorts of card games like a professional, and she dances expertly in any and every style. The chorus of the song is especially interesting, for, instead of drawing the listener's interest to unexpected chord changes or melodic leaps—as was his usual practice—Braham surprises the listener by rhythmical variations in the accompaniment.

On September 23, Harrigan produced the first version of *The Mulligan Guard Picnic*, an original musical sketch that ran in tandem with the usual variety bill until October 26. This entry in the Mulligan Guard series exploited the farcical mishaps that might befall a group of water excursionists in search of a picnic area. It introduced the new (and immediately popular) Braham-Harrigan patter song and dance "Casey's Social Club," advertised as sung by "The Royal Four": Edward Harrigan, Tony Hart, John Wild, and Billy Gray. *Our Law Makers*, Harrigan's "farcical, comical, and highly sensational drama," appeared on October 28, lasting three weeks until November 16, as the finale to a series of olios that included Zegrino and Legab and their astonishing feats on the double horizontal bars, Kitty O'Neil and her jigs, the famous Hibernian eccentrics Williams and Sullivan, Harry Osborne and Fanny Wentworth in their sketch "Lad and Lass from Ireland," and Andy Collum with banjo solos and marches. Braham composed a "New Introductory Overture" expressly for *Our Law Makers*, as well as a march and song designed to be sung as the finale by the "Miniature 79th" and titled "79th Brave Highlanders." Within the play itself, Braham composed incidental music played by a brass band on the promenade deck of a steamboat, and arranged Harrigan's new song "The Daly Serenade," performed to the accompaniment of the offstage brass band by Harrigan, Hart, John Wild, and Welsh Edwards.

On November 18, *Sullivan's Christmas* reappeared as the finale of a lengthy variety bill, but on November 25, the olio was dropped in favor of a single three-act Irish drama by Harrigan with music by Braham and called *The Lorgaire*. Considered "the best work" Harrigan had produced to that point, the play told the story of a young fisherman (Tony Hart) who is heir to a wealthy Irish landowner. When the child's father is about to return to Ireland, the steward (Welsh Edwards) in charge of the man's estate causes the boy to be arrested for robbery and murder so that his own son can take his place as heir. The Lorgaire (Edward Harrigan), a detective who happens to be in the vicinity, takes an interest in the boy's case and, through a series of clever disguises, eventually manages to expose the villain and reunite the young heir with his father. No specific songs were noted in the reviews of the play: all the attention was directed on Harrigan's virtuosic performance of the title character and the dance performed in the second act, accompanied by authentic Irish pipers.

The Lorgaire held the boards until December 23, when *Christmas Joys and Sorrows* was revived. The variety entertainment returned with the New Year, and the Mulligans were back as well. On January 13, 1879, Harrigan ended the olio bill with his new play *The Mulligan Guard Ball*, in which the Mulligan Guards and the Skidmore Guards both hire the same hall on the same night for their annual ball. A compromise is reached when the Skidmores agree to take the Red Men's Lodge, a room directly overhead, but their heavy stepping proves to be too much for the ceiling, and they come crashing down on the Mulligans below. A *Romeo and Juliet*–like subplot involves the elopement of Irish Tommy Mulligan (Tony Hart) with German Katy Lochmuller (Nellie Jones), the offspring of families who do not get along, and their subsequent efforts to bring about harmony and reconciliation.

In addition to reprising the tune of "The Mulligan Guard," the song that began the series at various points in the sketch, Braham composed the music for three new Harrigan songs in *The Mulligan Guard Ball*: "The Babies on Our Block" and "Singing at the Hallway Door," both sung by Harrigan in the role of Dan Mulligan, and "The Skidmore Fancy Ball," sung by John Wild and Billy Gray, in the blackface roles of Sam Primrose and Palestine Puter. All three follow the verse/chorus formula, with the chorus melody independent of the verse. Both of Harrigan's songs— bright, folklike ditties—are quite demanding vocally, requiring a singer with an expansive range and fine musicianship. The "Skidmore" song, full of playful leaps in the verse, has, by contrast, an exceptionally hummable chorus displaying yet another example of Braham's triadic melodies. All of the songs were well received by audiences and critics alike, and the gen-

The "Downfall of the Skidmores," from *The Mulligan Guard Ball.*

eral consensus was that, in every way, *The Mulligan Guard Ball* was "attractive and amusing" and an "emphatic hit."

Along with *The Mulligan Guard Ball* came the usual array of variety performers, including Fryer's Dogs; Jennie Morgan; Emma Hoffman; Jerry Cohan (George M. Cohan's father); the Four Aces; Billy Carter; and "dashing" Kate Castleton, "England's greatest comique," for whom Braham composed "Darling Little Harry" and "Evening Star," both to lyrics by J. C. Lampard. "Darling Little Harry" is a sprightly patter song about unrequited love:

While others betray their devotion,
And carry their hearts to my feet,
He shows not the slightest emotion,
Nor utters a word that is sweet.
He knows very well that I love him,
He knows he has stolen my heart.
How happy I'd be could I strike him,
That is in the tenderest part.
Chorus:
My Darling little Harry, is the man I like to marry,
But make him out I really never can.
He is so fascinating I really almost hate him,
For he is such a handsome little man.

Braham set Lampard's lyrics to the verse in a flowing barcarole style, while the chorus resembles the typical patter formula, with simple, unobtrusive harmonies, and a melody utilizing repeated notes and easily negotiated leaps. "Evening Star" displays a similar structure reversed. In this case, the chorus is a legato flowing waltz, with a shimmering eighth-note accompaniment pattern designed to evoke a celestial atmosphere. The transparent, chordless accompaniment also provides the illusion that the vocal line is floating in space, independent of harmony or meter.

On March 24, *The Mulligan Guard Ball* was joined by another Harrigan sketch, "The Great In-Toe-Natural Walking Match," satirizing the popularity of heel-and-toe competitions and six-day walking races in the 1870s and 1880s. Braham's son George was an expert walker and often demonstrated that fact to Harrigan's advantage—financially. When George was eighteen, Harrigan would take him to a bar and bet that the boy would beat anyone in the place in a heel-and-toe race to the next bar down the street. Invariably George would win, and Harrigan would collect a fair sum of money, which he would split with his brother-in-law. Although David Braham was not much of a gambling man himself, he was hard-pressed to begrudge his son or son-in-law the extra income generated by such a clever ruse. In addition to Harrigan's sketch on March 24 appeared the obligatory variety acts, including H. R. Archer in a musical sketch called "Music Lesson," and Johnson and Bruno performing two songs with lyrics by Harrigan and music by Braham: "Tom Bigbee Bay" and "Sweet Persimans."

On April 9, *The Mulligan Guard Ball* celebrated its one-hundredth performance, the first of the Harrigan-Braham collaborations to achieve so long a run. David Braham and John Cannon (Tony Hart's brother and treasurer of the theater) took their benefit performance together on May 15, to an overcrowded house, and the season closed on May 24 with *The Mulligan Guard Ball* still playing to large audiences. On the following Monday the show was transferred to the Park Theatre in Brooklyn, where it played a week's engagement, accompanied by an overstuffed variety bill, and from Brooklyn, the company moved to the Boston Museum for a four-week run. It is significant that during the second week of the Boston run, selections from Gilbert and Sullivan's *HMS Pinafore* were added to the olio. *HMS Pinafore* had received its American debut on November 25, 1878, at the Boston Museum in a performance that was conducted by David's nephew, John. The Boston critics found little literary merit in *The Mulligan Guard Ball* but enjoyed its "life, fun, and spirit," concluding that it was "well calculated to amuse warm-weather audiences." Large audiences were reported for the first week, good audiences for the second, but only fair business for the last two weeks of the engagement. The Walnut Street Theatre in Philadelphia was the next stop for the Harrigan and Hart Combination Company's *The Mulligan Guard Ball* tour, followed by a week in Jersey City beginning on July 14.

The tour closed on July 19 and the company returned to New York City where Braham and Harrigan immediately set to work polishing the third volume of the Mulligan series, *The Mulligan Guard Chowder*, scheduled to open the 1879–80 season at the Theatre Comique. During the summer recess the theater had been completely overhauled, inside and out. The walls of the lobby were painted in French gray with an elaborately ornamented border at the top, and wainscoting, representing dark wood, rising four feet from the floor. The auditorium was completely washed, and all the private boxes were freshly draped with red satin and white lace. The dome was newly frescoed in a "neat and chaste" manner, and all the decorations in the house were restored to their original luster. Welsh Edwards continued in his position as stage manager, but William Harrigan, Edward's father, assumed the post of treasurer in place of John Cannon, who was promoted to business manager. The admission prices continued to hold at seventy-five cents for the orchestra seats, fifty cents for the parquet, thirty-five cents for the dress circle, and fifteen cents for benches in the balcony. Private boxes ranged from four dollars to six dollars.

A mere three weeks after the summer tour, *Chowder* was served to a

David Braham

capacity audience on August 11 as the finale of the evening's variety entertainment. The audience, grown accustomed to the established pattern and anxious to revisit the glories of the previous seasons, greeted each act with the familiarity of old friends. Braham was applauded warmly as he led his orchestra into the pit and, after the customary overture, the curtain rose on the sketch "Tickle Me under the Chin" performed by John Shay, Edward Burt, Harry Fisher, and Mary Bird. Clara Moore followed with character songs, Goss and Fox with their new act, "Juliana Johnson," and other Ethiopian specialties, and Edwin Barry with a series of "motto" and topical songs. The olio portion of the evening ended with "C.O.D.," a sketch enacted by John Wild, Billy Gray, and Harry Fisher, all of whom were greeted enthusiastically by an exceedingly appreciative audience. The removal of the olio curtain was accompanied by a new and original overture composed by Braham to introduce the Mulligan festivities. The piece not only offered the audience a preview of the melodies they were about to hear but also recalled the familiar tunes of "The Mulligan Guard" and "The Skidmore Guard," in an attempt to capitalize on their popularity and remind the auditors of the previous episodes in the Mulligan series. As a kind of good-luck charm, a melodic motif from "The Mulligan Guard" would appear in virtually every overture Braham wrote for Harrigan, sometimes appearing as the opening fanfare, at other times disguised in the subtle variation of a countertheme. Braham certainly knew how to influence audience reaction through what they heard, and he was not above trading on the familiarity of popular songs to put the audience into the proper spirit to appreciate the dramatic offering that would follow.

The Mulligan Guard Chowder turns on the continued feud between the Irish Mulligan Guards and the African-American Skidmore Guards, both of whom had arranged an excursion, at exactly the same time, to exactly the same spot on the New Jersey shore: the Mulligans planning their annual chowder junket, the Skidmores seeking to decorate a Cuban general's monument. The confusion is intensified by the presence of yet another organization, the Fat Men's Club, who arrive at the same place for a clambake. Hand-to-hand combat ensues and, not unexpectedly, the Mulligans end up victorious. Braham composed three new tunes for this one-and-a-half-hour farce: "The Little Widow Dunn" and "O Girly! Girly!," both sung by Edward Harrigan in the role of Dan Mulligan, and "The Skids Are Out To-Day," sung by John Wild as Captain Simpson Primrose and the rest of the Skidmore Guard. The regulars of the

Mulligan series were also in attendance. Tony Hart appeared as Dan's son, Tommy, as well as in the transvestite role of Mrs. Welcome Allup. Annie Yeamans reappeared as Cordelia Mulligan, Dan's wife, and Annie Mack played Cordelia Lochmuller, her nemesis. H. A. Fisher acted Gustavus Lochmuller, and Jennie Yeamans, Annie's real-life daughter, played Katy (Lochmuller) Mulligan, Tommy's wife. Billy Gray played the Reverend Palestine Puter, a criminal who had been smuggled out to New Jersey in a coffin, and M. Bradley played Walsingham McSweeny, who is selected head chowder cook over the volatile Snuff McIntosh, performed by Edward Burt.

"The Little Widow Dunn," reminiscent of "Sweet Mary Ann" both in its use of a highly rhythmical accompaniment in the chorus and patterlike verse, was found to be tuneful and catching by the critics, who predicted it was destined to become popular and soon to be "whistled or sung upon our streets." "O Girly! Girly!," a patter song about chasing women to no avail, did not impress the critics as much, even though it was considered "a meritorious composition" and the chorus possessed a bouncingly infectious melody. "The Skids Are Out To-Day," a march in the style of "The Mulligan Guard," fared better, perhaps because of its triadic melody, easily digestible harmonies, and self-consciously playful lyrics:

> Plumes flying wenches sighing,
> Children cry, ha, ha.
> Oh, stop dat cart!
> Now don't you start!
> Oh, do you hear me, sar?
> Whew, whew, dandies,
> Oh, ain't we hot que hay!
> Sweet goodness sake,
> We take de cake,
> De Skids are out today.

Interspersing phrases of old, familiar melodies between the verses (a device Braham would employ again and again), "The Skids Are Out To-Day" made a hit with both audiences and critics, and it was predicted that this "bright and inspiring" number would be as popular as "The Little Widow Dunn." Although the critical reaction to the songs was less enthusiastic than it had been in the past, Braham was not concerned. The fact that his ballad "Over the Hill to the Poor-House," was in its tenth edition by 1879 proved that his music continued to be popular with the public and, as the *New York Times* of November 2, 1879, noted, "If popularity is a species of present immortality, then the composer, Mr. David Braham, should be a happy man." And happy he was!

In October, "The In-Toe-Natural Walking Match" reappeared in the olio portion of the evening, along with the popular serving of *Chowder* that reached its one-hundred-performance mark on November 5. While the third installment of the series was enjoying a popular run, Harrigan and Braham were busily at work on the fourth entry in the series, *The Mulligan Guards' Christmas,* which opened for holiday business on Monday, November 17, two days after *Chowder* closed. The new installment in the Mulligan saga was a complicated series of more or less interrelated stories. Mrs. Cordelia Mulligan (Annie Yeamans) is on her way up to Albany to fetch her belligerent and recently married brother, Planxty McFudd (Welsh Edwards). At the same time, Dan Mulligan (Edward Harrigan) leads the Guard, now sporting Indian costumes, to a shooting match against the Skidmore Guard at Spuyten Duyvil Creek on Christmas Day. Meanwhile, Mrs. Welcome Allup (Tony Hart) learns that the Reverend Palestine Puter (Billy Gray), with whom she is in love, is about to be reinstated as chaplain of the Skidmores (having repaid the money he embezzled from the organization) and made a member of the Order of the Full Moons. This dismays the present chaplain, Ferguson Clinton (Charles Shafer), who challenges Puter to hand-to-hand combat to determine the right to hold the office. All the complications resolve in the Mulligan tenement where Dan and the Guard have assembled to eat Christmas dinner (before Cordelia and her relatives return from Albany). They are surprised by the presence of Primrose, Puter, the widow Allup, and the Skidmores, who end up absconding with all the food before Mrs. Mulligan returns, and a fire breaks out in the neighborhood causing a general melee, on which the curtain falls.

Braham composed five new tunes for the show, in the following order of appearance: "Sweet Kentucky Rose," a mock pathetic ballad sung by Allup followed by an octet of the Full Moons, performing a medley of traditional camp-meeting hymns; "The Pitcher of Beer," a Bowery-style waltz performed by Dan Mulligan, offering Lochmuller (Harry Fisher) something to drink on Christmas Eve; "The Mulligan Braves," sung by Dan and the Mulligan Guard, celebrating their new Indian costumes; "The Skids Are on Review," the obligatory Braham military march (complete with bugle fanfare and "arata tata ta" in the lyric), sung by the Skidmore Guards en route to the shooting match, during which they perform a close-order drill; and "Tur-i-ad-i-lum, or Santa Claus Has Come," a jocund polka performed by the assembled company, during which toys are thrown out into the audience. Of particular interest is "The Mulligan Braves," with its incessant eighth-note accompaniment, percussively suggestive of tom-toms, and a chorus that switches from a modal chant to a sprightly, infectious march tune.

Christmas proved to be effective holiday fare. Business was so good that an extra matinee was added for Thanksgiving. The *New York Mirror* (December 13, 1879) reported that sold-out performances continued through the early part of December, attributing much of the success to Braham, "the musical director, who has certainly brought the musical part of the programme to a high state of perfection." On the afternoon of December 11, while *Christmas* was completing the olio bill at the Theatre Comique, Harrigan, Hart, and Braham performed selections from the show at the Academy of Music, joining with dozens of actors, singers, and dancers to raise money for the Roman Catholic Orphan Asylum.

On Thursday, January 29, 1880, a reception of the Members of Harrigan and Hart's Theatre Comique Association was held at Irving Hall, with music supplied by the Theatre Comique orchestra under the direction of "Professor McAdams." David's son George Braham was identified as a member of the "Floor Committee," and David was on the "Reception Committee," along with John Cannon, William Harrigan, and other members of the company. On the program of dance music for the evening, seven of the twenty-odd numbers identified were composed by Braham. These included "Quadrille: The Mulligan Guard Ball," "Polka: Tur-i-ad-i-lum, or Santa Claus Has Come," "Quadrille: The Mulligan Braves," "Waltz: The Skids Are on Review," "Quadrille: Nine-Pin-M.G.P.," "Lancers: The Mulligan Guards' Chowder," and a galop titled, "Sleigh Ride."

The Mulligan Guards' Christmas closed on February 14 after a highly respectable twelve-week run and gave way, on Monday, February 16, to the next installment of the series, called *The Mulligan Guards' Surprise.* Cordelia Mulligan (Annie Yeamans) convinces her husband, Dan (Harrigan), to leave their simple dwelling in Mulligan Alley and move to a "French flat" in a posh neighborhood, where the widow Allup (Tony Hart), now answering to the first name Rebecca, works as a domestic servant, and Simpson Primrose (John Wild) functions as a coachman. Feeling henpecked, Mulligan rebels against his wife's wishes and returns to his old surroundings, where he is welcomed by a surprise party, on the same night that a wedding reception is under way for an African-American couple in a nearby apartment. Add to this a marital squabble between the Lochmullers (Harry Fisher and Annie Mack), a poisoned liverwurst mistakenly delivered to the wedding reception, a mislaid document that holds up the wedding, and another rough-and-tumble melee that rings down the curtain. The Harrigan formula had become somewhat predictable, but that was a source of its appeal! An introductory olio featured John Wild, Billy Gray, and Harry Fisher in a sketch titled "Brothers in Misfortune," and Jennie Morgan singing popular songs, including the Braham-Harrigan parlor ballad "The Beauty of Limerick."

For this "fifth" entry in the series, Braham composed several new tunes, many of which were exceptionally popular. The first song in the show, however, was neither by Braham nor Harrigan but the interpolation of a ballad by George Cooper and John Rogers Thomas titled "Linger Not Darling," and performed as a duet between Mrs. Mulligan and Mrs. Lochmuller, the former appearing to accompany herself on the guitar. The first original melody in the score, "I'll Wear the Trousers, Oh!" reminiscent of an Irish folk song, is next sung by Dan Mulligan in an attempt to convince himself to take a stand against his wife. Although the song is quite tonal, it is very expansive in its vocal range and marked by extensive leaps, dramatically evoking Dan's state of inebriation and attempts at sober decision making. "The Full Moon Union," a martial production number sung by members of the "Full Moon" lodge, follows, complete with extended orchestral introduction, reminiscent of the *Lone Ranger* theme borrowed from Rossini's overture to *William Tell*.

Braham noted that the chorus to "The Full Moon Union" was the only example of a song composed during his entire collaboration with Edward Harrigan when the music preceded the lyrics. When Harrigan handed him the lyrics to the song, there was no chorus, and no matter how forcefully Braham pressed his son-in-law, he refused to write any more verses. A song without a chorus concerned Braham greatly, and, no matter how hard he tried, he could not come up with a melody for it. Months passed, and one day in August 1878, while Braham and Harrigan were on tour, they found themselves crossing a street in St. Louis when a melody came to Braham in a flash of inspiration. He stopped dead in his tracks and exclaimed, "Ned, I've got it." "Got what?" was the obvious reply, "The chorus for 'Full Moon.' Listen." As they stood in the middle of a busy intersection, Braham hummed Harrigan the new tune. Harrigan liked it so much that a horsecar nearly ran them down before they remembered where they were. When they returned to their hotel, Braham wrote out a lead sheet of the melody and, that night, after the performance, Harrigan finally wrote the lyrics to the chorus, and Braham completed the song.

"Hark, Baby, Hark" is sung at the wedding reception by widow Allup, followed by a lilting cakewalk and waltz, "Dat Citron Wedding Cake," performed by the company. "Never Take the Horseshoe from the Door," a jaunty schottische patter song sung by Dan Mulligan at his surprise party, is next in the running order, followed by the atmospheric "Whist! The Bogie Man," sung by the party guests. This ghost-evoking piece is filled with traditional "scary music" devices: string tremolos, minor and diminished chords, a melody filled with short rests that imply breathlessness, and virtuosic runs evocative of the "storm music" composed by serious composers. Ten years later, the number was interpolated into the British burlesque of Bizet's *Carmen*, *Carmen Up-To-Data* and quickly became even more popular in London than it had been in New York. Not only did "Whist! The Bogie Man" guarantee the success of the British show, the song itself turned into an international hit as well.

The *New York Times* of February 18, 1880, was complimentary of Braham's "very pretty and spirited" score, noting that "His songs are flowing, melodious, and will probably be popular, though they suggest at times other pieces, as, for instance, the waltz in scene five, which is embraced in a song and dance called 'Dat Citron Wedding Cake.' However, Mr. Braham deserves a great deal of credit for his work."

The financially successful seasons at the Theatre Comique enabled Braham not only to provide for his family in New York City, but also for his seventy-nine-year-old father back in England. A letter from the elder Braham, mailed on May 10, 1880, provides an important glimpse into David's supportive relationship with his father:

I received your kind letter this day with draft quite safe, for which I am truly grateful. I am [happy] to find you received my picture and you appreciate it. It was taken 12 months ago when I was in good health, but unfortunately, my illness is [*sic*] altered my looks wonderfully. I hope when I breathe the sea air as my doctor advises me, and your kind offer to pay the little expense, I trust it will make a great improvement to my constitution. Now, my Dave, you wrote in your letter dated 5th April, you wish to ascertain what the expense will be for a month or two. I have inquired, and lodgings this time of year is dear: not less than £5 or £6 a week. Then there is sea bathing and living which cannot be done less £10 a week. I think one month will be quite sufficient to recruit my health, but to be there two months—it will run up to a great expense to you. You see, my dear boy, it is not my wish to infringe on your good nature. You have a large family to consider of. Don't think I wish to dictate you in your kind intentions. On your behalf I merely say this and show you that your father does not wish to run yourself to too much expense. Nevertheless, I shall leave it entirely to your own discretion how to act. Either way, I shall be thankful because I know it will be a great benefit to me. Therefore, if I am to go, I should like to leave on my birthday, that is 24 June. If God spares me, I shall be 79 years old, and if I benefit by this trip, I shall have to thank the Lord and yourself, in taking a fresh lease of my life a few years longer. . . . Now I must conclude, wishing you answer this as early as possible. I have no more to say, but give my love to Annie, my dear grandchildren, and accept the same from your affectionate father, Joseph Braham.

Inevitably, Braham's father spent two months at the seashore, but his health did not improve as much as he anticipated. He died two years later, never having seen a single one of his son's musical productions.

The one-hundredth performance of *The Mulligan Guards' Surprise* fell on May 12, and every woman in the audience received a souvenir satin program. Three days later the season closed, a week earlier than had been advertised, to begin its summer tour. The Braham-Harrigan families had recently moved to new living quarters on 30 King Street on account of the birth of another son, Edward, to the Braham family in 1880. Although the new apartment was even more spacious than the last, it would be some time before either David Braham or Edward Harrigan would relax in the simple luxury of the family home.

Immediately following the end of the season in New York City, Harrigan and Hart and their "Great Comedy Company" moved to the Park Theatre in Philadelphia for a one-week engagement of *The Mulligan Guards' Surprise* beginning on May 17. On Thursday, May 20, members of the company performed "The Full Moons" at an afternoon benefit at the Walnut Street Theatre for George K. Goodwin, the manager of the Park Theatre. Although patronage was only moderate in Philadelphia, the next week at the Park Theatre in Brooklyn played to very good business, in spite of the sweltering weather. Another well-attended week at the Novelty Theatre in Williamsburgh sent the company on a northward loop to Poughkeepsie, Troy, Albany, Springfield, Worcester, Providence, Hartford, New Haven, Paterson, and Newark, with the tour scheduled to close in Jersey City on June 26, 1880. Returning to New York City, Braham and Harrigan used the month of July to complete the revision they had begun of *The Mulligan Guard Picnic* and to continue working on *The Mulligan Guards' Nominee*, both scheduled to appear in the 1880–81 season at the Theatre Comique.

Not untypically, the theater underwent another renovation during the summer months. The auditorium and hallways were painted white and the benches behind the orchestra seats and in the dress circle were replaced with folding chairs so that all the seats on the main floor and in the dress circle were alike. India-rubber matting was laid down in the aisles, and the floors underneath the chairs were stripped of any covering so they could be scrubbed before each performance. Edward Harrigan was advertised as stage manager for the new season, with William Harrigan and John Cannon returning in their roles as treasurer and manager, respectively. Prices were raised slightly from the previous season: one dollar to sit in the orchestra, seventy-five cents to sit in the parquet, seventy-five cents for a reserved seat in the dress circle, fifty cents for an unreserved seat, and $.25 for a space in the gallery. Private boxes were still valued at six dollars and four dollars.

A revised and expanded *Mulligan Guard Picnic* opened on August 9, 1880, sharing the bill with singer Jennie Morgan and another Harrigan farce, titled "Doctor Tanner Outdone," featuring Billy Gray and John Wild in the principal roles. In the reconstruction of *Picnic*, Gustavus Lochmuller (Harry Fisher), presumed dead, has returned disguised as a member of a German band, only to find Tommy Fagin (Billy Gray) a persistent suitor for the hand of his erstwhile widow, Bridget (Annie Mack). Dan Mulligan (Harrigan), recovering from his unhappy experience uptown in the French flat, and hung over from a party the night before, encounters a series of mishaps with a pair of ill-fitting trousers brought him by Roderick O'Dwyer (Edward Burt), the tailor who now occupies Lochmuller's former butcher shop. Mulligan expresses his frustration at the tailor in the first song of the play, a belligerent patter song titled "Roderick O'Dwyer." Braham sets the chorus of the song in a very high range, with many repeated notes that seem designed literally to hammer out the lyrics:

Roderick O'Dwyer, you are the biggest liar;
Your tongue will never tire;
Get out! get out! go an [*sic*]!
Now if you raise my ire, I'll throw you in the fire;
And then you will expire,
You little tailor man.

It is noteworthy that when Braham repeats the melodic phrase, he changes the harmony from the consonant chords of the first hearing to more dissonant diminished chords to emphasize the growing frustration of the character.

Widow Allup (Tony Hart) and Walsingham McSweeney (Michael Bradley) convince Mulligan to rent his yacht to the Full Moons, who want to go to Pleasure Grove, New Jersey, on a picnic, the very place where the Mulligan Guard has decided to hold its picnic. The Mulligans, unaware of the conflict of interest, prepare to depart for Pleasure Grove, singing "All Aboard for the M.G.P.," a buoyant march with an infectious, energetic tune making fine use of nonchordal tones that subtly evoke a driving-forward movement. The Full Moons then appear and counter with "Second Degree, Full Moon Union," a forerunner of the marches typically associated with John Philip Sousa, complete with trumpet fanfare and highly ornamented orchestral introduction. They board Mulligan's yacht and head toward New Jersey but are prevented from docking by a New Jersey sheriff, who demands payment of a five-dollar license fee. Unable to come up with the cash, the Full Moons sail off to another location, just as the Mulligan Guards arrive, pay the fee, and set up for their picnic. When the festivities get under way, Dan Mulligan sings "Mary Kelly's Beau," an Irish-style waltz anticipating such popular Irish ballads as "My Wild Irish Rose" (1899) and "When Irish Eyes Are Smiling" (1912), and "Locked Out after Nine," a vivacious, jiglike patter song with an extended dance break.

After the dancing of the quadrille that accompanies "Locked Out after Nine," Tommy Fagin announces his intention to marry Mrs. Lochmuller, arousing the immediate animosity of her husband, present in the disguise of a tuba player. The men get into a fight, during which both are arrested by the sheriff. The scene changes to Squire Cohog's grocery store and courtroom, where Mulligan, appearing as Fagin's lawyer, manages to get him acquitted by bribing the judge. Thrilled with his release, Fagin suggests to Mrs. Lochmuller that the judge marry them on the spot, when Lochmuller removes his disguise and claims his wife. Amid the excitement accompanying Lochmuller's return to the living, the whistle of a tugboat is heard, calling the picnickers for the return voyage home to New York City, with a reprise of "All Aboard for the M.G.P." On the way home, the Mulligan Guards' barge manages to rescue the foundering yacht on which the Full Moons, still looking for a place to picnic, have been stranded. In celebration, Mulligan sings "Sandy-Haired Mary in Our Area," another lilting patter song, the chorus of which is filled with unusual and unexpected harmonies and rhythmical phrases, as the harbor police board the barge and the curtain falls. Although it found the dialogue to be overwritten and in need of compression, the *Clipper* (August 21, 1880) predicted that in its revised form *The Mulligan Guard Picnic* would be as successful as any of its predecessors in the series and that "David Braham is to be complimented for the tuneful music of all the songs, as well as the taking overture, which gives a foretaste of the good things to come."

On November 3, *Picnic* attained its one-hundredth performance. On the afternoon of November 16, at the Academy of Music, along with performers from New York City's other legitimate theaters and variety houses, Harrigan and Hart's company performed scenes and songs from the show for the annual benefit of the Roman Catholic Orphan Asylum. Harrigan, Hart, and Braham enjoyed appearing on benefit programs, even though they added an extra performance to their already crowded workweek. Like Braham, Harrigan and Hart had emerged from humble beginnings. Each had managed, through talent, hard work, and good fortune, to realize the American Dream and, because of their success, each was driven to help the less fortunate members of the population. Besides, charity performances afforded Braham and Harrigan a wealth of free publicity for their new songs and routines, so clearly there were benefits on both sides.

By the time *The Mulligan Guard Picnic* closed on November 20, Harrigan and Braham had the next installment ready to open on November 22, *The Mulligan Guards' Nominee*. This new chapter in the series opens on Cunard wharf, where Gustavus Lochmuller (Harry Fisher), Mulligan's rival in the current election for alderman, awaits the return of his wife, Bridget (Annie Mack), from a recent visit to her relatives in Ireland. When she appears, she is followed by an English detective, Oliver Bullwinkle (Edwin Barry), who suspects her to be involved with the FNA (Fenian National Association) because of certain coded letters addressed to her that he had intercepted. Lochmuller's celebrated jealousy is aroused by what appears to be Bullwinkle's attentions toward his wife, and the scene closes with Bridget threatening to beat her husband if he does not behave himself.

In the Wee-Drop Saloon (Mulligan's establishment), a group of ladies are discovered making flannel shirts, and enthusiastically singing the lilting "Canada, I, Oh!," activities that confirm Bullwinkle's suspicions that the women are members of a secret organization. His attempt to purloin the yellow briefcase Mrs. Lochmuller brought with her from Ireland is stymied by Rebecca Allup (Tony Hart), who hides the contents while the ladies are singing "Down in Gossip Row." During this chatty musical interlude, the ladies exchange the latest neighborhood gossip in a chirpy patter song. The ladies flee when Dan Mulligan (Harrigan) appears with a crowd of ward politicians making plans for a ratification meeting and singing the campaign song "Hang the Mulligan Banner Up," a vivacious polka with a highly fetching tune.

Typical of the Mulligan series, the hall that had been leased for Dan's ratification meeting also has been rented by Lochmuller for *his* ratification meeting, and the Skidmore Guards for a masquerade party, all on the same night. But Dan's troubles come more from within his constituency, whom he tries to appease with a song, "Oh, He Promises," another dramatic musical scene in which Dan sings a lilting waltz and his followers respond in a bouncy duple-meter patter. The lyrical, almost schmaltzy, melody of Dan's verse underscores the overblown sincerity of his campaign promises, while the more angular, rhythmic chorus response of the men evokes their lively expressions of support. A fight ensues and the politicians tumble out of the room just as the Skidmores enter to begin their masquerade. Many of the sewing ladies from Dan's saloon also are present, including his wife, Cordelia (Annie Yeamans). Dan returns to fetch his overcoat and, mistaking his wife for a member of the Skidmore party, flirts with her while the dance begins with "The Skidmore Masquerade," an attractively tuneful, rhythmically stirring promenade that ends in a galop.

After an altercation with the Lochmuller contingent that leads the company down to the police station, Mulligan is elected alderman. In celebration, the Skidmore Guards appear in spiffy new uniforms and perform "The Skids Are Out To-Night," another "Sousa-like" march introduced by a long and elaborate orchestral prelude, and accompanied by marching and close-order drills. A striking feature of this number lies in the musical burlesquing of familiar songs such as "Hard Times," "Sally in Our Alley," and "Annie Laurie," where Braham again trades on audience recognition to good effect. At the end of the play, in the cabin of a steamboat, Detective Bullwinkle realizes that the sewing women belong to the Florence Nightingale Association, not the militant Fenian group, when he discovers that in the code being used, "c.s.," does not represent cavalry sabers, but cotton socks, and "f.s." means flannel shirts, not flying shells. After a jovial polkalike drinking song, "A Nightcap," a boiler explodes, wrecking the entire boat as the curtain falls.

Due, in no small part, to the contributions of David Braham, who provided incidental music as well as songs, and Charles W. Witham, who designed and painted the scenery, *Nominee* ran until February 19, 1881, accumulating more than one hundred performances. The outstanding hits of the evening were "Down in Gossip Row," called by the *Spirit of the Times* (November 27, 1880) "a masterpiece of musical fun," and "The Skids Are Out To-night," with the marching and close-order drill earning three encores on opening night.

All was not fun, however, in the final weeks of the run. The *Spirit of the Times* (February 12, 1881) reported that just before the curtain went up on Saturday, February 5, word was brought to the theater that Harrigan's baby girl Annie had died. Everyone backstage, including the child's grandfather in the pit, knew of the misfortune but kept it from the actor until the performance was over. The newspaper emphasized the ironic pathos of the situation: Harrigan performing at the top of his form, laughter filling the auditorium, while his wife was at home weeping over an empty cradle and the rest of the company trying to hold back their tears. Although Harrigan's grief after the performance was monumental, how much greater was Braham's pain, forced to maintain his composure for the good of the performance, privately grieving the loss of his grandchild, and sharing the sorrow of his wife and daughter.

Two weeks before the tragedy, Harrigan and Braham had commenced rehearsals for *The Mulligans' Silver Wedding*, the eighth installment of the Mulligan saga, and it was work on the new show that enabled the pair to overcome their personal anguish. The opening night on Monday, February 21, before a large and enthusiastic audience comprising every class of New York City society, was a triumph. As the *Spirit of the Times* (February 26, 1881) gushed: "Nowhere else in our experience can you find an audience who will sit for three hours and twenty minutes, without intermission or the relief of an act-drop, and laugh all the while, as at the Theatre Comique."

Cordelia Mulligan (Annie Yeamans) now rents out furnished apartments, counting among her tenants Lochmuller (Harry Fisher), whose wife has gone off to Europe and who now works as a trombonist at the Criterion Music Hall; Edgar De Angelles (Edward Burt), an actor who previously deserted Clorinda Perkins (Annie Mack); Washington Irving Crumbs (Michael Drew), an eccentric poet; Dennis Mulligan (Tony Hart), Dan Mulligan's cousin and mate on a ship recently arrived from Europe; and Clorinda Perkins, a passenger on the same ship, looking for the man who betrayed her. Alderman Dan Mulligan (Harrigan) enters and entertains his tenants liberally with drink, while Dennis vocalizes the first song, "The Castaways," a jolly hornpipe, recounting his virtuosic adventures as an able-bodied seaman, assisted by the ensemble joining in the chorus.

Clorinda Perkins secures a job at the Criterion Music Hall, and the scene changes to a performance at that theater, the interior of which is realistically depicted onstage. Jolly Johnson (Edwin Barry), acting as chairman in the English music-hall style, sings two olio numbers, "Don't You Miss the Train," a bouncy schottische ditty, and "The Mirror's the Cause of It All," an Irish-flavored ballad blaming the problems of unsuccessful courtships on a woman's vanity, in four verses and a chorus. Winsome Winnie (Emily Yeamans) follows with "I Am Such a Shy Young Girl," a mincingly flirtatious trifle that earns her the reward of a bouquet filled with peppered flowers thrown from the onstage audience. Mulligan enters to sing "John Riley's Always Dry," a bright drinking song—part stately gavotte, part Irish jig—trading on easily digestible ascending scales, followed by the Louisiana Serenaders (eight gentlemen from the company dressed as blackface swells and belles) singing "South Fifth Avenue," a minstrel-style production number beginning as an expansive waltz song and ending with a lively quadrille tune and dance break. This number is particularly interesting because of the subtle ways in which Braham modulates from one tonality to another without losing a sense of melodic flow. According to the *Clipper* (March 5, 1881), the number was encored several times before the play could move forward.

After Edgar De Angelles escapes being strangled by Clorinda Perkins during the performance of *The Lady of Lyons*, the dramatic sketch ending the olio at the Criterion, he hides, now in disguise, in a stable, where Captain Primrose (John Wild) is about to be initiated into the third degree of the order of Full Moons. The Moons enter with great ceremony to the ironically pompous "Third Degree Full Moon," an elaborately overblown march that aspires to be stately in spite of its schottis-che rhythms and playful melodic leaps. Dennis Mulligan, pursuing De Angelles, unwittingly witnesses the ceremony and is forced to become a member of the order.

Back at the Mulligans' home, Cordelia, dressed in her twenty-five-year-old bridal gown, opens a letter addressed to her husband and dis-covers it to be an anonymous love letter. Consumed with jealousy on this, their silver anniversary, she decides to commit suicide by drinking from a bottle of "Rat Poison" kept in the kitchen, unaware that the bottle con-tains brandy sequestered by her husband. She arrives inebriated at the anniversary celebration and scolds her husband for his infidelity. Clorinda Perkins sees the letter in question and explains that she wrote it to Dennis Mulligan, suggesting that Cordelia must have mistaken the "Den" for "Dan." With the plot thus sorted out, Dan and the anniversary guests sing "Wheel the Baby Out," a lively schottische finale into which well-known nursery rhymes are interpolated as the curtain falls.

Reviewers generally found *Silver Wedding* to be the best of the series, noting Harrigan's growth as a playwright and the unexpected presence of the wealthier classes in the audience (who actually seemed to be enjoy-ing themselves). Although the ever-supportive *Spirit of the Times* (February 26, 1881) called Braham the "Offenbach of the Comique" and predicted popularity for all of the new songs, the pervasive opinion was that Braham's music was not equal to his best work. Even so, the songs were found to be bright and melodic, and *Silver Wedding* played until April 30, when the season closed at the Theatre Comique. After that date, 514 Broadway ceased to function as a theater, and the building was converted into a large store. During the final week of the season, the scenery, drop curtain, and all of the theater fixtures were sold at auction, with Harry Miner buying all the folding chairs in the auditorium. It is an important historical note that Braham was a member of the first com-pany to use the building as a theater (Wood's Minstrels) as well as the last: The theater opened and closed with David Braham and his violin.

The annual summer tour began immediately on May 2 at the Globe Theatre in Boston, where *Silver Wedding* played to a large and apprecia-tive audience for two weeks. The next stop was the Park Theatre, Brooklyn, where *The Mulligan Guards' Nominee* and *The Mulligans' Silver Wedding* split a two-week engagement, followed by a week at the Novelty Theatre in Williamsburgh, where *Silver Wedding* closed the regular sea-son at that theater. From Brooklyn, the company boarded a train for

The exterior of Harrigan and Hart's Theatre Comique, 514 Broadway, New York City, 1881, from the Museum of the City of New York. Used with permission.

Chicago, where the two shows each played a week at Hooley's Theatre to good houses, if only lukewarm reviews. The Olympic Theatre in St. Louis welcomed the company with an enthusiastic full house on June 20, even though the weather was suffocatingly hot. At the opening-night performance of *Silver Wedding*, Captain Paul Boynton (the inventor of a pneumatic underwater life-saving suit) and companions filled one private box, while international singing star Emily Soldene and her party filled the other. After playing to a large and delighted audience for a week in St. Louis, the Harrigan and Hart tour disbanded for the season, and the performers returned to New York City.

While their husbands were off on tour, Annie Braham and Annie Harrigan set about moving the Harrigan household into its own home on 14 Perry Street, midway between Greenwich Avenue and Waverly Place. Every Braham child strong enough to carry a box was enlisted to help in the move uptown to the three-story town house, which had been paid for in full from Harrigan's profits at the Theatre Comique. It was not simply necessity that caused the women to engineer the move. The summer tour was a brief one, and the relocation could have waited if the men had to be necessarily involved. The fact was that, in household matters, the two Annies made the executive decisions. They hired and fired servants and nurses, dealt with creditors and banks, and did all the buying and selling necessary to maintain a comfortable and happy domestic environment for their workaholic husbands. Harrigan and Braham knew how to earn money. Their wives knew how to save it and use it wisely.

In July, after the move, Harrigan and his wife, Annie Theresa, went to Schroon Lake in upstate New York for a much-needed vacation. David and Annie Braham spent the summer at 30 King Street, looking after their grandson, three-year-old Eddie Harrigan, and enjoying the peaceful clamor of their seven children.

Chapter 8

Entr'Acte: "The New Comique"

ven before the 1880–81 season was completed, Harrigan and Hart had been apprised of the closing of 514 Broadway, and the pair began searching for a site for a new Theatre Comique. They latched on to another church-turned-theater building uptown, at 728–30 Broadway, which was slated for transformation into a block of retail stores, and began negotiations with Judge Hilton, who represented the Alexander Turney Stewart estate, to which the property belonged. An agreement was reached whereby Harrigan and Hart would lease the site for a minimum of seven years at sixteen thousand dollars per year, with the Stewart estate agreeing to construct the front wall of the theater at a cost of thirty thousand dollars, leaving the responsibility for rebuilding the interior to the managers, each putting up another thirty thousand dollars.

The location of the new Theatre Comique was not unfamiliar to the team. They had made their first appearance in New York City at 728 Broadway when it was called the Globe Theatre (one of its several names), although, by the time the new theater was ready to open, the earlier building was hardly recognizable, masked by an imposing new facade designed by E. D. Harris, made of Philadephia pressed brick, extending 90 feet along Broadway. The lobby was decorated in gold and bronze, with the floor covered in red, black, and buff tiles. From either side of the lobby were fireproof iron staircases leading to the balcony, and then continuing on to the gallery. A single central door, 6 feet wide, led directly from the lobby to the parquet for entrances to the auditorium, while two doors, each 5-feet wide, one on either side of the central opening, were to be used for exits. The parquet, designed in an oval, rather than the traditional horseshoe shape, was 50 feet deep and 70 feet wide and could seat 450 people, each with a clear view of the stage. The oval design also was useful in bringing the audience in closer proximity to the actors. The designers, Kimball and Wisedell, believed that the actors gave better performances when the audience was close at hand, a philosophy shared by the managers. The seats were upholstered to adapt comfortably to the shape of the body, in tinseled raw silk, with plaited brass bands at the top of the chairs. On either side of the stage were two canopied proscenium boxes, the larger of which was on continual reserve for the Stewart estate, and a single canopied box lined either side of the balcony, which was designed to accommodate about 400 people. The gallery, extending from the outer wall of the theater to the edge of the dress circle, was arranged to seat 800, making the total occupancy, exclusive of boxes and standing room, about 1,650.

The decorations of the new theater, like the kind of entertainment to be housed there, were light and cheerful, dispensing entirely with the masks of comedy and tragedy, ornaments that traditionally accompany theater architecture. The auditorium was painted in old ivory, buff, and bronze, and the balcony and gallery were surrounded by friezes depicting birds, animals, and foliage. The elaborately carved wooden frame around the proscenium opening was ornamented with antique bronze figures, two of which were salvaged from the previous Theatre Comique, and on the fronts of the private boxes were painted panels depicting flowers, birds, griffins, and lions. The drop curtain was painted with the words "To Be Continued," manifesting Harrigan and Hart's confidence in their own managerial skills.

The stage was 70 feet wide and 34 feet deep, outfitted with all the latest in stage machinery, traps, and scenic devices, and the proscenium opening was 29 feet wide and 32 feet high, allowing for about 20 feet of storage space on either side. Beneath the stage was a large cellar (with a subcellar) that could be employed for the special effects required in pantomimes and spectacles, with an electrical apparatus for igniting and controlling all the gaslights onstage and signals for the conductor and the various stagehands. The carpenter's shop, dressing rooms, boiler, and stage engine were all housed in a separate building to the rear of the stage, joined by a brick wall, 2 feet deep and connected through fireproof doors. An important feature of the new theater was the lighting system, which sought to dispense with the old practice of gaslight in the auditorium. The parquet was designed to be flooded with light from a prismatic chandelier containing 22,000 glass prisms suspended from the central dome and illuminated with electricity.

Although the new Comique was nearly twice the distance from 30 King Street than 514 Broadway, David Braham applauded the move. The acoustics of the new house were close to perfect, and the larger orchestra pit enabled his orchestra—comprised of two first violins, second violin, viola, cello, bass, flute, clarinet, first cornet, second cornet, trombone, and percussion—to perform in relative comfort. More space also afforded Braham the luxury of expanding the size of the orchestra—a typical practice for benefit performances—without musicians, stands, or instruments getting in the way, as they had at the old theater.

When the new Theatre Comique opened its doors on August 29, 1881, the house was packed to the rafters, with hundreds of people denied admittance, lingering outside the theater in hopes of catching a note or two of the music. The *Spirit of the Times* (September 3, 1881) reported: "It was a thoroughly American audience assembled in our first thoroughly American theatre, with no imitations of foreign fads, ancient or modern, and the first night was more like a genuine old Knickerbocker house-warming than a theatrical opening." Not untypically, as each familiar performer entered—beginning with Braham—the audience went wild, clapping and stomping in an enthusiastic demonstration of their sincere affection. After the obligatory welcoming speeches by the actors, the audience was induced to contain their enthusiasm so the play could proceed.

The work that opened the new theater was not part of the Mulligan series, though it was clearly designed in the Mulligan mold. *The Major* centered around the search of a mother, Arabella Pinch (Annie Mack), accompanied by her manservant, Henry Higgins (Tony Hart), for her daughter, Amelia (Marie Gorenflo), who fled from England with Granville Bright (Edward Burt), a photographer, and who subsequently married him. Arabella, however, was aware that Bright had been previously married, and enlisted the assistance of Major Gilfeather (Harrigan), an Irish shyster lawyer, both to find the girl and to ascertain the legality of her marriage. Various romantic subplots involved Miranda Biggs (Annie Yeamans), who doted on the major; Percival Popp (M. F. Drew), the fireworks manufacturer who first loved Miranda but who would end up marrying Arabella; and Henry Higgins and Henrietta (Gertie Granville), the housemaid, whose onstage marriage anticipated the real-life marriage of the couple the following year. Upon such a simple spine, Harrigan attached numerous opportunities for familiar performers to engage in their characteristic clowning, assisted by spectacular special effects. The scene in Popp's fireworks factory was, perhaps, the most notable. Having gone there to interrogate the owner, Major Gilfeather becomes preoccupied with the melodious music of a nearby camp meeting. When he unconsciously throws a lighted cigar to the floor, the room explodes in an extraordinary display of fireworks that ultimately blows the roof off the building and tosses the camp meeting singers amid the debris all over the stage.

In addition to providing the music incidental to all the theatrical effects in the play, Braham composed the melodies for four new songs in *The Major*. Harrigan sang the boastfully chauvinistic "Major Gilfeather," revealing the character's adeptness at manipulating people. Beginning with a jiglike patter, the song ends in a charming waltz, the melody of which revolves around accented nonchordal tones, adding a comically ironic edge to the piece by means of cleverly inverted word painting. A fine example of this lies with the word "under," which Braham sets with an ascending phrase that leaps "over," contradicting the lyric. "Miranda, When We Are Made One," Gilfeather's duet with Miranda Biggs, is an expansively romantic waltz in which the harmonic and melodic materials change with the speaker, each dreaming about the possibilities of marriage from his or her characteristic point of view.

The two most celebrated numbers of the score were performed by the African-American Veteran Guard Cadets, twelve boys dressed in Continental uniforms with tricorn hats over their powdered wigs, and assisted by a professional chorus called the Madrigal Boys. The cakewalk number "Clara Jenkins' Tea" is another of Braham's infectious schottische tunes accompanied by an extended dance break full of rhythmical variety, dynamic changes, and heavy accents, all designed to serve the high-stepping choreography on stage. Harrigan's lyrics not only trade on a "Sunday go to meeting" archetype, however; with the mention of the "citron cake," recalling "Dat Citron Wedding Cake" in *The Mulligan Guards' Surprise*, they even draw attention to earlier African-American numbers in the Braham-Harrigan canon:

Oh, now put on your Sunday clothes,
Get ready for the jubilee,
Dere's a mighty high time, when the clock strikes nine,
Oh, do come along with me.
All Methodist and Baptist too, oh, my!
Will sing about the old Red Sea;
De new church choir will sing a note higher,
At Clara Jenkins' socialistic tea.
Ladies, try this citron cake,
Pass it 'round for goodness sake;
Won't you try some lemon cream?
Oh! yes, now don't be mean, Oh!

Even more popular than the cakewalk, the "Veteran Guard Cadets," a number recycled from an earlier sketch, "Down Broadway," was the showpiece of the score, so beloved by the audience that it was encored twice on opening night. Another of Braham's Sousa-like military marches, it opens with an orchestral introduction that gradually mounts in intensity, both harmonically and dynamically. The "C" section of the march is especially effective in its use of a staccato, scale-generated melody complemented by alternating rhythmical phrases that energetically propel Harrigan's celebratory lyric.

On November 25, *The Major* celebrated its one-hundredth performance. The show continued into the New Year, closing on January 7, 1882, with 150 performances, the longest-running Harrigan-Braham work to date. Although the show had a long and successful run, the opening-night critics found much to criticize, particularly in the length of the performance. As the curtain rose at eight twenty-three and fell at eleven forty-eight, most reviewers found the four acts too long—especially since there were only four new songs in the piece, nearly half of the songs found in the Mulligan series. Still, the four were judged to be first-rate, with the *New York Times* noting on December 20, 1881, that "Mr. Braham's melodies are as attractive, and win as much applause now, at Christmas-tide, as last September."

The next Braham-Harrigan confection, *Squatter Sovereignty*, opened on January 9, 1882. Evidently Tony Hart had been dissatisfied with the non-singing role of Henry Higgins in *The Major*, so Harrigan and Braham appeased the actor with the transvestite role of the Widow Rosie Nolan, who is at the center of the new three-act comedy. The widow desires that her daughter, Nellie (Gertie Granville), marry Terence McIntyre (Michael Bradley), son of Felix McIntyre (Harrigan), a wandering astronomer who travels up and down the street with a huge telescope, charging ten cents a peep. A contract is drawn between the widow and Felix in which she bestows her daughter with a dowry of bedding and a billy goat, while he gives his son a pig and a goose, with the understanding that should either child refuse the marriage, the parent would forfeit the dowry. It develops that Nellie is in love with Fred Kline (James Tierney), the son of a wealthy glue manufacturer, Captain Kline (Harry Fisher), who is, himself, in search of a wife by means of the "Personals" column in the newspaper. When the widow learns of her daughter's marriage to Fred Kline, she refuses to give up her goat to McIntyre, igniting a feud between the entire McIntyre clan and the Maguire family, who side with the widow. Before the curtain falls on the third act, both families find themselves in another characteristic Comique melee in which the widow's shanty is torn down and all the animals are let loose from their cages.

Theatrically the comedy was unusual in the conspicuous absence of African-American characters in the *dramatis personae*. Musically the work was uniquely experimental because it dispensed entirely with the marches and schottische rhythms that had heretofore been associated with Braham's music. There were no songs and dances, walk-arounds, or military parades. Instead, Braham borrowed from European operetta and Irish jig patterns to create, arguably, his most original score to date.

The runaway song hit from *Squatter Sovereignty* was "Paddy Duffy's Cart," an ensemble number used at the beginning of the third act to announce the arrival of Paddy Duffy (Eugene Rourke), a character of tangential importance to the plot. Particularly notable is the antiphonal choral writing in the second chorus, the melody and lyric of which recall Harrigan and Hart's earliest theatrical success: "Little Fraud,/ Little Fraud,/ She's the daintiest darling of all." As the widow Nolan, Hart was provided with "The Widow Nolan's Goat," an attractive Irish jig with a chorus in the minor mode and a rather conservative melodic compass. It is significant to recall that Braham was extremely sensitive to the abilities of his performers when he composed. He firmly believed that the greatest difficulty in writing for the theater was making the music fit the voices and characters of the actors, because it was rare that a good actor was also an expert singer. Tony Hart's voice, for example, had to be nursed very carefully. Braham generally composed simple, scalelike melodies for Hart with a very limited range, typically emphasizing the middle and upper extensions of the voice. Harrigan, on the other hand, had a much more flexible instrument, and the music written for him characteristically reflects a much broader spectrum.

Demonstrating his vocal dexterity, Harrigan performed "Miss Brady's Piano For-Tay," a jiglike patter song trading on musical terminology, while the Maguires and the McIntyres each had self-revelatory numbers. "The Maguires" was a patter galop from the Offenbach school of operetta, while "The McIntyres" was an Irish quadrille preceded by an elaborately ornamented orchestral introduction. Perhaps the most interesting number in the score was "The Forlorn Old Maid," sung by Captain Kline and his sister-in-law Josephine Jumble (Annie Yeamans). Written and performed in mock-operetta fashion, with grandiose vocal cadenzas and pseudo-classical accompaniment, the lyrical duet ironically details the problems experienced by a woman with a wart on her nose in finding a husband. Whether or not the score was as "integrated" as other Braham-Harrigan compositions, the music for *Squatter Sovereignty* was filled with variety and humor, and the *New York Times* of January 10, 1882, judged it to be supplied with some of Braham's "most spirited melodies."

On April 4, the day after selections from the play were performed at an afternoon benefit for the Actors' Fund at the Union Square Theatre, *Squatter Sovereignty* reached one hundred performances, and continued on to June 3, when the season closed at the new Theatre Comique. On June 5, Harrigan, Hart, and Braham took the play to the Park Theatre, Brooklyn, for a two-week engagement to good business.

Following the engagement in Brooklyn, Harrigan and his wife returned to Schroon Lake, anxious to enjoy another summer holiday at the Taylor house, where they had spent the previous summer. They left four-year-old Edward Jr. to the loving care of his grandparents, who passed the summer months at their home on 30 King Street. Harrigan made two decisions that summer that had a profound effect on the Braham household. The first was to build a summer house on the southern shore of Schroon Lake, and the second was to send out tours of the Harrigan-Braham shows under the management of Martin W. Hanley.

Edward Harrigan's cottage at Schroon Lake.

The first decision resulted in an annual assembly of the Braham-Harrigan clan at Harrigan's 125-acre spread for fun, rest, and (of course) work on new projects. As the Schroon getaway became Harrigan's favored workplace, David Braham and his wife purchased a cottage close by so Annie Braham could stay in close contact with her daughter, and David could continue his work with Ned. From an undated letter Braham wrote to his daughter, Annie Theresa, it seems clear that she and her husband played an important part in making the summer home a reality for her parents:

> Yours to hand and glad to hear of your kind offer. Your ma is delighted at the location which she has always admired. She accepted the offer and will build a very handsome front building, reserving the old cottage as dining room, kitchen, etc. She is greatly improving and is going to take a walk in the sun.
>
> The moment our theatre closes we will start for Schroon . . . while the men are at work, so she can see what they are doing. We propose to lay out about one thousand dollars on it, so it will be a credit to you and Ned. Now, as they say in Mrs. Jack, "it is up to you."

As Annie Harrigan supervised the construction of the Harrigan estate at Schroon Lake beginning in the summer of 1883, so Annie Braham oversaw the remodeling of the Braham cottage nearby, leaving both of their husbands free to concentrate on musical and theatrical matters; the work they did best.

Harrigan's second decision that summer had even more far-reaching effects. He had originally resisted turning over his work to a third party because of the flagrant piracy of his material in the early days of his career. By 1882, however, he and Braham were sufficiently established for audiences all over the United States to recognize their names and properties, and his trust in Martin Hanley was absolute. Hanley was, after all, part of the family, and a skilled businessman. If there was money to be made from such an enterprise, Hanley would make it. In addition, Hanley was as proprietary over the Braham-Harrigan material as the authors themselves. In the Boston programs for *Dan's Tribulations*, for example, he pointedly warned against theatrical piracy, threatening immediate prosecution and heavy fines against any and all offenders. Hanley's tours of the Braham-Harrigan canon began with *Squatter Sovereignty* on August 28, 1882, with Chapin Lucy as musical director, and later continued with *McSorley's Inflation* and *Dan's Tribulations* after they had appeared in New York.

The *Squatter Sovereignty* tour, featuring Eugene Rourke as Felix McIntyre, the role originally acted by Edward Harrigan, began in Bridgeport and traveled along the East Coast as far north as Montreal and Toronto, as far south as Washington, D.C., then inland to Cincinnati, St. Louis, and Chicago. The tours increased David Braham's prosperity in several ways. Not only did they add to his steady flow of royalties, they also inspired him to tour in his own right, advertising the availability of the Theatre Comique Orchestra for concerts, balls, and parties during the 1883–84 season. He even took an office at 37 Bond Street to function as his business address.

By the end of the summer, Braham and Harrigan were back at the Theatre Comique rehearsing *The Blackbird*, a Scottish costume melodrama written by George L. Stout and featuring, in addition to the popular Theatre Comique regulars, the twenty-four-year-old DeWolf Hopper, a young, "legitimate" actor fresh out of a touring company, in the leading role. The original opening of the season, scheduled for an earlier date, was postponed to August 26, 1882, so Stout's five-act melodrama could be properly rehearsed and the complicated scenery readied for production. Always ready to experiment, Braham and Harrigan agreed that the time was right to steer away from their usual fare of local comedies and explore the more adventuresome terrain of romantic drama. Both men had for some time wanted to attempt a more serious tone in their work, and Stout's melodrama seemed to suit their purposes perfectly.

The complicated plot, set in Scotland in 1746 following the Battle of Culloden, deals with Redmond Darcy (DeWolf Hopper), believed to be dead, returning to find his wife and heir, Lady Helen (Mattie Earle), suffering the unwanted advances of Major Neville (Mark A. Price), a traitor who is in league with Perry Dunlevy (Harry Fisher), an English spy. The rest of the play follows Darcy's adventurous attempts to reclaim his wife and stay alive, often with the help of Con O'Carolan (Harrigan), a piper pretending to be blind, and always involving some sensational theatrical effect. The "Devil's Pool and Waterfall" sequence drew the greatest applause when Mona Mahr (Gertie Granville), having discovered papers that would convict Neville of treachery, is dragged up a rocky cliff and tossed into the rushing water below.

A backstage story is related to this production that is infinitely more interesting than the actual plot of the play. Gertie Granville, recently returned from her honeymoon as Mrs. Tony Hart, was dissatisfied with the roles Harrigan had provided her in her two previous outings at the Theatre Comique. She insisted that she play the role of the girl who is tossed into the whirlpool. Neither Annie Braham nor Annie Harrigan much liked Gertie, and lobbied against her with their husbands. Harrigan, attempting to keep peace at home and in the theater, persuaded Braham and his wife, Annie, to withdraw their objections, and cast Mrs. Hart in the desired role. On opening night, after the scene when Con manages to drag Mona out of the water, there were four curtain calls. After the first two, which Harrigan took alone, the audience shouted for Gertie. Harrigan took the third curtain call alone. The shouts for Gertie grew to deafening proportions. Harrigan stepped out and bowed alone for the fourth time, and as he passed the soaking-wet actress waiting in the wings, he called for the play to proceed, subtly exacting revenge for the trouble she had caused him in casting the play.

Except for the scenery designed by Charles W. Witham, the stage machinery developed by William McMurray, and the music composed and arranged David Braham, the critics did not speak highly of the production, claiming that much of the plot and many of the lines were stolen

John Franceschina

from popular Irish melodramas. The *Spirit of the Times* (August 19, 1882) even questioned the wisdom of Harrigan's choice of material:

> The public argue that, when a shrewd and clever manager like Mr. Harrigan changes the entire policy of his successful theatre; breaks away from all the traditions of his management; takes down his own name as author from the bills where it has stood for so many years; puts up the hitherto unknown name of George L. Stout, the prompter; transforms his entertainment from gay vaudeville to grave drama; discards the new tunes to which Dave Braham, the American Offenbach, can make the whole town keep time; substitutes the Jacobite period and the adventures of the Pretender for local hits at the present day, and engages DeWolf Hopper, the tallest actor in the business, as his leading man—the public argue, we say, when such facts are revealed to them, that Mr. Harrigan must have got hold of the best play ever written since Shakespeare tackled the historical drama and cut the chronicles of Hollingshead into blank verse. We should not be surprised to see, on Monday, a startling revelation in dramatic art. Nothing less than this will excuse the revolution in the policy of the Comique and the public's deprivation of our only local, original, vaudeville, American theatre.

Only DeWolf Hopper seemed to benefit by the experience: during the run of *The Blackbird*, he began to study singing under Luigi Meola at the New York College of Music and subsequently began a stellar career as a leading man in American musical comedy.

Braham arranged five overtures for the production, one before each act, and all based on traditional Scottish or Irish folk melodies. In addition, four songs were sprinkled throughout the production, two of which, "The Blackbird" and "Johnny Cope," had no claim to originality. The other two, composed by Braham to Harrigan's lyrics, were "The Mountain Dew," sung by Harrigan, and "The Trooper's the Pride of the Ladies," sung by William Merritt. Another Braham schottische ditty, "The Mountain Dew," was considered by the *Clipper* (September 2, 1882) an immediate hit, having a melody "quite within the comprehension of the masses, who, as soon as it falls upon their ear, will take to it as warmly as they would welcome an old friend." Here Braham uses a pentatonic melody characteristic of Scottish folk music to lend a note of authenticity to the original songs in the score. The obligatory Braham march "The Trooper's the Pride of the Ladies" began with the usual orchestral fanfare and ended predictably with an addictively hummable chorus. Both compositions were considered so tuneful and catching that the *New York Times* (August 27, 1882) predicted: "[B]efore long both airs will be sung from one end of the land to the other and be whistled at the street corners, just as its predecessor, 'The Mulligan Guards,' was."

Because of lukewarm notices and the departure from the usual topical fare, business was not good for *The Blackbird*, and late in September, Braham and Harrigan began polishing their next work, *Mordecai Lyons*, as a quick replacement should business not improve substantially. The new work was, in its own way, as experimental as Stout's melodrama. Mordecai Lyons (Harrigan), a Jewish pawnbroker living in New York City, has a daughter, Esther (Annie Mack), who grows up to become an internationally celebrated actress. In Europe, she falls in love with Charles Chester (Mark M. Price), who promises to marry her but forsakes her in favor of Mary Radcliffe (Gertie Granville). Having papers in his possession proving that Mary is, in fact, Chester's daughter, Mordecai encourages the marriage to revenge his daughter, whom he curses as a fallen woman. Esther begs Chester to reconsider but he refuses, claiming that it is forbidden for her to marry a Christian, and that he really loves Mary. Esther drinks poison and swoons; Mordecai goes mad, reveals Mary's parentage, and falls lifeless to the floor. Before the final curtain falls, Esther recovers from the poison and accepts Chester's hand in marriage.

Attendance at the Theatre Comique did not improve through the month of October, and *The Blackbird* was withdrawn after the Tuesday night performance on October 24. On Wednesday night the theater was closed for the dress rehearsal of the new play, and on Thursday, October 26, *Mordecai Lyons* opened to a large but baffled crowd, disappointed in its expectations of seeing another of Harrigan's amusing local plays. The only portion of the evening's entertainment that was judged an unqualified success was Braham's music, through which the audience was reminded of the lighthearted spirit and energy it had grown to expect from a Braham and Harrigan show.

There were five songs in *Mordecai Lyons*, three of which were waltzes, something of an oddity in a Braham score. "Cash! Cash! Cash!," sung by Tony Hart in the supporting role of Leon Mendoza, a rosy-cheeked, curly-headed Hebrew "masher," is a simple patter emphasizing the mercenary qualities of the female sex. After a verse that trades on ascending scale patterns, Braham makes an effective use of rhythmic variety and repeated melodic tones in the chorus, maximizing the limitations of Hart's voice. "Mordecai Lyons," performed by Harrigan as the Jewish pawnbroker, is a self-introductory waltz song with an incisive, staccato verse and a lyrical, almost plaintiff chorus in which the character promises to treat customers well. "The Old Bowery Pit," sung by Billy Gray in the role of Dad Bailey, the old stage-door man, lyrically recalls the theatrical past at the Old Bowery Theatre in a fetchingly simple Bowery-style waltz.

The tenor ballad "She Lives on Murray Hill," sung by George Merritt in the obligatory Irish role of Jimmy Reilly, demonstrates Braham's fondness for mixing meters within a single song to underscore the dramatic context (or subtext) of Harrigan's lyrics. In this case the patter verse dispenses the narrative exposition, while the romantic waltz of the chorus (with its elaborately ornamented accompaniment) gets to the heart of the matter. Reminiscent of "Hark, Baby, Hark" in *The Mulligan Guards' Surprise*, "When the Clock in the Tower Strikes Twelve," a drinking song sung by William Merritt as Barnaby Guy, is another of Braham's modified parlor songs. It is anthemlike in its expansive melody and accompanied with the harmonic texture and complexity of a classical art song. Of special interest is the chorus, in which the singing ensemble accompanies the melody with a contrapuntal intonation of the midnight bell.

Branded by the *New York Herald* (October 27, 1882) as Harrigan's "first distinct failure" and condemned by the *Clipper* (November 4, 1882) as an unwarranted experiment, *Mordecai Lyons* played only one month, closing on Saturday, November 25, the day the *Clipper* published the following doggerel verse, reprimanding Harrigan for his lack of judgment:

You've erred in judgment, Edward. You should know,
    Ere a Hebrew you sought to "do,"
It's a very cold day when one gets a show
    To "make anything" out of a Jew.
There was a Jew, 'tis very true,
    That Shakespeare drew, and crowned him,
But the pawnbroking Jew that Harrigan drew
    Hiplocked Ned and "downed" him.

Two days before the demise of *Mordecai Lyons*, the funeral of actor Billy Gray was held at St. Joseph's Church, the Roman Catholic church where Annie Theresa Braham and Edward Harrigan were married and where all the Braham children had been baptized. Gray, who had joined the Harrigan, Hart, and Braham team in 1876 as a blackface comedian, performed the character of Dad Bailey for the last time on Thursday November 16, 1882, and died five days later, at age thirty-six. The loss was significant for Braham and Harrigan. Much of their finest work had been written for Gray, the performer Harrigan called one of the funniest men he ever met and the finest actor who ever appeared in his company.

At times of great sorrow, Braham and Harrigan needed work to lift their spirits. It was serendipitous, then, that diminishing attendance at the Theatre Comique during the run of *Mordecai Lyons* forced the team to prepare a replacement in a hurry. On Monday, November 27, Braham and Harrigan's new show was ready and filled with more of what audiences expected at the Theatre Comique. *McSorley's Inflation* dealt with Peter McSorley (Harrigan), a tenement landlord and candidate for the local coronership. Ashamed of the successful poultry-stall run in Washington Market by his wife, Bridget (Tony Hart), McSorley attempts to destroy her seller's permit. Bridget hides the document in her mattress, which is subsequently taken away by a black politician, Rufus Rhubarb (John Wild), at McSorley's request. Bridget follows the mattress robber to his home, where a group of African Americans are assembled to hear the political platforms of McSorley and his opponent, Coroner Slab (Edward Burt). Bridget, with the help of the female constituency, manages to recapture the bed, and McSorley, who has been knocked out by Tom Tough (Michael Foley), a bruiser in the employ of Coroner Slab, decides against a political career and vows never again to try to interfere in his wife's poultry business.

Six new numbers were introduced in *McSorley's Inflation*, each receiving a "heel and toe" accompaniment in the gallery, which indicated immediate audience approval. "I Never Drink behind the Bar," sung by Harrigan, assisted by John Wild and James Fox (in the supporting role of Major Wabble), was a patter story song with a schottische "echo" chorus that proved quite popular with the crowd. "The Market on Saturday Night," sung by Tony Hart, was a self-introductory ballad with a plaintively modal verse and an ironically pretty chorus in which a lovely and expansive melody accompanies the itemizing of merchandise.

Harrigan's "McNally's Row of Flats," a lively hornpipe with another schottische dance break, Hart's jiglike "Old Feather Bed," and the energetic chorus number "The Salvation Army, Oh!" all won their share of generous applause. The hit of the score, however, was the finale march,

"The Charleston Blues," which employed all of the expected Braham devices: the military fanfare, the elaborate orchestral introduction, the Sousa-like refrain with its catchy melody and rhythmic variety, and the satirical medley of familiar songs, including "Maggie May" and "Annie Laurie." Add a drill routine and an elaborately staged parade, and it is no wonder that the number was encored several times on opening night. The *Clipper* (December 2, 1882) critic was less enthusiastic about Braham's music than usual, though he had to admit its mass appeal:

> It will hardly do to be captious concerning this stripe of song, or to lament the want of a higher musical education on the part of the masses who seem to relish it. It serves the purpose for which it was written, and therein fills the bill; and, though the alarming paucity of ideas fills the musical head with misgivings, the unconscious tap of the feet beats a merry opposition to serious objection, and exacting criticism is at once disarmed. . . . Nevertheless, it may not be considered entirely unreasonable if we yearn occasionally for just a bit, a trifle, a tinge of "something different" from the stereotyped shapes. . . . But when songs are sprung on us a half-dozen at a time, it may not be consoling to inquire too closely into their hasty manufacture. That the ones under review pleased the audience is beyond doubt, and double and triple encores were common.

Popular appeal seemed to be enough, and *McSorley's Inflation* marched brazenly into the New Year, celebrating its one-hundredth performance on February 19 and continuing healthily until March 31, 1883.

On April 2, 1883, Braham and Harrigan unveiled *The Muddy Day*, a three-act comedy with music, and their last new show of the season. *Muddy Day* is a mud scow commanded by Roger McNab (Harrigan), who is in competition with Herman Schoonover (Harry Fisher), the captain of the barge *King William,* over the affections of Mary Ann O'Leary (Tony Hart), a gold-digging widow, who is only interested in the man with the larger bank account. The rivalry between the captains is intensified by the belligerence of their crews, McNab's being Irish and Schoonover's comprised of Germans and Italians. In the second act, a floating African-American church called the *Bethel* holds a fair to raise money for the congregation, but the religious ship sinks into the East River before the fair even begins to show a profit. In the final act, the crew of the *Bethel* has been rescued from the river just in time to witness a procession of sixty maskers, half of whom carry giant caricatures of men who are prominent in entertainment and other social circles in New York City, while McNab and the widow O'Leary appear as *commedia dell'arte* characters Pantaloon and Columbine, respectively. During the parade, a dozen boys, appearing in the gymnastic uniform of the "Turners," execute a number of military maneuvers and sing the obligatory march song as the curtain falls.

Although Braham's score for *The Muddy Day* was in some way a continuation of old techniques and formulas, it still managed to get feet tapping and hands clapping in the audience, particularly in the gallery. The hit of the performance, "The Turnverein Cadets," borrowed from an earlier sketch, *Malone's Night Off*, was another of Braham's characteristic marches. Tony Hart had his usual self-introductory song and dance, "The Bunch o' Berries," with a predictable stepwise melody and schottische rhythms, and Harrigan sang another jovial hornpipe, "On Board o' the Muddy Day," somewhat reminiscent of Gilbert and Sullivan's "I Am the Captain of the *Pinafore*."

More interesting was "The Golden Choir," performed by the chorus in the *Bethel* scene, Braham's second experiment with the African-American spiritual (his first pseudo-spiritual was "Dip Me in de Golden Sea," a nonshow jubilee song and chorus set to words by Edward Harrigan and published in 1881). Anticipating the twentieth-century variety of "white" spirituals ("Blow, Gabriel, Blow," "Hallelujah," "Great Day"), Braham's composition makes effective use of major and minor modes in the verse, followed by a rhythmic chorus with a driving and soaring melody in the major mode. The obligatory dance break is a syncopated shuffle jauntily alternating between major and minor and filled with surprising rhythmical variety.

"The Silly Boy," another of Braham's multiple meter songs, sung by M. F. Drew in the same scene, was said to be a plagiarism of Eliza Weathersby's song "I'm a Swell." The polka patter song "The Family Overhead" was evidently poorly received because the reviewer for the *Clipper* did not remember having heard the number. Although most of the songs were encored, the public did not enjoy wading through *The Muddy Day* and, for the first time ever on an opening night at the Theatre Comique, the audience began to leave long before the play was over.

The Muddy Day closed on May 19, ending a lackluster season at the Theatre Comique. Braham and the rest of the company headed for the newly opened Mount Morris Theatre for a week's engagement of

McSorley's Inflation beginning on May 21. The opening-night audience was large and appreciative, and business was good for the remainder of the stay. The Park Theatre in Brooklyn was the next stop, where *McSorley* played to enthusiastic audiences until June 2. It is significant that during the same week, at the Novelty Theatre in Williamsburgh, Martin Hanley's Combination Company was performing *Squatter Sovereignty* to crowded houses. There is a subtle irony in the fact that Braham and Harrigan had two shows playing successful simultaneous engagements in Brooklyn during the last week of May, when their record in New York City was at a low point.

Of the year's four new shows at the Theatre Comique, only one, *McSorley's Inflation*, could be considered a success in any sense of the word. Even though Braham's music continued to weather the hazards of experimental libretti and lukewarm reviews, the composer knew that a writer of songs need not shackle himself to the demands of integrated plot progression, actors' egos, and theatrical performances simply to get a "hit." People all over the country were whistling and singing songs that emerged from minstrel and variety shows, music halls, and the mountains of sheet music published by the likes of William A. Pond, E. H. Harding, or A. J. Fisher. So even while composing and arranging the music for Harrigan's shows at the Theatre Comique, Braham continued to produce nontheatrical solo songs, permitting him greater musical freedom without denying his instinctive theatricality.

Braham had just revised for publication "My Pearl; or, The Old Water Mill," a romantic parlor song with lyrics by J. J. Kelly that had been originally introduced in an olio performance at the Theatre Comique in 1877. Chronicling the chance summer meeting of a young couple by an old water mill, their happy courtship, and subsequent marriage, the song employs "serious" musical devices such as the *Alberti* bass to provide a kind of forward motion to the narrative, and accented nonchordal tones to build tension and emphasize the active words of the lyrics. The chorus is especially effective in its use of musical pauses that evoke the excitement, confusion, and breathlessness attendant on meeting the love of one's life.

With Jeannie O. B. Sammis, Braham was working on two new compositions, an anthem apotheosizing the daisy and titled "The Flower of Columbia," and a bright Irish jig, "Granny O'Reilly's Wake!" In the first song, dedicated to Miss Anna Boyle, an actress at the Star Theatre, Braham deftly manages his musical material, not allowing the harmonic texture or expansive melody to overwhelm the simplicity of the emotions expressed in the lyrics. In the second, the words are of primary importance, so the melody and accompaniment, while musically not without interest, maintain a subordinate place, driving the lyrics forward by predictable melodic phrases and harmonies.

The composer also was laboring over lyrics written by William Carleton for a song to be dedicated to Miss St. George Hussey, "My Dad's Old Violin." Recalling her father's use of the violin to court her mother and play the children to sleep at night, the singer concludes that the man deserves a place in Heaven because of his music:

> You may talk about Apollo and his celebrated lyre,
> But my father and his instrument stood head and shoulders high'r;
> He was not a Paganini nor yet an Ole Bull,
> But when he played the fiddle, oh the coldest heart was full;
> But if in Heaven he's restin' he'll meet with Orpheus there,
> If they only have a fiddle how dad will make them stare.
> Do what they choose they can't refuse midst their throng to let him
>   in,
> For music's birth occured on earth
> In my dad's old violin.

These sentiments, which seemed to echo Braham's own fondness for the violin, were set with an almost childlike melody, alternating predictable stepwise movement with surprising leaps against a sophisticated harmonic accompaniment. Most appealing is the chorus, where the accompaniment is embellished with a violin obbligato.

Braham earned much satisfaction from his olio and parlor songs, both creatively and financially, but he knew that his main interest was in composing for the theater: not just writing hit songs for his son-in-law's shows, but also producing integrated, dramatic music (songs *and* underscores) that explored character, helped propel the situation, and made the actor look good, using an essentially popular musical vocabulary. Braham knew that operettas had achieved these goals with more serious-sounding music. However, that was the route to which his nephew John was drawn, not Uncle Dave. Braham was constantly searching for better ways of expression, using primarily a standard popular-song vocabulary and a traditional structure. Harrigan was doing the same thing dramatically: continually tightening and rewriting dialogue, constantly looking for better ways to play a scene, methodically reworking and revising old plays, and integrating successful pieces of business and popular routines into new ones.

The Brahams had moved into another apartment, at 175 West 10th Street, before the end of the season, and Harrigan was a frequent visitor during the summer of 1883 while construction of the new house at Schroon Lake slowly began to take shape, under the watchful eye of his wife. By the time the Theatre Comique season opened on August 6, 1883, Braham and Harrigan had completed revision of two of their earlier successes and were ready with another new local comedy to put into rehearsal. Marking the return of Annie Yeamans to the Theatre Comique after a season's absence, a new and improved two-act version of *The Mulligan Guard Ball* opened the season to a standing-room-only audience. To the popular songs of the original, Braham and Harrigan added a medley of songs from *The Muddy Day*, performed by Braham's orchestra during the intermission: "The Little Widow Dunn," from *The Mulligan Guard Chowder*; "The Pitcher of Beer" from *The Mulligan Guards' Christmas*; "Down in Gossip Row" from *The Mulligan Guards' Nominee*; and the newly composed "We're All Young Fellows Bran' New," for Tommy Mulligan (Tony Hart) and his band of "Young Mulligans." Another self-expository patter with a quadrillelike verse, the chorus changes to an overblown waltz as the lyric parodies the behavior of the upper classes, and Braham creates subtle dramatic irony through the juxtaposition of dance patterns. The new song was well received, but not everyone found *The Mulligan Guard Ball* improved by the new topical references and gags, and the show closed on September 22, giving way to *The Mulligan Guard Picnic* on Monday, September 24. *Picnic* offered two new songs: "Going Home with Nellie after Five," a lilting waltz for Harrigan; and "Hurry, Little Children, Sunday Morn!," a quasi-spiritual production number sung by the ensemble. In both songs, Braham continued to provide the catchy melodies and infectious rhythms that characterized the original score.

The hustle and bustle of the new season at the Comique were matched by the flurry of activity in the Braham household. Maids were hired and fired with great regularity by the mistress of the house, who tolerated no impertinence or challenge to her authority. Mary Ann, the domestic whom the Brahams shared with the Harrigan household, seemed to be doing fine, but the young and pretty lass whom Annie had recently engaged to replace a "terrible hoister" had become the apple of many a young Comique actor's eye, and Annie was dead set against anyone romancing the help. She was especially suspicious of Michael Bradley, who had lately begun to stop by the Braham home for drinks and conversation. She remembered what happened when Ned Harrigan used the same excuse. But marrying her daughter was one thing; marrying her maid was quite another.

Only six of the Braham children were now living at home, providing David and Annie the unaccustomed luxury of extra space in a perpetually crowded apartment. Following in his father's footsteps, eighteen-year-old George Braham was now on tour as the musical director for Hanley's production of *McSorley's Inflation*. Writing his sister Annie Harrigan on October 23, 1883, from Woonsocket, Rhode Island, he bragged about rehearsing his ramshackle three-piece band comprised of cornet, second violin, and bass (George played the first violin part) until they played perfectly. He also spoke of meeting Mr. Fulding, one of the few musicians who ever had anything bad to say about his father. Evidently Fulding had been hired to play in Braham's orchestra during one of the Boston engagements, and Braham fired him because of his poor playing. Although the musician continued to complain that he was inappropriately discharged, George noted that it was lucky that his father replaced the man, because his obvious lack of physical dexterity made him a liability in the pit of any Braham-Harrigan show. David Braham may have been the soul of kindness throughout his life, but it never got in the way of the efficient realization of his music.

Six weeks after *The Mulligan Guard Picnic* was revived at the Theatre Comique, on November 5, Braham and Harrigan's newest addition to the Mulligan series opened. *Cordelia's Aspirations* begins at Castle Garden, where Dan Mulligan (Harrigan) is waiting to greet his wife, Cordelia (Annie Yeamans), and her attendant, Rebecca Allup (Tony Hart), who are returning, after sixteen months abroad, with Cordelia's obnoxious relatives, led by the conniving Planxty McFudd (Harry Fisher). Also arriving are members of a demoralized *Uncle Tom's Cabin* combination, who join Rebecca Allup in singing "Just Across from Jersey," a pseudo-spiritual revival number, followed by a vigorous dance. Later that day, Dan confides to Walsingham McSweeny (Michael Bradley) that his wife, no longer wishing to live in Mulligan Alley, has bought a house on Madison Avenue and is selling all the family's old furniture. At the auction, when someone attempts to carry off an old dinner pail, an heirloom to Dan, he seizes it and sings "My Dad's Dinner Pail," a modified jig, in explanation:

Preserve that old kettle, so blackened and worn,
It belonged to my father before I was born,
It hung in a corner, beyant on a nail,
'Twas an emblem of labor, was Dad's dinner pail.
Chorus:
It glistened like silver, so sparkling and bright,
I am fond of the trifle that held his wee bite;
In summer or winter, in rain, snow, or hail,
I've carried that kettle, my Dad's dinner pail.

The second act changes scene to the Mulligan mansion on Murray Hill, where Dan is overwhelmed by the aristocratic airs of his wife and her relatives. During a reception, a cakewalk is performed by male and female servants under the supervision of Simpson Primrose (John Wild), a former pie salesman, now a coachman in the employ of the Mulligans. "Sam Johnson's Colored Cake Walk" is an elaborate production number, alternating between a self-consciously dignified ragtime march and a sweeping waltz with an infectious, soaring melody. At the same reception, the waiters go through their paces in a song titled "Waiters' Chorus; or, Two More to Come," an opéra-bouffe patter in the style of Offenbach, followed by a dance anticipating the "Waiters' Galop" in the twentieth-century blockbuster musical *Hello, Dolly!*

Attempting to alienate Cordelia from Dan to appropriate all of Mulligan's property, Planxty convinces his sister, Diana (Gertie Granville), to write a bogus love letter to Dan. Cordelia discovers the document and determines to kill herself by swallowing the contents of a bottle labeled "Rat Poison," after signing over all of her property to Planxty. However, due to the skill of her lawyer, who exchanged Dan's name for Planxty's on the document, and the fact that the bottle of "Rat Poison" was really a bottle of brandy, a reconciliation occurs between Dan and Cordelia at the end of the second act. In the last act, after horrifying Cordelia and her guests by his uncouth behavior at the dinner table, Dan decides to assert his authority and move back to Mulligan Alley, singing "I'll Wear the Trousers, Oh!," a modified Irish jig borrowed from the score of *The Mulligan Guards' Surprise*. Planxty orders him from the house, claiming to be the owner of the property (a scene borrowed from Molière's *Tartuffe*), but the lawyer exposes McFudd as the villain he is, and the Mulligans return to Mulligan Alley.

Notwithstanding the obvious borrowings from earlier episodes in

"Cordelia's Suicide," from *Cordelia's Aspirations*.

the Mulligan series, *Cordelia's Aspirations* was favorably received, the *New York Mirror* (November 10, 1883) calling it "very funny," and "one more success . . . added to the many at this house." The *Clipper* (November 10, 1883) added that "The applause accorded the new songs was remarkably enthusiastic, again illustrating that the audiences here are ever on the lookout for something fresh in the popular-ballad line." The comedy lasted well into the New Year, closing significantly past the one-hundredth-performance mark on April 5, 1884, by which time Braham and Harrigan had another Mulligan episode ready to view, *Dan's Tribulations*, opening on Monday, April 7.

In the new comedy, Dan Mulligan (Harrigan) and his wife, Cordelia

(Annie Yeamans), are back in Mulligan Alley. Virtually reduced to poverty, Dan is in the liquor and grocery business, and Cordelia operates a French academy out of their Upper East Side house, property that Dan was saving for his son, Tommy (Tony Hart), who has moved out West with his wife, Kitty (Sadie Morris). The Lochmullers, also on hard times, have given up their fashionable residence. Mr. Lochmuller (Harry Fisher) has returned to the butcher business, and his wife (Jenny Christie) works for Mrs. Mulligan as a cook. Because of a mortgage on the East Side property, and a threatened foreclosure because of unpaid debts, Mrs. Mulligan sells the house to Mrs. Lochmuller for "one good dollar," while she continues to advertise for borders to help pay off her debts. Tommy Mulligan and his wife respond to the ad and appear in disguise to get a firsthand view of how his parents are prospering. Just as they arrive, Cordelia's attempt to entertain her students in the parlor, while Mrs. Lochmuller is giving a party in the kitchen, results in a clash of wills between the women. Mrs. Lochmuller threatens to evict Cordelia from the house, but Tommy steps up in the nick of time, revealing that the dollar used in the bargain was counterfeit and the contract, predicated on the exchange of "one good dollar," is invalid. The return of the children fills both families with such joy that all recriminations are forgotten, and the curtain falls on hopes of peace and prosperity.

Four new "bright and catchy" songs were composed for *Dan's Tribulations*, all of which were given triple encores on opening night. "My Little Side Door," Dan Mulligan's customary expository ballad, continues in the Irish folk-song tradition with an especially florid orchestral introduction, lending an ironic seriousness to the simple triadic tune. "Coming Home from Meeting," sung and danced by Palestine Puter (George H. Wood) and a chorus of African-American friends, is another of Braham's hummable schottische rhythm numbers, with an interlude during which the orchestra echoes the lyric "Whippoorwill" with ornamented birdcalls, parodying the kind of word-painting prevalent in operettas of the day. "The French Singing Lesson," performed by Cordelia and her students, begins with another florid orchestral introduction, more at home in an operetta than in a popular song, followed by a contrapuntal chorus during which Braham effectively uses a drone pedal point to suggest the monotony of learning by rote. The number ends in a stirring march, sounding less like an American military band tune than the more florid operetta marches of Offenbach. "Cobwebs on the Wall," sung by Dan, Cordelia, Tommy, and

McSweeney near the end of the play, anticipates George M. Cohan's songs with its parlando verse and chorus, soaring melodic phrases, and simple harmonic structure emphasizing the philosophical message of the lyrics:

> I'm an old peculiar fellow, and I've some peculiar ways;
> I believe in sticking to a friend or anything that pays.
> There's one thing true in nature, old Time was made for all;
> Without your leave 'twill wind and weave like cobwebs on the wall.
> *Chorus:*
> Then here's to my old attic, a rusty dusty place,
> Where Pride, Deceit, or Envy, must never show their face;
> Then here's to my old slippers,
> My bottle, pipe and all,
> Likewise my old companions, oh! the cobwebs on the wall.

Dan's Tribulations earned good notices and continued through the remainder of the season, closing on May 31, when the Theatre Comique company left New York to begin its traditional summer sojourn at the Park Theatre in Brooklyn. *Cordelia's Aspirations* charmed audiences during the week of June 2, followed by *Dan's Tribulations* on the ninth. During the Brooklyn engagement, Harrigan told the *New York Mirror* (June 7, 1884) that he was finished with the Mulligan series and that the next Braham-Harrigan work, a satire of municipal government, was already completed and ready to be put into rehearsal for the following season. Claiming that the new play would possess many of the features that made the Mulligan series so popular, Harrigan promised that it would be "of a higher and better order than anything I have yet presented to the public." After the Brooklyn run, Harrigan and his family went up to their new home at Schroon Lake, while Braham and his orchestra finished the month of June performing at the Jerome Hotel on Sheepshead Bay.

Throughout the summer, the *New York Mirror* continued to buzz over the news surrounding the Theatre Comique and Braham and Harrigan's new satire. On July 19, the newspaper reported that the Theatre Comique had been outfitted with a brand-new stage. The following week, a letter to the *Mirror* from Harrigan, vacationing at Schroon Lake, contradicted rumors that the new work, scheduled to open the 1884–85 season, was a satire on local politics and announced that "Six original musical gems have been composed for the play by Mr.

Braham." In the August 16 issue, Harrigan was interviewed during a break in rehearsals for Martin Hanley's tour of *Dan's Tribulations* and *Cordelia's Aspirations*, scheduled to open in Bridgeport, Connecticut, the following Monday, with George Braham as musical director. He noted that *Investigation*—the title of the new play—would include choruses by pretty girls (real girls, not the traditional drag act typical of the Theatre Comique) and quipped, with a gleam in his eye, that David Braham was devoting "special attention to this department." Because Braham was always sensitive to the cast for whom he was writing, it made sense that he would be interested in the casting: yes, of course the girls had to be pretty, but they also had to be able to sing!

With a cast numbering forty-two actors, singers, and dancers, *Investigation* opened the Theatre Comique season on September 1, 1884, when the farcical plot was revealed to the customary large and encouraging audience. The New York State legislature has appointed a three-man committee (Michael Bradley, George Merritt, and Harry Fisher) to report on the unhealthy conditions at Hunter's Point, where Bernard McKenna (Tony Hart) is the proprietor of a glue factory. He and D'Arcy Flynn (Harrigan), a tenement agent, are rivals for the heart of Belinda Tuggs (Annie Yeamans), a rich widow, whose candle factory, inherited from her late husband, both men want to possess. The rest of the evening is spent with the attempts of McKenna and Flynn to outwit one another using a variety of subterfuges (including Flynn's disguising himself as Mrs. Hop Sing, an Italian woman married to a Chinaman). Their efforts are complicated by the presence of the state committee men, whose "investigations" lead them to an opium den, a cookery school full of beautiful girls (where glue is accidentally substituted for molasses in the plum duff), and the Theatre Comique (where they are, of course, discovered by their wives in the arms of ballet girls).

Flynn is successful in his suit with the widow, and in the last act, on what is supposed to be the stage of the Theatre Comique, the couple enact the balcony scene from *Romeo and Juliet* in an attempt to raise money for the cooking school. Their best efforts are foiled, however, by the orchestra's penchant for playing in the wrong places throughout the scene (precipitating an altercation between the actors and the onstage orchestra leader), and the elusive and wobbly limelight, forcing the pair to perform most of the action in the dark! The pointed satire of Henry Irving and Ellen Terry, who were performing in New York City that season, was obvious to both the audience and the critics. Noting that Annie

Yeamans's makeup in the scene was à la Ellen Terry, the *New York Mirror* (September 6, 1884) reported that when she invitingly asked Romeo, "*Do* I look like Miss Terry?" the audience "broke loose and wasn't gathered together for a full half minute."

Once again, Braham's melodies were encored throughout the performance and destined for immediate popularity. "Plum Pudding," sung by the girls' cooking club in the first act, is a catchy two-step, enumerating the dos and don'ts of the culinary arts. In the same act, Harrigan and the cooks perform "As Long as the World Goes 'Round," a lilting carousel-style waltz, with a hurdy-gurdy accompaniment that drives forward the romantically soaring melody. "The Boodle," an anthem to capitalism, sung by McKenna and the Committee in the second act, is an energetic quadrille, mining the potential of a scale-tone melody and very regular rhythmical patterns (as in most of what Braham composed for Tony Hart). Also in the second act, Charles Gilder (J. Hardman), Gaspard Pitkins (James Fox), and Hop Sing (Billy West) perform "Hello! Bab-by" to a real baby onstage. While the verse of the song follows the typical pattern of a modified cakewalk, the chorus is quite unique in its use of instrumental interludes between phrases of the lyrics, allowing for stage business and audience reactions. Typical of Braham's dance music, the extended instrumental interlude after the chorus is filled with contrasting rhythmic phrases and heavy accents, marking the changes in dance steps. In the third act, Flynn and chorus perform the politically satirical "The Man That Knows It All," a buoyant two-step with an elaborate choral arrangement that suggests that Braham was successful in casting real singers in the show. In addition to Braham's published music for the show, the *New York Mirror* (September 6, 1884) also noted the interpolation of an unaccompanied dialect song, "Find in Genoa," sung by Harrigan in the guise of the Italian woman, evoking the old variety days at the original Theatre Comique.

On November 26, *Investigation* celebrated its one-hundredth performance. Throughout the month of December, while performances continued, Braham and Harrigan put their next show, *McAllister's Legacy*, into rehearsal, planning to open it on January 5, 1885. The flurry and excitement of putting up a new show was not limited to the stage of the Theatre Comique, however. Braham's youngest daughter, Rose, and Harrigan's sister, Martha, had been cast in an amateur production of Douglas Jerrold's *The Rent Day*, scheduled for performance on December 15, at the Lexington Avenue Opera House. The weeks preceding the opening saw the girls in constant preparation at the Braham house: memorizing lines, perfecting their articulation, and rehearsing scenes with the maid. Annie Braham usually accompanied the girls to the theater for afternoon rehearsals. No stage-door mother, she retired quietly to the background, until the stage manager introduced a piece of business that offended her sensibilities. Then, and only then, would she make her presence known as the wife of David Braham and mother-in-law to Edward Harrigan. Not suprisingly, she always got her way.

The girls' successful theatrical debut imbued their families with the holiday spirit. Everything seemed to be going splendidly: rehearsals for the new show were ahead of schedule, and *Investigation* began its seventeenth week on Monday, December 22, with a fairly large and exuberant audience. Little did the Brahams or the Harrigans know that their holiday exuberance would be short-lived. After the performance, the cast remained in the theater to rehearse *McAllister's Legacy* until about 1:30 A.M., Tuesday morning, then went home. Harrigan, Hart, and Braham were among the last to leave, between 2:00 and 3:00 A.M. The night watchman, Austin Heffern (some accounts give his name as "Hefferan," others say "Heffernan"), Tony Hart's brother-in-law, remained until 6:45 a.m. when he went home to breakfast, leaving only a single light burning inside the theater: the "ghost" light on the stage. Five hours later, the building had burned to the ground, completely gutted by a fire, the origin of which remains a mystery.

According to the *New York Herald* (December 24, 1884), shortly before 8:00 A.M. a policeman named Clune noticed smoke coming out of the front windows of the building and ran to the fire box across the street at the New York Hotel and sent out an alarm. Another policeman, named Sullivan, attempted to enter the theater, but the entrances were covered in flames. The three-alarm fire drew such a crowd of onlookers that police captain Brogan quickly discovered that his police force was incapable of controlling them, and reserves from the Ninth, Sixteenth, Seventeenth, and Twenty-ninth Precincts had to be brought in to preserve order. At 8:30 A.M., a deafening crash signaled the tumbling of the theater's roof, followed a short time later by the crumbling of the rear wall, as well as the top part of the front wall.

When Braham learned of the fire, he rushed to the theater, hoping to salvage his precious Stradivarius violin and scores: all the incidental music he had written for Harrigan's plays, the orchestra parts, and the manuscripts for songs that had yet to be published. When he arrived, however, he was met at the New York Hotel by Harrigan and Hart, whose expressions convinced him that the music was lost forever. Since the managers had allowed the insurance on the theater to run out, their loss was substantial, well-informed sources appraising it in the neighborhood of seventy-five thousand dollars: the theater, fifty thousand dollars; scenery, twenty thousand dollars; and costumes, five thousand dollars. In addition, all of the actors' wardrobes and musicians' instruments were destroyed, including David Braham's violin, valued between $500 and $1000. After watching the fire for some time from the windows of the New York Hotel, Harrigan, Hart, and Braham traveled to Sinclair House, where they set up temporary offices. Tensions were high, and not even the usually unperturbable David Braham could hide the strain.

Surrounded by his friends and supporters, Harrigan immediately began contacting theater managers to book space for the remainder of the season. Neither the Star nor the Fourteenth Street Theatre were available, so he sent a message to Hyde and Behman of Brooklyn, inquiring into the availability of their New Park Theatre, located between Broadway and thirty-fifth Street in Manhattan, and gave the following announcement to the *New York Herald* (December 24, 1884):

> We are waiting for Hyde and Behman to come, and then I think we
> can arrive at some decision. I think it probable that we shall by next
> week be quartered in the New Park Theatre, and if all goes well we
> shall begin rehearsals tomorrow. As to the origin of the fire or any of
> the details don't ask me. I know nothing of it and have been too wor-
> ried and harassed to bother myself about it. All I know is that my
> property has been destroyed and that I have not a cent of insurance. . . .
> I have the original manuscript of my new play and the public will
> soon be able to judge whether it was to their advantage that it was
> saved.

After seven hours of negotiations, the deal was finalized with the Brooklyn managers, and Harrigan, Hart, and Braham began planning the move to the new house. Because the New Park Theatre had recently been employed as a menagerie and dime museum, all the animals and grotesqueries had to be removed before the stage could once again function as a performance space. In the interim, Tony Pastor had generously offered the use of his theater for afternoon rehearsals. So at 2:00 P.M. on December 24, the Theatre Comique company gathered at Tony Pastor's to continue rehearsals of *McAllister's Legacy*. Depressed, tired, and emotionally drained, the actors moped through the early part of the work. Being in a new theater, nothing felt right. None of the old business that had always worked before was working; none of the lines felt funny. Then David Braham appeared to rehearse the company in "Oh, My! How We Posé!," an elaborate song and dance. As the music began to echo through the empty auditorium, the actors' spirits changed. Depression became exultation, and everyone suddenly remembered that it was Christmas Eve.

Chapter 9

Act Five: "Triumphs at the Park"

The new year began as Harrigan had predicted on the day of the fire. The company was housed uptown in Hyde and Behman's New Park Theatre, Museum, and Menagerie at Broadway and thirty-fifth Street, and rehearsals for *McAllister's Legacy* continued for the scheduled January 5, 1885, opening. Braham had been busy redrafting the songs that had been lost in the fire, reorchestrating the score, and rehearsing the orchestra in the new space. The cast and orchestra continued rehearsing until opening night, finally abandoning the stage as the sound of an audience waiting to get in grew louder and louder. Outside, the crowd began to assemble at 7:00 P.M., every horsecar on the Broadway and Sixth Avenue lines stopping in front of the theater over the course of nearly an hour. The performance was completely sold out, and the ticket scalpers who were familiar appendages to the openings of Braham and Harrigan plays were particularly well rewarded for their efforts. Everyone wanted to see the first performance after the fire, and most people were willing to pay premium prices for the opportunity. More than two hundred members of the Seventh Regiment, wanting to demonstrate their appreciation to Harrigan for kindnesses he had shown them in the past, bought tickets in a block at the front of the parquet, while the private boxes were crowded with the famous and the infamous.

At 8:20 P.M., when Braham entered with his musicians, he was greeted with applause and cheers, the audience chiming in chorus, "How are you, David Braham?" He acknowledged the ovation with a bow and a smile and took his seat in the orchestra, giving the tempo for the overture with the tip of his bow. When the old familiar faces from the Theatre Comique appeared in the performance, the reception was no less enthusiastic, with shouts of "How are you, Mr. Harrigan?" "We're wid yer, Eddie!" and "One! two! three! How do you do, Mr. Hart?" ringing through the auditorium. At the end of the first act, Braham was presented with an expensive violin, intended to replace the one he had lost in the fire. Abe Hummel, a New York City lawyer, made the presentation speech, remarking about the replacement violin, "I do not know how old it is, but it is older than any of Washington's nurses." Braham was urged to say a few words but, characteristically, he chose to let his orchestra speak for him and struck up a stirring march, to which the audience replied, "Who was David Braham? First in war, first in peace, and first in the hearts of his countrymen."

McAllister's Legacy turns on a will left by Morgan McAllister, an eccentric Irishman who lived in Australia. At the reading of the will by lawyer Valentine Clancy (Harry Fisher), most of the McAllister clan are bequeathed unsubstantial legacies, such as a pair of leather pants, or a wooden leg. Only two of his relatives receive significant bequests, Dr. Patrick McAllister (Harrigan), a veterinarian who is left a plot of land on Thompson Street, and his sister, Molly McGouldrick (Tony Hart), who is given the tenement house standing on the property. Patrick responds to his inheritance by trying to sell the lot and ousting his relatives from the tenement where Molly had permitted them refuge, to court Mrs. Helvetia Van Dusen (Annie Yeamans). She's a rich widow who is addicted to the stock market and is looking after her father's lunatic friend Stephen Tewksbury (Michael Bradley), who has a mania for millinery. Patrick's nephew, Richard (W. J. Dagnan), is hired by Van Dusen as her coachman, and he falls in love with her daughter, Tillie (Annie Langdon). Ultimately it is discovered that Morgan McAllister did not actually die, but is alive in the person of lawyer Clancy, having concocted the ruse to test the moral fiber of his relatives. Only Molly passes the test, and she is rewarded with his entire estate and the hand of one Baldy O'Brien (John Sparks) in marriage, while Patrick pairs up with Van Dusen, and his nephew is matched up with her daughter.

Braham composed five new melodies for *McAllister's Legacy*. "Pat and His Little Brown Mare," designed for Harrigan, evokes the Irish ballads so long associated with that performer, while Tony Hart's song "Molly" is a simple ballad of the Stephen Foster mold, employing the typical scalewise melodies and conservative harmonies typically associated with Hart. "Mister Dooley's Geese," a narrative patter song complaining about a noisy neighbor, has an attractive march chorus evoking the quacking sounds of geese, the gobbling noises of turkeys, and the rooster's cock-a-doodle-doo, and "Blow the Bellows, Blow!" is a lusty chorus work song highly evocative of the sea chantey "Blow the Man Down." The showstopping song and dance "Oh, My! How We Posé!," in which the blackface chorus puts on aristocratic airs, is another of Braham's quadrilles, moving from the duple meter verse to a waltz chorus and finally to a schottische dance break. The *Clipper* (January 10, 1885) found the number to be especially charming and predicted that it would exceed the popularity of "Coming Home from Meeting," from *Dan's Tribulations*. It is noteworthy that the *Clipper* review discussed Braham's work before Harrigan's, explaining that "much of the success of a Harrigan and Hart production lies in the popularity of the music therein introduced—a fact, we think borne out by figures."

On February 28, dissatisfied with the attendance at the New Park Theatre and concerned that the new theater was too far uptown to draw good business, the Harrigan and Hart Company closed *McAllister Legacy* at that house. They moved to the "unlucky" Fourteenth Street Theatre, where the production opened without fanfare (and without the usual opening-night performance of "The Mulligan Guard" for luck) on March 2, a move that was christened for David Braham by the birth of a new grandson, George, to Harrigan and Annie Theresa. After two weeks of only moderate business, *McAllister's Legacy* was replaced by *The Major*, reworked and revitalized with four new songs recently composed by Braham. Called by the *New York Times* (March 17, 1885) "one of the most taking songs that the composer has recently produced," "4–11–44," a gambling song sung by the blackface chorus, is a soaring revival number alternating between minor and major modes and ending with a frenetic dance. "Henrietta Pye," a self-introductory song sung by Henry Higgins (Tony Hart) and Henrietta (Gertie Granville Hart), is another catchy Braham dance tune, emphasizing a triadic melody, a limited vocal

David Braham

range, and easily accessible harmonies. "I Really Can't Sit Down," a repeated-note patter song with an expansive waltz-time chorus, and "Oh, That's an Old Gag with Me," another of Braham's modified jig tunes with a lilting chorus, round out the new material that the *Spirit of the Times* (March 21, 1885) called "as tuneful and catching as any of his previous melodies." Both Braham and Harrigan must have felt as strongly about the new songs as the reviewers because, for this revival, they retained only two numbers from the original score: "Major Gilfeather" and "Miranda, When We Are Made One," both old favorites.

On April 18, *The Major* closed, giving rise to a revival of *Cordelia's Aspirations* beginning on April 20. Braham's familiar melodies were still crowd pleasers and were repeatedly encored throughout the three-week run that closed on May 9, with Harrigan and Hart agreeing to dissolve their partnership. Rumors had been flying all through the winter that Harrigan and Hart were not on good terms. Everyone knew that, even though David Braham had tried to maintain a professional relationship with Hart's wife, Gertie Granville, both his wife and his daughter disliked her, and barely tolerated her presence in the company. Every time Hart expressed the urge to go off on his own, Gertie was blamed for feeding his insecurities and fomenting distrust between the partners. The "Giddy Gusher," writing in the *New York Mirror* (May 9, 1885), seemed to echo the popular opinion:

> If the two men were unmarried the harmony would be undisturbed;
> but there you are—the dear good friends and life-long pards must
> have wives. And of all the wedges in the world give me a woman. I'd
> split the universe into two distinct halves with the right kind of
> woman for that work and a mallet that wouldn't break her head
> before I drove her in. You can break up lots of things with a man, but
> a woman is the daisy tool of destructive invention.

Whether or not Gertie was the cause of the trouble, Hart gave Harrigan a week's notice on May 2, announcing his resignation, forcing Harrigan to renegotiate the contracts (that specified the appearance of Harrigan *and* Hart) for the summer tour that was due to begin on May 11. The closing night in New York City was an especially emotional one for Harrigan and Braham. Not only did they lose their longtime friend and colleague, but also, in the early-morning hours preceding a two-performance day, two-month-old George Harrigan died of acute bronchitis.

Sunday was a day of mourning and, because it was a time of sorrow, Braham and Harrigan buried themselves in work. Immediately following the funeral, Harrigan rushed to the Fourteenth Street Theatre to supervise the dress rehearsal of Martin Hanley's Company, scheduled to open there the next day in his farce *Are You Insured?*, and Braham set off to work with Richard Quilter, the actor replacing Tony Hart on the summer tour.

A revision of Harrigan's 1878 sketch *Love vs. Insurance*, dealing with two ambitious insurance agents who woo old ladies to get them to purchase insurance policies, *Are You Insured?* had a score that included five new melodies by David Braham's son George, who also was the musical director for the production. A trial run of the show in Philadelphia during the week of April 13, 1885, drew large houses and encouraging reviews that were particularly complimentary to Braham's music. Critics were less kind in New York City. Although all found promise in young Braham's music (because it was written in the same popular style as his father's), most found the work a failure—well beneath Harrigan's talents—with the *Spirit of the Times* (May 16, 1885) wishing that the show had expired in Philadelphia!

While the younger Braham was leading the orchestra for *Are You Insured?*, the elder Braham was conducting Harrigan's first tour without Hart since the pair united fifteen years previously. After stops in Newark, Plainfield, and Jersey City, the tour moved on May 18 to Philadelphia's Chestnut Street Theatre, where *Cordelia's Aspirations* was warmly received by an audience that included the mayor and visiting councilmen from Boston, and Braham's songs were encored again and again. *The Major* opened the following week to a smaller audience, which included millionaires Elkins and Widner, who celebrated the opening of their new cable road by attending the Braham-Harrigan comedy. Because Colonel Sinn, the proprietor of the Park Theatre in Brooklyn, refused to renegotiate his contract, and threatened to sue if Harrigan *and* Hart did not appear, Tony Hart rejoined the company for two weeks only, beginning June 1, reprising his roles in *The Major* and *Investigation*.

On June 15, Harrigan's Company moved to the Boston Museum, where it was given an exuberantly hearty reception, indicative of its popularity in New England. Before leaving Boston on June 28, Martin Hanley announced that Harrigan would return in August to the New Park Theatre, which would be rechristened "Harrigan's Park Theatre," under his (Hanley's) management. He also promised that the Harrigan

Company would return to Boston every summer for a month's engagement, rather than the usual two-week stay, a prospect that was cheered by Bostonians and Braham alike. David Braham always enjoyed working in Boston. The musicians were first-rate, the food was excellent, the accommodations were always comfortable. And he got to spend time with his favorite nephew, John, who had already acquired a reputation as musical director and composer for Rice's Extravaganza Combination. After Harrigan's company returned to New York City, Hanley began hiring performers for the following season, and Braham and Harrigan took their families to Schroon Lake for the month of July.

Following a quiet summer of work and relaxation, Braham and Harrigan were back in New York on August 10, when three weeks of rehearsals began for *Old Lavender*, an expanded version of one of Harrigan's favorite shows, with an entirely new score by David Braham. On Tuesday, September 1, the refurbished, repainted, and rechristened Harrigan's New Park Theatre opened its doors for the 1885–86 season. The season had been scheduled to open on Monday, August 31, but Braham and Harrigan felt that the production needed an extra day of rehearsal, so a dress rehearsal was held instead of a performance. The delay caused the management some embarrassment, because the newspaper advertisement for *Old Lavender* published on Tuesday described the show (that had yet to open) as a success the night before!

Developed from an extended character sketch about a good-natured, lighthearted alcoholic, *Old Lavender* tells the story of Old Lavender (Harrigan), disowned by his brother, Philip Coggswell (E. A. Eberle), an inveterate teetotaler, as soon as he smells liquor on his breath. Philip's wife, Laura (Stella Boniface), becomes enraptured with a home-wrecking miscreant named Paul Cassin (H. A. Weaver Jr.) and runs away with him, only to find herself ultimately abandoned and tossed into a river. By happy coincidence, she is rescued by Old Lavender's confederate Dick, the Rat (Dan Collyer), and reconciliations follow on all sides.

Braham composed six new songs for the production, each of which was rapturously applauded and encored on opening night. "Extra! Extra!" the newsboy's song for Dick, the Rat, is a repeated-note patter song clearly designed for an actor with only a modicum of musical ability. What it lacks in melodic interest is relieved by an inventive and energetic accompaniment. "Get Up, Jack—John, Sit Down," sung by Old Lavender, is a jaunty sea chantey with a busy hornpipe accompaniment and a vigorously "manly" chorus. "The Owl," sung by Zolia Brown

(George Merritt), is a lilting serenade reminiscent of "Tit-Willow" in Gilbert and Sullivan's *The Mikado*, employing a highly atmospheric accompaniment evoking the sound of birds in the moonlight. The polka "Please to Put That Down," sung by Old Lavender, is a study in accented nonchordal notes and reveals the character's philosophy:

> When sorrow sits down on your brow,
> And sadness peeps out of your eye,
> Don't stop to think, but take a drink
> Of old Kentucky Rye;
> Twill lighten up your burden, boys,
> And banish ev'ry frown;
> That's one good thing of which I'll sing,
> Oh, please to put that down.

"Poverty's Tears Ebb and Flow," also sung by Old Lavender, is an old-fashioned verse/chorus ballad highly reminiscent of Braham's more serious compositions, with a willowing accompaniment and soaring melodic lines. The *New York Times* (September 2, 1885) found this number to be especially effective, predicting that it would become as popular as the Italian woman's lament "Find in Genoa" in *Investigation*. "Sweetest Love," a rhythmical blackface serenade and dance with a highly rhythmical verse and legato refrain, evokes Stephen Foster in its long melodic lines, but is pure Braham in its rhythmical surprises. The *Clipper* (12 September 1885) found it the most meritorious of Braham's compositions and predicted that it would become a substantial hit.

Early in November, Braham and Harrigan began rehearsals for *The Grip*, their next local comedy, designed to succeed *Old Lavender*. By the end of the month the new show was ready and, on November 30, it was hailed with screams of laughter and hearty applause by the usual large and appreciative audience. During the Civil War, Colonel Patrick Reilly (Harry Fisher) and his friend Captain Phil Clancy (George L. Stout) had contracted the betrothal of their infant children, sealing the agreement with the grip of the secret order to which they both belonged. After the war, the friends moved to different parts of the country, Reilly moving to Cooperstown, New York, and Clancy going off to a cattle ranch in Galveston, Texas. The play begins in Cooperstown when the children have attained a marriageable age and Reilly receives a letter informing him that John Clancy (H. A. Weaver Jr.) is on his way to claim his bride. The colonel had received another letter from Texas the previous year claiming that the Clancys had fallen into ill repute, and he had no intention of seeing his daughter, Rosalind (Stella Boniface), marry into a family of drunks and swindlers. To avoid having to fulfill the contract, he decides that he and his daughter will exchange identities with his stableman, a soldier who served under him in the war and, coincidentally, also named Patrick Reilly (Harrigan), and his spinster sister, Rosanna (Annie Yeamans), a former governess at a girl's seminary who now works as a maid for his daughter. The "second" Patrick Reilly had been the proprietor of an alehouse, "The Canteen," before coming into his employ, and the colonel is convinced that Reilly's lack of breeding and Rosanna's age will discourage the Clancy boy from pursuing the match. When John arrives, he is, of course, disenchanted with the woman he believes he is supposed to marry, but he finds himself quite attracted to her maid, the real Rosalind, and she, in turn, falls in love with him. A delegation of the Board of Alderman who spend the night drinking and carousing with the bogus lord of the manor so upsets Rosalind (who, as the maid, has to serve the inebriated men) that she reveals the ruse to John Clancy. John's father arrives and explains that it was he who sent the letter blackening their reputations to test the colonel's friendship and dependability. In the end the families are reconciled, and the children make plans for their wedding.

Patrick Reilly (Harrigan), acting as the proprietor of the alehouse, sings "A Soldier Boy's Canteen," a rousing Irish ditty reminiscent of Thomas Moore's "The Minstrel Boy" (1813), accompanied by his sister, Rosanna, on the drum. He also performs "No Wealth without Labor," a majestically soaring march, lionizing the value of work: "Then cheer for the wage worker and toiler,/ He's the builder of home and joys;/ All riches must come after hard labor,/ There's no wealth without it, boys." Braham's setting of this chorus places an odd and awkward emphasis on the lyrics for comic effect and character development. For example, in the second line, the word "he's" is a pickup note and the words "the" and "of" are on strong beats, suggesting that the character is rather unsophisticated, clearly the point of the personality exchange.

As the captain of a canal boat, Erasmus Pebble, (John Wild) sang "Oh! Dat Low Bridge!," another of Braham's pseudo-African-American spirituals. This one has a chorus interrupted by musical interludes to allow for stage business and an extended dance break evocative of the "Virginia reel." The self-aggrandizing Aldermanic Board sang an easily hummable march, "The Aldermanic Board," from Braham's growing catalog of self-revelatory songs, and Handsome Grogan (Michael Bradley) sang another, this time a waltz and dance, "Grogan, the Masher," remotely suggestive of Buttercup's waltz in *HMS Pinafore*. Another infectious, memorable waltz sung by the girls at the seminary, "School Days," employing Braham's favorite device of a simple tonal melody, rounded out the score. Although the songs were repeatedly encored, and sung with vigorous energy, the critics felt that they were below Braham's usual standard, and no real hits emerged from the show.

The Grip ambled along into the New Year, undoubtedly helped by members of the Seventh Regiment, who returned over and over again to support Harrigan and Braham (on December 21, for example, they occupied 530 seats in the orchestra, virtually buying out that portion of the auditorium). In January, the next show was already in rehearsal, and by the middle of February it was time for a change. The New Year was already a full one for David Braham: at the theater, writing and rehearsing during the day and conducting at night; and at home, preparing for the wedding of his second oldest daughter, Adelaide. Not untypically, everything happened at once: on Saturday, February 13, *The Grip* closed; the following Monday, a revised version of *Christmas Joys and Sorrows* titled *The Leather Patch* opened; and later in the week, Adelaide got married.

The Leather Patch is named for a pair of old worn trousers patched with leather in which a secret codicil to Dennis McCarthy's will is secreted. McCarthy (George Merritt), a widowed undertaker, had married again, this time to a shrewish wife, Madeline (Annie Yeamans), who convinced him to bequeath all of his property to her. Guilt-ridden, the old man adds a codicil to the will, leaving the property to his son, Jeremiah (Harrigan), also an undertaker. To teach Madeline a lesson, old McCarthy feigns death, undergoes a mock funeral at night, and hides in the attic, ready to materialize as a ghost to frighten his widowed wife. She is already engaged in a courtship with Roderick McQuade (John Sparks), an undertaker and business rival to her stepson, Jeremiah. When Roderick needs an old pair of trousers in which to bury the corpse of an Italian, Madeline offers him the pants with the leather patch. After the burial, the trousers are stolen by Jefferson Putnam (John Wild), a grave robber, who sells them to a Baxter Street clothier, Moses Levy (Joseph Sparks), who, in turn, hangs them over his door as an advertisement for his shop. Jeremiah goes in search of the pants and finds that the trail leads to Putnam, who, sensing the importance of the commodity, steals the trousers back from the clothier and sells them to Jeremiah, currently disguised as Judge Doebler, in the process of marrying his stepmother to his business rival. In the end, old McCarthy reappears and sets everything right. McQuade is disappointed in his suit; Madeline learns her lesson; Jeremiah is rewarded with the hand of Libby O'Dooley (Amy Lee), the girl he loves; and the curtain falls on a jovial wedding dance.

Despite the fact that the show produced no enduring hits, the four new sprightly and catchy tunes Braham composed for *The Leather Patch* were considered to rank among his best. As Jeremiah McCarthy, Harrigan sang "Denny Grady's Hack," a spirited march with an effective use of sound effects (the cracks of a whip) to suggest a journey in a hack, and "It Showered Again," an old-fashioned Irish ballad about meeting and wooing a girl in a rainstorm. Moses Levy performed "Baxter Avenue," a self-revelatory waltz ethnically flavored by the alternation between the minor and major modes, and an old-style chorus reiterating the final melodic phrases of the verse. The most popular number in the score was sung by the blackface ensemble on the occasion of Jeremiah's marriage to Libby O'Dooley at the end of the comedy. "Put On Your Bridal Veil" is another of Braham's pseudo-spiritual revival numbers in the familiar quadrille pattern of verse/chorus/dance, all in different meters or tempos. Here the chorus is a romantic and soaring waltz tune that leads to a mazurka-like dance break.

The published copy of "Put On Your Bridal Veil" was dedicated to Mr. and Mrs. William E. Burke, Braham's daughter Adelaide and her husband, who were married on Thursday, February 18, at 6:30 P.M. at St. Joseph's Roman Catholic Church by Father J. Francis Fitz Harris, the priest who had officiated at Annie Theresa's marriage to Harrigan at the same church ten years earlier. Adelaide's sister Alice (Ida) acted as her maid of honor, and Sheriff Hugh J. Grant was the best man. Following the ceremony, attended by the Braham family, the Harrigan family, Martin and Marietta Hanley, Patrick H. Burke, and a host of city officials, a reception was held at the Brahams' apartment at 175 West 10th Street and continued throughout the night, reaching its peak at about 11:00 P.M., when Braham, Harrigan, Annie Yeamans, John Wild, and a large contingent from the theater arrived after the performance of *The Leather Patch*. Members of the theater orchestra stopped in to serenade the bride and groom and to congratulate the proud father, who had managed to steal a few hours from his chores as musical director to attend his daughter's wedding.

The Leather Patch played merrily through the end of the season on

A portrait of David Braham's five daughters, known as the "Five Sisters." Top, left to right, are Adelaide, Annie, Henrietta; bottom, Ida and Rose. From the collection of Ann Connolly.

Saturday, May 1, 1886. The following Monday, Harrigan and his actors began a three-week engagement at the Grand Opera House in Brooklyn, accompanied by Braham and his orchestra. *Old Lavender* opened to excellent business on May 3, followed by *The Grip* on May 10, and *The Leather Patch* on the seventeenth. When the Brooklyn run closed on May 22, the company boarded a train for Philadelphia for a two-week stay at the Chestnut Street Opera House, where *The Leather Patch* drew poor attendance but *Old Lavender* did markedly better. A week's stay in Newark beginning on June 7, led to three weeks at the Boston Museum, beginning on June 14 with *The Leather Patch*, followed on the twenty-first by *The Grip*, and the last week by *Old Lavender*. On July 3 the Boston engagement ended, and the next day the company was back in New York City. Harrigan packed up his family and headed out to Schroon, followed by Braham a short time later with his wife and children. The season had been busy and successful. It was time to rest and write.

During the summer, Braham and Harrigan completed a revised version of *Investigation*, adding a new song, "On Union Square," a tribute to the old stars of the variety stage and capitalizing on the kind of material and performance styles used by Pat Rooney, Johnny Wild, and Tony Pastor. Because Braham had worked with all of them at one time or another, the way he characterized each performer was credibly authentic: the "Pat Rooney" caricature was an overblown, heavily accented, Erin-flavored march; the "Johnny Wild" section was set as a blackface spiritual; and "Tony Pastor" was a waltz full of long-held notes perfect for crooning. When the season began at Harrigan's Park Theatre on August 23, the newly refurbished *Investigation* was the opening show, and the new song was singled out as a hit by critics (who found it "catchy") and audiences (who spiritedly requested that it be sung again and again).

In September, Braham and Harrigan began rehearsals for *The O'Reagans* with the opening scheduled for October 4. As opening night grew closer, it became clear that the production needed a little more work, and the date was postponed to October 11. When it finally opened, the show was greeted by another crowded house, whose continued laughter and earnest applause led Braham and Harrigan to believe that they had yet another "hit" on their hands. The story begins in "The Locker," a saloon owned by Bernard O'Reagan (Harrigan), who is visited by his Irish cousin, Bernard O'Reagan, M.P. (Joseph Sparks), on behalf of the Parnell Fund. The American O'Reagan is engaged to marry Bedalia McNeirney (Annie Yeamans), a keeper of a boardinghouse, but he secretly marries her daughter, Kate (Amy Lee), instead. The first act ends when Silas Cohog (John Wild) drops through a skylight while attempting to hang up a banner for Darrell Kilhealy (Michael Bradley), a candidate for assemblyman.

The second act opens on Gilligan's Court, where a haircutting contest between African-American barbers is under way. Bedalia McNeirney, who suspects the relationship between the American O'Reagan and her daughter, enters with her confidante, Sylvie Dreams (Emily Yeamans), to spy on him and his friends. Bedalia appropriates the thousand dollars raised for the Parnell Society in order to bribe O'Reagan's friends into telling her the truth about him, but somehow the money gets lost—accidentally becoming attached to a plaster attached to the American O'Reagan's back and discarded with the plaster—and the rest of the play revolves around recovering the cash.

The third act opens on Sheepshead Bay, where there is a clambake, plenty of dancing and singing, and Silas Cohog is selling bets on the racehorses. He accidentally falls into one of the open fires used for cooking, and the thousand dollars are discovered on him. The scene changes to the interior of the Cunard Wharf, where the "Gilded Zephyr Burlesque Troupe" is waiting to board ship. The real Bernard O'Reagan, M.P., appears, the other having been his valet in disguise, and the money is delivered to the true custodian of the Parnell Fund. The Burlesque Troupe, along with a company of U.S. black Marines heading for Egypt, board the ship and, as the boat begins to sail away, the curtain falls.

Braham composed five new tunes for the production, of which Harrigan performed two, "The Little Hedge School" and "Mulberry Springs," the first an old-style Irish ballad, the second a waltz exhibiting Braham's fondness for using unusual musical forms as dramatic devices. The chorus of "Mulberry Springs" employs unexpected harmonies and breaks out of the traditional song pattern, typically structured in four-, eight-, or sixteen-bar phrases, by the inclusion of a fourteen-bar interlude (evoking the vender cries on the street) before the final eight-bar restatement of the theme. "Strolling on the Sands," another Braham schottische dance tune (this time labeled "Tempo di Gavotte") opened the third act, while "U.S. Black Marines," a military march with an elaborate orchestral introduction and military drill, ended the show.

The hit of the evening, however, earning five encores on opening night, was the pseudo-spiritual "When de Trumpet in de Cornfield Blows," a work song in the minor mode, evoking the spirit of traditional African-American gospel hymns, and anticipating Oscar Hammerstein II's verse to "Old Man River." A frenzied dance break followed, choreographed by Michael Bradley, who was praised for his "nimble and tripping" dancing throughout the entertainment. Special mention must be made of Annie Yeamans who played a solo on the one-string Chinese fiddle and performed a Chinese song and dance with her real-life daughter, Emily. Braham did not compose new music for them, but simply dusted off material that Yeamans had used in her act back in the old variety days. The audience members old enough to have seen the original laughed in happy recognition, while those too young to remember judged the routine sufficiently humorous to encore. The *New York Times* (October 12, 1886) found only two of Braham's songs worthy of praise, the "U.S. Black Marines" and "When de Trumpet in de Cornfield Blows," calling the latter a "gem" with an especially effective dance orchestration.

On Saturday, January 29, *The O'Reagans* closed its sixteen-week run and, on the following Monday, *McNooney's Visit* was ready to open. Written and rehearsed hurriedly, Braham and Harrigan's new local comedy turns on an Irishman named Martin McNooney (Harrigan), who comes from Yonkers to New York City to court the widow Gilmartin (Annie Yeamans), who keeps a nursery and sells goat's milk, and to march in the St. Patrick's Day Parade. On the train trip into Manhattan, his suitcase is switched with that of a burglar, causing him to be arrested on suspicion of burglary. The second act opens at the Court of Special Sessions, with Judge Halzweiser (Harry Fisher) questioning a number of performers seized in a raid on a concert garden. Interrogated about their profession, the actors give way to hysterical histrionics, aggravated by the sudden appearance of an escaped lunatic that quickly clears the courtroom. Because the real Yonkers burglar was apprehended while Martin was sitting in the courtroom, McNooney is ultimately released. In the third act, after McNooney escapes the massage parlor into which he marched for a quick respite from the St. Patrick's Day Parade, Mrs. Gilmartin comes into money, and McNooney marries her, goat and all.

Braham contributed only three original songs to this farce: "Ho, Mollie Grogan," a pert Irish song and dance performed by Harrigan and the chorus, with exuberant choral shouts ("How, wow, Yow, yow," "Whoop") leading into, and throughout, the dance music; "The Black Maria, O!," an unusually catchy dirge borrowed from an olio number dating back to 1875, sung by prisoners on their way to Blackwell's Prison; and "The Toboggan Slide," an extended quadrille performed by the blackface chorus. The number begins with an elaborate orchestral fanfare followed by a satirical minuet, a flowing waltz that slips and slides melodically, a pseudo-spiritual section in a minor mode, and a vigorously rhythmical dance. The *New York Times* (February 1, 1887) found "The Toboggan Slide" particularly pleasing but predicted that all three numbers were destined for popularity.

Early in March the *New York Mirror* (March 12, 1887) reported that seats were scarce for *McNooney's Visit*, claiming that the show was the hit of the season at the Park Theatre and synonymous with the expression "Standing Room Only." On March 26, the *Mirror* reported that Braham and Harrigan had added a song to the show that was still drawing full houses. The song was "Have One with Me?," a heavily syncopated drinking song that ends in a "Virginia reel." It anticipates the syncopations in the work of George Gershwin and Vincent Youmans in songs such as "Heaven on Earth" or "I Want to Be Happy," where the accented word in the lyric falls on a normally unaccented beat in the music. On April 16, a month after the new song was added, *McNooney's Visit* closed and was replaced on the eighteenth by a two-week revival of *Cordelia's Aspirations* that added little in the way of new music. On April 30 the regular season closed at the Park Theatre, and Braham and Harrigan were again on the road.

Traveling with a repertory that included *The O'Reagans*, *Cordelia's Aspirations*, *The Leather Patch*, and *Investigation*, Harrigan's forty-five-member company (including Braham and his orchestra) began a month's engagement at the Grand Opera House in Brooklyn on May 2. They opened at the Chestnut Street Opera House in Philadelphia on May 30 for a week's engagement, then moved to the Opera House in Pittsburgh, for another week, beginning on June 6. On June 12, the company boarded their private coach and Pullman car for Chicago where two weeks at the Columbia Theatre awaited them. The rest of the month, into the beginning of July, was filled with shorter engagements and one-night stands in St. Joseph, Lincoln, Council Bluffs, Omaha, Cheyenne, and Salt Lake City, until the tour settled into five weeks in San Francisco, starting July 11, at the Bush Street Theatre. The company always enjoyed San Francisco, and with husbands, wives, children, and pets along for the ride, this tour seemed more like an extended vacation than work.

After a delightful and highly remunerative engagement in the Bay Area (where *Cordelia's Aspirations* and *Old Lavender* were preferred to *Investigation* and *The O'Reagans*), the company headed East, stopping again at Salt Lake City, then Denver, Leadville, Pueblo, Colorado Springs, and Kansas City, finishing with a week of only "fair" business at the Olympic Theatre in St. Louis on September 24. According to the *New York Mirror* (September 10, 1887), the scenery for every show except for *Old Lavender* and *Cordelia's Aspirations* was erroneously shipped directly from San Francisco to New York City, necessitating a change in the bills throughout the eastern leg of the tour.

When the company returned to New York City at the end of September, the opening date of the 1887–88 season was only two weeks away. To give the actors and musicians some rest after the arduously long—although enjoyable—summer tour, Harrigan and Braham, who had been working on new material all through the summer months, decided to open with one of the touring shows, saving the new work for later in the fall. Martin Hanley did not have the luxury of time, however, and labored feverishly night and day to get the theater in order for an October 10 opening. So strenuously did he work that when *The Leather Patch* opened on that date, Hanley was nowhere in evidence. He had been felled by an apoplectic stroke the week before, and Braham began the season with visits to his brother-in-law's bedside between rehearsals during the day and performances in the evening. By happy coincidence, Braham's nephew John was in New York in October for a production of *The Corsair*, for which he composed the music with E. E. Rice. John had been a great consolation to his uncle when Joseph died, and David was always grateful for his company, especially during times of stress.

By the beginning of November it was clear that *Pete*, the new work, was not yet ready for performance, so on November 21, 1887, *Cordelia's Aspirations* appeared for a two-week run. The theater was dark on Monday, November 21, for a final dress rehearsal for the new show, and, on Tuesday, the twenty-second, *Pete* gave its first performance before an enthusiastic audience. The crowd was so enthusiastic that because of the repeated encores, ovations, and entrance speeches, the performance lasted until midnight.

Based on an earlier sketch, "Slavery Days," and set in Florida—an exotic locale for a Braham-Harrigan show—*Pete* tells the melodramatic saga of an African-American slave, Pete (Harrigan), whose master, Colonel Randolph Coolidge (Marcus Moriarty), has had a daughter by a secret marriage. When the colonel is killed in the Civil War, it falls to Pete to tell his daughter, Little May (Kate Patterson), what has happened to her father, and to protect her from the colonel's gold-digging second wife, who wants to rob the girl of her rightful inheritance by questioning her legitimacy. The original marriage license between the colonel and May's mother had been cleverly defaced by Mrs. Coolidge's cronies, who shot bullet holes through the names of the witnesses. Pete painstakingly recovers all of the missing scraps of paper, but is beaten with a whip for his efforts and left to bleed to death. Little May nurses him back to health and is thrown into a millpond for her kindness. Her charity does not go unrewarded, however, for Pete rescues her as she descends the millrace, proves her legitimacy, and vanquishes the villains for a happy ending. Local color was provided by the presence of Vi'let (Dan Collyer), a half-mad slave girl who engages in voodoo, and comedy was present in the personalities of a New York alderman, Constantine Brannigan (Joseph Sparks), his maid and wife, Mary Duffy (Annie Yeamans), and his servant, Gaspar Randolph (John Wild).

In addition to producing a vast amount of incidental music, Braham composed ten new songs for this production, all praised as "bright and infectious." "As We Wander in the Orange Grove" is another example of his use of the quadrille format, alternating among a schottische tune; a lyrical waltz arranged for full chorus; and a playful, meandering dance routine. The work song "Haul the Wood Pile Down" is another fine example of Braham's pseudo-spiritual numbers in the vein of "When de Trumpet in de Cornfield Blows," with an imaginative juxtaposition of major and minor modes that also characterizes "Heigh Ho! Lingo, Sally," a somber work song with a dance. Opening with a bright fanfare, "Massa's Wedding Night" is characteristic of Braham's "Jubilee" songs trading on a syncopated, cakewalk style of march. "The Old Barn Floor" is another celebration song with unexpected harmonic changes; a chorus that imitates the sounds of dogs, pigs, chickens, ducks, and roosters; and an extended schottische dance break. The penchant for animal sounds is again found in "The Old Black Crow," where the call of the crow, "Caw! caw! caw!," is repeatedly given prominence. This memorable ditty alternates between minor and major modes and anticipates (at least in its verse) the theme and tone of "The Buzzard Song" in Gershwin's folk opera *Porgy and Bess*. "Slavery's Passed Away" is a stirring anthem arranged for full chorus, and "Where the Sweet Magnolia Grows," employing a mandolinlike accompaniment in its verse, is a minstrel ballad in the style of Stephen Foster. Two other songs advertised for the production, "The Bridal March" and "The Stonewall Jackson," appear not to have been published and do not survive in manuscript.

Not untypically, the reviewers praised Braham's music, enjoyed much of the spectacle and many of the performances (especially Dan Collyer as Vi'let, and the live oxen onstage), but found the kicking mule intrusive, Harrigan's slave to be too Irish in his mannerisms, and the show far too long in performance. To remedy the problem of length, an entire character (Mary Morgan, played by Lavinia Shannon) was cut from the play at the beginning of the second week of the run. *Pete* continued happily into the New Year when, during a performance in January 1888, Harrigan noticed that Tony Hart was sitting in one of the private boxes, watching the performance. After the show, Hart went backstage to visit some of his old friends, and Braham, Harrigan, and Hart caroused into the morning hours, reminiscing about the old days and sharing plans for the future. It was a happy reunion and the last time Braham and Harrigan would see Hart alive.

Following the dissolution of the partnership, Tony Hart and his wife, Gertie, took to the road, touring with second- and third-class comedies and melodramas in a futile attempt to sustain a career. By the summer of 1887, when Hart closed in the Harrigan-like melodrama *Donnybrook*, in Boston, newspapers were running stories about his deteriorating physical condition: the lisping and stuttering that haunted his performances, the lack of muscular coordination, the abrupt changes in personality, the delusions, depressions, and rumors of insanity. A month before Braham and Harrigan were reunited with their old partner, the *New York Herald* (December 15, 1887) gave the rumors a name: paresis, a third-stage form of untreated syphilis, affecting the brain and spinal chord and occurring as much as twenty years after the initial infection. Six months later, in June 1888, an incurable invalid, Hart was admitted as a private patient to the State Lunatic Hospital in Worcester, Massachusetts.

On January 19, 1888, the Braham-Harrigan company moved to the Metropolitan Opera House for a matinee performance organized by Augustin Daly to benefit the Roman Catholic Orphan Asylum. With Braham at the podium, the company performed selections from *Pete*, approaching its 100th performance on Valentine's Day, February 14. A month later, the show was still going strong, but tragedy had struck the company once again. Early in March, Michael Bradley, who was acting the blackface role of Sunset Freckles, ruptured a blood vessel in his stomach. He continued performing, so no one in the cast had the slightest inclination of his condition. He finally collapsed on March 28, the day before *Pete* reached its 150th performance, and was taken to New York Hospital, where he died on April 2. His funeral took place on April 5 at the Harrigan residence, where Braham and members of the orchestra "played Bradley off" to his final resting place in Evergreen Cemetery. Two weeks later, *Pete* finally closed on April 21, leaving a revival of *Old Lavender* to finish out the season.

Throughout his collaboration with Harrigan, David Braham always seemed to have the time to work on other projects, ranging in scope from single songs to fully orchestrated incidental music for plays. Because he had scored only one new show for Harrigan during the season, Braham had time to dust off the nearly four-year-old incidental music and songs he had composed for a play by Fred Williams and starring Braham's old friend Maggie Mitchell. *Maggie the Midget* had originally opened on December 3, 1884, at Boyd's Opera House in Omaha, Nebraska, as part of Maggie Mitchell's touring repertory. After a disappointing reception at Colonel Sinn's Park Theatre in Brooklyn during the week of December 6, 1886, the play would finally receive its New York City premiere at the Fourteenth Street Theatre on March 12, 1888, for a two-week engagement.

Maggie the Midget tells the Cinderella story of Margaret St. George, alias the "Midget" (Maggie Mitchell), who, on the death of her father, is sent by her stepmother to the south of France in the charge of a governess who ignores her. As a result, after years of neglect, Margaret becomes the tomboy Maggie and returns to her father's house, where her stepsister's lover, Jack Falconer (Charles Abbott), falls in love with her. A series of family squabbles ensue, leading to a plot to kill Maggie by forcing her to ride an untamed horse, a scheme she manages to foil because of her skill as a rider. Maggie is followed to London by Ishmael Akbar (Earle Stirling), a Spanish Gypsy and playmate from her youth, who murders the stepsister after he realizes that she is intent on killing the midget. The crime, of course, is attributed to Maggie, but Ishmael arrives in the nick of time to confess his guilt and send Maggie from the gallows into the arms of Jack Falconer.

In addition to the incidental music for this four-act play, Braham composed a "Chorus and Fandango" performed by Muleteers and Gitanos at the end of the first act, a "Bull Fighter's Dance" performed by Maggie Mitchell and Earle Stirling between the first and second acts, and a "Tarantella," danced by the same pair, between the second and third acts, none of which appears to have survived, either in published or manuscript form. Although Braham was usually more comfortable conducting his own work, his responsibilities at the Park Theatre made that impossible. Luckily, the musical director of the Fourteenth Street Theatre was William Lloyd Bowron, one of his oldest friends, and Braham was confident that his musical intentions would be observed meticulously.

After the Park Theatre closed its regular season on May 5, 1888, Braham, Harrigan, and company were back in Brooklyn, at the Grand Opera House, with a week of *Old Lavender* beginning on May 7 and *Pete* playing the following week. A week in Philadelphia at the Chestnut Street Opera House and two weeks at Boston's Hollis Street Theatre completed the short summer tour, and the company returned to New York City on June 17 for a full two months off, just enough time for Braham and his wife to spoil their grandchildren.

Attempting to abandon the practice of repeated revivals and to reduce the number of blackface roles in the productions, Harrigan's Park

Maggie Mitchell.

Theatre opened on September 3, 1888, with Braham and Harrigan's latest effort, *Waddy Googan*, in which Harrigan plays two roles: Waddy Googan, a ubiquitous Irish cabdriver, and Joe Cornello, an old Italian sailor controlled by a band of Neapolitan thugs. An Italian heiress named Bianca (Annie O'Neill) is Waddy's ward, rescued by him from a shipwreck and educated in a convent. Because he holds a deed guaranteeing him possession of Bianca's wealth in the event of her death, her cousin, Antonio Ronzani (Marcus Moriarty), arranges for the girl to be lured to the riverfront, where she is locked up (presumably forever). Her cries for help (and her singing of a plaintive song) attract the attention of Joe Cornello, who tries to help her, but he is easily overtaken and dragged away by Ronzani's henchmen. Bianca is left to meet her dire fate, until Waddy appears with fists flying, and the girl and her fortune are saved.

Much of the play is devoted to the portrayal of local color, including a shipyard at Red Hook, a Bowery saloon called the "Willow Garden," the old Spring Street Market, and an Italian hideout under the dump on the riverfront. Braham composed five new songs for the entertainment (though the *New York Times* of August 21, 1888, claims there were six). "Isabelle St. Clair," another self-introductory song utilizing the quadrille formula, begins as a sprightly polka and ends with a sweeping waltz, caricaturing the imported "Chappy" from England:

I'm a chappy, and my pappy is a jolly old millionaire,
I'm a chummy, and my money,
Oh, I spend it ev'rywhere,
But my lovey and my dovey,
She has gone,
I do declare, with a bald-head lilly lally,
My Isabelle St. Clair.

"The Midnight Squad" is a vigorous policemen's march, recalling Braham's fondness for accented nonchordal tones, and "Old Boss Barry" recalls Braham's patter parlando style, with a repeated-note melody and schottische rhythms accompanying Harrigan's trenchant satire of Tammany-style politics. "Where the Sparrows and Chippies Parade" continues the satire of low life in New York City with a pleasantly hummable waltz tune sung in the "Willow Garden" scene in the Bowery. This last number was considered most likely to attain the widest popularity by the critics, although the entire score was found to be melodious and pleasing. The *New York Times* of September 4, 1888, singled out the performance of the Italian tarantella, "Italian Joe" as particularly noteworthy (but that song was not published) and predicted that before week's end, all of New York City would be whistling Braham's tunes.

Braham, Harrigan, and company were back at the Metropolitan Opera House on November 22 for Augustin Daly's annual benefit for the Roman Catholic Orphan Asylum. The first act of *Waddy Googan* was their contribution in the afternoon portion of the bill. Two weeks later, on December 8, *Waddy Googan* closed, and the following Monday, December 10, Harrigan's Park Theatre introduced *The Lorgaire*, revised and enlarged from the play Harrigan had produced more than ten years before. The plot still turned on Sir Robert Elliott (Frank E. Aiken) returning for his son, clandestinely begotten of an Irish peasant girl, and receiving in his place the wayward son of an unscrupulous squire who is a drunk and a thief. After a murder is committed, the real son, brought up by Widow Mullahey (Anne O'Neill), is arrested on circumstantial evidence, and it takes the Lorgaire (Harrigan), an officer from Scotland Yard, to sort everything out. The role of the Lorgaire gave Harrigan the opportunity to appear in a great many disguises throughout the play: a long-winded intellectual, a hearty French smuggler, a commercial traveler, a crusty old sailor, and an itinerant peddler. The work also gave Braham the opportunity to produce seven new songs, including his personal favorite, "Dolly, My Crumpled-Horn Cow," an old-style folk ballad of Mozartian simplicity and grace about a farmer's devotion to his cow. "I'm a Terror to All," a macho male duet, begins like a Gilbert and Sullivan patter song and ends in a military march, complete with an elaborate "trumpets and drums" orchestral finish. "Oh, My Molly Is Waiting for Me" is a highly memorable ballad, with the transparent simplicity of an Irish folk song and a subtle pulsating accompaniment. "Paddy and His Sweet Poteen" is a lilting hornpipe drinking song. "La Plus Belle France" is an atmospheric barcarolle with a melody and accompaniment that evoke undulating waves and the rocking of a ship, highly appropriate word-painting for Harrigan's lyrics:

I am one smuggler bold,
That loves the rolling sea;
I sail from France to Spain,
With brandies, spices, and tea;
Oh all of you should voyage with me, with me, with me,
We ev'ryone should visit Parie, Parie, Parie.
Oh I dance and sing with sweet demoiselles,
With them I drink the sparkling Moselles,
Vive la joie. Vous santé? Vive la plus belle France!
To the revenue I say, "Pooh, pooh."
In race of chase I bid them adieu,
Vive la joie. Vous santé? Vive la plus belle France!

The opening number, "List to the Anvil," encored on opening night, and "The Snoring Song" were not published and do not survive in manuscript.

The Lorgaire closed on January 30, 1889, and *Pete* returned the follow day and remained at the Park Theatre until March 2. *The O'Reagans* reappeared on March 4 and stayed until the twentieth, making room for a newly improved *McNooney's Visit* on the twenty-first. The play was revived under the name *4-11-44*, after the popular song from *The Major* that was added to the production. The Tombs prison scene and the song "Black Maria, O!," from the original production, were deleted. *The Grip* played the week of April 8. After the Saturday night performance on April 13, 1889, Braham and Harrigan withdrew from the Park Theatre, and rested for a short time before beginning the customary summer tour of Brooklyn and New Jersey.

After a week of *Pete* at the Amphion Academy in Williamsburgh starting on April 29, a week each of *Waddy Googan* and *The Grip* at the Grand Opera House in Brooklyn, and stops in Jersey City and Philadelphia, Harrigan and Braham began making preparations for fifty-two weeks on the road. Many of Harrigan's stock performers had elected to remain in New York so the month of June was spent recasting and rehearsing the touring repertoire, which included *Pete, Waddy Googan, Old Lavender, The Leather Patch, Cordelia's Aspirations, The Lorgaire, Squatter Sovereignty,* and *4-11-44*. Braham was now assisted by his son George, also an expert violinist, and a seasoned conductor (having gained experience working on Hanley's tours). At the end of June, a company of fifty performers and musicians that included Braham's daughter, Annie Theresa, his son Dave Jr., and his grandson Eddie Harrigan Jr., began the trek to San Francisco.

The company commenced its eight-week engagement at San Francisco's Alcazar Theatre on July 1, 1889, with a performance of *Pete* to a crowded house, and reports of unprecedented advance sales seemed to guarantee the financial success of the Bay Area leg of the tour. On August 26, after two months of standing-room-only business, the company played a series of one-night stands in California before stopping for a week in Denver to play the famous Tabor Grand Opera House. Chicago was the next major stop, with a week of *Old Lavender* at the Columbia Theatre starting on September 30. After a short respite, the company spent the fall touring the Midwest before settling down for a week each at the Grand Opera House in St. Louis and the Academy of Music in Buffalo, where they spent Christmas.

After a brief New Year's holiday, during which most of the company returned to New York City to visit friends or family, the tour picked up on January 3, 1890, in Utica, moving up and down the East Coast throughout the spring and ending with full week stops in Newark, Washington, and Philadelphia. George Braham was designated as conductor in Washington, and it is likely that he split the conducting chores with his father throughout the tour. On June 2, 1890, the company settled in at the Boston Museum for a month-long residency, performing *Squatter Sovereignty* for the first two weeks, *Cordelia's Aspirations* in the third week, and completing the engagement with *Old Lavender*. Finally, on June 28, 1890, the year-long peregrination ended and the company dispersed for the summer, Braham and Harrigan going to Schroon Lake to evaluate the past and plan for the future.

MR. EDWARD HARRIGAN IN HIS LEADING CHARACTERS.

Mr. Edward Harrigan in his leading characters.

Chapter 10

Act Six: "Harrigan's Theatre"

The 1889–90 season had been a full one for Braham and his family. Not only had David and his sons spent nearly the entire year on the road, but also his household moved uptown, to 75 West 131st Street in Harlem, where Braham would comfortably reside for the rest of his life. In the 1880s and 1890s, the elevated railroad in New York City had enabled Harlem to become a haven for the affluent middle classes who desired easy access to the city, but not its crowds and hectic pace. Even the long ride downtown on the "L" was useful to Braham, because it enabled him to get work done on an arrangement or a composition. His way of working might appear unorthodox, but it was amazingly efficient, as he explained to the *New York Herald* (July 12, 1891) about his collaboration with Ned Harrigan:

> After he gives me [the lyrics] I read them all over a number of times until I get a good idea of the time and style of the music each calls for. Then I select one to work on and put it in my pocket with a sheet of blank music paper which I always carry. On my way down

town in the elevated train I take out "Ned's" manuscript, hold my music paper over it so that I can just see one line. Then I hum that line over until I get something that suits me and jot it down on the paper. If I can't find any air I like, I skip it and go on to the next line. . . . "The Babies on the Block" was so written. I don't recollect any others now that were entirely composed on the "L," but I have caught a great many strains on the cars that form parts of songs. It's a long trip from here down town, and I have got into the habit of utilizing the time in composing.

The 1890 Police Census identified eight residents in the Braham household: David, now fifty-six; his wife, Annie, forty-four; his daughters Alice (Ida), twenty, Etta, eighteen, and Rose, twelve; and his sons George, twenty-five, David Jr., sixteen, and Edward, ten.

Young David and Eddie Harrigan, who had virtually grown up together, were inseparable friends. During the previous year's tour, they began imitating their fathers, sketching out song ideas and comic routines for a children's theater company, not unlike the "Grand Duke's Opera House" in the 1870s that Harrigan and Braham had so admired. Although the material the boys produced was derivative and not especially good, Braham and Harrigan continued to encourage their efforts, proud that their offspring wanted to follow in their footsteps. This was, of course, not unusual in the Braham-Harrigan circle. Annie Yeamans had acted with her daughters Jennie, Emily, and Lydia; Ed King Jr., the son of the xylophonist in Braham's orchestra, would travel with Harrigan's shows in the 1890s; and Martin Hanley's son, Willie, would grow up to be a theater manager with great initiative. The story goes that once he took a circus to Europe but business was so bad that the company was unable to afford a return ticket home. Willie managed to come up with the cash for the trip by selling one of the circus elephants to a French farmer, after convincing him that it would enable him to plow his land more efficiently. Not only had he inherited his father's honest face and salesmanship, but a bit of the blarney as well!

On September 4, Braham and Harrigan returned to New York from Schroon Lake to begin rehearsals for a short fall tour before the opening of a new Harrigan's Theatre at 63–67 West 35th Street. On Monday, September 8, the company met at 11:30 A.M. in Harrigan's home at Perry Street prior to beginning rehearsals for *The Leather Patch* and *Squatter Sovereignty* that afternoon at the Bijou Theatre. A mere seven days later,

A photograph of David Braham's children and grandchildren. Top, left to right, are Tony Harrigan, Rose Braham, Eddie Braham; bottom, Henrietta Braham, Willy Harrigan, Annie Harrigan, Adelaide Harrigan. From the collection of Ann Connolly.

on September 15, the Harrigan Company opened at the Academy of Music in Jersey City for a week's engagement, splitting *Squatter Sovereignty* with *The Leather Patch*. Coincidentally, the following day, at Green's Opera House in Cedar Rapids, a medley overture of Braham's popular songs opened a production of Milton Nobles's romantic melodrama *From Sire to Son*. On September 22, the Harrigan troupe was back at the Amphion Academy in Williamsburgh for a week's stay, while on 26 September, at Greene's Opera House in Cedar Rapids, Dan McCarthy's Irish comedy-drama *The Dear Irish Boy* was introduced by another overture comprised of songs composed by David Braham. After a three-week engagement at the Tremont Theatre in Boston, the tour continued on October 20 at the Academy of Music in Brooklyn, where another week was split between *Squatter Sovereignty* and *The Leather Patch*.

Braham spent the early part of November preparing the orchestrations for the show intended to open Harrigan's new theater, and helping his wife manage preparations for their daughter Ida's wedding. On Tuesday, November 18, at 10:30 A.M., under a marriage bell of white roses and chrysanthemums, Ida married John J. Farley in All Saints Roman Catholic Church at 129th Street and Madison Avenue, with the Reverend James W. Power, rector of the church, celebrating the Mass. Brother George and sister Etta were among the ushers and bridesmaids who, coincidentally, included Annie Morrisey, the woman George would marry, and the maid of honor was Adelaide Harrigan, Ida's seven-year-old niece. After the ceremony there was a breakfast reception at the Braham home, catered under the meticulous supervision of the bride's mother.

After Ida's wedding, Braham's major concern was whipping the new show into shape, rehearsing at Tony Pastor's during the day, since the new theater was not yet finished. Under the supervision of Francis H. Kimball, the designer of the Madison Square Theatre, the Casino Theatre, and the new Theatre Comique, workmen labored feverishly in the early days of December to complete Harrigan's Theatre. Because of Harrigan's past experiences, the building was erected with a great many fire escapes, eighteen possible exits from the auditorium, and six different outlets from the stage, including two escapes from the fly galleries. A sprinkler system was installed, and dressing rooms, as well as the main curtain, were completely fireproofed to prevent, in every way possible, damage to the building by fire.

Designed in an Italian Renaissance style, the exterior of the building was composed of cream-colored brick and white terra-cotta, creating the effect of white marble. On an overhead panel was inscribed "Harrigan's Theatre," ornamented on each side and above by a variety of theatrical emblems, and in the frieze above the panel, just below the roof covered in Spanish tile, were eighty heads in bas-relief, representing different expressions of the face. The lobby was painted in soft blues and dull reds, with stenciled designs in silver and gold, and an ivory-colored molding. The theater proper, painted in a light red color with silver and gold decorations, was arranged in three levels: the parquet, seating 375; the balcony, seating 265; and the gallery, accommodating 275. Although it could be enlarged somewhat by using the space behind the parquet as standing room, the small seating capacity of the house, 915 people, guaranteed the comfortable and intimate surroundings that Harrigan and Braham preferred for their shows. In addition, there were six proscenium boxes—four on the parquet level and two in the balcony.

The stage was 73 feet wide and 35 feet deep, behind a proscenium opening that measured 28 feet wide and 26 feet high. The auditorium was illuminated by a central chandelier of 40 incandescent lights, surrounded by a circle of gas jets, only to be used out of necessity. Four other hanging fixtures, each carrying 10 electric lights, and an abundance of sidelights and staircase illuminants gave the interior a bright and airy atmosphere.

The opening of the theater was advertised for December 22, 1890, and at eleven o'clock on the morning of Thursday, December 18, an auction sale for opening-night seats was held at the Madison Square Theatre. According to the *Clipper* of December 27, 1890, the sale of the orchestra and balcony seats amounted to $5,240. The gallery seats were not put up for bid. Instead, according to Harrigan's wishes, they would be sold on a first-come basis at the regular price, starting at 7:30 P.M. on opening night.

The theater did not open as advertised on the twenty second. Neither the building nor the play were entirely ready, and the date was postponed, first to the twenty-seventh and then to the twenty-ninth. Finally, on Monday, December 29, the line for gallery tickets extended all the way to Fifth Avenue by 5:00 P.M., two hours before they were to go on sale. Barely ten minutes after the house opened, every seat in the gallery was filled, the lucky occupants anxiously gawking at the celebrities who filled the boxes and the parquet, and breathlessly awaiting the initial appearance of their old favorites in a new theater. David Braham was the first to enjoy the uproar when his familiar red hair appeared from under the stage as he led his musicians into the orchestra pit. In his characteristic way, he counted off the overture with the tip of his violin. The orchestra began to play, and the new Braham-Harrigan comedy *Reilly and the Four Hundred* had begun. After a thunderous ovation, the curtain went up on the first act, crawling to a halt every time a popular performer appeared.

Reilly and the Four Hundred begins in the pawnshop of Wiley Reilly (Harrigan), who is assisted in his work by Mary Ann Dooley (Annie Yeamans). He learns that the plans of his lawyer son, Ned (Harry Davenport), to marry a blue blood named Emiline Gale (Isabelle Archer) are endangered by one Herman Smeltz (Harry Fisher), who threatens to reveal Ned's humble beginnings so he can marry Emiline for her money. To provide Ned with the proper pedigree, Reilly decides to appear among the upper crust masquerading as Sir William Reilly, an Irish baron and Ned's uncle, aided and abetted by Mary Ann Dooley (disguised as Lady Isabelle Reilly) and Commodore Toby Tow (James Radcliffe), Reilly's old friend and Emiline's uncle. Reilly also knows that Smeltz is not himself a member of the Four Hundred, but a Dutch butcher who stole a pig and went overboard when he was stationed aboard the commodore's ship *Mary Ann* in the Philippines. However, he needs the ship's logbook to prove the fact, but the book manages to get mixed up with another called *Illustrated Ireland*, the prize in a dance contest, through the efforts of Salvator Maginis (John Wild), the commodore's butler, and his girlfriend, Bessie Barlow (John Decker). Much of the rest of the evening is spent hunting down the book, which is finally recovered by the end of the third act. The drama ends happily when Ned is reunited with his Emiline, Mary Ann with the commodore, and Reilly with Lavinia Gale (Hattie Moore), Emiline's aunt.

Braham composed seven new numbers for *Reilly and the Four Hundred*, each of them among his finest work. The first act offers two self-expository numbers, "The Jolly Commodore," sung by Toby Tow, detailing his adventures on board the *Mary Ann*, in a bright hornpipe patter, and "Uncle Reilly," sung by Wiley Reilly, a bright polka with a subtly syncopated chorus reminiscent of "Have One with Me?" from *McNooney's Visit*.

The second act begins with a short musical introduction, followed by a lilting ballad in the style of a Bowery waltz titled "I've Come Home to

Stay." Sung by Percy Oggles (Fred Peters), the song lyrically portrays the ennui of the wealthy, a subject Cole Porter would mine until the vein ran out in the middle of the twentieth century. Commodore Toby and a chorus of sailors later chime in with "Jim Jam, Sailors Superfine," a schottische hornpipe celebrating life at sea, with an immediately memorable chorus and an energetic dance break. Waltzing music from an onstage orchestra leads into "Maggie Murphy's Home," an exceptionally catchy waltz describing tenement life in New York City and performed by Maggie Murphy (Emma Pollock). Before the end of the second act, Reilly sings "Taking in the Town," a jovial and remarkably infectious Irish jig beginning with the usual parlando verse but ending with a driving and heavily rhythmical chorus. An eight-minute jig follows during which Maggie Murphy and Bessie compete in challenge dancing. The music does not survive for this routine and, although it has been suggested that a reprise of "Taking in the Town" was used, it is doubtful that Braham would have simply repeated Reilly's song for an eight-minute routine, because in all of his published music, Braham typically composes dance music that is different from the song it accompanies (even if it is simply a variation of the tune).

The third act begins with another musical curtain-raiser accompanying the performance of a quadrille onstage. After a long scene, Reilly, in the disguise of Sir William Reilly, sings "The Great Four Hundred," a spirited satire of the New York City elite in march time, followed by a dance in the schottische style. There is a reprise of the chorus of "Jim Jam, Sailors Superfine," sung by the blackface chorus of sailors as they haul out the villain, and the act ends with a reprise of "Uncle Reilly" sung and danced by the ensemble.

The critics had nothing but praise for the score. The *Clipper* (January 3, 1891) found it to be in Braham's "sprightliest and most enticing vein" and predicted that at least five of the seven numbers would quickly become hits. The *New York Times* (December 30, 1890) agreed, noting that "Not the least pleasant feature of the performance is the incidental music furnished by Mr. Dave Braham, who occupied his old place as leader of the orchestra, and received a full share of the honors of the evening. He exploited eight new songs in all, and some of these are certain of receiving that tribute of popularity—to be soon whistled on the streets of the city." On January 3, 1891, The *New York Dramatic Mirror* added that "although David Braham's melodies are not strictly original, they possess his characteristic jingle, which seldom fails to impress itself on the musical memory," and predicted that "Maggie Murphy's Home" would soon put "Annie Rooney" to sleep.

In an interview with the *New York Herald* (July 12, 1891), David Braham described the creation of "Maggie Murphy's Home." When asked how long it took to write the song, he replied:

> Oh, about five minutes. I wrote it right off in its present form. It's a little odd that I did not want to write that song, which has proved to be the most popular of any I have written for several years.
>
> You see the songs for "Reilly" had all been written and got out of the way. Then "Ned" came to me and said he had got another song for the soubrette. She had one already. I thought that was quite enough and I objected to another. But at any rate I took the verse and chorus "Ned" had written and said I would do what I could.
>
> After reading it over several times the chorus rather stuck in my mind. It had a certain swing to it that I liked. It kept running in my head, while the verse did not impress me.
>
> One night after I had gone to bed I was thinking of the chorus and an air came to me that just fitted it. I got up, lit the gas, sat down at the table and began jotting it down on music paper. It went along perfectly smooth and straight to the last two bars. Then I hummed over two or three different endings, as you must be very particular to get the right snap in the ending to make the tunes go. The third one I hummed just suited me, and I jotted it down.
>
> Then I went up to "Ned's" room and knocked. He hadn't gone to bed, but was reading. I hummed the air over to him.
>
> "It's just the thing," he said.
>
> To make a sure test of it right then and there I wrote out a pianoforte score, which, of course, as all musicians know, is only a matter of a few minutes, and purely mechanical work, and calling Rose, my youngest daughter, asked her to go down and play it on the piano while "Ned" and I listened. We both liked it, and Mrs. Harrigan prophesied that it would take better than any air in the piece. She was right.

Emma Pollock, the newcomer who introduced "Maggie Murphy's Home," was noticed by all the critics because of her pretty face and graceful dancing. To Braham's dismay she was also noticed by his son George, a violinist in the orchestra, who initiated a romantic affair with the actress early in the run of the show. All was proceeding nicely

Facsimile of Braham's manuscript sketch for "Maggie Murphy's Home," published by
the *New York Herald*, July 12, 1891.

between the two lovebirds until George's other vice—betting on horse
races—necessitated his pawning a ring Emma had given him to place a
bet on a horse that simply could not lose. The horse, of course, lost, and
young Braham was unable to reclaim his love token.

To George's dismay, it was Pollock's practice, during the performance of "Maggie Murphy's Home," to stand close to the footlights and
smile dotingly on her boyfriend in the band. Realizing that Emma would
notice the absence of the ring when she looked in his direction—a violinist's hands are always visible when performing on the instrument—as
soon as her number began, he abruptly doubled over and began to play
with the violin in his lap.

David Braham, used to a well-disciplined pit, jumped to the conclu-
sion that his son was drunk. "What's wrong with you?" he whispered, not
missing a beat. "Pain in my shoulder. Can't lift my arm," was George's
whispered reply. "Ridiculous. Never heard of such a thing," David shot
back, still leading the orchestra unperturbedly, "Lift up that fiddle and
play." The younger Braham hesitated, hoping to play for time until the
song was over, a strategy that ultimately worked. The next day he talked
Harrigan into resuscitating their old walking contest scam, and the pair
spent the day going from bar to bar until George had earned enough
money to buy back the ring. That night, when Emma Pollock looked

down into the pit during "Maggie Murphy's Home," the ring was on his finger, and his violin was held high.

Reilly and the Four Hundred remained through the end of the season, closing on June 20 after 202 performances. Late in the run, a special benefit was held at Harrigan's Theatre for the widow of Captain Healy of the Sixty-ninth Regiment, one of the longtime supporters of Harrigan, Hart, and Braham. On Sunday evening, May 1, members of the *Reilly* company, as well as Burt Andrews, the Reed Family, and John Walsh, performed a variety bill accompanied by the orchestra, conducted by Braham, who seemed to enjoy returning to his roots, if only for a single evening.

July and August were spent working on new material with Harrigan, but, unlike previous summers, this year Braham was home with his family. He even had the time to take out a copyright registration (#1542) on a collection of "Braham's New Songs," published by J. W. Johnson. Braham rarely copyrighted his music; he let his publishers, or his son-in-law, take care of that part of the business. When copyrights begin to appear under his name in the 1890s, it is because he finally had the time to concern himself with such things. What had been an endless flow of compositions, arrangements, orchestrations, rehearsals, and performances had finally eased up.

On September 14, 1891, Harrigan's Theatre reopened with a continuation of *Reilly and the Four Hundred*. Braham was back in the leader's chair in the pit, his son-in-law starring in the play; his brother-in-law, Martin W. Hanley, managing the front of the house; his nephew, Hanley's son, Willie, running the box office; and his grandson, Eddie Harrigan Jr., selling tickets. The following week, Braham and Harrigan began rehearsals for *The Last of the Hogans*, planning to open the new show sometime in October. However, audiences for *Reilly* showed no signs of diminishing, so, after a few weeks, rehearsals for the new play were suspended. *Reilly* continued into November, when tragedy again struck. On Wednesday, November 4, 1891, Tony Hart died at the State Lunatic Asylum in Worcester, Massachusetts, at age thirty-six. He had not been seen in public since March 16, 1890 when, accompanied by an attendant from the asylum, he attended his wife's funeral. The *Worcester Gazette* of August 25, 1955, recalled that Hart's last days were spent in an almost unconscious reverie, seated in a large stuffed chair, staring blankly through a window that overlooked a lake nearby. The funeral took place on November 6, beginning at 8:30 A.M. at the home of Hart's niece, Mrs. P. H. Murphy, and moving to St. John's Church, where a solemn requiem High Mass was celebrated, ending with his interment in St. John's Cemetery. Braham and Hanley packed their families onto the train the night before to get to Worcester in time to pay their final respects.

By the middle of December it finally appeared as if *Reilly* had run its course, and the new show was quickly dusted off for a holiday opening. On Monday, December 21, Harrigan's Theatre was closed for a dress rehearsal, and the following day, *The Last of the Hogans* opened to the customary crowded and fashionable audience. The first act begins in the law offices of Judge Dominick McKeever (Harrigan), an even-tempered, fair-minded, Irish-American lawyer and adventurer. He is immediately involved in two cases: one involving a legacy left to the "last of the Hogans," a bricklayer supposed to be dead, and pursued with great energy by the man's wife (Emma Pollock); and an African-American congregation seeking to sell their church for five hundred dollars above the mortgage debt. The second act takes place on the waterfront, where an old oyster boat, supposedly used as a Bethel chapel for the congregation, is, in fact, the meeting place for a secret society called "The Mystic Stars," led by Esau Coldslaw (John Wild). During an initiation ritual, the mooring becomes untied and the boat floats out to sea, banging into a tugboat carrying the judge, two prizefighters, and a crowd of sporting enthusiasts, all being pursued by the police. The boxing match is transferred to the old oyster boat–Bethel chapel, to avoid suspicion, but the proceedings are halted when the bow of a yacht, sailing in the harbor, barges through the ship. The third act opens in the Gull Club House, a boating establishment on the Harlem River, and involves a boat race between the judge and Esau. Due to Esau's tying a heavy anchor to the judge's boat, the judge loses the race, but he discovers that a museum freak called "the wild man of Borneo" is, in reality, the supposedly dead bricklayer, and the last of the Hogans has been found.

Braham's songs for the production drew the usual popular and critical reactions, calling for repeated encores, and predicting immediate popularity. "Danny by My Side," a song about the Brooklyn Bridge and another of Braham's infectious waltzes, was expected to be as popular as "Maggie Murphy's Home," and whistled throughout the city. Although there are many similarities structurally between "Danny" and "Maggie Murphy," suggesting that Braham was hoping to capitalize on his previous hit, the chorus of the new waltz is much more expansive and soaring, almost reaching the realm of operetta. The *Spirit of the Times* (December 26, 1891) agreed, noting that "'Danny by My Side' convinces the audience that our local Offenbach is at his best."

"Knights of the Mystic Star" is another of Braham's African-American military marches, beginning with a long orchestral introduction and ending with a highly memorable chorus melody. The *New York Dramatic Mirror* (December 26, 1891) found that it compared favorably to "The Charleston Blues," in *McSorley's Inflation*. The title song is a self-expository ballad, evocative of Irish folk music in its melodic and harmonic structures, and was called "whimsical, catchy, and charming" by the critics. "De Rainbow Road" returns to Braham's usual spiritual-revival formula, with a verse in the minor mode followed by a spirited chorus in the relative major. An energetic and highly rhythmical dance, in a minor mode, ends the number. The vainglorious "Hats off to Me," another example of the quadrille formula, begins with a schottische patter, followed by a lilting waltz, and ending with a playfully rhythmic dance. The *New York Clipper* (December 26, 1891) was especially fond of these two numbers, giving Dan Burke's choreography particular praise. Also mentioned as noteworthy was "Take a Day Off, Mary Ann," a pleasantly hummable ballad cut from the same cloth as many of Braham's parlor songs.

The Last of the Hogans ran happily into April 1892, only to be replaced on April 18 by a return engagement of *Reilly and the Four Hundred* that rounded out the season with a two-week run, ending May 7, 1892. Two days later, the *Reilly and the Four Hundred* summer tour began with a week's engagement at the Opera House in Jersey City. George Braham accompanied his father on the tour, generally playing in the orchestra but often conducting the performances; the *Clipper* (May 21, 1892) noted that George did "yeoman service" with the Opera House orchestra during the engagement.

The next week was spent in Newark, followed by an engagement at the Chestnut Street Opera House in Philadelphia, where the xylophone solos, usually performed by Ed King, were rendered by Emil R. Seitz. On May 30, the company was back at the Amphion Academy in Williamsburgh, moving to Colonel Sinn's Park Theatre in Brooklyn on June 6, and finally, on June 13, to the Columbia Theatre in Boston, where the short but successful summer tour closed on July 2, 1892.

A week later, relaxing at Schroon Lake with his family, David Braham learned that he had lost another friend. Kate Castleton, an internationally acclaimed vocalist and comedienne for whom he composed olio material early in their careers, died of blood poisoning in Providence on July 10 at age thirty-six. The summer this year at the lake would be one of reflection and, although work had always provided an escape from the tragedies that interrupted their many successes, neither Braham nor his son-in-law felt especially driven to produce.

When Harrigan's Theatre opened on September 19, 1892, it inaugurated the new season with a tenth-anniversary revival of *Squatter Sovereignty*, with a cast that included Edward Harrigan, John Wild, Dan Collyer, Joseph Sparks, Harry Fisher, Emma Pollock, Ada Lewis, Annie Yeamans, and Dave Braham Jr. as John Brennan, one of the Maguires. Braham Sr.'s melodies seemed as fresh as ever to the audiences, which continued to clamor for encores, and the reviews predicted that the show would run for several months. The predictions overshot the mark, however, and the show closed on November 28, 1892, followed by a revival of *The Mulligan Guard Ball* with a pastiche score drawn from the Braham-Harrigan canon. This incarnation of the show included "The Pitcher of Beer," originally in *The Mulligan Guards' Christmas*; "The Little Widow Dunn," from *The Mulligan Guard Chowder*; "Going Home with Nellie after Five," from the revised *The Mulligan Guard Picnic*; "Our Front Stoop," from *Sullivan's Christmas*; "Down in Gossip Row" and "The Skidmore Masquerade," both from *The Mulligan Guards' Nominee*; and two songs from the original score, "The Skidmore Fancy Ball" and "Babies on Our Block." On March 18, 1893, *The Mulligan Guard Ball* closed, replaced, on March 20, by a revival of *Cordelia's Aspirations*, which held the stage until the end of April. On May 1, *Reilly and the Four Hundred* returned to bring the season, comprised entirely of revivals, to an end on 13 May 1893.

Two days later, the company opened a two-week engagement at the Chestnut Street Opera House in Philadelphia, with a week each of *Reilly and the Four Hundred* and *The Mulligan Guard Ball*. Eight performances at Miner's Theatre in Newark led to the annual visit to the Amphion Academy in Williamsburgh on June 5, and two weeks at the Park Theatre in Brooklyn. With the performance of *The Mulligan Guard Ball* on Saturday evening, June 24, the tour ended, and the company dispersed for the season. Invigorated by their continued popularity on the road, Braham and Harrigan retired to Schroon Lake to revise and refresh the old shows and to work on a few new ones.

The fruits of their summer labors appeared in the 1893–94 season at

Harrigan's Theatre. First came a revival, on August 28, of *Dan's Tribulations*—an installment of the Mulligan series that had not been played in New York in nine years—and later *The Woollen Stocking*, the first new piece to be mounted since *The Last of the Hogans* in December 1891. Like many of the previous Braham-Harrigan revivals, *Dan's Tribulations* featured a number of songs added from other shows: "Full Moon Union" from *The Mulligan Guards' Surprise*, "Roderick O'Dwyer" from *The Mulligan Guard Picnic*, "Hurry, Little Children, Sunday Morn!" from *The Mulligan Guard Picnic* (revival), and "The Bunch o' Berries" from *The Muddy Day*. In September, while *Dan's Tribulations* was playing to capacity crowds with a cast that included David Braham Jr., Braham and Harrigan began rehearsals for *The Woollen Stocking*, opening the show on October 9, 1893.

The Woollen Stocking is the name of a coal mine in Pennsylvania, bequeathed to Paddy Dempsey (Edward Mack) because he had, at one time, saved the owner's life. Unfortunately, Paddy loses the deed, goes blind, and is reduced to begging on the streets of New York, playing an accordion, and accompanied by his beautiful daughter, Nellie (Emma Pollock), who is a street performer. The mine subsequently falls into the hands of Cornelius Callahan (Harry Fisher), whose son, Dick (Harry W. Wright), falls in love with Nellie. Dempsey tells his story to Larry McLarney (Harrigan), a boss stevedore in love with the widow Hickey (Annie Yeamans), and McLarney begins the search for the deed, which turns up in a Bible inherited by Cool Clinker (John Wild). Typical of a Harrigan farce, the document then passes through the hands of a lawyer, a Jewish landlord, and a dealer in secondhand books before it ends up at McLarney's boardinghouse, where he manages to convince Callahan not only to restore the mine to Dempsey but also to bless the marriage of his son to Dempsey's daughter.

Braham composed five new tunes for this piece, each of which was eagerly encored. "Little Daughter Nell," a self-expository ballad performed by Nellie Dempsey, is an especially tuneful waltz, with a chorus that rises and falls against a wistful accompaniment, complemented by an energetic ascending countermelody that adds the ambience of perpetual motion to an exceptionally conservative harmonic structure. The simple beauty of the melody, combined with the ingenious and winsome performance by Emma Pollock, resulted in the number receiving five encores on opening night. Harrigan was equally as successful with "Sergeant Hickey of the G.A.R.," a "rattling" march comprised of a verse that is highly reminiscent of Sir Arthur Sullivan's comic operas, and a chorus coming right out of the popular military march tradition. The *New York Times* (October 10, 1893) predicted that the number would be on the streets within a week, and in the hand organs before the month was out.

A song about New York City's East Side, "They Never Tell All What They Know," sung by Isidore Rosenstein (James B. Radcliffe) and a chorus of Hester Street Jews, is another of Braham's rhythmical Bowery-style waltzes with an elaborate accompaniment, followed by a dance full of surprising, syncopated accents that lend a kind of ethnic flavor to the music. "Callahan's Gang," performed by a chorus of Irish workers, is an energetic polka followed by an exuberant jig, while "The Sunny Side of Thompson Street (Away Down Town)," sung and danced by the African-American characters in the play, is another of Braham's minstrelsy tunes, beginning with a chorus in the schottische style and ending with a highly syncopated "ragtime" chorus. An extended dance break follows, filled with the composer's characteristic unexpected accents and schottische rhythms.

Although Braham's songs were found to be "spirited, quaint, and catchy," they were insufficient to guarantee *The Woollen Stocking* a long run. On December 16, 1893, the production closed and was replaced, two days later, by a revival of Harrigan's favorite, *Old Lavender*. After a five-week run, *Old Lavender*, in turn, gave way to a revival of *The Leather Patch* on January 22, 1894. Audiences were not as friendly toward Harrigan's revivals as they had been when the shows were novelties, and *The Leather Patch* finally gave out on February 17. The *Woollen Stocking* returned on the nineteenth in the hopes of finishing out the season, but the threadbare audience attendance forced the show to close at the end of the week. Harrigan and Braham, feeling that their time had passed on Broadway, once again took to the road under the management of Martin W. Hanley, with a company that included their sons, George, David Jr., and Eddie Jr.

On February 26, the tour opened at the Grand Opera House in Bridgeport, Connecticut, with *Reilly and the Four Hundred*. The company was en route to a month's engagement at the Columbia Theatre in Boston, where it played *The Leather Patch*, *Reilly and the Four Hundred*, *The Woollen Stocking*, and *The Mulligan Guard Ball* to large crowds at reduced prices. On April 2, the tour moved to the Harlem Opera House for a two-week engagement, playing all four shows. Built on 125th Street between Seventh and Eighth Avenues by Oscar Hammerstein in 1889, the theater was a comfortable walking distance from Braham's 131st Street residence, and Braham, who had just turned sixty, appreciated being able to enjoy the comforts of home on tour. On April 15, the company boarded the train for Philadelphia, where they enjoyed a month-long run at the Chestnut Street Opera House. The opening week of *The Woollen Stocking* grossed nearly eight thousand dollars, topping every other theater in the city.

The engagement in Philadelphia closed on Saturday, May 12, with a performance of *McSorley's Inflation* (having just been added to the repertory). On the following Monday the company returned to the Park Theatre in Brooklyn, where they performed *The Mulligan Guard Ball*, *Reilly and the Four Hundred*, and *McSorley's Inflation* over a two-week period. It is interesting to note that as Braham was leaving the Park Theatre, his nephew, Harry, was arriving with the cast of W. H. Crane's production *On Probation*. Harry's show at the Park opened on May 28, the same day that Braham opened *The Mulligan Guard Ball* at the Amphion Academy in Williamsburgh.

Following the Williamsburgh engagement, the company started packing for another lengthy West Coast summer tour. Beginning on June 6 with stops in Albany and Troy, the tour immediately headed West, opening at the California Theatre in San Francisco on June 18, with *Reilly and the Four Hundred*. Hattie Moore, who had joined Harrigan's company during its last engagement in San Francisco, was given an exuberant homecoming, and the house was sold out as soon as the doors to the theater were open. During the following weeks, *The Mulligan Guard Ball*, *Old Lavender*, *The Leather Patch*, *Cordelia's Aspirations*, *McSorley's Inflation*, and *Squatter Sovereignty* were played to consistently sold-out houses. When the two-month run in San Francisco ended on August 11, Harrigan and Braham were satisfied that their work was appreciated.

On September 3, the tour began to work its way back to the East Coast, stopping first at the Tabor Grand Opera House in Denver and next at the Columbia Theatre in Chicago. An engagement at the Columbia Theatre in Brooklyn from September 21 to 29 led to one-night stands in a variety of northeastern cities, including Worcester, where Braham and Harrigan stopped to visit Hart's grave. A week in Baltimore was followed by short stays in Scranton, Wilkes-Barre, Philadelphia, and Jersey City (where David Braham Jr.'s dancing was singled out by the critics), and concluded with a week at the Park Theatre in Boston beginning on November 26, during which the company performed *Old Lavender*, *Reilly and the Four Hundred*, and *Cordelia's Aspirations*. The next day, a train transported the company back to New York City, where the performers had just enough time to unpack before rehearsals began for *Notoriety*, the newest Braham-Harrigan collaboration, on Monday, December 3.

After a week's rehearsal in New York City, *Notoriety* opened at Harrigan's Theatre on December 10, 1894, and Braham and Harrigan were welcomed back to New York City like conquering heroes. The short rehearsal time does not infer a lack of preparation among the cast. Both Braham and Harrigan had been working on the show all through the long summer and autumn tours, and, according to the *New York Dramatic Mirror* (December 1, 1894), the production had been staged during the Boston leg of the tour.

In any event, what the audience saw in New York City on December 10 was typical Harrigan fare. Barney Dolan (Harrigan), a retired policeman and proprietor of a popular tavern, is called in to solve the problem of a letter sent by members of an African-American "Accident Society" to Frederick Hoffman (Harry Fisher), a German millionaire, threatening to "blow his Dutch head off" unless he sends one hundred dollars to a specified address. While Barney is busy solving the blackmail mystery, his daughter, Bessie (Emma Pollock), falls in love with Dr. Charles Atwater (Edward Harrigan Jr.), an amateur boxer known as Rainbow Charlie and the son of Ariminta Atwater (Hattie Moore), who runs a mission in the Tenderloin district. She is being courted by Ollie Montague (Harry Wright), a traveling Englishman with an eye for fashion, and also by Frederick Hoffman, whose bicycle-riding daughter, Frankie (Queenie Vasser), happens to be engaged to Charles Atwater as a convenient family arrangement. The other characters that, more or less, figure into the plot are Barney's girlfriend, Molly Malone (Annie Yeamans), a wealthy dealer in junk, horses, and stocks, who also is being chased by Carlos Cassidy (Charles F. McCarthy), a rent collector; her brother, Paddy (George Merritt), a landscape gardener; Mealy Moon (John Wild), Hoffman's African-American bodyguard and a fight trainer in love with a secretary named Linda Linseed (Dave Braham Jr.); Melancholy Mary (Vivian Bernard), a denizen of the slums; and Barnum Brock (William West), the African-American proprietor of the "Burnt Rag," where students from Yale and Princeton collect to "paint the town" after a football game.

To this patchwork, Braham contributed six songs, each of which was repeatedly encored, even though the score follows his usual patterns, without much variation. "The Girl That's Up to Date," Frankie's self-introductory song, is in Braham's schottische vein, with sprightly musical interludes in the chorus designed to accompany the stage business of riding a bicycle. "Melancholy Mary," another eponymous self-expository number, follows in Braham's parlor-song tradition, with a lovely and expansive melody accompanied by a classically flavored pseudo-*Alberti* Bass. Barney's paean to Cherry Hill, "The Old Neighborhood," is a reminder of Braham's fondness for mixing meters within a single song; here the verse is a waltz, and the chorus, a rousing march. Unlike the earlier songs written for Harrigan, the vocal compass of this number is very conservative, suggesting a slight compression of the actor's singing range. The chorus, "Out on a College Rah! Rah!," is an extremely catchy waltz tune that would sound appropriate in an early-twentieth-century musical comedy. The same could be said for the polka "Tally Ho Song," in which the chorus tunefully narrates off-the-stage action:

Now, who's that in the distance?
Does he need assistance?
Bless me, it is Charley,
He's out to take a blow;
He looks a little foggy,
Driving rather groggy,
Oh, please don't sound the Tally Ho,
You'll wake him, don't you know!
Here comes a wealthy brewer in his single seated trap,
He's ogling all the ladies, for he has a smile on tap,
And also Miss O'Grady with her second cousin Joe,
A merry lot of people, don't you know?

"Up in the Tenderloin," performed by the denizens of the Tenderloin district, is another of Braham's pseudo-spirituals, beginning with solos and choral responses in a minor mode and ending up in a bright, driving chorus with a dance break, alternating between major and minor modes. The opening-night audiences treated the songs as if they were among Braham's best, although the critics were less impressed, the *New York Times* (December 11, 1894) arguing that "the songs were up to the ordinary level of variety farce—and no higher." Ultimately the audiences became less and less enchanted with the show and, after sixty-four performances, it was withdrawn, followed on Tuesday, February 5, 1895, by a revival of *The Major*.

The run was proceeding exceptionally well until the beginning of the second week. On Sunday, February 17, Harrigan's oldest son, Eddie, died of a ruptured appendix and peritonitis. The Braham-Harrigan family rallied together to mourn the loss, and the boy's father and grandfather elected to continue the performances through the week, hoping that the work that had gotten them through so many other tragedies would help them overcome this as well. At the end of the week they realized that an immediate continuance would be impossible. Eddie was not only a member of their family, he was also a member of the company, and his loss was felt by everyone involved with the theater—from the stagehands to the ticket sellers. Supported by Braham and his wife, Harrigan decided to close the theater and allow his family the time to mourn. All of New York City mourned with them. On March 16, 1895, the *New York Dramatic Mirror* reflected the feelings of many in the metropolis:

> Edward Harrigan has labored long and successfully to amuse the
> New York public. Since the days of the old Theatre Comique his
> busy and prolific brain has furnished forth an unbroken series of local
> plays whose mirth, melody and skilful characterization have provided
> unique and constant diversion.
>
> Within the limitations of his own field Mr. Harrigan has upheld
> the native play. During all these years, almost single-handed, he has
> held the fort against every form of opposition and counter-allure-
> ment, with prodigious industry, originality, and talent, triumphantly
> combining the functions of author, star, and manager.
>
> It seems to me that a man with such a record for perseverance
> and individual resource deserves the highest commendation, espe-
> cially in view of his bereavement, illness and other troubles, and it
> does not appear in the papers that there is a disposition to give him
> all the credit, the encouragement and the praise that are unquestion-
> ably his due.

By the end of March, Harrigan needed to work again, so he and Martin Hanley convinced Harrigan's aging father-in-law to join them on another tour. Soon the trio began reassembling a company, hoping to include their old friends Annie Yeamans, John Wild, and Harry Fisher. Everyone Harrigan approached agreed to the tour, and suddenly, on April 1, 1895, it was like old times again when *The Major* crossed the

Mr. Edward Harrigan,

AND HIS NEW YORK COMPANY.

Under the Management of M. W. HANLEY.

Presenting Mr. Harrigan's great comic play, in Three Acts, entitled

"THE MAJOR"

DAVE BRAHAM'S ORIGINAL SONGS:

"Major Gilfeather,"   "I Really Can't Sit Down."
"Miranda, When We Are Made One,"   "4-11-44."

Cast of Characters.

Major Gilfeather	Mr. Edward Harrigan
Phineas Bottlegreen	Mr. John Wild
Mike Gillespie	Mr. Joseph Sparks
Herman Buckheister	Mr. Harry Fisher
Helen Murphy	Mr. Charles F. McCarthy
Henry Higgins	Mr. Harry Wright
Percival Pop	Mr. George Merritt
Caleb Jenkins	Mr. Wm. West
Granville Bright	Mr. Dan Burke
Harriet Jenkins	Dave Braham, Jr.
Spotem	Mr. W. H. Gunning
Aunty Green	Mr. Ed. Burke
Mr. Shroud	Mr. John Brennan
Thomas Tape	Mr. John Mayor
Helen Gladdes	Mr. John Flynn
Mr. Whelt	Mr. Nelson Curtis
Harriet Pinch	Miss Hattie Moore
Henrietta	Miss Emma Pollock
Amelia Bright	Miss Lillian Stuart
Ellen Coombs	Miss Cora Marsh
—AND—	
Miranda Biggs	Mrs. Annie Yeamans

Touring playbill for *The Major*.

boards of Miner's Theatre in Newark. After a successful run in New Jersey, they were off to the Columbia Theatre in Boston for two weeks at the end of April, and on to the Columbia Theatre in Brooklyn (May 6–18), where every song was encored and, to quote the *New York Dramatic Mirror* (May 11, 1895), the company was made to feel "as welcome as the flowers of May." From the Columbia Theatre, it was back to the Amphion Academy in Williamsburgh and the Chestnut Street Opera House in Philadelphia, with *The Major* enjoying a profitable week at each house.

Even though the tour had been an artistic success, finances were not good with the Harrigan organization, and rumors of salary cutbacks begin to spread like wildfire. Late in May, while the company was performing in Philadelphia, Annie Yeamans told a reporter from the *New York Dramatic Mirror* (June 1, 1895) that she would not be a member of Harrigan's company during the 1895–96 season. She insisted that she would not consent to a reduction in salary with Harrigan's organization and announced her availability to other managers in the coming season. Harrigan accepted her resignation without malice, and, after the evening performance of *The Major*, on June 1, 1895, they parted friends. Her departure was a severe blow for David Braham, who had been involved with the Yeamans family since the outset of his career. Annie's daughters grew up with his own children, and they had adopted her as a surrogate aunt. But it was time for her to move on to other companies and other roles, and Braham began to consider whether the same might be true for himself as well.

Chapter 11

Grand Finale: "I Have Had My Share of It"

In June, after the engagement in Philadelphia ended, David Braham and Edward Harrigan had a talk about the future. Harrigan and Hanley were already planning an extensive tour up and down the East Coast, but to Braham, who had recently turned sixty, the touring circuit that he once regarded as a familiar and welcome friend had become more taxing than enjoyable. Now that his children were grown, he became more concerned about leaving his wife, particularly after his sons, George and David Jr., had joined the Harrigan company. He told Harrigan that he wanted to remain in New York City, and he encouraged his son-in-law to hire George Braham as his new musical director. Harrigan was easily persuaded and left for Europe, taking David Braham Jr., whom he was grooming to take Hanley's place eventually as manager of the company. When the pair returned aboard the steamship *Etruria* on July 13, the newspapers announced that Harrigan would open his new road season at the Chestnut Street Theatre in Philadelphia on September 8. The tour, extending from Maine to Florida and from the Atlantic Ocean to the Mississippi River, would be devoted exclusively to

Augustus Pitou.

Old Lavender and Harrigan's new comedy *My Son Dan*, both advertising songs by David Braham.

The summer of 1895 marked a turning point for the Braham family. George and David Jr. were now firmly entrenched in the Harrigan organization, and Rose, who had made her professional debut the year before as Juliet in an afternoon benefit at the Fifth Avenue Theatre, was in high demand by theater managers and directors. Another aspiring actress, daughter Ida, was having marital problems, sparked in part by her husband's unemployment and his habit of spending too much time "with the boys," and sister Etta was planning for her marriage to A. H. Benoit. After Eddie died suddenly in 1894 at age fourteen, virtually all of the children were out of the house, and David and his wife decided to take

Interior of the Grand Opera House, from the collection of Robert Davis Inc.,
Theatre Consulting Services.

in borders, a decision that was as sentimental as it was practical, because
they had become accustomed to the noise and mayhem of a large family.
The couple who ultimately filled the gap in the Braham household were
twenty-five-year-old Margaret Lindsay, and her twenty-three-year-old
brother, Edward, students from Pennsylvania.

After retiring from the Harrigan tours, Braham did not wait long for
a new position to come his way. Augustus Pitou had just become the new
lessee and manager of the Grand Opera House in New York City, and
he wanted to turn the theater into a first-class stock house, typically with
a new play every week. He needed a musical director who was conver-
sant with all styles of music and theatrical production, and someone who
could churn out, quickly and efficiently, orchestrations of popular songs
for *entr'acte* entertainment. Of course, the first person he contacted for
the job was Braham, and for the next three seasons Braham and his
orchestra were advertised beneath the banner of the Grand Opera
House.

The first season was full of interesting challenges for Braham, beginning on August 31 with *The Passing Show*, a musical review by Sydney
Rosenfeld (words) and Ludwig Englander (music), which had opened at
the Casino Theatre on May 12, 1894, with a cast of a hundred perform-

ers. The satirical songs, living pictures, burlesques of familiar plays, and acrobatics reminded Braham of the old days, and he found himself in his element, even though his work was limited to intermission entertainment, because the review traveled with its own conductor. A series of plays followed in September, allowing Braham somewhat more creative freedom in providing incidental and curtain music. The Lewis Morrison production of *Faust* during the week of September 9, for example, included vocal and organ music that needed to be coordinated with the action of the play.

In October, Herrmann the Magician arrived with his spectacular illusions, including the disappearance of his wife in front of a giant mirror, a transformation trick called "The Asiatic Trunk Mystery," in which two girls exchange places in a locked and sealed trunk, and "The Artist's Dream," in which a girl appears and disappears into a picture painted on canvas. Throughout the entertainment, Madame Herrmann performed a number of spectacular and exotic dances, accompanied by Braham and the orchestra, who excelled at accompanying dancers. Herrmann was followed by the Charles M. Barras spectacular melodrama *The Black Crook*, and an assortment of other plays and musicals. At holidaytime the gymnastic extravaganza *Superba,* took the stage, conceived and written by the acrobatic Hanlon Family with a little help from playwright John J. McNally and featuring spectacular scenic effects, ornately costumed ballets, and a villain named Wallawalla. The new year brought Braham back to his roots in minstrelsy with the arrival of *Primrose and West's Minstrels* on January 27, 1896, sporting a company of seventy performers. The entertainment featured patriotic songs and choruses, the barbershop harmonies of the Dorian Quartette, and the familiar comic antics of George H. Primrose, George Wilson, and Jimmy Wall. The minstrels were followed by the Garrick Burlesque Company with a production of *Thrilby*, a spoof of Paul M. Potter's popular melodrama *Trilby*. Braham was again in his element, not only because of his familiarity with the burlesque form but also because the production ended with a ballet.

While Braham was enjoying the return to old forms as a musical director, he and Harrigan were still attempting to produce new work. At the same time as the Harrigan company was in residence at the Park Theatre in Brooklyn (April 6–11), performing *Old Lavender* (with Dave Braham Jr. in Hart's old role of Dick, the Rat), the new Harrigan comedy, with music by David Braham, *My Son Dan*, was in rehearsal, for an opening planned at the Amphion Academy in Williamsburgh on the six-

The *New York Dramatic Mirror* (April 18, 1896), advertisement for Braham and Harrigan's *My Son Dan*.

teenth. The show played four performances at the Amphion and was subsequently withdrawn from the tour, never to resurface. Although the *New York Dramatic Mirror* (April 18, 1896) suggests that the score was merely a pastiche of earlier material, reporting that Braham's "popular songs were liberally encored," no specific titles are indicated. If any original music was composed for the production, it was not published.

Only marginally more successful was Braham and Harrigan's next musical, *Marty Malone*. It opened at the beginning of the 1896–97 season on August 31, at the Bijou Theatre in New York City (after three try-out performances in New Jersey), with George Braham as musical director and Dave Braham Jr. in the role of Easter Munday. The familiar, convoluted plot always associated with Harrigan's comedies is again evident. Marty Malone (Harrigan), an aging though hearty sailor, had been cast away on the island of Ghoola-Ghoola, where he had become the inamorato of the queen. That not unpleasant predicament was soured by the fact that Marty had a sweetheart back home, Sally Jordan (Catherine Lewis, the international musical theater star), who ran a boardinghouse for sailors. Marty returns home only to find that Sally's affections have turned to the cook working on a yacht owned by Heinrich Vanderdam (Harry Fisher), a bogus German baron who won a yacht race under mysterious circumstances. The cook wears a gold medallion, supposedly given him by the baron for "secret services." Lord John Foxwood (John Hollis), the loser in the race, tries to get the medal to prove that the race was rigged. But before he can, the trinket is stolen by a Haitian prince, Hippolite Ducrow (Dan Collyer), doing menial labor in New York City, who needs it for a prize in a cakewalk contest. From him it is purloined by Asa Munday (William West), who gives it to his girlfriend. By the end of the play the medal winds up in the hands of Marty Malone, bearing evidence of the true identity of Pauline Jordan (Pauline Train), a street waif whom Marty and Sally Jordan had adopted and who has become a popular music-hall singer. By the time the curtain falls, the girl, having become an heiress, marries Lord Foxwood, and Marty wins the hand of Marie Pinto (Maggie Fielding), the former Mary Kelly, a music teacher, now the female leader of the Cuban cause in New York.

Braham provided four songs to this effort. "The Hole in the Wall," a lusty sailor's song lionizing one Mary McCan and her bar, displays the composer's continued use of a fetchingly hummable triadic melody. Celebrating Pauline's music-hall successes, "The Pride of the London Stage," which Braham dedicated to Mrs. John J. Farley (his actress daughter Ida), is another example of the quadrille formula, with a polka verse and a waltz-time chorus. "Sweet Mary Mullane," about a woman selling songbooks for her crippled brother, Joe, is yet another of Braham's expansive ballads evocative of many of Stephen Foster's romantic melodies. The hit song of the show, however, was the blackface trio and dance "Savannah Sue," which critics compared to "Paddy Duffy's Cart" and "The Full Moon Union." Although reviewers predicted that the number would become part of the standard repertory for college glee clubs, brass bands, and street organs, no extant copy of the song (published by John Church with the rest of the score) appears to exist. In spite of the fact that the songs were repeatedly encored—ever the rule at a Braham-Harrigan opening—they were only sufficiently popular to sustain the show for thirty-two performances. From the Bijou Theatre the show moved to the Park Theatre in Brooklyn and the Amphion Academy in Williamsburgh, where a boy contralto, Dan McCarthy, who was not included in the cast in New York City, performed olio numbers to the delight of the audience.

At the Grand Opera House, the season did not begin much better. *The Cotton Spinner*, a melodrama by Scott Marble, chosen as the opening bill, only served to alienate the reviewer for the *New York Dramatic Mirror* on September 5, 1896, who concluded:

> There is really no use in saying anything of a critical nature in regard to the play. Unless the author, Scott Marble, sees fit to rewrite it, the best thing to do with it would be to take it off the boards as quickly as possible. . . .
>
> The acting was much better than the piece, but was far from brilliant. As it is doubtful whether even the author knew what it was about, the actors were excusable in looking rather bewildered after the second act, and as if they wished the performance were over.

Not even Braham's popular intermission medleys were enough to reverse the misfortunes of the production.

However, on October 5, *Sandow's Olympia*, a huge vaudeville company, stormed into the Grand with a dramatic sketch titled "Cleon," written expressly for Eugene Sandow, the strongman billed as the "Monarch of Muscle" by his manager, the young Florenz Ziegfeld Jr. Set in ancient Rome, the climax of the drama occurs when Sandow holds up the pieces of a broken bridge so a horse can cross it unharmed. An olio bill including the Rossow Midgets; Alcide Capitaine, "the perfect woman"; Wood and Sheppard, musical comedians; vocalist Jessie Merrillees; Mandola, a juggler; and Muldoon, a "wrestling pony," completed the evening's entertainment. Braham was back in the nest of variety entertainment, from which he and Harrigan had emerged years before. A week of Sandow gave way to *On Broadway*, a melodrama constructed by Clay M. Greene and Ben Teal around the talents of Maggie Cline, whose renditions of "Arrah, Go On!" and "Throw Him Down, McCloskey," to the accompaniment of Braham and his orchestra, were the hits of the evening.

A Night at the Circus tumbled in on October 19, combining farce with the ring show, followed by E. E. Rice's popular burlesque, *Excelsior Jr.* with its pretty girls, dazzling costumes, and spectacular scenery, and May Irwin in *The Widow Jones*, providing New Yorkers with their last opportunity to hear Irwin belt out "The Hoodoo," "The New Bully," "Hot Tomale [*sic*] Alley," and "The Old Oak Tree." Primrose and West were back with their minstrel company in November, followed by three weeks of plays, for which Braham and his orchestra supplied curtain and incidental music. Charles H. Hoyt's military satire *A Milk White Flag*, reminding Braham of the old "Mulligan Guard" days, appeared in December, sporting a fine array of talented singers and dancers. It was followed by John J. McNally's farce-comedy *A Good Thing*, featuring Peter F. Dailey performing "Your Baby's Comin' to Town," and Flora Irwin singing the popular "Honey, Does Yer Love Yer Man?" *Superba*, the Hanlons' spectacular pantomime, rematerialized on December 21 and remained until the New Year. For the holiday entertainment the theater was outfitted with Christmas trees and holly wreaths, and Braham prepared special medleys for the children's matinees while toys and games were distributed to the five hundred or six hundred girls and boys in the audience. The *New York Dramatic Mirror* (January 2, 1897) reported an incident at the Christmas matinee when a happy father led his two small children to the toy counter:

> The little man was given a game and his sister a doll, but he did not seem satisfied.
> "What's the matter?" inquired the parent. "You've got a game."
> "I know, papa," replied the hopeful, "but I'd rather have a doll."
> "A doll!" gasped the father. "Why, boys don't want dolls!"
> "Well, you see," explained the tiny man, "Sister will break her dolly and then if I have one, I can give her mine."
> He got a doll.

Coincidentally, the 1896 "holiday issue" of the *New York Dramatic Mirror* published a new Braham-Harrigan composition, "Her Broken Toys," which was inspired by the incident and dedicated to David's daughter Rose. An old-style verse/chorus ballad in the art-song tradition with a soaring and expansive melody, the piece describes the sentiments of a grandfather watching his granddaughter cry over her broken toys at Christmas. The third verse seems especially evocative of Braham and Harrigan's philosophy:

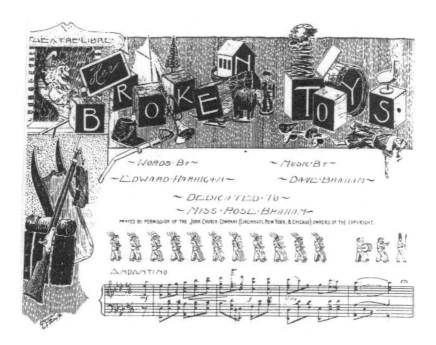

The illustrated title page for Braham and Harrigan's "Her Broken Toys," printed in the *New York Dramatic Mirror* (Holiday Issue 1896).

He thought as he gazed at the sweet little child,
So sad on this bright Christmas day,
The tear is the suitor so gentle and mild,

Of laughter so hearty and gay.
They never will part, both spring from the heart,
They're lovers in sorrows and joys.
The grave's a relief from this life oh so brief
That's burdened with poor broken toys.

The Byrne Brothers moved into the Grand Opera House on January 11, 1897, with their characteristic mixture of spectacle, farce, pantomime, burlesque, and circus acts in an entertainment called *Eight Bells*, and Rose Coghlan followed in a play, *The Sporting Duchess*, on the eighteenth. The next week, while Braham and his orchestra were accompanying Al G. Field's Minstrels at the Grand Opera House, Braham's incidental score for Augustus Pitou's play *Sweet Inniscarra* was being performed at the Fourteenth Street Theatre, under the expert musical direction of his old friend William Lloyd Bowron.

Starring Chauncey Olcott (who had previously appeared at the Grand Opera House in Jessop and Townsend's play with music *Mavourneen* at the end of the previous season), *Sweet Inniscarra* is named for a village on the Lee River in Ireland. In 1812, Gerald O'Carroll (Chauncey Olcott), a wealthy young man, tired of life in London, settles and meets an heiress, Kate O'Donoghue (Georgia Busby), who had volunteered to teach school until the new teacher arrives. Gerald assumes the role of the schoolteacher and the couple fall in love, although, because Kate's father, Squire O'Donoghue (Daniel Gilfether), had chosen another husband for her, the pair are forced to meet secretly in a glen, where they are eventually discovered by the squire and Creswick (W. J. Bean), the preferred suitor. O'Donoghue arranges to have Gerald carried away by a press gang, but he manages to escape the man-of-war ship, return home, and prove that Creswick is only interested in Kate's money. Squire O'Donoghue, impressed by O'Carroll's perseverance and the fact that he is a young man of means, finally allows him to marry his daughter. During the performance, Olcott sang four songs he wrote expressly for the play: "Sweet Inniscarra," "Kate O'Donoghue," "The Old-Fashioned Mother," and "The Fly Song," all of which were well received. David Braham is credited with the composition of "Dramatic Music," designed to establish the tone and atmosphere of the play. *Sweet Inniscarra* remained at the Fourteenth Street Theatre for 104 performances. Then it was withdrawn for one week, during which time the third act was rewritten, and the play reopened for another 24 performances.

While *Sweet Inniscarra* was enjoying a profitable engagement at the Fourteenth Street Theatre, Braham continued to accompany plays and melodramas at the Grand Opera House, as well as the Irish comedians Barney Gilmore and John F. Leonard, in their conglomeration of specialty acts, songs, and dances called *Hogan's Alley*. In March, while *On Broadway* was crossing the boards again at the Grand, Harrigan and company were at the Murray Hill Theatre for a week, performing *Old Lavender*; when Harrigan moved the production to the People's Theatre on March 29, Braham was busy providing incidental and intermission music to Sardou and Moreau's play *Madame Sans Gêne*.

May brought *The Cherry Pickers*, *An Enemy to the King*, and *Uncle Tom's Cabin* to the Grand Opera House, and Braham had his hands full. At the same time, on May 3, 1897, Harrigan began an eight-week vaudeville engagement at Proctor's Twenty-third Street Theatre, under the management of Robert Grau. The centerpiece of Harrigan's performance was a one-act sketch called "Sergeant Hickey," an abbreviated version of *The Grip*, with music by David Braham. In the cast were the old standbys Harry Fisher, Michael Keirney, and Hattie Moore, as well as Dave Braham Jr. and his sister Rose. As was their usual practice when altering or reviving shows, Braham and Harrigan created a pastiche score for "Sergeant Hickey," utilizing their most popular numbers, as well as the songs Harrigan most enjoyed singing.

For David Braham, the 1897–98 season at the Grand Opera House was little more than a reiteration of the previous two years. The fall was a hodgepodge of straight and musical plays seasoned by an occasional minstrel show and acrobatic extravaganza. Early in November, while Braham was accompanying the songs in Edward W. Townsend's Harrigan-like comedy *McFadden's Row of Flats*, Harrigan's production of *The Grip* (with "The Mountain Dew" interpolated from *The Blackbird*) appeared at the Third Avenue Theatre for a week's engagement before going out on the road. Later in the month, Braham was providing intermission music to *The Silver King*, a melodrama by Henry Arthur Jones and Henry Herman, while his own score for *Sweet Inniscarra* was playing at the Columbus Theatre. The new year brought *Sweet Inniscarra* back to the Fourteenth Street Theatre for forty performances, while Braham continued providing incidental music for Franklyn Fyles's Civil War drama *Cumberland '61*, T. R. Birmingham's sex farce satirizing Victor Herbert *Never Again; or, The Tricks of Seraphin*, and Edward E. Rose's period costume melodrama *Under the Red Robe*, in addition to minstrel turns and accompaniments for Primrose and West. Braham and his orchestra finally had the opportunity to perform his score for *Sweet Inniscarra* when the play arrived on March 14 for a week's engagement, performing a special matinee on St. Patrick's Day.

A month earlier, Braham had lost another friend and colleague when John Wild died of pneumonia in Troy, New York, on March 2, 1898. The body was transported to the Elks Lodge at Broadway and Twenty-seventh Street, where it lay in state until noon on Sunday, March 6, when the Elks' ritual funeral services began. Following a eulogy delivered by Arthur T. Moreland, the former interlocutor of the San Francisco Minstrels, the ceremony of the "amaranth and the ivy," and the singing of "Auld Lang Syne," Wild's body was escorted in procession to the Little Church around the Corner, where Reverend Houghton performed the burial service of the Episcopal Church. Joining Braham and his family at the funeral were many of the most famous names in the theater:

Tony Pastor, Harry Fisher, Daniel Frohman, Charles Frohman, Charles Hoyt, Oscar Hammerstein, Weber and Fields, Augustus Pitou, Col. William E. Sinn, Augustin Daly, DeWolf Hopper, Chauncey Olcott, and William H. Crane. Edward Harrigan, who was performing in Chicago at the time, sent a very large bouquet of white roses.

The season at the Grand Opera House ended with Edwin Barbour's production of *The White Squadron*. War pictures added a visual emphasis to Braham's *entr'acte* entertainment during the first two intermissions, and Minnie Emmett, dressed as Columbia, performed a new "National Hymn," written by Albert Ellery Berg, between the third and fourth acts. Braham and his orchestra accompanied the proceedings until the theater closed for the summer, when Braham packed up his violin and moved uptown to Wallack's Theatre at Broadway and Thirtieth Street. Even at sixty-four, David Braham was not ready to retire.

With the 1898–99 season, David Braham began his association with Theodore Moss, the manager of Wallack's Theatre, who had something to offer that was somewhat more attractive than the weekly changing bills at the Grand. Moss was interested in developing longer runs at Wallack's Theatre, more along the lines of Braham's later work with Harrigan. The one-a-week stock at the Grand had taken its toll on the musical director. He found himself mass-producing arrangements simply to meet deadlines and, while he was still eminently capable of churning out the work, the process no longer satisfied him. Even though his orchestra was still considered one of the tightest and most efficient in the city, his musical direction at the Grand had stopped being creative, becoming instead merely an exercise in technique. Braham knew it was time for a change and, encouraged by his wife, change he did.

Early in September, while Braham and his orchestra were accompanying a production of Augustus Thomas's play *The Meddler* at Wallack's, the ubiquitous *Sweet Inniscarra* had returned to the Columbus Theatre for a week's stay. Braham also was hard at work on the incidental music to a loosely plotted variety show, *The Finish of Mr. Fresh*, scheduled to open at Butler's Grand Opera House in Washington, D.C., on October 25, 1898, in preparation for a November 7 premiere at the Star Theatre in New York City.

Designed to exploit the "comicalities" of Al Wilson, *The Finish of Mr. Fresh* tells the story of a man who marries a woman with an "Oklahoma divorce." Her mother promises to deed him a valuable piece of property, provided he pay off a mortgage, which he does in good faith.

John Franceschina

Just as Mr. Fresh tries to take possession of the property, his mother-in-law repudiates her agreement and refuses to vacate the premises. In retaliation, he locks the woman in the house, shuts off the water and the gas, and, effectively, attempts to starve her into submission, unaware that she has managed to smuggle in water and food through the help of friends. When Fresh is ultimately brought to court for the mistreatment of his mother-in-law, he discovers that his wife's divorce was illegal and that he is, subsequently, a free man—that is, until the judge sentences him to marry his mother-in-law in reparation for his misbehavior.

Irrespective of the plot, the real entertainment in *The Finish of Mr. Fresh* came out of the actors' performing their various specialties (just like the old days at the Theatre Comique). George W. Day's comic monologues and songs, for example, were so well received on opening night that the performance had to be suspended while the actor answered the audience's demands for encores. The Stewart Sisters were popular in their songs and patter, Al H. Wilson told funny stories in a German dialect, Fannie Bloodgood sang saucy soubrette songs, Kathryn Klare effectively chirped Braisted and Carter's "She Was Bred in Old Kentucky," and Charles B. Ward characteristically sang songs about the Bowery. After a week at the Star Theatre, *The Finish of Mr. Fresh* traveled to the Metropolis Theatre at 142nd Street and Third Avenue for another eight performances, then abruptly disappeared.

Braham had a week off at the beginning of January 1899, but it was back to business as usual when diva Olga Nethersole, who had been absent from New York City for several seasons because of extensive touring engagements, began performing Beatrix in *The Termagant*, a poetic drama written for her by Louis N. Parker and Murray Carson. Frederick Corder composed the incidental music for the play, performed with dramatic sensitivity by the orchestra under Braham's direction. As if in anticipation of the furor Ms. Nethersole would create during the next season by appearing in the play *Sapho*, the season closed with two comedies by the French playwright Henri Meilhac: *The Cuckoo*, adapted by Charles Brookfield, and *My Cousin*, adapted by Frank Tannehill. Both plays traded on marital infidelity and sparked the moral indignation of the critics, who condemned them not only from an ethical perspective but from a dramatic one as well. Virtually oblivious to the highly charged atmosphere surrounding the plays, Braham continued to do his job and achieved the same high standard of orchestral efficiency that had been his trademark since the Canterbury Music Hall.

Olga Nethersole.

Although Braham's second season at Wallack's was marred by controversy and scandal, it was also a source of great personal satisfaction for him. The production of Victor Herbert's comic opera *The Ameer*, starring Frank Daniels, beginning on December 4, 1899, was praised by the critics for its strong chorus work and for the sensitive playing of the orchestra, held in perfect balance with the voices onstage. Though he did not conduct the performance, Braham, who knew the acoustics of the theater, worked closely with Herbert's musical director, Louis F. Gottschalk, to attain the desired orchestral sound and meticulous chorus work. Following Herbert's comic opera came Clyde Fitch's adaptation of Alphonse Daudet's novel *Sapho*, starring Olga Nethersole as Fannie Legrand. This foray into the demimonde filled with illicit passion, obsessive love, and an illegitimate child was one of five plays running in New York City that were considered "indecent," the others including the musical *Papa's Wife* by Harry B. Smith and Reginald de Koven at the Manhattan Theatre, and the farce *Naughty Anthony* by David Belasco at the Herald Square Theatre. Because *Sapho* was considered the most immoral of the lot, Wallack's Theatre was closed on March 5, 1900, by order of the New York City police. In an attempt to continue her engagement at the theater, Nethersole quickly dusted off a production of *The Second Mrs. Tanqueray* by Arthur Wing Pinero on March 6 and played it for two weeks, moving on to Pinero's *The Profligate* on March 17. On March 22, Olga Nethersole and Hamilton Revelle, the protagonists of *Sapho*; Theodore Moss, the proprietor of the theater; and Marcus R. Mayer, the manager of the company, were indicted for the crime of unlawfully committing and maintaining a public nuisance. Nethersole was so emotionally drained by the experience that, under the advice of her physician, who claimed she was suffering from nervous prostration, she refused to finish the run of *The Profligate*, and the theater closed for two weeks on March 22.

The *Sapho* trial began on April 3 before Justice Fursman in the Criminal Branch of the Supreme Court of New York City, with Assistant District Attorney Charles Le Barbier prosecuting, and Abe Hummel, the lawyer who presented Braham with the replacement violin in 1885, representing the accused. For three days, witnesses for both sides argued the concept of decency in artistic matters. On Thursday, April 5, after ten minutes' deliberation, the jury returned the verdict of not guilty, causing Olga Nethersole to engage in the kind of hysterical histrionics typically found in the sensation scene of a melodrama. As soon as the verdict was made public, with the announcement that performances of *Sapho* would recommence on Saturday, the street in front of Wallack's Theatre was crowded with people from all walks of life, ready to wait in line for hours to buy a ticket.

The seasons began to accumulate at Wallack's Theatre, one running into the other without too much distinction, except for the long runs such as *A Gentleman of France* (December 30, 1901), which played 120 performances, *The Show Girl* (May 5, 1902) with 64 performances, *The Sultan of Sulu* (December 29, 1902), with 192 performances, *Peggy from Paris* (September 10, 1903) playing 85 times, *The County Chairman* (November 24, 1903), with 222 performances, and *The Sho-gun* (October 10, 1904), accumulating 125 performances. During the run of

Peggy from Paris, Harrigan reappeared at the Murray Hill Theatre on September 14, 1903, with a new show called *Under Cover*. This time George Braham provided the "catchy" music and musical direction, and his sister Ida was a member of the cast, along with the old standbys, Annie and Jennie Yeamans, Dan Collyer, Harry Fisher, George L. Stout, and Joseph Sparks. Missing from the roster was Dave Braham Jr., who had left the Harrigan organization to join the cast of *Checkers*, Henry M. Blossom's popular play that opened at the American Theatre, 260 West 42nd Street, on September 28, 1903.

On January 24, 1905, *The Yankee Counsul*, a comic opera by Henry M. Blossom and Alfred G. Robyn that had premiered at the Broadway Theatre in February 1904, opened at Wallack's and remained there for forty-seven performances. It was to be David Braham's last production. During the latter part of the run, he complained of severe abdominal pains and sought advice from his doctor. He was diagnosed with kidney disease and bedridden for several months, during which time his son George took over the musical directorship of Wallack's Theatre. Early Tuesday morning, April 11, 1905, surrounded by his children and grand-children, David Braham died in the arms of his wife of forty-five years. The funeral was held two days later at the Braham residence, 75 West 131st Street, attended by an enormous crowd of musicians, performers, producers, and friends, including ventriloquist Alexander Davis and con-ductor William Lloyd Bowron, two of Braham's oldest companions.

Outside the residence were assembled fifty musicians from Wallack's orchestra and the Aschenbroedel Verein, a local brass band, who played Chopin's "Funeral March" under the direction of Edward King, xylo-phonist in Braham's orchestra and assistant director of the Seventh Regiment Band, on the way to All Saints Roman Catholic Church at Madison Avenue and 129th Street. After a requiem Low Mass cele-brated at the church by the Reverend Cornelius F. Crowley, the coffin was buried in the family plot at Calvary Cemetery, where Mozart's librettist Lorenzo da Ponte and the celebrated bandmaster Patrick S. Gilmore also were laid to rest.

On February 26, 1907, Mrs. Annie Braham took out a copyright on "The Babies on Our Block," the song usually cited by Braham as his most popular composition, to help support her in her old age. In the fall of 1908 the Harrigans moved back to Manhattan, at 249 West 102nd Street, from Brooklyn, where they had resided since 1896, so Annie could be closer to her aging mother. Two years later, on March 16,

Edward Harrigan made his last public appearance as the guest of honor at a Friends of Ireland dinner held at Shanley's Restaurant at Broadway and Twenty-ninth Street, where the orchestra, accustomed to playing hits from current Broadway musicals, struck up a medley of Braham-Harrigan tunes. In the same year, Dave Braham Jr. gave up acting and retired to a farm in Dutchess County, New York, where he died, five years later, on June 30, at age forty-one. On June 6, 1911, Edward Harrigan died of heart disease, followed by his wife, Annie Theresa, on March 24, 1918. Annie Braham followed two years later, on October 8, 1920, leaving behind George, Ida, and Rose. Ida, whose daughter, Alma, became a Ziegfeld Girl, divorced John J. Farley and later married Sam McKee before her death in 1944. In their later years, George (who had become the musical director for David Belasco) and Rose shared a house at 545 West 125th Street where they enjoyed a kind of *Cox and Box* lifestyle; she never leaving the house in the daylight, he never leaving at night, except to subway down to Times Square to count the house for *Mister Roberts*, the long-running comedy cowritten and directed by Joshua Logan, the husband of his niece, Nedda Harrigan. George died in 1952 at age eighty-seven, and Rose joined him four years later, at age seventy-eight.

David Braham, the American Offenbach, gave only two public interviews in his entire career. Both exhibit a self-effacing, gentle man who lived only for his family and for the work he did so well. "It's very hard work making songs for the people. I have had my share of it," he said in a joint interview with Edward Harrigan in 1891, following the remarkable run of *Reilly and the Four Hundred*, possibly the greatest success of Braham's long career. With hundreds of songs to his credit, most of them popular hits, thousands of arrangements, and countless pages of musical continuity designed to propel and punctuate the dramatic action of plays and musicals, Braham certainly did have his share of the work—and a little of the fame that extended beyond the ephemera of popular taste.

Writing about Braham and Harrigan's Mulligan series, the *New York Mirror* of May 9, 1885, concluded:

> Low life in the Metropolis was converted into comedy and flavored
> with melody, and it was a most palatable dish. The music of the
> Comique found its way to the hand-organ; but before it reached that
> humble instrument it had not been scorned by dignified orchestras. It
> found a place in concert and between the acts in leading theatres.

In addition, many of Braham and Harrigan's songs became huge international hits. By the time Braham died, "Whist! The Bogie Man" and "Maggie Murphy's Home" were played and sung around the world, and civilians and enlisted men, from New York to London to Paris to Bombay, marched to the tune of "The Mulligan Guard," the Braham-Harrigan composition memorialized by Rudyard Kipling in his 1901 novel *Kim*.

But regardless of a life marked by popular and critical success—and an inordinate amount of personal sorrow—Braham would always be the family man, wearing the tennis cap, sitting on the front stoop, smoking a cigar. In 1898, when his name was known across the world and his songs and musical arrangements had influenced the way the musical theater in America sounds, he left an interviewer from the *New York Dramatic Mirror* with only one request: "I haven't talked so much about myself since I was born. Now, don't make me appear egotistical, whatever you do. Good-bye!"

Songs by David Braham

Songs by David Braham and Edward Harrigan

"The Aldermanic Board" (1885), in *The Grip*

"All Aboard for the M. G. P." (1880), in *The Mulligan Guard Picnic*

"Are You There, Moriarity?" (1876)

"As Long as the World Goes 'Round" (1884), in *Investigation*

"As We Wander in the Orange Grove" (1887), in *Pete*

"The Babies on Our Block" (1879), in *The Mulligan Guard Ball*

"Bard of Arinagh" (1872), in *Shamus O'Brien*

"Baxter Avenue" (1886), in *The Leather Patch*

"The Beauty of Limerick" (1880)

"The Beggars" (1888), in *The Lorgaire*

"The Black Maria, O!" (1887), in *McNooney's Visit*

"Blow the Bellows, Blow!" (1884), in *McAllister's Legacy*

"The Blue and the Grey" (1875), in *The Blue and The Grey*

"Bold Hibernian Boys!" (1876), in *The Bold Hibernian Boys*

"The Boodle" (1884), in *Investigation*

"The Bradys" (1878), in *The Bradys*

"The Bridal March" (1887), in *Pete*

"The Broadway Statuettes" (1876)

"Bum's Refrain" (1875), in *Down Broadway*
"The Bunch o' Berries" (1883), in *The Muddy Day*
"Callahan's Gang" (1893), in *The Woollen Stocking*
"Canada, I Oh!" (1880), in *The Mulligan Guards' Nominee*
"Casey's Social Club" (1878), in *The Mulligan Guard Picnic*
"Cash, Cash, Cash" (1882), in *Mordecai Lyons*
"The Castaways" (1881), in *The Mulligans' Silver Wedding*
"The Charleston Blues" (1882), in *McSorley's Inflation*
"Clara Jenkins' Tea" (1881), in *The Major*
"Cobwebs on the Wall" (1884), in *Dan's Tribulations*
"Colored Cadets" (1881), in *The Major*
"Coming Home from Meeting" (1884), in *Dan's Tribulations*
"Cruel Slavery Days" (1877–87)
"Danny by My Side" (1891), in *The Last of the Hogans*
"Dat Citron Wedding Cake" (1880), *in The Mulligan Guards' Surprise*
"De Rainbow Road" (1891), in *The Last of the Hogans*
"Denny Grady's Hack" (1886), in *The Leather Patch*
"Dip Me in de Golden Sea" (1881)
"Dolly, My Crumpled-Horn Cow" (1889), in *The Lorgaire*
"The Donovans" (1876), in *The Donovans*
"Don't I Love My Dolly! (1885), in *Lancashire Songs and Dances*
"Don't You Miss the Train" (1881), in *The Mulligans' Silver Wedding*
"Down in Gossip Row" (1880), in *The Mulligan Guards' Nominee*
"Duffy to the Front" (1876)
"Extra, Extra!" (1881), in *Old Lavender*
"The Family Overhead" (1883), in *The Muddy Day*
"Find in Genoa" (1884), in *Investigation*
"The Forlorn Old Maid" (1881), in *Squatter Sovereignty*
"4–11–44" (1885), in *The Major* (revival)
"The French Singing Lesson" (1884), in *Dan's Tribulations*
"The Full Moon Union" (1880), in *The Mulligan Guards' Surprise*
"The Gallant '69th'" (1875), in *Down Broadway*
"Gentle Gennie Gray" (1879), in *The Mulligan Guards' Surprise*
"German Turnverein Song" (1876), in *Malone's Night Out*
"Get Up Jack, John Sit Down" (1885), in *Old Lavender*
"The Ginger Blues" (1876)
"The Girl That's Up to Date" (1894), in *Notoriety*
"Gliding Down the Stream" (1875)
"Going Home with Nellie after Five" (1883), in *The Mulligan Guard Picnic* (revival)
"The Golden Choir" (1883), in *The Muddy Day*
"The Great Four Hundred" (1890), in *Reilly and the Four Hundred*
"Grogan the Masher" (1885), in *The Grip*
"Hang the Mulligan Banner Up" (1880), in *The Mulligan Guards' Nominee*
"Hats Off to Me" (1891), in *The Last of the Hogans*
"Haul the Woodpile Down" (1887), in *Pete*

"Have One with Me?" (1887), in *McNooney's Visit*

"Heigh Ho! Lingo Sally" (1887), in *Pete*

"Hello, Bab-by!" (1884), in *Investigation*

"Henrietta Pye" (1885), in *The Major* (revival)

"Her Broken Toys" (1896)

"Ho! Molly Grogan" (1887), in *McNooney's Visit*

"The Hole in the Wall" (1896), in *Marty Malone*

"Hurry, Little Children, Sunday Morn!" (1883), in *The Mulligan Guard Picnic* (revival)

"I'll Never Get Drunk Any More" (1874)

"I'll Wear the Trousers, Oh!" (1880), in *The Mulligan Guards' Surprise*

"I'm All Broke Up Today" (1876), music adapted by David Braham

"I'm Going Abroad with Pa" (1878)

"I'm a Terror to All" (1889), in *The Lorgaire*

"I Never Drink behind the Bar" (1882), in *McSorley's Inflation*

"I Really Can't Sit Down" (1885), in *The Major* (revival)

"Isabelle St. Clair" (1888), in *Waddy Googan*

"Isle de Blackwell" (1878), in *A Celebrated Hard Case*

"It Showered Again" (1886), in *The Leather Patch*

"Italian Joe" (1888), in *Waddy Googan*

"I've Come Home to Stay" (1890), in *Reilly and the Four Hundred*

"Jim-Jam, Sailors Superfine" (1890), in *Reilly and the Four Hundred*

"John Riley's Always Dry" (1881), in *The Mulligans' Silver Wedding*

"The Jolly Commodore" (1890), in *Reilly and the Four Hundred*

"Jolly Factory Boy" (1885), in *Lancashire Songs and Dances*

"Just Across from Jersey" (1883), in *Cordelia's Aspirations*

"Knights of the Mystic Star" (1891), in *The Last of the Hogans*

"Knights of St. Patrick" (1878), in *Patrick's Day Parade* (revival)

"*La Plus Belle France*" (1889), in *The Lorgaire*

"The Last of the Hogans" (1891), in *The Last of the Hogans*

"List to the Anvil" (1878), in *The Lorgaire*

"Little Daughter Nell" (1893), in *The Woollen Stocking*

"The Little Green Leaf in Our Bible" (1879)

"The Little Hedge School" (1886), in *The O'Reagans*

"The Little Widow Dunn" (1879), in *The Mulligan Guard Chowder*

"Locked Out after Nine" (1880), in *The Mulligan Guard Picnic*

"London Comic Singers" (1875), in *The London Comic Singers*

"The McIntyres" (1881), in *Squatter Sovereignty*

"McNally's Row of Flats" (1882), in *McSorley's Inflation*

"Maggie Murphy's Home" (1890), in *Reilly and the Four Hundred*

"The Maguires" (1881), in *Squatter Sovereignty*

"Major Gilfeather" (1881), in *The Major*

"The Man That Knows It All" (1884), in *Investigation*

"The Market on Saturday Night" (1882), in *McSorley's Inflation*

"Mary Kelly's Beau" (1880), in *The Mulligan Guard Picnic*

"Massa's Wedding Night" (1887), in *Pete*

"Melancholy Mary" (1894), in *Notoriety*

"The Midnight Squad" (1888), in *Waddy Googan*

"Miranda, When We Are Made One" (1881), in *The Major*

"The Mirror's the Cause of It All" (1881), in *The Mulligans' Silver Wedding*

"Miss Brady's Piano-Fortay" (1881), in *Squatter Sovereignty*

"Mister Dooley's Geese" (1884), in *McAllister's Legacy*

"Molly" (1884), in *McAllister's Legacy*

"Mordecai Lyons" (1882), in *Mordecai Lyons*

"The Mountain Dew" (1882), in *The Blackbird* (play by G. L. Stout)

"Mud Brigade" (1875), in *Down Broadway*

"Mulberry Springs" (1886), in *The O'Reagans*

"The Mulligan Braves" (1879), in *The Mulligan Guards' Christmas*

"The Mulligan Guard" (1873), in *The Mulligan Guards*

"My Dad's Dinner Pail" (1883), in *Dan's Tribulations*

"My Little Side Door" (1884), in *Dan's Tribulations*

"Never Take the Horseshoe from the Door" (1880), in *The Mulligan Guards' Surprise*

"A Night Cap, A Night Cap" (1880), in *The Mulligan Guard Nominee*

"No Wealth without Labor" (1885), in *The Grip*

"Oh! Dat Low Bridge!" (1885), in *The Grip*

"O Girly! Girly!" (1879), in *The Mulligan Guard Chowder*

"Oh, He Promises" (1880), in *The Mulligan Guards' Nominee*

"Oh, My! How We Posé!" (1884), in *McAllister's Legacy*

"Oh, My Molly Is Waiting for Me" (1889), in *The Lorgaire*

"Oh, That's an Old Gag with Me" (1885), in *The Major* (revival)

"The Old Barn Floor" (1887), in *Pete*

"The Old Black Crow" (1887), in *Pete*

"Old Boss Barry" (1888), in *Waddy Googan*

"The Old Bowery Pit" (1882), in *Mordecai Lyons*

"The Old Feather Bed" (1882), in *McSorley's Inflation*

"The Old Neighborhood" (1894), in *Notoriety*

"On Board o' the Muddy Day" (1885), in *The Muddy Day*

"On De Rainbow Road" (1891), in *The Last of the Hogans*

"On Union Square" (1886), in *Investigation* (revival)

"Our Front Stoop" (1878), in *Sullivan's Christmas*

"Out on a College, Rah! Rah!"(1894), in *Notoriety*

"The Owl" (1885), in *Old Lavender*

"Paddy Duffy's Cart" (1882), in *Squatter Sovereignty*

"Paddy and His Sweet Poteen" (1889), in *The Lorgaire*

"*Parlez-vous Français?*" (1876)

"The Pat Daly Song" (1878), in *Our Law Makers*

"Pat and His Little Brown Mare" (1884), in *McAllister's Legacy*

"Patrick's Day Parade" (1874), in *Patrick's Day Parade*

"Patriotic Coon" (1898)

"The Pitcher of Beer" (1879), in *The Mulligan Guards' Christmas*

"Plain Gold Ring" (1878)

"Please to Put That Down" (1885), in *Old Lavender*

"Plum Pudding" (1884), in *Investigation*

"Poverty's Tears Ebb and Flow" (1885), in *Old Lavender*

"The Pride of the London Stage" (1896), in *Marty Malone*

"Put On Your Bridal Veil" (1886), in *The Leather Patch*

"The Regular Army O!" (1874), in *The Regular Army, Oh!* Written and composed by Edward Harrigan. Music adapted and arranged by David Braham

"Roderick O'Dwyer" (1880), in *The Mulligan Guard Picnic*

"Salvation Army, Oh!" (1882), in *McSorley's Inflation*

"Sam Johnson's Colored Cake Walk" (1883), in *Cordelia's Aspirations*

"Sandy-Haired Mary in Our Area" (1880), in *The Mulligan Guard Picnic*

"Savannah Sue" (1896), in *Marty Malone*

"School Days" (1885), in *The Grip*

"Second Degree, Full Moon Union" (1880), in *The Mulligan Guard Picnic*

"Sergeant Hickey of the G. A. R." (1893), in *The Woollen Stocking*

"79th Brave Highlanders" (1878), in *Our Law Makers*

"The S.G. Marche Comique" (1875), music by William Carter, arranged by David Braham

"She Lives on Murray Hill" (1882), in *Mordecai Lyons*

"The Silly Boy" (1883), in *The Muddy Day*

"Singing at the Hallway Door" (1879), in *The Mulligan Guard Ball*

"The Skidmore Fancy Ball" (1879), in *The Mulligan Guard Ball*

"Skidmore Guard" (1874), in *The Skidmores*. Music by William Carter, arranged by David Braham

"The Skidmore Masquerade" (1880), in *The Mulligan Guards' Nominee*

"The Skids Are Out To-Day" (1879), in *The Mulligan Guard Chowder*

"The Skids Are Out To-Night" (1880), in *The Mulligan Guards' Nominee*

"The Skids Are on Review" (1879), in *The Mulligan Guards' Christmas*

"Slavery Days" (1876), in *Slavery Days*

"Slavery's Passed Away" (1887), in *Pete*

"The Snoring Song" (1888), in *The Lorgaire*

"The Soldier Boy's Canteen" (1885), in *The Grip*

"Sons of Temperance (S.O.T.)" (1876), in *S.O.T. (Sons of Temperance)*

"South Fifth Avenue" (1881), in *The Mulligans' Silver Wedding*

"Stem the Tide" (1878)

"Stonewall Jackson" (1887), in *Pete*

"Strolling on the Sands" (1886), in *The O'Reagans*

"Sunday Night when the Parlor's Full" (1877)

"The Sunny Side of Thompson Street" (1893), in *The Woollen Stocking*

"Sweet Mary Ann [Such an Education Has My Mary Ann]" (1878), in *Malone's Night Off*

"Sweet Mary Mullane" (1896), in *Marty Malone*

"Sweet Persimans" (1879)

"Sweet Potteen" (1876) in *Iascaire*

"Sweetest Love" *(1885), in Old Lavender*

"Take a Day Off, Mary Ann" (1891), in *The Last of the Hogans*

"Take My Arm, The Other Side" (1876)

"Taking in the Town" (1890), in *Reilly and the Four Hundred*

"Tally Ho Song" (1894), in *Notoriety*

"They Never Tell All What They Know" (1893), in *The Woollen Stocking*

"Third Degree Full Moon [Union]" (1881), in The *Mulligans' Silver Wedding*

"The Toboggan Slide" (1887), in *McNooney's Visit*

"Tom Bigbee Bay" (1879)

"Tom Collins" (1874), in *A Terrible Example*

"The Trooper's the Pride of the Ladies" (1882), in *The Blackbird* (play by G. L. Stout)

"The Turn Verein Cadets" (1883), in *The Muddy Day*

"Tur-ri-ad-i-lum; or, Santa Claus Has Come" (1879), in *The Mulligan Guards' Christmas*

"Uncle Reilly" (1890), in *Reilly and the Four Hundred*

"Under the Green" (1878)

"Up at Dudley's Grove" (1878)

"Up in the Tenderloin" (1894), in *Notoriety*

"U.S. Black Marines" (1886), in *The O'Reagans*

"Veteran Guard Cadets" (1881), in *The Major*

"Waiters' Chorus; or, Two More to Come" (1883), in *Cordelia's Aspirations*

"Walking for Dat Cake" (1877), in *Walkin' for Dat Cake*

"We're All Young Fellows Bran' New" (1883), in *The Mulligan Guard Ball* (revival)

"Wheel the Baby Out" (1881), in *The Mulligans' Silver Wedding*

"When the Clock in the Tower Strikes Twelve" (1882), in *Mordecai Lyons*

"When the Trumpet in the Cornfield Blows" (1886), in *The O'Reagans*

"Where the Sparrows and Chippies Parade" (1888), in *Waddy Googan*

"Where the Sweet Magnolia Grows" (1887), in *Pete*

"Whist! The Bogie Man" (1880), in *The Mulligan Guards' Surprise*

"The Widow Nolan's Goat" (1882), in *Squatter Sovereignty*

Songs by David Braham and Assorted Lyricists

"Adolphus Morning-glory" (1868), words by J. B. Murphy

"The Babies of Our Street" (1880), words by J. Bishop (a parody of "The Babies on Our Block")

"The Bold Hibernian Boys" (1885), words by Harry Hunter (a parody of Bold Hibernian Boys!")

"The Boot Black" (1874), words by Gordian K. Hyde

"The Boys of Lancashire" (1885), in *Lancashire Songs and Dances*, words by John Williams

"Bring Flowers; Red, White, and Blue" (1884), words by Jeannie O. B. Sammis

"Bull Fighter's Dance" (1888), in *Maggie the Midget*

"Chorus and Fandango," (1888), words by Fred Williams, in *Maggie the Midget*

"Dance Diabolique" (1873), in *Gabriel Grub*

"Darling Little Harry" (1879), words by J. C. Lampard

"The Eagle" (1875), words by G. L. Stout

"Eccentrique" (1873), words by Fred Lyster, in *Gabriel Grub*

"Eily Machree" (1876), words by G. L. Stout

"Emanicipation Day" (1876), words by G. L. Stout

"Evening Star" (1879), words by J. C. Lampard

"Flirting in the Twilight" (1870), words by Jennie Kimble

"The Flower of Columbia" (1884), words by Jeannie O. B. Sammis

"The Foot-print in the Sand" (1869), words by W. E. McNulty

"Fred Lay's Bogie Medley up to Date" (1894), words by Fred Lay

"Garfield Our Best Man" (1878), words by O. E. Henning

"The Giddy Old Owl" (1887), words by F. Bower

"Granny O'Reilly's Wake" (1884), words by Jeannie O. B. Sammis

"Grecian Bend" (copyright 1897)

"Hush! Hush!! Hush!!! Here Comes the Broker's Man" (1890), words by George
    Dance (a parody of "Whist! The Bogie Man")

"The Idol of My Heart" (1874), words by Gordian K. Hyde

"In April when the News Did Come" (1879)

"Janice Meredith. March" (1900)

"A Jolly Christmas Party" (1873), words by Fred Lyster, in *Gabriel Grub*

"The Lancashire Dance" (1885), in *Lancashire Songs and Dances*, words by John
    Williams

"Lingard Quadrille" (1868)

"Little Green Veil" (1870), words by W. E. McNulty

"Maggie Murphy's Flat" (1891), words by J. S. Evalo (a parody of "Maggie
    Hurphy's Home")

"The Man That Knows It All" (1887), words by E. French

"Monday Was the Day" (1891), in *Reilly and the 400*, words by Alfred J. Morris

"Money the God of the Purse" (1877), written by Geo. H. MacDermot, music
    arranged by David Braham

"The Money, the Money for Me" (1887), words by E. French

"The 'Muffs' Are Out To-Day" (1880), words by F. Green (a parody of "The Skids
    Are Out To-Day")

"My Dad's Old Violin" (1884), words by William Carleton

"My Pearl; or, The Old Water Mill" (1883), words by J. J. Kelly

"Our Welcome Guest" (1873), words by Fred Lyster, in *Gabriel Grub*

"Over the Hill to the Poor-House" (1874), words by George L. Catlin

"Par Excellence" (1870)

"Quadrille Domestique" (1873), words by Fred Lyster, in *Gabriel Grub*

"Rest, My Darling, Slumber Now" (1876), words by G.L. Stout

"Sailing on the Lake" (1874), words by Gordian K. Hyde

"Sally Waters; or, The Babies in Our Row" (1885), words adapted from Edward
    Harrigan by William Charles Levey

"A Sandy Haired Fairy is My Mary" (1881), words by T.S. Lonsdale (a parody of Sandy-Haired Mary in Our Area")

"The Spider and the Fly" (1873), words by Fred Lyster, in *Gabriel Grub*

"Such a Heducated Girl Is Mary Hann" (1879), words by T. S. Lonsdale (a parody of "Sweet Mary Ann")

"The Summer Wind" (1884), words by Jeannie O. B. Sammis

"Sway the Cot Gently for Baby's Asleep" (1876), words by Hartley Neville

"Tarantella" (1888), in *Maggie the Midget*

"'Tis All One to Me" (1884), words by Jeannie O. B. Sammis

"To Rest Let Him Gently Be Laid" (1876), words by George Cooper

"Waiting at the Ferry" (1869), words by Lina Edwin

"We Are so Volatile" (1873), words by Fred Lyster, in *Gabriel Grub*

"We Have Our Brave Hearts Still" (1875), words by H. B. Farnie

"We're About to Have a Baby" (1877), words by A. Anthony

Appendix B
Songs by the Braham Family

Songs by George Braham and Edward Harrigan

"The Actors Who've Seen Better Days" (1885), in *Are You Insured?*
"Advertising Man" (1885), in *Are You Insured?*
"Are You Insured?" (1885), in *Are You Insured?*
"A Coon Will Follow a Band" (1903), in *Under Cover*
"Don't Tell Maria!" (1897)
"The First Sweetheart I Ever Knew" (1894)
"The Fringe of Society" (1903), in *Under Cover*
"Hodge's Country Dance" (1885), in *Are You Insured?*
"Limerick's Running Yet" (1903), in *Under Cover*
"Lulu 's Honeymoon" (1903), in *Under Cover*
"Oh, What's the Use?" (1903), in *Under Cover*
"Only a Tear" (1895)
"Pretty Little Laundry Girls" (1885), in *Are You Insured?*
"She's My Girl" (1897)
"We'll Drink to Our Friends Not Here" (1898)
"When Mamie, Sweet Mamie's a Bride" (1903), in *Under Cover*

Songs by George Braham and Assorted Lyricists

"April Showers. March" (1907)

"Elysia. Valse Lente" (1906)

"Four in Hand. March and Two-Step" (1906)

"Rolling Home. Convivial March-Two-Step" (1906)

"True Love Should Never Change" (1898), words by John J. McIntyre

"What the Butler Saw? March" (1906)

Songs by John J[oseph] Braham and Edward Harrigan

"The Day That I Kem Over" (1874)

"Little Old Dudeen" (1875), in *The London Comic Singers*

"N.E.F.C. (North End Fishing Club)" (1874)

"Poor Little Tom" (1875)

"Steady Company" (1872), in *The Little Fraud*, music arranged by John Braham

Songs by John J[oseph] Braham and Assorted Lyricists

"Alexander Crow" (1874), words by Harry Bloodgood

"Answer to Crime" (1874), words by Harry Allen

"Army So Grand" (1874), words by W. Cavanagh

"The Babes in the Wood Waltzes" (1878), music arranged by John Braham

"The Ballerina's Vision. Valse Lente" (1908)

"Barcarolle" (1878), from *Conrad, the Corsair*, words by J. Cheever Goodwin

"Blue Are the Eyes of My Kathleen" (1875), words by Samuel N. Mitchell

"Broken Down" (1879), words and music by Gus Williams, arranged by John
    Braham

"Brothers Dobkin" (1881), words by John P. Kelly

"Buckets of Gore" (1887), in *The Corsair*, words by Henry E. Dixey

"A Capital Good Fellow" (1874)

"The Cigarette" (1889), in *Bluebeard Jr.*, words by Clay M. Greene

"Coney Island down the Bay" (1880), words by Charles H. Duncan

"Corsairs Bold" (1887), in *The Corsair*, words by J. Cheever Goodwin

"Daisy Dunbar" (1875), words by Samuel N. Mitchell

"Don't Forget a Friend" (1880), words by Charles H. Duncan

"Don't Take Me Back to Slavery" (1878), words by William B. Dever

"Dutch Policeman" (1874), words and music by Gus Williams, arranged by John
    Braham

"The Fire in the Grate"(1877), music by G. W. H. Griffin, arranged by John
    Braham

"Geranium Leaves and Roses" (1883), words by Bobby Newcome

"Good Night" (1878), from *Pippins, a Musical Travestie*, words by J. Cheever
    Goodwin

"He's Afraid (Conrad and Chorus" (1887), in *The Corsair*, words by J. Cheever
    Goodwin

"Hiawatha" (1913)

"Huldy Ann [Hulda Ann, How Is Your Mother?]" (1877), words by Sidney Burt

"Idyl" (1878), from *Pippins, a Musical Travestie*, words by J. Cheever Goodwin

"I Am the Author of Divorce" (1889), in *Bluebeard Jr.*, words by John Braham

"I'm a Pedagogue" (1878), from *Pippins, a Musical Travestie*, words by J. Cheever Goodwin

"I'm Weary, So Weary" (1877)

"Johanna Louisa McGuire" (1880), words by Charles H. Duncan

"Kaloolah" (1875), words by W. B. Cavanah

"Killarney Quadrille" (1877)

"Like June Skies" (1889), in *Bluebeard Jr.*, words by John F. Harley

"Lulu Darling" (1873), words by Arthur W. French

"Margretta Polka" (1874)

"A Marionette's Courtship" (1908)

"The Mayflower Waltz" (1886)

"The Monarch of the Woods" (1900)

"My Dancing Days Are Over" (1878), from *Pippins, a Musical Travestie*, words by J. Cheever Goodwin

"A Night in Japan" (1908)

"No Hayseed in My Hair" (1874), words by Fred. Stimson

"Of All the Maidens" (1878), from *Pippins, a Musical Travestie*, words by J. Cheever Goodwin

"Oh! Dat Watermelon" (1874), words by Luke Schoolcraft, music arranged by John Braham

"Our Peculiar Style" (1881), words by Frank Binney

"Picadilly: Favorite Songs" (1872), music arranged by John Braham

"Picadilly Galop" (1872), music arranged by John Braham

"Pizzicato. Polka de Concert" (1913)

"Poor Old Uncle Rufe" (1876), words by Harry Bloodgood, melody by James Maas, arranged by John Braham

"Rowing on the Lake" (1871), words by J. Cohan

"Schoolcraft and Coes Quadrille" (1877)

"Shine On" (1874), by Luke Schoolcraft, arranged by John Braham

"Sights of Ireland" (1874), words by E. D. Davies

"Speak to Me Flow'rets" (1878), from *Pippins, a Musical Travestie*, words by J. Cheever Goodwin

"Strolling in the Woodlands" (1899)

"There's a Sweet Smile Awaits Me at Home" (1874), words by Gussie Crayton Maas

"Ven My Band Begins to Play" (1872), words and music by Gus Williams, arranged by John Braham

"The Way to Kiss in Style" (1874), words by Samuel N. Mitchell

"Who Would Be Beautiful to Be Sold" (Slave Chorus)" (1887), in *The Corsair*, words by J. Cheever Goodwin

"Why Don't You Tell Me So" (1874), words by Samuel N. Mitchell

Songs by Harry [A.] Braham

"Adelaide Caprice" (1905), in *Easy Dawson*, words by Edward E. Kidder
"Auto Galop" (1905), in *Easy Dawson*, words by Edward E. Kidder
"Burnaby the Brave" (1885), words by J. S. Haydon
"Comedy" (1905), in *Easy Dawson*, words by Edward E. Kidder
"The Danger Signal" (1881), words by T. Brown
"Dat Heabenly Balloon" (1897), words by Chas. A. Pusey
"Easy Dawson March" (1905), in *Easy Dawson*, words by Edward E. Kidder
"Some Other Evening" (1885), in *A Rag Baby*, words by C[harles] H. Hoyt
"Zabelle Waltz" (1905), in *Easy Dawson*, words by Edward E. Kidder

Songs by Joseph Braham

"O Dutch Pull Down Your Vest" (1876), words by H[arry] B[loodgood]

The Repertoire during Braham's Employment at the Grand Opera House

1895–96 Season

August 31, 1895: *The Passing Show* (review) by Sydney Rosenfeld (libretto) and Ludwig Englander (music) (8 perf.)

September 9, 1895: *Faust* (play) by W. G. Wills, adapted from Goethe's tragedy (8 perf.)

September 16, 1895: *Fantasma* (spectacle) by W. M. Hanlon (8 perf.)

September 23, 1895: *Sowing the Wind* (play) by Sydney Grundy (8 perf.)

September 30, 1895: *The Twentieth-Century Girl* (musical comedy) by Sydney Rosenfeld (libretto) and Ludwig Englander (music) (8 perf.)

October 7, 1895: *Herrmann* (magic show) conceived and performed by Herrmann the Great (8 perf.)

October 14, 1895: *The Black Crook* (extravaganza) by Charles M. Barras (8 perf.)

October 21, 1895: *The Man Upstairs* (play) by Augustus Thomas (8 perf.)

October 28, 1895: *Charley's Aunt* (play) by Brandon Thomas (8 perf.)

November 4, 1895: *Rory of the Hills* (play) by James C. Roach (8 perf.)

November 11, 1895: *For Fair Virginia* (play) by Russ Whytal (8 perf.)

November 18, 1895: *The Bicycle Girl* (musical farce-comedy) by Louis Harrison (8 perf.)

November 25, 1895: *The Cotton King* (play) by Sutton Vane (8 perf.)

December 2, 1895: *A Bowery Girl* (play) by Ada Lee Bascom (8 perf.)

December 9, 1895: *Camille* (play) by Alexandre Dumas, fils (8 perf.)

December 16, 1895: *Ups and Downs of Life* (play) by F. A. Scudmore (8 perf.)

December 23, 1895: *Humanity* (play) by Sutton Vane (8 perf.)

December 30, 1895: *Superba* (extravaganza) by the Hanlons with John J. McNally (8 perf.)

January 6, 1896: *The Masqueraders* (play) by Henry Arthur Jones (8 perf.)

January 13, 1896: *A Milk White Flag* (musical burlesque) by Charles Hoyt (8 perf.)

January 20, 1896: *The Night Clerk* (farce comedy) by John J. McNally (8 perf.)

January 27, 1896: *Primrose and West's Minstrels* (8 perf.)

February 3, 1896: *Thrilby* (burlesque) by Joseph W. Herbert (libretto) and Charles Puerner (music) (8 perf.)

February 10, 1896: *The Gay Parisians* (play) by Georges Feydeau and Maurice Desvalliere (8 perf.)

February 17, 1896: *In Old Kentucky* (play) by C. T. Dazey (8 perf.)

February 24, 1896: *A Mid-Summer Night's Dream* (play) by William Shakespeare (8 perf.)

March 2, 1896: *Little Christopher Columbus* (musical comedy) by George R. Sims and Cecil Raleigh (libretto) and Ivan Caryll and Gustave Kerker (music) (8 perf.)

March 9, 1896: *1492 Up To Date* (musical comedy) by R.A. Barnet (book and lyrics) and Carl Pflueger (music) (8 perf.)

March 16, 1896: *The Cruiskeen Lawn* (play) by Daniel McCarthy (8 perf.)

March 23, 1896: *A Run on the Bank* (play) by Charles E. Blaney (8 perf.)

March 30, 1896: *The White Slave* (play) by Bartley Campbell (8 perf.)

April 6, 1896: *The Fatal Card* (play) by C. Haddon Chambers and B. C. Stephenson (8 perf.)

April 13, 1896: *The Two Orphans* (play) by Hart Jackson, adapted from the French of Adolphe D'Ennery and Eugene Carmon (8 perf.)

April 20, 1896: *Coon Hollow* (play) by Charles E. Callahan (8 perf.)

April 27, 1896: *Rob Roy* (musical comedy) by Harry B. Smith (libretto) and Reginald de Koven (music) (8 perf.)

May 4, 1896: *Trilby* (play) by Paul M. Potter, based on George Du Maurier's novel (8 perf.)

May 11, 1896: The Tavary Grand Opera Co. (16 perf.)

May 25, 1896: *Mavourneen* (play with music) by George H. Jessop and Horace Townsend (8 perf.)

1896–97 Season

August 31, 1896: *The Cotton Spinner* (play) by Scott Marble (8 perf.)

September 7, 1896: *The War of Wealth* (play) by C. T. Dazey (8 perf.)

September 14, 1896: *Chimmie Fadden* (play) by Edward W. Townsend (8 perf.)

September 21, 1896: *The Land of the Living* (play) by Frank Harvey (8 perf.)

September 28, 1896: *The Last Stroke* (play) by I. N. Morris (8 perf.)

October 5, 1896: *Sandow's Olympia* (vaudeville) (8 perf.)

October 12, 1896: *On Broadway* (play) by Clay M. Greene (8 perf.)

October 19, 1896: *A Night at the Circus* (circus spectacular) produced by H. Grattan Donnelly (8 perf.)

October 26, 1896: *Excelsior, Jr.* (musical comedy) by R. A. Barnet (libretto) and George Lowell Tracy, A. Baldwin Sloane, and Edward E. Rice (music) (8 perf.)

November 2, 1896: *The Widow Jones* (play with music) by John J. McNally (8 perf.)

November 9, 1896: *Primrose and West's Minstrels* (8 perf.)

November 16, 1896: *Shaft No. 2* (play) by Frank L. Bixby (8 perf.)

November 23, 1896: *The Power of the Press* (play) by Augustus Pitou and George H. Jessop (8 perf.)

November 30, 1896: *A Naval Cadet* (play) by Charles T. Vincent (8 perf.)

December 7, 1896: *A Milk White Flag* (musical burlesque) by Charles H. Hoyt (8 perf.)

December 14, 1896: *A Good Thing* (play with music) by John J. McNally (8 perf.)

December 21, 1896: *Superba* (extravaganza) by the Hanlon Brothers, with John J. McNally (16 perf.)

January 4, 1897: *In Old Kentucky* (play) by C. T. Dazey (8 perf.)

11 January 11, 1897: *Eight Bells* (spectacle) by John F. Byrne (8 perf.)

18 January 18, 1897: *The Sporting Duchess* (play) by Sir Augustus Harris, Cecil Raleigh, and Henry Hamilton (8 perf.)

January 25, 1897: *Al G. Field's Minstrels* (8 perf.)

February 1, 1897: *Under the Polar Star* (play) by Clay M. Greene (8 perf.)

February 8, 1897: *Hogan's Alley* (play) by Barney Gilmore and John F. Leonard, together with *The Yellow Kid* (play) by W. F. Carroll (8 perf.)

February 15, 1897: *The Woman in Black* (play) by H. Grattan Donnelly (8 perf.)

February 22, 1897: *Siberia* (play) by Bartley Campbell (8 perf.)

March 1, 1897: *The Lady Slavey* (musical comedy) by George Dance (libretto) and Gustave Kerker (music) (8 perf.)

March 8, 1897: *Jim the Penman* (play) by Charles Young (8 perf.)

March 15, 1897: *On Broadway* (play) by Clay M. Greene and Ben Teal (8 perf.)

March 22, 1897: *The Prisoner of Zenda* (play) by Edward E. Rice, based on the novel by Anthony Hope (8 perf.)

March 29, 1897: *Madame Sans Gêne* (play) by Victorien Sardou and Emile Moreau (8 perf.)

April 5, 1897: *The Politician* (play) by David D. Lloyd and Sydney Rosenfeld (8 perf.)

April 12, 1897: *Sowing the Wind* (play) by Sydney Grundy (8 perf.)

April 19, 1897: *Two Little Vagrants* (play) by Charles Klein, adapted from Pierre Decourcelle's *Les Deux Gosses* (8 perf.)

April 26, 1897: *The Heart of Maryland* (play) by David Belasco (8 perf.)

May 3, 1897: *The Cherry Pickers* (play) by Joseph Arthur (8 perf.)

May 10, 1897: *An Enemy to the King* (play) by Robert N. Stephens (8 perf.)

May 17, 1897: *Uncle Tom's Cabin* (play) by C. W. Taylor from the novel by Harriet Beecher Stowe (8 perf.)

1897–98 Season

August 21, 1896: *A Fight for Honor* (play) by Frank Harvey (10 perf.)

August 30, 1897: *A Black Sheep and How It Came to Washington* (musical farce) by Charles H. Hoyt, with songs by Richard Stahl, Charles H. Hoyt, William Devere, Otis Harlan, Mr. Conor, and Mr. Kelly (8 perf.)

September 6, 1897: *A Contented Woman* (play) by Charles H. Hoyt (8 perf.)

September 13, 1897: *At Gay Coney Island* (musical farce) by Levin C. Tees (book), and J. Sherrie Matthews and Harry Bulger (music and lyrics) (8 perf.)

September 20, 1897: *Man-O-War's Man* (play) by James W. Harkins, Jr. (8 perf.)

September 27, 1897: *Primrose and West's Minstrels* (8 perf.)

October 4, 1897: *Eight Bells* (spectacle) by John F. Byrne (8 perf.)

October 11, 1897: *For Liberty and Love* (play) by Lawrence Marston and Albert B. Paine (8 perf.)

October 18, 1897: *The Sporting Duchess* (play) by Sir Augustus Harris, Cecil Raleigh, and Henry Hamilton (8 perf.)

October 25, 1897: *McSorley's Twins* (play) by Sidney Wilmer and Walter Vincent (8 perf.)

November 1, 1897: *Courted into Court* (play) by John J. McNally (8 perf.)

November 8, 1897: *McFadden's Row of Flats* (play) by Edward W. Townsend (8 perf.)

November 15, 1897: *Cymbeline* (play) by William Shakespeare (8 perf.)

November 22, 1897: *What Happened to Jones* (farce) by George Broadhurst (8 perf.)

November 29, 1897: *The Silver King* (play) by Henry Arthur Jones and Henry Herman (8 perf.)

December 6, 1897: *Half a King* (musical comedy) by Harry B. Smith (libretto, from the French of Mm. Leterrier and Vanloo) and Ludwig Englander (music) (8 perf.)

December 13, 1897: *A Happy Little Home* (play) by Charles Klein (8 perf.)

December 20, 1897: *The Secret Enemy* (play) by Elmer Grandin and Eva Mountford (8 perf.)

December 27, 1897: *A Hot Old Time* (play with songs) by Edgar Selden (8 perf.)

January 3, 1898: *Captain Impudence* (play) by Edwin Milton Royle (8 perf.)

January 10, 1898: *My Friend From India* (play) by H. A. du Souchet (8 perf.)

January 17, 1898: *A Ward of France* (play) by Franklyn Fyles and Eugene W. Presbrey (8 perf.)

January 24, 1898: *In Old Kentucky* (play) by C. T. Dazey (8 perf.)

January 31, 1898: *Cumberland '61* (play) by Franklyn Fyles (16 perf.)

February 14, 1898: *Never Again; or, The Tricks of Seraphin* (play) by T. R. Birmingham, adapted from the French of Anthony Mars and Maurice Desvalliere (8 perf.)

February 21, 1898: *Primrose and West's Minstrels* (8 perf.)

February 28, 1898: *Under the Red Robe* (play) by Edward E. Rose (8 perf.)

March 7, 1898: *Oliver Twist* (play), adapted from the novel by Charles Dickens (8 perf.)

March 14, 1898: *Sweet Inniscarra* (play) by Augustus Pitou, with songs by Chauncy Olcott and incidental music by David Braham (8 perf.)

March 21, 1898: *The Swell Miss Fitzwell* (farce) by H. A. Du Souchet (8 perf.)

March 28, 1898: *East Lynne* (play) by B. E. Woolf, from the novel by Mrs. Henry Wood (8 perf.)

April 4, 1898: *Eight Bells* (spectacle) by John F. Byrne (8 perf.)

April 11, 1898: *What Happened to Jones* (farce) by George Broadhurst (8 perf.)

April 18, 1898: *Gettysburg* (play) by Frank G. Campbell (8 perf.)

April 25, 1898: *A Bachelor's Romance* (play) by Martha Morton (8 perf.)

May 2, 1898: *Little Lord Fauntleroy* (play) by E. V. Seebohm, adapted from the novel by Frances Hodgson Burnett (8 perf.)

May 9, 1898: *Lord Chumley* (play) by Henry DeMille and David Belasco (8 perf.)

May 16, 1898: *The Man from Mexico* (play) by H. A. du Souchet (8 perf.)

May 23, 1898: *The White Squadron* (play) by James W. Harkins, Jr. (16 perf.

The Repertoire during Braham's Employment at Wallack's Theatre

1898–99 Season

September 1, 1898: *The Meddler* (play) by Augustus Thomas (27 perf.)

September 26, 1898: *The Fortune Teller* (musical comedy) by Harry B. Smith (libretto) and Victor Herbert (music) (40 perf.)

October 31, 1898: *A Lady of Quality* (play) by Frances Hodgson Burnett and Stephen Townsend, adapted from the novel by Frances Hodgson Burnett (24 perf.)

November 21, 1898: *Ingomar* (play) by Munch-Bellinghausen, translated by Maria Lovell (8 perf.)

November 28, 1898: *As You Like It* (play) by William Shakespeare (8 perf.)

December 5, 1898: *Pygmalion and Galathea* (burlesque) by W. S. Gilbert, and *Mercedes* (play) by Thomas Bailey Aldrich (24 perf.)

December 26, 1898: *A Lady of Quality* (play) by Frances Hodgson Burnett and Stephen Townsend, based on the novel by Frances Hodgson Burnett (8 perf.)

January 2, 1899: Theatre closed for one week

January 9, 1899: *The Termagant* (poetic drama) by Louis N. Parker and Murray Carson (20 perf.)

February 6, 1899: *At the White Horse Tavern* (comedy) by Sydney Rosenfeld, adapted from the German play *Im Weissen Röessl* by Oscar Blumenthall and Gustav Kadelburg, with incidental music by Frank A. Howson (64 perf.)

April 3, 1899: *The Cuckoo* (play) by Charles Brookfield, adapted from the French of
Henri Meilhac (56 perf.)

May 22, 1899: *Ma Cousine* (play) by Henri Meilhac (8 perf.)

1899–1900 Season

August 28, 1899: *A Little Ray of Sunshine* (farcical comedy) by Mark Ambient and
Wilton Heriot (22 perf.)

September 18, 1899: *The Gadfly* (play) by Edward E. Rose, adapted from his novel
(14 perf.)

October 2, 1899: *Peter Stuyvesant* (comedy) by Brander Matthews and Bronson
Howard (28 perf.)

October 31, 1899: *A Rich Man's Son* (comedy) by Michael Morton, based on the
German play, *Das Grobe Hemd*, by H. Karlweiss (36 perf.)

December 4, 1899: *The Ameer* (comic opera) by Fred M. Rankien and Kirke La
Shelle (libretto) and Victor Herbert (music) (51 perf.)

February 5, 1900: *Sapho* (play) by Clyde Fitch, based on the novel by Alphonse
Daudet and the play by Mme. Daudet and A. Belot (29 perf.)

March 6, 1900: *The Second Mrs. Tanqueray* (play) by Arthur Wing Pinero (13 perf.)

March 17, 1900: *The Profligate* (play) by Arthur Wing Pinero (4 perf.)

March 27, 1900: Theatre closed for two weeks

April 7, 1900: *Sapho* (play) by Clyde Fitch, based on the novel by Alphonse Daudet
and the play by Mme. Daudet and A. Belot (55 perf.)

1900–01 Season

September 3, 1900: *Prince Otto* (play) by Otis Skinner, based on the novel by
Robert Louis Stevenson (40 perf.)

October 8, 1900: *The Greatest Thing in the World* (play) by Harriet Ford and
Beatrice de Mille (41 perf.)

November 12, 1900: *Sapho* (play) by Clyde Fitch, based on the novel by Alphonse
Daudet and the play by Mme. Daudet and A. Belot (28 perf.)

December 10, 1900: *Janice Meredith* (drama) by Paul Leicester Ford and Edward E.
Rose, based on the novel by Paul Leicester Ford (92 perf.)

March 19, 1901: *Manon Lescaut* (drama) by Theodore Burt Sayre, based on the
novel by Abbé Prévost (15 perf.)

April 1, 1901: *Are You a Mason?* (farce) by Leo Ditrichstein, adapted from the
German of Lauf and Kraatz (32 perf.)

April 26, 1901 (special matinee): *King Washington* (drama) by Robert Louis Weed,
based on the novel by Adelaide Skeel and William H. Brearley (1 perf.)

April 29, 1901: *Mistress Nell* (play) by George C. Hazleton (40 perf.)

1901–02 Season

September 3, 1901: *Don Caesar's Return* (play) by Victor Mapes (87 perf.)

November 18, 1901: *Colorado* (drama) by Augustus Thomas, with incidental music by William Furst (48 perf.)

December 30, 1901: *A Gentleman of France* (play) by Harriet Ford, based on the romance written by Stanley Weyman (120 perf.)

April 14, 1902: *The Last Appeal* (play) by Leo Ditrichstein (24 perf.)

April 24, 1902 (special matinee): *The City's Heart* (play) by Maude Banks (1 perf.)

May 5, 1902: *The Show Girl* (musical comedy) by R. A. Barnet (book), H. L. Heartz and E. W. Corliss (music) (64 perf.)

May 8, 1902 (special matinee): *Little Miss Mouse* (comedy) by Dore Davidson and Katherine Berry di Zerga, from the French of Edward Pailleron (1 perf.)

1902–03 Season

September 2, 1902: *Mrs. Jack* (comedy) by Grace Livingston Furniss (72 perf.)

October 6, 1902: *The Sword of the King* (play) by Ronald McDonald (*Mrs. Jack* moves to the Victoria Theatre) (48 perf.)

November 17, 1902: *The Crisis* (play) by Winston Churchill, based on his novel (50 perf.)

December 29, 1902: *The Sultan of Sulu* (musical satire) by George Ade (libretto) and Alfred G. Wathall (music) (192 perf.)

1903–04 Season

September 10, 1903: *Peggy from Paris* (musical comedy) by George Ade (libretto) and William Lorraine (music) (85 perf.)

November 24, 1903: *The County Chairman* (comedy) by George Ade (222 perf.)

April 14, 1904 (special matinee): *Love's Pilgrimage* (play) by Horace B. Fry (1 perf.)

1904–05 Season

October 10, 1904: *The Sho-gun* (comic opera) by George Ade (book) and Gustave Luders (music) (125 perf.)

January 24 , 1905: *The Yankee Counsul* (comic opera) by Henry M. Blossom (book and lyrics) and Alfred G. Robyn (music) (47 perf.)

Index